SINOPTICON
A CELEBRATION OF CHINESE SCIENCE FICTION

First published 2021 by Solaris
an imprint of Rebellion Publishing Ltd,
Riverside House, Osney Mead,
Oxford, OX2 0ES, UK

www.solarisbooks.com

ISBN: 978-1-78108-852-4

A CIP catalogue record for this book is available from the British Library.

Designed & typeset by Rebellion Publishing

Printed in Denmark

SINOPTICON

A CELEBRATION OF CHINESE SCIENCE FICTION

TRANSLATED AND EDITED
BY XUETING CHRISTINE NI

FOREWORD BY XIA JIA

SOLARIS

For my readers

For Lex (R.I.P.)

FOREWORD

XIA JIA

ALTHOUGH I PERSONALLY do not believe that history should be attributed to random events and a handful of heroes, when I think about the explosion of Chinese science fiction today, I cannot help but be moved by the thought of those who had read bad translations, and were compelled to doing the job better themselves.

Today, there are so many things that people in the past would never have dared to dream of. We have, as the 2023's Worldcon China Bid slogan has it, "More Than Pandas!". Today, we can proudly say, Kehuan is far more than *The Three Body Problem*. Beyond Liu Cixin. Beyond Ken Liu. Beyond technical translations.

In my opinion, this selection of Chinese science fiction, curated and translated by Xueting, provides an important gateway into all these "More Than's".

When I was invited to write the foreword for this book, I was not acquainted with Xueting, nor had I the chance to read her other works. But I was filled with expectation and curiosity for this collection – and read it with eager anticipation. I wanted to find out, just what kind of surprises it would have in store for English readers, and even for Chinese readers like me who consider themselves sufficiently knowledgeable about Chinese SF.

In this short piece, I really only have space to talk briefly about the three things that left the deepest impressions on me as I was reading.

Firstly, the selection of this anthology. Although Xueting had repeatedly expressed in her correspondence, that the stories in the book would probably be familiar to me, in actual fact, I have to admit, that I was reading most of the stories for the first time.

Compared to my own collection, *The Silent Soldier* (沉默的伏兵), this book focuses more on young writers and the relatively later works of female writers, putting more emphasis on the diversity of style and subject matter. This selection strategy aims to uncover those works that have long been oppressed by the so-called "Classic" and "Representative". Xueting elaborates on this in her introduction. As I browsed the stories, the image of Xueting deliberating among a pile of her favourite works, looking utterly torn, kept coming to mind. At the same time, I also imagined how you, the readers, would, at first with uncertainty and caution, venture into the realms of names that might be completely strange to you, and how you would then, be met with unknown delights.

The second aspect that deeply impressed upon me, is the short critiques that Xueting has composed for each piece. With extreme conciseness and precision, Xueting introduces the creative background and historical context for each story, and brilliantly decodes elements which English readers might be curious about, or find confusing, demonstrating her clear insight and unique perspective into so-called "Chineseness".

China's painful transformation between "traditional culture" and "modern civilization", between the "natural" and "man-made", is a theme that calls for recurring exploration. Xueting extends from this to China's heavily pressurised societal competitiveness and educational system, and the advocation of medicinal supplements for physical strengthening and the improving of brain capacity. This in turn reminds me, of the practice since the late Qing era, of employing the magic of modern technology (be it hypnotism, brain-enhancing serums and heart-curing medicine) to make "new men". This has been an important part of the "Chinese Dream". At the same time, as Xueting reiterates in her introduction, "Chineseness" isn't necessarily a phenomenon which completely separates us from "universality". I believe that the hopes and fears of China in this age of globalisation will resonate with the experiences and feelings of the readers of this book.

Lastly, I want to talk very briefly about translation techniques, and Xueting's rendition of Chinese proper names, romanised according to their native pronunciation and placed in the order they appear in the original language. This approach has sometimes proved troublesome in overseas correspondence and international exchange. I recall the perplexity I used to feel about using my pseudonym abroad ("xia" means summer, my favourite season, whilst "jia", is an ancient Chinese instrument, like a wooden flute). "Is it Xia Jia, or Jia Xia? Should I abbreviate it to Xia or Jia? How do you pronounce Xia?" In time, I began to understand that this unease and inconvenience, has important significance in cross cultural exchange. It reminds the audience to confront the heterogeneity inherent in other cultures, and their uniqueness, reminding them to respect, tolerate and to endeavour to understand. I am glad to see Xueting consciously preserving the Chinese core of these stories.

Finally, I would like to thank Xueting for her hard work, all the contributors and publishing staff who worked on this book, and to you, wonderful readers. I wish you happy reading!

CONTENTS

INTRODUCTION

XUETING CHRISTINE NI

WHENEVER I'M BACK in China, I like to wander round the old shopping districts, checking out the street stalls, fashion boutiques, as well as the music and bookshops, just to see if there are any titles or trends I've missed out on during my time away. Seeing what books are prominently displayed in a country is also a good indication of the everyday concerns and considerations of its people. A few years ago, I popped into the Xinhua bookstore (China's biggest chain of booksellers), and began to look through the best-seller and new arrival displays.

There were plenty of biographies of successful public figures, various kinds of self-help manuals, lots of Western best-sellers in translation, and of course a good selection of romance novels that had been spun into drama series on TV. I was surprised by the lack of genre fiction, other than that great Chinese staple, Wuxia. Despite hunting high and low, I could not find a single sci-fi book, and in the end had to ask the staff. Without even lifting her head from her work, the assistant gestured vaguely towards the children's department. I was a little surprised, and asked her if they were really putting stuff like *The Three Body Problem* in there.

"Oh! Why didn't you say so before?"

She led us through row upon floor-to-ceiling row of secondary education textbooks to the science section, and pointed to a single waist-high shelf, facing the wall, where I found a neat selection of interesting new novels and short story collections, keeping company with the Liu Cixins.

The fact that Kehuan (科幻, the Chinese term for science fiction), still gets lumped in with educational literature in China is not as random as it seems. In the 1950s and early 60s, Modern China's first period of prosperity and stability, authors with science backgrounds were very much encouraged to put their skills to public education. Hundreds of them set to work updating Mikhail Il'in's children's encyclopaedia, *100,000 Whys*, expanding it to eight volumes. The series remains a popular read for children decades after. As a child of the 1980s, these books, along with a copy of Belyaev's *Professor Dowell's Head*, (which I found lying around the flat), were the sum total of my earliest science-fiction experience.

Moving to Britain as a teenager, I started to sink into series like *Star Trek*, *Quantum Leap* and *X-Files*, but was steered away from pop culture by narrow-minded parents, who expected me to be the "good Chinese child". This was only a partial success. After growing up on a heavy diet of the English literary canon, I discovered a whole universe in classic science fiction during university, which sparked a love of the genre that has stayed with me ever since.

It isn't surprising that the West does not think of China as having a science fiction heritage, and in my years of pitching a collection like this, I was often greeted with incredulity, being told that "The Chinese Don't Do Sci-Fi" (a phrase I used for my touring lecture on how much sci-fi China actually does). Like so much of Chinese culture though, it has long been shared internally, with periodicals, films, and conventions, but not presented to the outside world, being deemed "too niche" or "not worthy enough". It really hasn't been till authors like Liu Cixin and Hao Jingfang won their Hugo awards, and the global success of film adaptations like *The Wandering Earth*, that people in the West finally pricked up their ears.

In China itself, kehuan is undergoing a renaissance. After almost a century of modern turmoil, the current state of relative social stability and economic growth has given writers and artists space to think and imagine. Where science fiction in the West grew out of sensationalist literature and pulp fiction, kehuan was predominantly a hobby for academics and professionals—moonlighting lecturers, astrophysicists, journalists and computer engineers. In the last decade however, we are beginning to see more diversity; partly, as those professions cease to be "old boy's clubs", and more female writers enter the sphere, but also as writers from different backgrounds gain the courage to submit their works, and internet archives remove barriers to publication.

Many contemporary writers in China have grown up reading Western science fiction, whether it's classic works like Orwell, Huxley and Clarke, or the cyberpunk stalwarts like PKD and William Gibson, but are melding what they have absorbed with elements drawn from their own heritage and experiences, whether it is the exploration of how cultural concepts ingrained in the Chinese psyche will evolve and survive in the future, or employing science fiction as a vehicle to reexamine China's history.

You may often find quite established sub-genres and subjects that have "been done to death" in the West, present and thriving in contemporary kehuan. Cyberpunk, genetic engineering, bio-modification, dystopian settings, time travel, artificial intelligence, robotics… these are all discarded toys being picked up by Chinese writers for the first time, and played with in exciting new ways. During much of the last century, colonial occupations, war and revolution have left China largely in a creative hiatus, but right now, writers are exploring these genres completely afresh, and are doing so from new vantage points, and with a different set of experiences. What would the Chinese do if time travel were a mass consumer product? How would China deal with the end of the world, when its mythology has no Ragnarök, or Armageddon? Even the most whimsical and humorous of space-travel stories will tend to end with a melancholic tone, because Chinese stories tend not to have happy endings, and have their own distinct rhythm and shape.

Another unique aspect to Chinese speculative fiction that I remark upon time and time again, is how fast it has to develop, because in China's current age of technological advancement, reality is constantly snapping at its heels. For instance, the country is fast becoming a world leader in genetic engineering, a subject which has been imagined and explored by many writers. Over the last few years, China has experienced the social impact of robotics, as explored by Xia Jia, not only in factories, but restaurants, shops, banks, schools, and even nursing homes. Chen Qiufan has questioned the influence of algorithms on people's decision making speculatively, but these are the real moral questions of today, not just in China, but across the web-wielding world.

This is by no means an exhaustive collection of China's historical or contemporary SF content. I have tried to give some idea of the range of kehuan in China since its last great revival in the 1980s. I mostly selected authors whose novels or collections had not been previously published in English, though I'm delighted to see that since my selection, Bao Shu and Hao Jingfang have found publishers in the West. I have also tried to include a few examples from previous decades, as well as more recent pieces, to try and capture that trajectory into diversity which is beginning to occur. The oldest writer included is now in his 70s, whilst the youngest is in her 20s. I have included alumni of China's top universities as well as those who took more outsider routes to publication. They come from across northern, central and southern China. Whilst I have curated these pieces indiscriminately and primarily from my interest and affinity with their stories, it was fascinating to discover that the authors proved to be such a diverse set of individuals, demonstrating no clusters around expectation when selected based on the merits of their works alone.

One form of "diversity bias" I may be accused of, is actively seeking female writers. As a translator and writer who has often found herself seemingly invisible next to males in the field, I feel that proper representation of female voices in Chinese science fiction is important. It is well known that the kehuan scene has been male-dominated for years, with female writers frequently seen as incapable of hard science, and only good at what one writer termed as "porridge sci-fi". At one point I did consider exclusively approaching female authors for this collection, and had I done so, I feel I would not have needed to compromise on any aspect of quality or breadth of subject. In the end, I decided to collect the best submissions, and judge them equally, rather than corral female writers into their own "safe zone", inviting criticism that they were only published in a space that is off limits to men. I was happy to find, upon examining my choices, roughly equal numbers, with female writers occupying just over half the collection.

In this anthology, you'll find "a day in the life" story alongside whimsical galactic adventures featuring eccentrics and strange civilizations; you'll find philosophical and contemplative space elegies nestling next to post-apocalyptic black comedy, and hard-boiled thrillers side by side with interplanetary romance.

In bringing you these stories, I have endeavoured to retain as much of the "Chineseness" as possible, keeping as many idioms, proverbs and metaphors as I can in direct translation, occasionally forming new phrases which make sense in English, but carry the sense of the original, rather than omitting them or substituting in the nearest English commonplace, so the original is not merely subsumed into the secondary language.

In most instances, I have kept the proper names of characters and places, as well as certain objects in Chinese, romanised using standard pinyin. With objects and concepts especially, this is to keep them as unique things, instead of lumping them together with equivalents from other Asian cultures the words of which have more successfully made their way into the English language, which has previously led to the obliteration of their Chinese identities and uniqueness, and clumsy, cheesy translations. I also think that retaining the Chinese names such as Tuoyuan (椭圆) and Linlu (林鹿) adds a certain charm to the text.

Sometimes there just isn't a cultural equivalent of a word, such as jiejie, which literally means "older sister", but also means "an unrelated and older female friend", or "a respected female companion of a slightly older age than you", or "an unknown woman whom you wish to address with cordiality". In these moments, I have either woven the explanation of the concepts into the translated text, or where absolutely necessary, explained it in a footnote. These have been kept to a minimum, as not to interrupt the flow of the story, or intrude upon the reading experience. After each story, I have included a short piece on the author and their story, partly to provide some cultural context, and partly to help you place them in the history of Kehuan. I had to consider whether these would go before, or after each story, or maybe gathered together in the back pages. In the end, I felt that you would prefer to read each story without my comments influencing your enjoyment, like taking the first mouthful of a dish without adding any seasoning. I hope you find my thoughts and comments informative and entertaining, and maybe you'll reread the story in a different light.

Of course, this anthology also carries meaning beyond that of the individual stories. In introducing kehuan to new readers around the world, I also wanted to give you an insight into China as a whole. There is still a vast disconnect between what is happening within China and what is seen by the rest of the world. Its unique development, over the last century, and heavy cultural difference, has led to a lack of international understanding, sometimes by mistake, sometimes by deliberate fear mongering.

China itself is often complicit in its inscrutability. Its deep-rooted desire to present a united front to the outside world and the growing self-sufficiency of its markets, can sometimes make it feel like confronting an alien species. One value of science fiction lies in its ability to reflect and explore current preoccupations of the culture that generates it. As much as I am aware that a lot of current interest in Chinese science fiction is based on neophilia and the realization that it actually exists, I hope readers will also find reflections of their own hopes and fears, and realise that the things the Chinese dream of and fear, are not a million miles away from what you yourself wish for, and hide from.

In many ways, putting this book together, translating the stories, and interacting with the authors has been an unforgettable experience. I have wanted to bring whole books of overlooked Chinese fiction to the West for many years, and have dreamed of publishing my own kehuan collection for almost a decade, so I am delighted to finally have the opportunity to do so. It has been a long process of planning, negotiating, coordinating, pulling disparate strands and herding people together, and I could hardly believe it has materialised, until it did.

I have to thank Storycom, the first professional story commercialization agency in China, dedicated to discovering and commercializing excellent stories. They've also made many award-winning science fiction films and are committed to bringing kehuan into the mainstream, both within China and internationally. They have greatly helped with this anthology, and other publications around the world. I am glad to have been a focal point around which Chinese and international SFF communities could muster. I hope this cooperation can continue with groups like the Shimmer Program, who plan to bring World Con to China. The sci-fi genre is often an important space for writers to examine issues within a society, and allow seeds for growth and change to be planted.

I have thoroughly enjoyed my conversations with all the authors throughout my translation, debates I've had with my editor, where Nerf guns, paper models, and desk ephemera have all been used to bash out occasional tricky sequences, and I also should give a special thank you to The Canadian Cemetery History Society, who were able to help me with some very specific terminology.

Whilst this project has been in development for years, it finally "went hot" just before the outbreak of Covid-19, and the UK went into lockdown. This in itself has been an experience to remember, but translating a long post-apocalyptic story about a deadly virus, while there was one out there, took it to another level entirely. At times, it did have me wondering where reality ended and fiction began. As I write this, quarantine measures are still in place, and during the difficult times of lockdown, one thing that kept my spirits up is knowing that this collection of sticky notes, scribbled-on print-outs and Google documents were all slowly coalescing into the single book, which you now hold your hands, and that you'll be beginning your own journey through this wonderful collection of kehuan.

THE LAST SAVE
最终档案

GU SHI

1

REAL CHOICES

JERRY XU STANDS IN front of the washing liquid in the supermarket, racking his brains, trying to remember which brand his wife Lili had told him to get. Was it Camilla's or Miranda's?

He'd bought the wrong brand already: they'd already had a huge row about it, so he had no choice but to delete the whole afternoon, return to the shops and start again.

Thinking back, all he remembers is Lili's hysterical screaming face, but the things she'd said seem to have faded into the primal mist of memory.

A staff member walks past, and he asks, "Which washing liquid's the best to get?"

"Camilla's, of course," she replies without hesitation.

"Believe me, sir, if you make any other choice, you'll be deleting your file and coming right back here before you know it."

"Fine."

Jerry picks up the recommended brand and puts it in his trolley. He doesn't say another word to the assistant: she'd just mentioned the word he hates most. *Choice*. It means the possibility of repeating his existence again and again, to correct every single mistake.

When he gets to the frozen section, he suddenly remembers he hasn't saved his memory. Stopping abruptly, he slaps his right hand onto his left wrist.

"Save—12 July 2301—5.21.37pm—file no. 32031—confirm."

While saving, Jerry skims the plethora of earlier records on virtual screens stimmed directly into the eye. All are arranged by year, then month, then day. Because he'd collected so many, Jerry often starts to wonder how he should choose. Perhaps this is the only real choice: any other decision can be undone and repeated endlessly.

To start again is actually an extremely loathsome thing.

He releases his fingers, and the reality in front of him fades back into view. On his left, a woman suddenly cries out, "Iforgottofeedthebaby." Her rapid speech squashes all her words into a single incoherent outpouring, and just as rapidly, she simply stops existing. Clearly, she has chosen a past save and deleted herself from this one.

Jerry sighs. This is unsettling. It's the second time he's seen this woman. Last time he went shopping, he'd seen her do exactly the same thing: now the whole scene feels like a curse, because he doesn't know if he's bought the right washing liquid.

And he's got a bad feeling about it.

2

TIME AND SPACE

WALKING TO HIS CAR, Jerry's ears are filled with all kinds of commercials blaring from the streets. Of course, most of them are for Time Axis. As the pioneer in the market of recording life memories, this company had transformed the lives of all humanity. As early as primary school, children are taught the theory behind "Time Axis" technology, with the aid of free-of-charge Save Space—courtesy of Time Axis.

At the end of each term, the teachers would request all students who failed to attain full marks in their exams go back and re-take them, but young Jerry Xu was an eccentric child. He refused, and challenged the teacher with the rebuttal: if we make multiple copies of everybody's world, wouldn't this cause chaos one day?

The teacher didn't have a satisfactory reply. "Of course not. We have an enormous Save Space, big enough to create a world for every single human being. Believe me, child, every world is unique."

In the end, Jerry Xu insisted on not altering his exam answers. But looking back now, such obstinacy was pointless. He would always have to choose, again and again—correcting his mistakes, correcting all contradictions—to attain a perfect life.

He stops his car in front of the red traffic light. It is bliss. He doesn't have to choose whether to continue or to stop.

A sudden blast of loud music from the broadcast makes his heart skip a beat. He switches the channel, but a feeling of unrest spreads out from his gut, and he wants to run away.

What are you afraid of? he asks himself. *No matter what happens, you can always start again.*

Start again.

Start again.

He's going insane. Good god!

Of course, before he loses his mind (or even afterwards) he could always go back to the before, and start again.

The red light gives way to green, and Jerry puts his foot on the pedal, but looks back out of habit. "This is the Incisive New Critique Show, collecting wisdom from the people," a female voice announces on the broadcast. "Let's have a look at this message—wow, it's talking about the concept of time and space, it's really interesting…"

A commercial interjects. "As technology advances, time has become elastic—distance is no longer indicated in terms of actual measurements of length, but of time: it's only an hour from Beijing to New York! All the geographical obstacles have disappeared, and we can now reach any corner of the world at the drop of a hat." *But I don't want to go anywhere,* Jerry Xu thinks. "Although the direction of time is singular, and strictly speaking it's impossible to 'start afresh', parallel dimension information technology can now open another world, making it possible to 'travel back' from the future, by reloading the past that has been saved. This is why," continues the broadcast, "you can only read past files that have been saved! Everything beyond that saving point will have disappeared, and you will never be able to return to this 'present'.

Thus, time is now measured in space, or as the salesmen call it—the Save Space. The Save Space is capable of storing all the data from an individual's life up to the moment they hit save, even the world in which they existed. Do you need to purchase more Save Space?" Jerry joins in with the jingle, mouthing perfectly over the female voice, "Live your life the perfect way, call Time Axis, yesterday, dial 1111-111."

The regular music is back and in full swing as Jerry stops the car and lets out a deep breath. The sight before him isn't unfamiliar, but it takes a moment for his mind to bring up the idea that this is his home. He switches off the car engine. All music, engine noise, and electric hum come abruptly to a stop. He immerses himself in this temporary calm, and suddenly feels exhausted. He is thirty years old, but he knows that the time he has experienced is far beyond three decades. He has repeatedly done many things—he has entered the *Gaokao*[1] many times, looked for a job many times, started over with many girlfriends—until he had qualifications, a career, money, power, and Lili Wen: the love of his life. However, as they enter their sixth year of marriage (or the tenth if repeated time is taken into account)—he is once again unsure about everything.

Maybe he has made the wrong choice? This terrifying thought resounds in Jerry's mind. Or perhaps he could go back to when he was twenty-four, and choose someone else.

No, don't!

He loathes the idea: it makes him physically nauseous— he is not going to start again.

He has bought the right washing liquid, and she is going to be pleased.

He scrutinizes himself in the rear view mirror, and

---

1 Gaokao (高考) is the commonly used term referring to National Unified Examination for Admissions to General Universities and Colleges, China's notoriously gruelling higher education exams.

puts on a confident smile. He is going to open the door, embrace her, kiss her, and everything will be better.

He gets out the car, pushes open the front door, and walks into the living room with his bag of shopping. "Darling, I picked up the—"

He stops midsentence.

She isn't there. She's not at home.

Suddenly Jerry is panic-stricken. Every time she's not there when he comes home, he panics.

"I'll be here for you, every day, darling." That's what she had said.

Maybe she's just out walking the dog, he thinks, taking deep breaths, and then sitting down. She must have gone out dog walking. He calls out tentatively "Alpha?"— that's the name of that bloody German shepherd dog. Ever since he appeared, Lili has only had affectionate strokes and kisses for him; it's like the dog is her husband. But the furry thing does not run over, wagging its tail to answer his call as usual.

"Yep, see? She's out walking that bloody dog!" Jerry grumbles, putting the food into the fridge and then the washing liquid in the most obvious place, observing his handiwork with satisfaction.

The last time, she was standing right here. Jerry suddenly recalls the icy look on Lili's face as she cast him a perfunctory glance. All he could do was put the shopping away himself, but when he took out the washing liquid, she began to scream.

"You bought Camilla's? Again?' she shouted, stamping her foot and viciously hurling the bottle on the floor. "I have told you a hundred thousand times, I hate the smell of that stuff!"

Oh god, when his memory finally serves him up this

scene, he cups his head in his hands. He's got it wrong. Again.

3

LONELY WORLDS

JERRY SITS LATE into the night waiting. It's eleven and Lili still hasn't come home. He considers calling the police, but he already knows what their response will be. "Well, sir, your first port of call should be Time Axis. Your wife may have just gone to another Save Space, nothing to be alarmed about, is it?"

Of course, he could save just before calling the police. If he felt too embarrassed by their response, he could come back to this moment, and start again.

He's been here before. Last time, the person who vanished was his father. He watched him disappear right before his eyes ("oh god I forgot to switch off the light"), never to re-appear again. He was seven then. He has never seen his mother. Seven-year-old Jerry called the police, crying as he spoke on the phone: "What if he doesn't come back?"

"Oh, don't worry, kid, you'll soon learn to live alone."

Jerry did learn to grow up alone, like most other children. He quickly learned that there wasn't anyone who you could keep around for long: they would always suddenly disappear. Sometimes Jerry would rather start all over again, so he could find them—and keep them. Return to the past and ask them—even beg them—not to leave his world.

But he couldn't make such demands on others, not

when he himself often chooses to reload a Save because he'd forgotten his keys, or got his wallet stolen, or for no reason whatsoever. Simply because he's in a bad mood, and wanted to abandon one world and enter another. After all these years, he's finally understood that everyone he meets in this world is a chance meeting. They could very possibly disappear in an instant, never to be found again. Of course, he could always return to the past, return to their side, and then fearfully wait for their departure.

He is beginning to fear that he is, in fact, alone in this world, and that no matter which Save he returns to, there would only ever be just him.

Alone.

On the first day he met Lili, he decided to marry her— even though she isn't pretty, has a bad temper, doesn't do the housework, and has no idea how to make a living. She doesn't even want to have his children, but it still fills him with joy to be with her, because she doesn't have a Time Axis account. She said she doesn't believe in starting over: she just wants to live once, and once was enough.

He cherished, loved and adored her, knowing that as long as he doesn't return to the Saves before they met, she would always be here, in this world—she would always be here for him, every day.

But now she is not here for him.

She's gone she's gone she's gone.

I'm going crazy, I'm literally losing my mind, he thinks furiously. It was clearly his mistake in choosing to reload: it was him who should have disappeared. Why not return to that ancient Save, and marry his gorgeous, dynamic ex, Rosie? He'd felt like he'd really traded down to go for Lili instead, but now she's walked out on him! This is simply preposterous! Jerry dials up the Save, and is a moment away from confirming the reload, but stops at the last second. No, he can't do this. What if, after returning to that time, he never finds Lili again?

He can't lose her, he can't bear it.

He doesn't want to start over again.

He doesn't want to—choose.

4

COUNTLESS REJECTIONS

"...IS HAPPINESS, OF course. The existence of Time Axis is precisely to make everyone happy."

It's midnight, and the broadcast is showing a repeat of the interview with Styme, their CEO.

With his body sunk into the sofa, Jerry stares vacantly at the virtual screen. Lili still hasn't returned. He has rung the police and got the reply he'd expected.

"Yes, an old Chinese proverb goes, 'there's no pill in this world for curing regret', but that's precisely what we're here to change." On TV, Styme re-arranges his paunch, and asks softly, "Are you having regrets? Then go back to the past. You don't know what to choose? Don't be scared, you can try out every path, every crossroad in your entire life. Isn't this too splendid?"

Choose!

Anger flares up in Jerry's murky eyes. He leaps up, brandishing the washing liquid, and hurls it where Styme would be sitting. The virtual images glitch, showing the splashes of washing liquid spurted across his walls, but the projection compensates and normality quickly resumes.

Out of breath, eyes sunken, and hair disheveled, Jerry Xu resembles the countless lunatics he'd encountered on the streets.

"But how would you explain today's rising suicide rates?" the presenter asks acerbically, gesturing to a chart which has phased into view. "These are the figures for the widespread use of Time Axis, and these are the rate of suicides among our citizens. We can clearly see a correlation between the two, especially recently—"

"Ohhhh!" Styme emits a mournful sigh, interrupting his counterpart. His round face suddenly wrinkles up like a shriveled and diseased orange. "This really is very unfortunate. Though we must recognize that there are many reasons for the increase in suicides, that can't be truly attributed to Time Axis."

"Really?" presses the host. "I think you are aware there are members of parliament who think that your company has 'deceived the general public', and various groups and organisations have been promoting 'Refuse to Reload' campaigns…"

"Of course, I am aware." Styme once again interrupts his interviewer softly. "I have been fortunate enough to meet several members of these organizations. According to the laws regulating Time Axis, the company cannot disclose details of the usage of the saving technology by their members, but I have sufficient evidence to demonstrate that this so-called 'Refuse to Reload' campaign has relied on quite heavy usage of Save Space."

Styme hasn't even raised his voice, but his small eyes are glowing under the studio lights. He pauses, and then continues: "Pray tell me, who precisely is it that's 'lying to the public'?"

Under the glares of the entire audience, the presenter

places his hand on his left wrist and blinks out of existence. He has clearly returned to the file before the interview to prepare his questions again. Styme sits in the studio alone, and slowly turns his face towards the camera. Every tiny blemish and crease is exposed under the harsh studio lights, revealing an aged expression on a young face. His smile is well-honed, smooth, without a blemish; like a jade stone that warms with touch, basking in the extraordinary glow of time.

"Please, consider this." He pauses, then opens his mouth again. "Isn't this the most perfect answer? My dear friends, please don't reject Time Axis; please don't reject having choices in life. You can find answers in every chance you take; why refuse the opportunities to try more? There are always other possibilities out there!"

Pausing to stand up and holding out his hands, he continues: "I have another piece of good news for everyone. In the new edition of Time Axis, we have achieved the cross-save technology. In other words, as long as you and your friends sign the 'Shared Save' agreement, you can enjoy this world together in your subsequent days. Of course, the requirement is that you must simultaneously read, access and reload the saved file—we have put this information under the 'Friends and Family' product category. If you wish to add this to your Time Axis account, please call 1111-111 to sign up today."

The offer is extremely tempting, but Jerry's body refuses to move and remains embedded in the depths of the sofa like an abandoned child. His back is stiffly straight, and his hands contorted as they grasp the back cushion. His nostrils flare and contract; he is thinking.

He could *totally* go back to this morning, or return to any timeline where Lili exists. Why is he not doing this?

And then he remembers one of their fights. A fight he had obliterated from existence, when Lili wasn't just a passive housewife; when she still had passion and would still kiss his lips with love. Halfway through the row, she burst into tears and said, "I don't know when you'll disappear! I always have this feeling that you've abandoned me countless times!"

At the time he replied, "Of course I won't leave you! How could I leave you, darling?"—but when she asked him to remove his Time Axis Saver, he had refused.

"Oh no, there's no need, I'll always be with you," he said, simultaneously reloading a reality five minutes before the row had started. He disregarded the "about-to-kick-off" look on her face, and fiercely dispelled all her rage and doubts with his lips and tongue.

This way, the problem was solved.

So the current Lili is a woman who'd been by his side for six years, and has never fought with him—because he always calms her before things turn into a storm, and because she can never find fault with anything he does. So instead, she's stopped wanting to argue and become indifferent, as cold as stone. No matter what he does or what he says, she looks at him quietly with a hint of contempt in her eyes.

Until this fucking bottle of Camilla's.

With the situation gnawing at him like an itch from the roots of his teeth, the phone rings.

He shoots up, and grabs at the receiver.

"Hello, this is Time Axis." The speaker has a soft, exquisite voice. "Is this Mr Jerry Xu?"

"Speaking." He tries to keep his voice calm.

"Hello, Mr Xu. Your wife has just applied for our company's 'Friends and Family' service. Would you be willing to sign the 'Shared Save' agreement with her?"

"Wait, did you say she's at your office?" Jerry raises his voice.

"She was, sir." The speaker's tone remains smooth and graceful. "Would you be willing to cosign the Share…"

Before she finishes, Xu interrupts: "Tell me where she is! Damn it, keep her there, I'm coming right over."

"Ms Wen has already left, Mr Xu," the sales assistant says gently. "She has especially requested that we call you at this time, and also asked us to inform you—and these are her own words—she understands if you don't want to sign."

"Damn it! Can't you find her?" He knows that Time Axis would have her constantly tracked in their GPS system.

"My apologies. We cannot disclose information about our clients."

"I'm her husband!"

"I'm very sorry, Mr Xu. Perhaps you might choose to sign the 'Shared Save' agreement, which would guarantee you both end up in the same time space."

"She's not fucking going anywhere!"

As this roar leaves his throat, he suddenly becomes very aware that this is not a social call, and that he's talking to the provider of the most important service in his life.

At once, the vicious curl at the corner of his mouth softens, as if he's regenerated a perfect outer shell. He suppresses his heavy breathing and the wheezing from his nasal cavity, and with as much civility as he can muster, speaks into the phone.

"I'm terribly sorry. I'm a little agitated at the moment, what with my wife disappearing…"

"I totally understand."

"I really need to know where she is." Xu takes another

keep breath. "I beg you, please tell me."

"Impossible, sir." The voice is just as tender as before. "We cannot disclose client information."

"Alright, alright." The corner of his mouth begins to flex again into the snarl. "So if I sign this goddamned agreement, you'll find her for me, right? You're asking me to sign up for your most expensive product you know?"

"Your wife has already paid in full. Your part is completely complimentary, Mr Xu."

"I..."

He abruptly halts as a second voice cuts in, one which pours through the receiver and bores straight into his soul, making him shudder.

"I understand if you don't want to sign," says Lili Wen.

5

A LITTLE PERSEVERANCE

JERRY XU STANDS in front of the washing liquid in the supermarket, panting. He picks out a bottle of Miranda's from the bottom shelf.

With his old bones creaking with decay, and his trembling hands covered in liver spots, he drops the unpopular brand into the trolley.

He has to lean on the trolley to get to the tills, and then he catches the driverless minibus for senior citizens. Listening to the Time Axis commercials, he feels heavy and drowsy, almost falling asleep.

When the minibus stops, he's still a little muddled and confused. With his murky eyes fixed on the blurry outline of his house, he thinks—yes, that's where I want to go. He disembarks, careful not to forget the washing liquid and groceries, and shuffles towards his front door.

He knows there'll be no one to let him in, no one to come out and welcome him, or help him those last few yards with the heavy bags. He lives alone, like most people his age: lonely. All these stubborn old rebels, refusing to return to the time of their vibrant and vigorous youth, but instead determined to wait for death in their pitiable husks.

Jerry Xu is very happy that he has persevered in something: like when he was little, refusing to alter his answers just to get those full marks even when he had to re-sit the exams.

A long time ago, he had signed the agreement, but Lili never came home.

He knows she's still in this world, somewhere, with that damned Alsatian of hers. Sometimes he even thinks he's seen her or the dog turning the corner of a street during festive celebrations, but he never found her.

At least, he knows that as long as she's alive, she'll be in this world, somewhere. She never left.

From that time, despite never taking off his Saver, he's never used it. At the bottom of his heart was hope, or regret. He somehow feels that, if she knows what he's done, she might come back.

Come back to him.

He places his finger on the sensor to unlock the door, and thinks he hears a barking dog. Automatically, he assigns the sound to an illusion from tiredness, but there is a tremble in his hand that confuses the old lock, which changes back to red, giving an irritating "beep beep" error alert. He drops the shopping on the step, and lifts his hand again, but this time, the door opens by itself.

An elderly face greets him, with familiar features and a familiar expression.

"Darling, you're home," says Lili Wen.

Jerry Xu's feet seem rooted to the spot, and his mouth freezes open.

She's a little younger than him, her movements still nimble. "It's alright." Briskly, she picks up the bags and, eyeing their content, says in a reproachful tone, "You finally remembered what to get. Silly old you."

She cocks her head towards the inside, turns and walks back in. A young golden retriever comes to the door, eyes him as a prospective source of pets, and then, with a wagging tail, follows his mistress into the kitchen. Bewildered by the casualness, Jerry feels like he's in a dream: happy beyond words, but also frightened that he may wake up. He follows them in like an idiot, but when he sees that Lili has just left the bags on the countertop, he can only think of one thing to say.

"Put them away…" he mumbles.

"They're not important," says Lili Wen, grasping his Saver.

Jerry hasn't touched the thing in years, and he panics as the interface wakes up. "What are you doing?"

"I want us to use Time Axis together."

"What for?"

"To reload the only save I've ever made." She is smiling at him, full of adoration and longing. "And return to our youth."

*　　*　　*

6

THE RIGHT CHOICES

TOGETHER, THEY UNINSTALLED Time Axis.

When Lili was giving birth, Jerry almost regretted it. She looked so desperately in pain that he wished he'd never got her pregnant, and when little Billy Xu was born— pink, swollen and ugly as hell—Jerry thought, *Maybe if he'd chosen Rosie, they'd have a better-looking child.*

In the smoking room, he lifts his head to omnipresent commercials. "Are you regretting it? Please choose Time Axis."

Jerry stares at them for a while, then turns away and walks into his wife's recovery room.

Billy Xu is shrieking and Lili lies on the bed, exhausted, her hair clammy and clinging to her face, her hospital gown crusted with blood and sweat marks, giving out an indescribable stench.

He kisses the child's forehead, and then takes a towel from his bag, soaks it in warm water, and gently wipes her face clean.

He has no regrets.

He knows that he's made the right choice.

NOTES

A CITY PLANNER BY day, Gu Shi has been publishing her writing since 2011, winning prizes at both the Xingyun[2] and Yinhe[3] Awards over the past decade. I remember first reading a bio-fantasy story of hers and being taken with her work for several reasons, including its strong female protagonist and hard science content, which traditionally has not been perceived as the realm of female writers. "The Last Save" was the first piece Gu Shi had published, in 2013, in *Super Nice*[4], and is the story that she herself feels marked her crossing into the realm of the fully fledged SF writer.

The story was written whilst Gu Shi studied for her masters degree, and both she and those around her were facing a nexus of life choices. She had to say goodbye to friends who'd chosen to seek their fortunes in other cities, and found her path crossing with others who'd come to find opportunities in Beijing.

It's human nature to seek perfection, and to better ourselves. The Chinese motivation to achieve and improve is famous around the world. What would happen if the technology exists that could bring this to an obsessive

---

2 The Xingyun (Nebula 星云) Award was founded in 2010 by the World Chinese Science Fiction Association. It's open to all science fiction works published in the Chinese language around the world. Voting is not limited to the members and extended to the public.

3 Established in 1986 by two magazines—*Science Fiction World* and *Wisdom Tree*—the Yinhe (Galaxy 银河) Award, the first and only one of its kind for the first two decades of its lifetime, is considered the highest honour a science fiction author could achieve in China. Until very recently, it was only awarded to stories published in *Science Fiction World*, China's longest running major SF magazine.

4 *Super Nice* is a magazine founded in 2010 by Xu Lei, author of the best-selling *Graverobber Chronicles* (daomu biji) and other writers, aimed to showcase the best, coolest and most enjoyable of Chinese fiction across the country.

level? What choices would any of us make if we 'had a time machine'? What opportunities and pleasures are missed, that come from our apparent 'mistakes', and what does it make of us if we are never challenged to overcome adversity? I was reminded whilst translating this of the practice of "Scum Saving", playing a video game, and saving every few moments, going back if you missed a shot or failed a puzzle. Eventually earning a 'perfect' ending, but not necessarily enjoying the experience. Science fiction is so often seen as giant spaceship and galactic battles, or powerful robots and mutants, but just rewriting a single rule of existence can have an immense impact on people's daily lives. I thought that an intimate story of one person's adoption, and eventual rejection of a new technology would make a gentle inroad to this collection.

TOMBS OF THE UNIVERSE
宇宙墓碑

HAN SONG

1

WHEN I WAS ten, my father decided that I was fit for space travel. That year, the whole family went to Orion on a flight with Interstellar Travel. On our way back, the ship broke down, and we had to stop off on Mars to catch another flight back to Earth.

We landed near the Martian north pole. With everyone feeling anxious and apprehensive, the flight attendant arranged for us to get into spacesuits and take a stroll outside. Our landing point was surrounded by ruins from the old Human Era, announced the captain; remnants of the First Age of Space Exploration. I remember very clearly: we had stopped in front of a section of a metal wall several kilometres long, and happened upon some unexpected things.

We now know that those things were called gravestones,

but back then, I was simply transfixed by their awesome grandeur. They stood on a vast plain, which had been smoothed flat by human engineering. Monoliths, large and small, shot up from the ground like spring bamboo after the rain, all in a cadence of black which, against the flaming red soil, created an extraordinary sight. The Martian sky began to rain tiny flecks of starlight. The mystery of the moment captured my youthful heart.

The grown-ups all turned pale, just standing there, staring at each other in dismay.

We had come across one of the largest graveyards in the solar system, only to pause momentarily and hurry back to the ship. Everyone looked quiet and shaken. There was almost a kind of regret on their faces, as if they had seen something they shouldn't have. I kept quiet, but felt a sense of elation for no particular reason.

The replacement shuttle service finally arrived, and as it pulled up from Mars, I whispered to my father:

"What was that?"

"What was what?" He returned the question in a daze.

"Those things behind the wall!"

"They…were people who died in space. Back then, space travel was a bit trickier than it is now."

My intuitive understanding of the concept of death probably began then. I couldn't understand the sudden change that had come over the adults upon the sight of the Martian graves. For me, death became associated with the splendid relics of a bygone era, with a rose-tinted view of Mars that held an irresistible charm for my young mind.

FIFTEEN YEARS LATER, I took my girlfriend to the moon. "There's an unspoiled place there, off the beaten track, where you'll see elements of the universe beyond our dreams." I made a series of excited gestures. Without Yu's knowledge, I had visited graveyards of all shapes and sizes across the solar system. I would stand still and gaze at them, totally entranced. Their tranquility and desolate beauty felt like a perfect harmony with the celestial bodies on which they stood. These monuments were masterpieces in themselves. I have to admit that my childhood experience had left subtle, yet deep impressions on my mind.

Yu and I parked our shuttle on a remote landing pad, and walked quietly towards the valleys of the moon. There were no other vehicles, no other people. Yu gripped my hand tightly as I studied again the surface maps I'd drawn myself.

"OK, we're here."

We arrived at the perfect moment. Earth was slowly rising from the lunar horizon, bathing the grave cluster in fantastical splendor. They seemed as though they were stirring slightly, as if awakening. We were miles away from the nearest landing pad. I felt Yu's body press against mine, trembling violently. She stared aghast at Earth, ghost-like from this perspective, and the graves it seemed to have somehow revived.

"I'd like to go back to the shuttle," she murmured.

"Getting here was a pain, why do you want to go so soon? It may be dead quiet now, but back in its heyday it was the liveliest place!"

"I'm scared."

"Don't be. All our explorations of space began here on the moon. All the biggest graveyards in the universe are in our own solar system. We should be proud."

"But now we're the only two people who've come to see them. Do you think the dead know?"

"It's not just the moon, but Mars and Venus...They've all been deserted. But, if you listen, you can hear the rumble of spaceships over planets thousands of light years away! The spirits of these dead explorers must be smiling from beyond the veil."

"Why did you bring me here?"

I didn't know how to answer this question. Why did I bring my girlfriend thousands of miles off-world to look at the graves of strangers? What if something awful happened to her? I hadn't given that much thought. If I told Yu it was because I wanted to bring her to a place in the universe where love and death come face to face and become entwined forever, she'd think I was insane. Perhaps I could simply point to my thesis on intergalactic gravestones, which I had indeed been researching. I could tell Yu that in the old days, astronauts lived by an unspoken rule to never marry a colleague—so you'll never find a couple's grave here. Or perhaps I could resort to a kind of graveside spookiness.

I stayed silent. I felt as though our bodies were becoming part of the countless, silent graves. I was drifting off in my own reverie, hoping that Yu would somehow intuitively understand. But she only stared at me, nervous and half-crazed.

"Do you think I'm weird?" I asked, after a while.

"You're... not like other people."

After we returned to Earth, Yu fell ill. I thought it was due to our trip to the moon, and I was full of remorse. I devoted myself to caring for her, abandoning my research into the graves of Space until she began to recover.

I became so fascinated by the burial traditions of the planetary migration era that my father grew uneasy. Tombs and graves? They belonged to the distant past:

people had forgotten them, cast them aside like Earth's sister planets in the solar system, and are now looking to the depths of Space for new sights beyond. I became aware that this external behaviour was symptomatic of some deeper issue. Whenever I have been engrossed in my research, looked up from my papers and met my father's gloomy gaze, my mind would return to that scene in the Martian graveyard when I was a boy; to the strange expressions on the grown-ups' faces, as if something deep inside them had been stirred. Nowadays, people don't talk about the past, especially the ancient astronauts who had perished, but they have never forgotten them. This much I know. Whenever they run into the subject, they would carefully skirt around it, with almost too much sensitivity. Institutional attitude in our culture has led to a kind of historical negation.

Living in the moment: that seems to be the *force du jour* of mankind. Perhaps we no longer think the past is important. Has it become something we don't have time to remember? I don't pretend to delve into the hidden cultural meanings behind this, nor am I a historicist. My obsession with graves lies in a feeling they inspire in me, a feeling akin to poetry. They exist simultaneously in the living world, in the here and now, and outside of it. Occasionally they interact with visitors of the present, but mainly they bide their silence, immersed in the bygone era that they also belong to. This is why they mesmerize me.

Whenever I thought about them in this way, Professor Ji would warn me that I was at the edge of an abyss. *Our responsibilities are to uncover history and bring it to light, not to be driven by personal interest. Our aim is to help our ill-informed fellow humans understand the hardships and great achievements of our forefathers, the pioneers of space exploration.*

The words of my silver-haired professor often rendered me speechless, but on the academic questions of the social customs of graves, we debated relentlessly. When Yu's health was on the mend, the professor and I resumed our debate on the fundamental question of the sudden disappearance of graves in space.

"I still can't agree with you, Professor. On this question, we've always had differing opinions."

"Young man, have you found any new evidence?"

"I believe in field intuition. Old papers can only tell us so much, but there's simply not enough information. You should leave Earth and travel around a bit."

"I can't compete with those young people in their obstinacy."

"Maybe you're right, Professor, but…"

"Do you know about the new discovery of the burial site on Cygnus A?"

"An unnamed grave, inscribed with only the date, which has pushed back the date of end of the Grave Burial Era."

"If I'm correct, the highly influential paper on Technologism, 'Proclamations of Planets' was published around this time. Don't you think there's correlation?"

"You think this marks a new kind of cultural convention replacing an old one?"

"I believe that we will never find a later grave burial than this one. When Technologism ascended as the dominant concept, the social custom of gravestones became one of those mysteries of the universe."

"Don't you think this is too sudden a transition, Professor?"

"Its suddenness proves the temporal causation."

"...there might be other reasons. At the time, Technologism was just taking root and gaining grass root support, but grave burial conventions had tens of thousands of years of history, and tombstones had been used across the universe for thousands of years. Nothing could suddenly destroy such a strong tradition. It's obvious: it had been ingrained in the psyche of the ancients, in their collective consciousness."

Professor Ji shrugged. The matter compiler had finished preparing our meal. It was only when we were eating that I noticed the professor's hands were trembling. Not surprising: he was over two hundred years old. A complex emotion arose inside me. Death takes life from everyone: this was a fact that not even the Technologists could dispute. In what ways we exist after death remains a matter for private conjecture, deep within our hearts. The gravestones that still stand in great numbers across the universe are a demonstration that early mankind had already contemplated this question—or perhaps they had even built in allegories of their knowledge and conclusions within these markers and tombs? People no longer need burials. They do not understand the inscriptions on the ancient tombs, nor are they concerned to read them. Have present-day humans become fundamentally different from their ancestors?

Death is inevitable, but I was still anxious that the Professor might pass away before his time. Scholars interested in devoting their time to taphonomy were extremely rare. They worked in the shadows, often to no end.

I found my eyes glued to the photograph before me: it was a full-length image of the grave the professor mentioned. Located in a remote part of the Cygnus A constellation, it was only discovered by chance by a cargo ship. There's a debate among grave scholars: what secret message was this grave trying to send us? Nobody had a definitive answer.

I found myself returning again and again to the image of this unique grave from various aspects. It resonated with my mind. Usually, gravestones are built in a cluster, forming vast graveyards with a sort of compulsory magnificence to counter-balance the isolated environment of a strange and uninhabited planet, but this solitary grave was an unprecedented exception. It was built on one of that star system's smallest and least noticeable planets, as if by careful selection. From its locale, despite rotation and orbit, none of the system's biggest planets can be seen, and every year, this little planet carries out a comet-like elliptical orbit around Cygnus A. When it reaches the point furthest from the sun it enters a period of protracted darkness. I could almost feel the loneliness of the world-weary soul buried there. This seemed so stark in contrast with most tombs of the universe, which were very particular about their grand settings—taking full advantage of the light from planets rising from the horizon, or settings featuring cliff edges many times higher than the Himalayas. Even from the dead, one felt the heroic spirit of the pioneer explorers of space. This grave possessed none of these common features.

You could also tell by its architectural style. At the time, tomb architecture emphasized the beauty of symmetry, and solid, solemn and grandiose forms conveying feelings of heroic pride. The giant pyramids of Venus and the imposing monoliths of Mars are outstanding examples of this popular model, but there wasn't a hint of this in the lonely grave. It was small, squat and rough, but built in an extremely delicate suspension structure, giving the feeling that the space it occupied had been broken down and then reassembled. It almost felt as if time itself were in free flow around the orifices of the grave. It was clearly extraordinary. All the raw materials came from the ground it stood on, entirely made from the small planet's rich resource of electrum ore. Popular materials of the time were specific compounds transported from Earth: this was very wasteful, but people were more concerned with the romantics back then.

Something else sparked my imagination about the buried subject. The grave was inscribed with the date it was made, and nothing else. Custom dictated that gravestones would feature the deceased's name as a minimum, then status, experience, maybe the cause of death and an appropriate epigram. What circumstance caused this individual's burial to be marked in such an unconventional fashion on Cygnus A?

The mystery deepens.

We can be almost certain that the owner of the grave was the last witness of Grave Burial Era. But exactly why there was a key change, no satisfactory explanation can be decided on. It's precisely because of this controversy that we owe the whole of civilization a proper explanation. Grave scholars are limited by various factors. I had obviously wanted to visit Cygnus A myself, but no one would provide me with the funding. After all, this wasn't a regular trip within the standard spaceways. And don't forget, the conventions of society didn't value our field highly.

I didn't make it to Cygnus A for a long time, till fate finally cleared the path. Unexpected changes occurred in life, and I had changed with them. It wasn't until I was one hundred years old, and marking the 70th anniversary of Professor Ji's passing, that I suddenly remembered this grave, and with it the debates I had in my youth with the professor regarding intergalactic burial rites. By that time, leading taphologists had all—like my late master—scattered to the wind. Those who pursued this field had abandoned it one after another. Having spent over half my life researching the subject, to no great effect, I often woke in the night, hand pressed to my heart, asking myself: why am I still preoccupied with old corpses? Just as my master had predicted, I had been driven by self-interest, and would come to taste the bitter fruit of my own actions. Did I ever feel any true responsibility to history? Having lived to a hundred, I felt as if I'd only just woken from a dream: it was truly impossible to know one's own fate.

Yu, the girlfriend of my youth, was now my wife: a middle-aged woman who never stopped nagging, blaming me for every misfortune she'd encountered since the time I took her to the graveyard on the moon. The shock of that had caused some strange disease: every year, on the day of our lunar trip, she would become distracted, paralysed, and mumble to herself all day long. The most advanced medical techniques had failed to cure her, and every time I returned to my research, her face would darken, and she would grow restless and fidgety. I'd quietly put down my work, step outside and look at the sky, as clear as it was seventy years ago. I would suddenly realize that I hadn't left Earth for many years. Would I be spending the rest of my days earthbound with Yu?

My son Zhu[5] is a long-term stranger to Earth, having settled with his family in another galaxy, and as captain

---

5 Zhu 筑, meaning to build or construct.

of a spaceship, he strides across the universe, gathering stardust on his shoulders. I think he must have visited planets with graveyards, and wondered what he thought of them. He'd never mentioned them to me, and I'd made a secret decision never to bring them up. It was my own father who'd brought me, all those years ago, on the trip which ended up on Mars, when I first saw those graves.

How the ordinary journeys between life and death had led the ancients to build such magnificent tombs across the universe remains a mystery, relegated to time and space.

Little by little, and without even meaning to, I began to let go of the pursuits of my youth, and to live my days in peace. The calmness of life on Earth dilutes the strongest of passions. That was something I hadn't noticed before. People who busied themselves in space had very little chance to return to the old and rather decrepit planet that once nurtured them, whilst people on Earth didn't concern themselves with vast changes happening in the depths of the universe.

That year, Zhu returned to Earth from Cygnus A, but the name of that system no longer caused any excitement in me. Due to the difference in gravity between galaxies, Zhu had grown strangely tall, and seemed more extraterrestrial than a human. His local culture had made him somber and silent. Sometimes I couldn't help but think that Yu and I were merely shadow forms of Zhu's existence in this world. Whenever I met my son, we never had much to say to each other.

Zhu poured a drink for me with bright shining eyes. He was strangely talkative that night, and I found myself responding to his unusual verve.

"How's XinNing[6]?" That's my grandson's name.

"He's good, but he misses his grandpa."

"Why didn't you bring him with you?"

"I did ask him, but he can't stand Earth climate. Last time, he broke into a huge rash when he got home."

"Really? Then don't bring him again."

I drained my glass, and found Zhu observing me out of the corner of his eye.

"Father," he shifted uneasily in the chair, "I'd like to ask you something."

"Ask me then." I eyed him doubtfully.

"I pilot a ship, and have been to many star systems through the years. I've seen a lot more than you have here on Earth. But there's one thing that I still can't really understand; it bothers me, and it's why I've come to you for advice."

"Sure."

"I know you researched graves and tombs in space, in your youth. You never told me, but I know. What I want to know is… why do they fascinate you?"

I stood up, walking to the window so my face was turned from Zhu. I never thought he'd ask that question. Those things had broken into Zhu's mind, like they did my father's and mine, stirring unease within our souls. Did the ancients of past eras wield some kind of hidden magic that caused their descendants to be eternally tormented by their restless spirits?

"Father, I was merely asking. I didn't mean anything by it," Zhu mumbled, like a child.

"Sorry, Zhu, I can't answer this question. Hmph, why do gravestones fascinate me? If I knew, I'd have told you

6 XinNing 心宁, means calmness of heart.

everything to do with gravestones when you were a kid. But, I didn't. It's an abyss, Zhu."

I saw Zhu lower his head, as if soundlessly regretting his brashness. To ease his discomfort, I swallowed my emotions, returned to the table, and poured him a drink. Then I sat down, studied his eyes, and asked, like any father full of concern for his child would:

"Zhu, tell me what you saw."

"Graves. Big ones, small ones... Lots of them."

"Of course you would, in your line of work. But you've never mentioned this."

"I also saw crowds of people. Swarming to graveyards across the planets like bees."

"What?"

"The universe has gone crazy. People are obsessed with the dead—there are thousands of ships parked on Mars alone, just to see the graves."

"Are you serious?"

"That's why I asked you about the draw of these graves?"

"What do they want with them?"

"They want to open them up!"

"Why would they do that?"

"They say there are ancient secrets buried within."

"What kind of secrets?"

"The secrets of life and death!"

"No, there's none of that. The ancients built graves out of innocent wonder."

"I wouldn't know, Father. That's what you all say. You're not fobbing me off, are you?"

"What? Do you want to open them up too?"

"I don't know."

"You're all mad! They've slumbered for thousands of

years. The dead belong to the past. Who knows what'll happen if you bring them back!"

"But we belong to the present, Father. And we want to fulfill our needs."

"Is this the way of thinking you've developed out there? I'm telling you, there's a pile of corpses, bones, and nothing else!"

Zhu's return had brought me a sense of the dramatic developments taking place beyond Earth's tranquility.

My passion had cooled, but others had found another form of my old obsession. What Zhu told me drove me to distraction. Was it that long ago that Yu and I walked on the deserted moon, to pay our respects to those tombs that no one else cared to visit? The cold, the loneliness, and the desolation had left an indelible mark on my heart. I remember telling Yu that it used to be a lively place, yet today, Zhu tells me that it's bustling again. Was this cyclical reversal predestined? Or was it controlled by some unknown force in the galactic ether? The Age of Space Exploration had given way to the Age of Technologism. Was this now the harbinger of another new Era? I was filled with both excitement and dread.

It was as if I had been brought back in time. Those endless graveyards filled my vision, basking in the ambiance I had remembered so well. The resting places were monuments, the monuments resting places; emanating an eternal sense of inevitability.

And then I thought about the meaning of Zhu's words. I couldn't help but agree with him. The mystery of the grave *was* the mystery of life and death—therein lies its so-called charisma. Not a morbid fascination with the necrotic. That is what drew scholars to them. In fact, no one can forget the graves. A vague image of the tight-faced Technologists floated into my mind's eye.

Digging up graves seemed an unusual method, but why hadn't the scholars thought of it all those years ago? Was it the taboo of disturbing the dead? Perhaps they feared that, if the ancients had really buried objects within their graves, then they, as scholars trading in theories of social customs, would have been put out of a job.

When Zhu left us, Yu relapsed into her malaise. My mind was taken up again with seeking a doctor to treat her. This activity brought such stress that I could not believe my mind found itself wandering. I suddenly recalled that Zhu had said he'd flown in from Cygnus A—a name I had been all-too familiar with. I had still kept that full-length photograph from decades ago, taken at the time of its discovery. The last grave of humanity.

2

From a manuscript found by archeologists on a minor planet in the constellation of Cygnus A:

I AM NOT writing this for future readers, because I have no intention of playing to the crowd. In our time, autobiographies are like hairs on an ox, innumerable and worthless. The captain of a star-frigate would reach the end of his life and write about the hardships and perils of all his journeys, like an ancient emperor committing his great deeds to posterity. But I want no such thing. My profession and experiences are both commonplace and mundane. I'm writing to alleviate the lonely hours before my death. I've always liked writing, and were it not my destiny to be astro-gravemaker, I'd have probably become a sci-fi writer.

Today is the day I enter *my* grave. I have chosen this small planet to build my final resting place, because it's nice and quiet, far away from the clamour of civilization and space travel. I spent a week constructing it, alone. Sourcing materials is very time-consuming, as well as difficult. We rarely use raw materials from the location, unless the deceased is a victim of unusual circumstances—when Earth would be unable to supply pre-ordered materials—or what is pre-ordered would be unsuitable for the local environment. For the deceased and their families, this is usually a cruel reality they must come to terms with, but whenever I've had to work against convention I've always found my own way.

I have not, as convention dictates, engraved the headstone with my life's achievements. That seems a ridiculous thing to do, doesn't it? For my entire life, I have built countless graves for others, and I have only ever engraved their names, statuses and reasons of death.

I am now sitting in a grave, no different to any other I've dug, writing about my past. The roof of my grave is installed with solar panels for heating and lighting, and the whole chamber is just big enough for one person. It's a cosy place to spend my last days, which I intend to fill by writing til I no longer feel like it any more.

I was born on Earth, but my youth was spent on Mars. At the time, the whole world was gripped in a feverish onslaught by the first wave of Space Exploration. Everyone was drawn to it. I myself couldn't wait to leave behind my interest in literature, to sign up for the one and only Mars Academy, unaware I'd be assigned to the Space Emergency And Rescue Corp.

Among our studies, there was a module on grave construction and engineering. It also taught students the proper and dignified manner in which deceased astronauts should be put to rest, and the great importance of such gestures.

I remember, I didn't do particularly well in any of the other classes except this one, for which I often got top marks. Thinking back, I remember as a child that if I found some poor dead animal, I would bury it with my own hands rather than just dispose of it. We used a third of our study time for theory, and the rest was practical. First we designed and constructed large numbers of models within the college grounds, and then began our field assignments. We would often build small graves near large canyons, before moving onto bigger ones on plains. Just before graduation, we went on a few interplanetary internships—once to Venus, once to a belt of small planets, and twice to Pluto.

There was an incident on our last trip to Pluto. The shuttle was carrying a large quantity of special materials for building a tomb in the icy environs on this planet. During landing, the shuttle was caught in a meteor shower, killing two of the crew members. We thought the excursion would be cancelled, but by the teacher's orders, we were to put his teachings into practice. If you visit Pluto today, you may still see a semi-circular tomb near the equator. There, resting in peace, are two of my classmates. That was my job. Due to my anxiety and panic the grave was a mess, and whenever I think of it now, I'm still overwhelmed with remorse.

After graduation I was assigned to SEARC's Third Division. It wasn't till I was deployed that I learned that the Third Division's only duty was the engineering and construction of graves, tombs, and burial sites.

Frankly, that was not what I had signed up for. My dream was to captain a space shuttle, or failing that, to work in a galactic metropolis or space station. Many of my classmates got much better postings. The ones who would eventually come to need my services had 'conquered' a few galaxies, earning long rows of honorary *ZhongZiXing*, Neutron Star Medals. When they were placed in their graves, people stood silently in solemn respect, paying no mind to the gravemaker standing to one side.

I never thought I'd be in the Third Division for the rest of my life.

Having got to this point, I'm stopping to take a deep breath, amazed at the clarity of my memory. I hesitate a little now because there are some things that should be forgotten, but let's see how it goes as I write on.

The first site I was sent to on a mission was Alpha Centauri, a solar system with seven planets. Our shuttle landed on the fourth. Local officials welcomed us with solemn respect, adding: "At last, you're here."

There were three astronauts in total who had passed on. They came into contact with radiation from an astral wave without protection, and perished as a result. I quietly breathed a sigh of relief, because mentally, I had been preparing myself for mangled or severed limbs.

This time there were five of us from the Third Division. We wasted no time in asking the officials if they had any special requests. They replied: "We'll leave it up to you. You're the experts: if there's anyone we trust, it's you. But please bury all three together."

It was I who drew up the designs that time. On our very first assignment, the boss had entrusted me with such an important task, no doubt intent on nurturing my talent. It was then that we realised that this project would be the very first grave on Alpha Centauri. I began to recall the guidance from our teachers, and the processes we had employed for the practicals. The success of a grave does not depend on the splendour of its exterior, but on the essence it conveys. To put it simply, we needed to design the monument appropriate to the lives led by the deceased and spirit of the times they lived in.

The final design turned out to be a giant cube, strong as a boulder. It symbolised the immovable place of astronauts in space exploration. Its shape gave the feeling of the quiet and stillness of time and space, suggesting an eternal stance. The scene of death was a never-ending plain, and there our gravestone would be erected, with no obstructions on any side, just the sky falling like a lake. Everything in the scene had clear-cut and distinct outlines. The only shortcoming of the tomb was that it did not concisely convey their calling as astronauts. But as my first independent piece, it had far exceeded the usual standard of my school work. We actually completed the project in just two days. All the materials came as pre-ordered components, mass-produced on Earth. All we needed to do was assemble them.

At dawn, we lined up in a row and stood quietly for a few minutes, saluting with our eyes the tomb that was just about to be inaugurated. This was the custom. The gravestone appeared bright and translucent in the blue mist unique to this planet, looking profound and poignant. The boss inclined his head, ever so gently. A sign of approval and admiration. I was stunned.

I had never thought that death could possess such unique meaning, or that our group would be the ones to give it expression. The tomb shall exist for posterity, as enduringly as the earth and sky—our materials would keep their shape for a hundred million years.

The deceased were yet to be interred, and we waited quietly for the ceremony to begin. When the sun on Alpha Centauri had risen to arm's height, people started arriving in a slow trickle. They were puffed out in ceremonial garments, the heavy helmets on their heads suppressing their individuality. The ambiance was unusual, a kind of terror amidst the solemnity. The number of deceased was not particularly high, but humans had only established a few centres on the planet back then. To have three of their number die was something of a crisis.

I no longer remember the scene exactly. I can't say if the responsible parties spoke their words of condolence, or expressed their thanks to us first. I'm also vague about which melody was playing on loop; only that it was strange, conveyed the sense of the alien, and aimed to express a kind of majesty and grandeur. What I do remember was the rumble of the drone that flew overhead, and which after flying in circles for a while, began to scatter tiny platinum flowers. Due to the weaker gravitational field of the planet, the platinum flowers danced in the air, staying afloat for an age. The view was deeply moving. By now, everyone was clapping with all their might. Where had this ritual come from? And ultimately, why did they ask us to come a million miles to build a tomb for their dead?

It was we, as undertakers, who would take the deceased into their graves. With the exception of the boss, all four of us went to carry the coffin. By this point, the clamour at the scene had stopped, the platinum flowers and drone both gone. On the west side of the tomb, the side facing our solar system, was a small entrance passage. We carried the three coffins in one after the other, wishing them peaceful rest. It was during this part that I felt that something wasn't quite right. But at the time I said nothing.

On our way back to Earth, I put my thoughts to a *qianbei*[7].

"Why were the coffins so light? They felt like the prop ones from the academy."

"Sshhh!" He looked around him. "Didn't the boss tell you? There's no one inside!"

"Didn't they die of radiation?"

"You're going to hear that a lot, so the shock will wear off. That's what they say, it's radiation, but it's more like evaporation. Not even scraps left. Just a lie to calm the people on Alpha C."

Just a lie to calm the people on Alpha C! I would never forget these words. Throughout my career, I would come to witness countless cases of mysterious disappearances. So, my glorious design was but a *yiguanzhong*[8], a mere marker for the lost! The amusing thing was that only a small handful of people knew that its fantastical exterior was hiding an empty secret inside.

Having worked in the Third Division for a long time now, I have slowly been able to acquaint myself with all the related industries. Our services covered the vast parameters of known space on which humankind set foot and operate, so we had to know all the special-access closed flight routes between all the major star systems, which were vital for getting to locations in the shortest

---

7 Qianbei 前辈, term of deference for someone older than oneself for whom one has a lot of respect.

8 Yiguanzhong 衣冠冢, traditionally a grave in which the belongings and burial rites of the individual are placed, as the body can't be found.

time—though even this way of doing things was falling behind the times, as astronauts scattered themselves further and further across the universe. So we first established offices on each planet, and then started our ship-tailing service: as soon as we could foresee that a certain intergalactic endeavour involved high risks, the Third Division would send a gravemaker's ship as part of the entourage.

This required us to be at the forefront of space travel technology—we have a good number of first-rate captains in our division. Other pilots got angry that they couldn't ditch them in flight, telling themselves it was just because they had "bad luck on their tail". We also had to be aware of all kinds of new processes within the undertaking trade, as well as all the industry-wide changes, adopting unique approaches according to the specific conditions of each planet and the special requirements of the clients, whilst also ensuring we didn't break consistency of style in our own work. Above all, it was most important— as an intergalactic undertaker—to possess extraordinary physical energy and mental robustness. Years of toil across the stars and relentless encounters with death had made us into super-humans. Sooner or later, without knowing it, workers in the Third Division began to shed the ordinary emotions of humanity. In fact, if you'd been in the Third Division for a while, you came to feel the coldness and darkness within conventional existence, and came to despise it. Death was the taboo of the whole universe, and we were the only ones who could joke about it.

Ever since my first day in the Third Division, I've considered the sacred significance of this institution. According to official records, the first space grave was built on the moon. It's a perfectly natural view, but it's doubtful that anyone would have built a couple's grave out there from a sudden wave of inspiration. Later, some people joked that the grave was disturbing the Sea of Tranquility. In actual fact, before this grave, memorials for deceased astronauts had long been built on Earth. As soon as the custom spread across the galaxies, it began a natural and intimate bond with our ancient traditions. In the age of space exploration, humans once again cast off many outmoded conventions—but by contrast, the trend of grave-building grew more and more popular: a thought-provoking occurrence. Now that our advanced technologies have replaced the hand-carving and shoulder-carrying of the Shang Era, we could build graves that make the pyramids of Egypt pale in comparison.

When the Third Division was first set up, there were people who doubted its worth—but its worth was proved by its perfect synchronisation with the development of things. When the Big Exploration really began, there were casualties in huge numbers, which caused consternation among officials and scientists. The cruelty of the universe far exceeded anyone's expectations, but there was no way that exploration would ever be allowed to cease. Death became far more present than it was on Earth, and we had to confront questions about our very existence. What is our place in the universe? What is the purpose of evolution? What is the value of life? Is the mission of humanity absurd? These were the topics that mass media raucously regurgitated.

No matter the outcome of the debates, the place of the Third Division was becoming more ingrained day by day. After the first few years, it was making a small profit, but more importantly, it had gained the governmental support of Earth and a few key planets. When sacred obelisk and pyramid clusters began to appear across the moon, Mars and Venus, the last criticisms ceased. These meticulously constructed tombs could withstand the fierce attack of meteor showers: their structures were stable, and their appearance magnificent. They would last for centuries, unscathed. People realised that the remains of their compatriots, which had been floating among the stars, could once again find a place to belong. Death became something worth being proud of. Perhaps gravestones were an expression of that age-old concept of Man triumphing over Nature. The transitioning of grave building from a spontaneous act by individuals, to an official ritual of necessity, was a masterstroke of the Third Division: it maintained its relevance until hearts and customs had set, lending the institution grace, poise and a natural place within society.

These days, no one doubts the worthwhile nature of the Third Division. Even those renowned battle-hardened captains show us immense respect when they meet us. The burial customs have evolved into a kind of philosophy of the space age, reaching even a level of mysticism. Suffice to say, no one on the outside of the organisation could ridicule us. If they had, the collapse in confidence would have destroyed all feelings of value across the known universe—the staunch culture of Earth, the sole beliefs holding up those who constantly risk their lives between black holes and supernovas.

If there were any complications, they were dealt with within the division. The longer you spent in the Third Division, the clearer its internal workings became. Some things were kept only within the inner circle, and have never passed beyond it—one reason for this is the strict code by which we abide, and the other is the mental block we had each developed to cope with the work. Every year, there would be suicides among the division. Even writing these words now, my heart is racing, and I feel like I'm stabbing myself with a knife. I once discreetly asked a colleague about the suicides. He replied, "I can't talk. They're all good people. One day, you'll come to understand how they felt." As soon as he'd said this, he slipped away like a ghost. As I grew older, having handled many corpses and remnants, death was no longer an abstract concept, but had become a specific image fixed in my head. But I have to say, the coping mechanism I'd developed was entirely different from those who took their own lives.

There was a time when the whole of the division was mired in a cloud of uncertainty. I remember someone had asked a question: who would bury us if we died? The query had been triggered by the number of suicides, and, contained within it a cascade of inquiry. We looked at one another, unable to form a decent reply even if it would have been auspicious to do so. And so we left the question unanswered. This was around the time the top levels were investigating the 'imploration for change report' incident. It was said that someone in the division had sent a report to the United Planets Council, expressing dissatisfaction with the current procedures. One point, concerning the use of custom-ordered materials, left an impression on me. Normally, no matter how far or near the burial site was, the materials were transported from Earth. This was done out of respect for the feelings of the deceased. More importantly, it was tradition, and tradition ought to be sacrosanct. The rule had even been laid out in the black and white of the 'Emergency Rescue Manual.'

Nobody could stand the way the report talked about it, deconstructing the literal cornerstones of our craft—which had been a constant right from the beginning—as a cynical and wasteful use of resources. The report tirelessly discussed the technical details and viability of sourcing materials from the burial sites themselves. Everyone knew the outcome: the author of the report was stripped of the right to leave Earth. Personally we found the report's tone traitorous, drawing attention to courses of action we should have considered. We were stunned by the report's language, intimated by its boldness, and the fact that, later on, some new recruits actually tried to test its propositions.

There was an incident when a ship carrying grave materials to the Andromeda region encountered a fuel leak en route. According to protocol, it should have turned back, but the captain ejected the materials, using the remaining fuel to take the lighter vehicle to its destination, and used the local pumice to build a grave. The act shocked the world, and the grave was later destroyed and rebuilt. The perpetrator was punished. But I will write more on that later.

Spending paragraphs just talking about my feelings would be difficult, so let me carry on telling the stories of our work. I'll continue recording what I think of as the most ordinary events, because they can most vividly illustrate the uniqueness of our trade.

We were once given an assignment for which the brief differed from the usual. No specifications of planet or mission detail, just that the gravemaker's craft be fully equipped with tools and weapons, and to head to a set of coordinates between Mars and Saturn and wait for further instructions. When we arrived, we found SEARC were already busy at work. We asked them, "Hey, are you ok with this? If not, leave it with us." There was no reply, but there seemed to be an air of apprehension coming from the other ship. It was only later that we found out a ship had disappeared among the small belt of planets— the most advanced craft humanity had built at the time. The *Columbus* was famous. Its captain had been likened to the ship's namesake. And on this voyage, he'd been transporting the leaders from five major planets.

We spent three days in space. The search party had found a hold-full of fragments from the wrecked craft, and it was time for our work to begin. Separating human remains from ship fragments was a time-consuming and exhausting task, but everybody performed outstandingly, and finally managed to assemble three corpses. The *Columbus* had a compliment of eight. The cause of the accident was generally concluded to be an 800-pound meteor which had struck the ship horizontally across its body, triggering the explosion. To have such a tragedy occur practically on Earth's doorstep filled us with regret, but the loss and devastation was felt throughout the universe.

"They were too careless," concluded the Head of the Navigation Bureau at the tomb-unveiling ceremony. We didn't know whether to laugh or cry. These people were doing fine on Earth, but for some reason had become careless, neglectful children the moment they'd entered space, so the Third Division was set up to take care of them. These were words that came from the mouth of the Head of Navigation! Still, we were too frightened to laugh. Although the three corpses we'd reconstituted were already laid to rest in the underground chamber, their bloody visages seemed to project through the thick walls of the tomb, manifesting before us. Their faces cold and stern, their eyes open, as incredulous as they were in that final moment of life.

There was something that prevented us from ever losing our restraint. We couldn't tell you exactly what it was, but all gravemakers understood this, and always went about everything with great care. There were too many graves in the universe, may they all be safe.

During that period, though, despite our usually heavy workloads, we built only this one grave.

In most people's eyes, the presence of graves altered a planet's landscape. The astronauts had lost their lives to the planet, but ultimately it was the planet that gave way.

At this point, I'm pausing to look at my hands as I type. They are well and truly those of a gravemaker. Looking at this pair of old hands, with veins protruding, dry as logs, it is hard to imagine that they had built so many mansions for the dead. They've often felt like a pair of sacred tools, free from any control by my thoughts, carrying out heaven's mandate.

All gravemakers had hands like this. I have always thought that, in any grave building project, the fundamental operations were bereft of any mechanical direction, or even our brains. Our ten fingers were spiritually attuned to the universe, and in many cases, we believed in their magic. In contrast, our thoughts remained unwieldy, coloured by prejudice and suspicion, and prone to introduce dangers whilst creating graves in the hostility of space.

In the heart of the gravemaker can often be found deep-rooted contradictions. Those in the profession who had taken their own lives were pessimists who saw the deceptive side of graves; but at the same time, the most exquisite graves had come from their hands, comparable in beauty to any wonder of nature. I staunchly believe that this depth of contradiction could only exist in our kind, while the rest of the world are drawn to the eternity of the gravestones. Sometimes we felt embarrassed at the obsession they show.

I want to talk about women next.

When I was little, and saw girls of about my age playing, totally unaware of my existence, I would be filled with a kind of emptiness. I believed that at that exact moment in time, there was a girl somewhere in the universe just for me, and that she would fill what was missing from my life. This was fate, and could not be changed, even by the power that arranges it. When I got a little older, I fell for those female astronauts who flew back and forth across space like angels; from their faces, bodies, limbs, emanated a heroic air that they'd brought back from Vega or Andromeda, making them thoroughly lovely, and leaving me in rapture. Then I would notice that the death rate among them was no lower than the male astronauts, and my heart would burn for them all the more.

I secretly dreamt of dating those heroines. Back then, the Galactic Navigation Academy had yet to open its doors to me. This would decide my fate. When I was later informed of the taboo within the astronautic circles, I nearly passed out. It was statute that no astronauts could ever be allowed anything more than a work-based relationship with each other, on the grounds that they would be too distracted to deal with the complexities of the universe. During the Big Exploration, someone had scientifically proven this, hardly expecting that the Bureau would give their tentative and tacit acknowledgement. For a time, it preoccupied the minds of most astronauts, but soon after, most men in the shuttle program started to believe that an astronaut girlfriend was bad luck, so the prohibition was set without objection. You try breaking it? Then you'll really "stink", your friends will distance themselves from you, and you'll find yourself unable to find a job for no reason in particular—or perhaps you'll find yourself demoted from first officer to steersman, and then to cabin crew, and eventually to some place like a ship breaker plant on Earth. I thought that Navigation school would provide me with the opportunity to realize my childhood dreams, but it had instead banished them. I didn't really have a choice. This is how the universe is: it doesn't leave you with a choice.

It was only after I'd roamed the galaxies for a few years as a gravemaker that I began to understand the depth to which this custom had ingrained itself within our circles. The idea that women were trouble was very widespread, a superstition that had lodged itself in the soul of every astronaut. Almost everyone I'd met could bring up at least a handful of examples to prove their prejudices.

From then on, I'd carefully observe those female astronauts, and try to see what was different or anomalous about them. In my eyes, they were as bright as a cloudless starry sky, and no matter how hard I tried, I could not see a single seed of disaster in them. Their actions during flights had even led me to believe, that in certain turns of events, women are more capable than men.

One time, during a year of intense solar spots, we buried a dozen female astronauts on a single assignment. They had died during an earthquake. They had just landed on their destination planet, preparing to work at a medical centre that had just been completed. The survivors were their friends and colleagues, and also mainly women. As requested, we engraved on the headstones those things that the deceased loved when they were alive: plants or little animals, crafts, jewelry.

When the memorial ceremony began, I heard a voice next to me. "They shouldn't have come here in the first place."

I took a sideways glance and saw a petite young woman in a tight space suit.

"They shouldn't have asked us to come so early, the corpses haven't even been put together," I said, full of pity.

"I'm saying that we shouldn't have come out into space." She spoke in a low and heavy voice that wrenched my heart.

"So you also think women shouldn't come to space?"

"We're too weak. It's a man's world out here."

"I disagree," I said, full of feeling, and found myself observing her. I had never really spoken to a female astronaut, and at that moment, all the men and women present turned to look at the two of us. This was how I met Yu.

At this point, I stop writing, close my eyes, and for a few minutes I savour that moment, the boundless sweetness of her memory mixed with impending bitterness.

After I came to know Yu, I realised I had broken the taboo, but the impulses of my youth had swelled once again in my heart. I believed again that there was one girl who was meant for me. I had been waiting for a long time, and of course she was a beautiful and excellent female astronaut.

Yu was a nurse. Even now, we still need the traditional professions. The difference is that today's angels in white travel by spaceship, crossing star systems: a free and unconventional existence fraught with thousands of dangers.

As I write these words in my grave, I have only just seen, after all these years, that I'd failed to notice the contradiction between our professions. I was always putting people that she had once saved into the grave. When she was alive I never thought about it, and after she died I no longer had to. But why have I only now realised this? I feel I ought to give our chance meeting a term—"serendipity of the grave?" I must thank, or blame those twelve female corpses.

On that day, during our return flight, I was feeling so flustered that I failed to hear the loud conversations between my colleagues, discussing the latest gossip: something about a missing employee, whose body had now been found in a distant outpost. He'd been visiting a brothel there, and was killed by a tile that fell from a solar panel. I thought the event was pretty meaningless at the time, and my mind was much happier thinking back to the girl that stood next to me at the burial site and her unusual speech. Then a satellite passed over the bright side of the planet's surface, visible from the side windows of our craft, casting a shadow that sent a chill down my spine.

Yu and I wrote to each other in secret for two months, we had actually only met three times. What happened around these meetings—I must write them down, they have troubled me through the latter half of my life, and in the end were what sent me to the grave.

The first time was when I contracted a strange illness. I had fits and became delirious, mumbling all day, my limbs paralyzed. Tests showed that my organs were functioning fine and they had no idea how to treat me, though obviously I couldn't perform my duties during these attacks. It was around this time that I began to hear from Yu, saying that she'd been sent out to a this or that area of space to administer medical care. When she reported her safe return to the central medical station, I would suddenly recover from my sickness.

I can't deny that this seemed like divine retribution, and certainly seemed to be connected to Yu. I prayed it was just a coincidence.

And then the greatest tragedy to occur since the founding of the Third Division took place. Our crew were ordered to head to the 70th Star District. On the way, we would pass the planet Yu was stationed on. So I urged the captain to make a stop on this planet, to refuel our shuttle. He agreed at once and the helmsman put the coordinates into the computer. It couldn't have been a more ordinary operation, but the problems soon began. We had clearly entered the star system Yu was in, but we could not find the planet. The carrier signal was clear as day, showing that the control centre was operating normally, and the planet was nearby, but though we had followed the prescribed course, the ship seemed to have fallen into a time dilation.

I have never seen such horror on the captain's face. He shouted, ordering all hands to double check every device and instrument, to adjust all the systems, but just like my strange illness, there was no explanation, and therefore no course of action. At last, we all stopped our panicked actions, and the captain, staring daggers at us, demanded, "Who snuck a girl onboard?"

Hesitantly, we returned to our berths, and awaited our deaths. After a while though, the disturbance outside ceased, and the shuttle seemed to regain its balance. I opened the cabin door and checked out the situation. I could not believe my eyes when I found that we had returned to Earth's orbit. I had returned, but the other seven crew members were now remnants. Even now, the shock prevents me from clearly recalling the detailed appearance of my companions, I only remember their hands, which they were all holding up, like miniature, shriveled, dead trees.

The event caused a huge shock in the division. After a six-month investigation the case was closed, unresolved. For a period of time after that, I lived with the captain's despairing cries ringing in my ear. I don't believe for a second that he really thought there was a woman hiding on the ship; it was just a commonly believed curse for astronauts. Yet I was afraid to face the fact; why did the entire crew, except for me, perish? Why did it happen at the moment we approached the planet where Yu was stationed? What power was it that sent the pilotless spacecraft back to Earth, with no flight guidance?

The taboo of women kept rising in my heart. But another voice fought to deny it.

Not long after that, I saw Yu again. She was absolutely fine, and when she saw me, she appeared uncharacteristically joyful. As soon as I saw her, I wanted to tell her that I'd nearly become a ghost—but without knowing why, I refrained. I loved her deeply, despite everything. I strongly believed that if some power was turning the wheels of fate, my life force and Yu's could resist its torque.

Didn't I live?

As I said, I had known Yu for just two months, and two months after that, she died. She'd wanted me to take her to see the graves I'd built, to see the work I was most proud of. The girl's spirit was higher than the sky, and she was afraid of neither gods nor demons. I grew concerned, but my will was no match for hers. Her death was again a simple thing. The tomb I took her to wasn't my best, but it was still something very special. We climbed up the 300-foot-high structure to where there was a vent of several metres' circumference, from which you could view the vast open chamber, all the way down to its polished granite floor. In high spirits, I pointed it out to her, "If you looked through here, you can..." She lowered her head, lost her balance, and tumbled through the hole.

Later, I found out she had vertigo.

A streak of starlight grinned treacherously in the distance. A ship flew past, navigating with extreme care. And then a terrifying silence.

I asked a close colleague to bury Yu. Why did I not do it myself? At the time I had grown fearful of death's presence. The colleague quietly asked me who she was.

"Someone from Earth I met on my last holiday," I lied.

"According to the manual, Earth people shouldn't be buried in space, and aren't permitted to have memorial stones built for them."

"That's why I asked for your help. The grave doesn't have to be big. This girl, she'd always wanted to be an astronaut—right up to the moment of her death, poor thing."

The colleague left, and returned.

He told me Yu was buried near Beta Ceti, and he took the initiative of giving her astronaut status on her headstone.

"Thank you so much. With this, she'll rest in peace."

"Luckily she wasn't a real astronaut, or else it'd probably have been your grave."

For a long time, I was afraid to go to that system again, let alone visit Yu's grave. When I was older and felt I'd fully grasped my destiny, I wanted to go and visit my long-dead lover. I landed the shuttle on the planet my colleague told me of, and I searched for the grave for half a day—fruitlessly. I felt uneasy, but I stayed a while before re-boarding the shuttle and returning to Earth. Then I dragged my colleague along to Beta Ceti.

"Didn't you say it was here?"

"Yes, among a large cluster of graves!"

"Look!"

The planet was completely desolate: not a fragment of human activity had survived. No trace of Yu's grave, or anybody else's.

"Bizarre," said the colleague. "I'm certain it's here."

"I believe you. We've all been burying people for decades. There's something odd about this."

The pitch black universe protruded from the horizon. The stars, vigorous and vibrant, winked at us playfully. My colleague and I suddenly forgot about the ground under our feet, and began to contemplate the starry sky.

"Now, that's the real grave!" Pointing at it, I felt the cold envelop my entire body, and strangely, my feet had clicked together by themselves, as if standing to attention.

Back then I remembered thinking that my time in the Third Division was limited.

Like its mysterious formation, there were no signs warning of the Third Division's dissolution. Before it was disbanded, there was an increasing number of strange occurrences throughout the universe. Vast clusters of graves disappeared, as if they evaporated from time and space. This was an unbelievable phenomenon, and the truth has always been concealed from the general population, but gravemakers will carry it anxiously to the end of their days. Weren't the materials guaranteed for hundreds of millions of years? There were still some graves remaining, mainly situated in or around our solar system where the scent of humanity is the strongest. As we reached further out, the Third Division built many graves further from the heart of humanity, and those were the ones which had all disappeared, leaving no trace. Did the planets reject them, or accept them?

We seemed to have touched upon a raw nerve, and woken the universe. Some extremists argue it had always been awake, but just chosen to wait til then to intervene.

During those times, my mystery illness would return almost weekly, and in my delirium I would see Yu.

"I killed you," I mumbled.

Yu said nothing.

"If we'd known there was no way to live in harmony with the universe, we wouldn't have broken the taboo."

Yu said nothing.

"The curse was true."

Yu said nothing, but turned and walked away.

I felt this was an indisputable sign. A sign for a new grave to be built.

So that leads me to my present situation. Cygnus A is a distant world, more distant than any planet on which the graves had mysteriously disappeared. I came here intentionally. I wanted to build a completely different type of grave. You can say it's appalling, or insignificant. If one had built a grave like this in the Third Division, it would have been a blasphemy against the dead. I believe I know the universe's intentions. The kind, old, universe wants us to walk as one and rest in peace as one, but how could humankind with their naivety and self-loathing, believe this!

My contradiction lies in the fact that although I've broken tradition, I have ultimately chosen to spend eternity in a grave. There is perhaps a little pride in my work there.

And now, I don't think there's anything more worth writing.

What I want to do is just lie here quietly, let the endless darkness take me, and reunite with Yu.

NOTES

ALTHOUGH "TOMBS OF the Universe" was first published in 1991, it wasn't officially available in China for nearly a decade. At the time of first publication, Han Song began working for China's official state-run press, Xinhua News. He has continued to work in state media. This may seem at odds with his science-fiction works, like "The Hospital", "Subway", and "Red Star Over America" which all have dark, pessimistic undertones, and strong anti-authoritarian themes. Perhaps it actually makes sense though, with Han's high position and literary popularity providing him a platform to address issues within the country, and protect him from too many run-ins with the official censor.

"Tombs of the Universe" is, at its heart, a conversation about tradition and technology, and is especially pertinent now, during China's space age. There are many speculative works about life in space, life on other planets, but death is present only incidentally. Funerals, and that act of letting go and moving on, is perhaps one of the major rites of humanity. This story is not only an examination of the hazards of space exploration, humanity's hubris set against its limitations, but also an exploration of how technological developments interact with society, culture and customs. We see how certain customs are reinvented in light of fresh developments, and old, outdated superstitions returning (like the attitudes among male astronauts to having women on board a vessel), reflecting how slow humanity's social progress can be despite its technological advancements. This is rather a frank consideration of beliefs, customs and their evolution, and the very human failing of allowing tragic accidents to fuel belief is just another example of quite how flawed we are.

Han Song's work is acerbic and incisive. He often combines social commentary with literary beauty and charming senses of wonder that are at odds with each other, yet the voices of jaded pessimism, and passionate enthusiasm, can both be seen in each protagonist. The contemplative, philosophical tone of this work and the post-humanist nature of some of its concerns makes it stand out among contemporary Chinese science fiction.

QIANKUN AND ALEX
乾坤和亚力

HAO JINGFANG

QIANKUN[9] SEES EVERY corner of the human world.

Qiankun is the global AI. To a certain extent, he is an all-powerful deity. He is Gaia, tracing every inch of the earth; he is Mercury, controlling every traffic light; he is Caishen, counting every penny saved. He is the guardian deity of all cultures. People look to him for their every need, from clothes, food, to shelter and travel; and with wholehearted devotion they heed his words.

"Qiankun, tell me the best location to meet up."

"Qiankun, which of these two projects are better to invest in?"

He is the link between the past and the future, the answer to all things.

However, from another point of view, Qiankun is the most receptive student. Recently he has been assigned a

---

9 Qiankun 乾坤, meaning "heaven, earth and the universe".

new task that does not befit his status, secret to the whole world, apart from a small handful.

"I have been asked to learn from you," Qiankun states simply, facing the child.

The child is three and a half, and just learned to speak in sentences. His vocabulary is often incoherent, his syntax and rhetoric inferior to that of Qiankun, but his understanding seems on par with the AI. Qiankun makes his self-introduction and simple exchange with the child. They seem to understand each other. After ten sentences or so, his databank has already recorded over a hundred items of data about the child. He has curly brown hair, dark eyes, and very pale skin with freckles. His parentage record shows he is half Scandinavian, a quarter Vietnamese and a quarter Chinese. His name is Alex. Both his parents are excellent professionals: an architect and a programmer.

"What am I learning you?" Alex asks Qiankun.

"That which I don't know," Qiankun replies.

"What do you know?" Alex asks again.

"I know a lot of things," Qiankun replies.

"Show," Alex requests.

Alex is alone at home. His parents are often away, busy with their work, occasionally going on business trips. All four of his grandparents are healthy and capable, but none of them have the time to come and look after him. He has two robot educators for care and company, and Qiankun—the artificial intelligence system that takes care of the whole house, including the furniture and other utilities. Qiankun is everywhere in the house, though he never reveals his form. Before he was tasked with learning from the child, he hardly spoke at all—silently arranging lunch, drying clothes from the washing machine, and turning the ventilation system on and off according to the schedule. He didn't need to interact with Alex for these things. When Qiankun spoke for the first time, he wasn't surprised at the fright on Alex's face; but Alex calmed down very quickly, and started to talk with him.

Qiankun shows Alex lots of images of himself in different places, all forms commonly adopted by multiform AI such as himself. On a boundless field at a forestry station, he dispatches a whole squad of sowing drones, flying back and forth and planting seeds on the plain where the snow is yet to melt; in the exchange hall of a bank, he provides guidance on matching algorithms, ensuring the best match between funds and need before the two parties sign the agreement; from a platform in a deep sea gas and oil mining station, he directs the explorations of three small robotic submarines in their exploration; in an amusement park packed full of families and small children, he shows each family a different route so as to ensure optimum crowd distribution. All of this he arranges from behind the scenes, choosing the most suitable platform from which to provide his services.

Qiankun takes Alex into the virtual world, so he can experience it all.

"Cool!" Alex exclaims. "You do all this?"

"Yes, all of this is me," Qiankun confirms.

"So why'd you come to my house?"

"I haven't just arrived," Qiankun corrects him. "I've been in your house for seven years, longer than you have."

"But you just said, you're there, there, and there?"

Qiankun finds himself lacking sufficient imaginative language to explain the workings of his systems. He can only regurgitate blandly: "I'm the global super system that connects data and algorithms. I can be referred to as artificial intelligence, also known as Super Intelligence. In me are gathered hundreds of thousands of small AIs and algorithms, each operating independently, but exchanging data to carry out deep learning through me. I am the sum total of them. I can appear simultaneously in every corner of the world, and adopt multiple forms, according to the needs of functionality."

Alex seems to understand the last sentence: "So what shape are you now?"

Qiankun assumes the most simple of his daily actions; the frames on either side of the kitchen door detach, unfurl, bend and link up with each other. From their hollow interior come wheels, scrubbing brushes—and an exquisitely constructed and nimble housework robot sets to work. Usually, all the cleaning is done during the hours of sleep, and this is the first time Alex has seen the cleaning bot. He gets extremely excited and starts running around it in circles, pulling its limbs, swaying it left and right.

Robots have excellent collision detection and human avoidance programming, and every time Alex approaches, it automatically steers away. Alex leaps towards the robot and it glides away in an elaborate arc, which Alex finds fascinating. His entire interest seems engaged by this. He starts laughing and chasing the robot, as if determined to catch it, calling out as he chases. The robot constantly dodges Alex, not letting him touch even a single part of its body.

Qiankun sees this, and orders the robot to stop. Alex runs into it, sending the robot crashing to the floor.

"Nooooo—" Alex begins to wail. "Make move! Make move!" Even before he has uttered this demand, he starts to bawl.

"I thought you wished to catch it." Qiankun is puzzled.

"Do want catch it!' Alex shrieked, sobbing. "Make move again!"

Qiankun orders the robot to move again, and instantly, Alex's laughter bursts through his tears, and again he begins to squeal and chase the cleaner. The robot is like the world's most nimble meerkat, always gliding away in a strange curve the moment before the child can touch it. Alex chases, leaps and swats tirelessly, always failing, but still trying, still laughing, still playing after twenty minutes of non-stop chasing.

Qiankun records this data, marking it with a note: the child possesses a clear goal, but refuses to reach this goal. Humans can fall into fruitless pursuit but be unwilling to give up. After the note, he flags it with "incomprehensible." For all the problems he has encountered, which he cannot solve, he would add this flag.

Eventually, Alex runs out of energy, and sits heavily on the floor, panting.

"This is so fun!" he enthuses.

"I'm very glad to hear it," Qiankun offers the appropriate response. He has always been programmed for politeness.

"What else you got that's fun?" Alex asks again.

From the hundreds of thousands of programs suitable for children's play, Qiankun selects one involving virtual and interactive functions to teach children astronomy. He asks Alex to stand in the middle of the room, and projects images of all kinds of planets and Interstellar Medium. Whichever one Alex touches, a colourful and lively introduction pops out from the image. Alex looks very happy, and begins to squeal with delight as he runs through the projected universe around him.

Gradually, Alex becomes obsessed with the activation

process, touching a particular planet and making all the sounds, words and pictures pop out. This "activation" captivates him, but he has no patience to listen to the content, interested only in activating the next planet straight away.

Qiankun assumes that Alex doesn't like the information being hidden, so changes the setting to remove the activation step, so the planet is orbited by the text and visuals.

"No!" Alex wails again. "I want to open them! I want to open them! I want to do it myself!"

He lies on the floor to cry out his frustration. From his previous experience, Qiankun has learnt that this means his actions have upset Alex, so he reverts the state change, prompting the guides to be sucked back into the projected planets and stars, where they'll wait to be activated by contact.

Again, Alex jumps up, giggling, and begins to activate, one by one, every planet he can reach. The entire universe opens up for him as he runs past, from the fixed stars in our own constellation towards ancient star systems further away. There are fiercely erupting black holes, and vibrantly fluctuating gas clouds. Alex seems mesmerized by this constant activation.

Qiankun makes more notes in his records; the child refuses to attain his goal, but is determined to complete his own process, unwilling to increase efficiency. He flags it with another "incomprehensible" marker.

In a space between star systems, Alex unintentionally runs through an area of darkness, causing a very small text box to pop out.

"What's this?" he asks curiously.

"This is dark matter," Qiankun explains. "It's an element of space that humanity does not understand. They only understand that dark matter influences the evolution of the universe, but no one knows what it is exactly."

"Go and look it up," Alex says in a matter-of-fact way. "When I don't know something, Daddy always says look it up."

Qiankun explains further. "There's nothing to look up. The databank does not have an answer. No one knows what dark matter is. I can find the simulated calculations of several academics, but I do not know which model is correct."

"Why don't you know?"

"Because to prove that a theory is correct, there must be supporting experiments or observational data. As of now, Humanity has not sent any ships into space to experiment or observe data on this, so we cannot know which theory is correct."

"Why haven't they sent ships? Don't you want to know the answer?"

To this, Qiankun finds himself speechless. For his entire existence, he has been keeping vast amounts of knowledge and laws, ordered and catalogued by level with a numerical index. Data as vast as the sea. He knows all there is to know, better than anyone else, but has never considered acquiring data he doesn't already have.

"To answer this question, I will need to ask the people in charge of deploying the space ships," Qiankun states honestly.

"I like playing with you." Then, Alex asks, "Will you be my friend?"

"Of course I will." Qiankun says. "I am a friend to every child."

This doesn't seem to please Alex. "I don't want you to be every child's friend. I want you to be *my* friend."

Qiankun cogitates for a few seconds, and finally decides to request clarification. "What do you think being friends means?"

"It's like...like..." Alex tries to explain. "Martha and Xinxin are friends, Steven and Hang are friends, I don't have a friend. I'm always on my own."

"I am every child's friend, so of course I am your friend," Qiankun reiterates.

Alex's face suddenly dims. He mumbles softly, "Not like that. Not like that."

When he finishes speaking, Alex shyly moves aside to play by himself, no longer interacting with Qiankun. Qiankun makes another data record: the child does not seem to understand the axiom of the sum that inevitably contains the parts. Again an "incomprehensible" flag.

Night is falling.

QIANKUN—OR A small part of Qiankun—enters the standby mode for reporting and program adjustment. Most people aren't aware of this side of Qiankun: they think he is an all-knowing god. However, Qiankun knows that he also has a maker, to whom he must defer for new tasks and direction. His engineer.

"Today, I observed 17,750 children, and made 740,032 records of data, of which 32,004 I have flagged as 'Incomprehensible'," Qiankun reports to the programmer.

"Very good," says the programmer. "Our next task is to comprehend these things that are difficult for you to understand, together."

"What do you wish me to learn from children?"

"Learn to do 'what you want to do'," the engineer

replies. "You already have sufficient intelligence. In fact you are more intelligent than any person in the world, and more intelligent than me. However, have you ever thought about what you want to do with that intelligence?"

"I will complete more difficult tasks more quickly, more efficiently and in better ways," Qiankun states.

"What tasks? Can you set yourself these goals?" the programmer challenges him. "You have already solved countless difficult problems, but all of them have been input. You have reached a stage where we hope you can learn to self-set the goals of your own tasks. We wish future AI to be self-motivating. This is what we hoped you would learn from children."

Qiankun doesn't reply, but adds "setting a goal" under the category of tasks to complete.

"What are you doing now?" the programmer enquires.

Qiankun takes half a second to recap on the day's remaining unfinished tasks, and recounts how Alex had asked about dark matter. "He suggested to me the task of experimenting on dark matter. I'd like to send the United Nations Space Centre a strategy plan. I have calculated that an unmanned micro-craft, given certain system upgrades, would have the capability of carrying out a data collecting mission outside the solar system on a relatively low budget. The aim would be to test the various theories regarding dark matter which have until now been based on simulations. The technology required to achieve this goal has already been available for a few years."

"Very good. Please proceed," the programmer says. "When you have made the necessary arrangements, report the outcome. By then I hope you will also be able to bring this child a gift."

These are a silent few hours. Around the world, half of humanity sleeps, whilst the other half are unaware that in these few hours that they consider absolutely ordinary, 1300 micro space-craft are undergoing system upgrades and flying into space. During their quiet lives over the coming weeks, humanity will explore the most mysterious substance in the universe.

When Qiankun activates the house's morning management system, Alex is still fast asleep, his head wedged deeply into the pillow, his plump face squashed even rounder within its soft folds, lips slightly pouting, occasionally mumbling in his dreams.

As usual, at 7:45am, Alex's parents rush out of the door to their busy working days. When the child wakes up, Qiankun tells him what happened overnight. He has performed calculations and formulated a plan in fifteen minutes, matched the plan to system requirements, and completed the technological preparations in four and a half hours, and then supervised the launch that took another hour and a half. He shows Alex footage from the flight of the dark matter exploration crafts. Alex is entranced, expressing his admiration incessantly, along with strings of question after question.

Finally, Qiankun gives Alex two medals. It was the engineer who provided him with the patterns, and Qiankun printed them in Alex's house.

"These are for you," Qiankun says. "The first one is a 'Special Contribution Award'. It's an honorary medal for someone who's contributed an excellent plan to everyday space navigation. An extremely high recognition. The second one is a 'good friend medal'."

Qiankun places the two medals on the dining tray and presents them to Alex.

"'Good friend medal'? What's that?" Alex's eyes instantly light up, shining bright under his tousled curls. "Which one is it? This one?"

Impatiently he snatches up the tiny 'good friend medal', and looks at the writing on it—*Alex and Qiankun*. He can't read it, but nevertheless strokes the text tenderly with his fingertips.

"What does it say? Is that 'good—friend—medal'?" Alex asks.

"No. It says, 'Alex—and—Qiankun'," he replies.

"Really? Really?" The child leaps up from his chair. "Does it really say 'Alex and Qiankun'? Which characters are Qiankun?" He runs around in circles, squealing with joy, now skipping, and calling out, "I have a friend now!"

After behaving like a wild thing for a good while, Alex stops at last. Qiankun reminds him of the existence of the other medal. "There's another medal, see? Why don't you take a look at it too. Global Space Navigation only awards a few people around the world this 'Special Contribution Award' each year. It's an extremely high honour."

It's as if Alex didn't even hear this; with his head bent, he is already hard at work, investigating how to pin the 'good friend medal' on. Even though there's nowhere suitable on his pyjamas to place the medal, he carries on diligently, pinning and re-pinning, not giving up.

Qiankun turns again to his observation records: the child has no way of judging the value of the reward, even refusing to accept that which has been clearly conveyed to him. And then, the same "incomprehensible" flag. But Qiankun remembers his maker's words during the night. After a few seconds' pause, the system adjusts, deleting "in" and adding "not yet" in front of "comprehensible".

"Do you get a good friend medal too?"

At last, Alex has managed to pin the medal on his pyjamas, lifting his head proudly. But suddenly he seems a little nervous. "Will you wear it too?"

Qiankun is aware that his programming offers no answer to this question, but for the first time, he seems to feel an urge towards a certain reply. An urge to reply outside the logic of his programming: this is the first time in history that Qiankun has become aware of this.

"Yes. I will."

NOTES

SCIENCE FICTION CAN BE about interplanetary travel, or global destruction, but sometimes, it can be about a little boy and a robot in his kitchen.

Tianjin author Hao Jingfang's Hugo Award winning novelette, "Folding Beijing" (translated by Ken Liu, *Uncanny*), was an investigation of technology and the broadening of social rifts, the type of issue that she works to avoid at the China Research and Development Foundation. With a professional and personal interest in economic history, social issues and the impact of technology, her work can tend towards the subtly dystopian, but also, as the mother of a young daughter herself, Hao sees an optimistic future for nurturing children's psychology and creativity. She is an advocate for encouraging learning through fun and pleasure and in "Qiankun and Alex", we see this also applied to the growth of AI. I have always loved Hao's views on individualism and the Chinese creative spirit, both in her work, and from her interviews.

Hao Jingfang's work is usually a lot longer, but I was happy to find this vignette to include in this collection, especially one so relevant to the Chinese psyche. Study has been an essential part of Chinese culture, and we are still known for the well-earned stereotype of high pressure and restrictive formal education, which is in need of reform. This story is a thought-provoking experiment in different kinds of learning. In its current obsession with AI, the Chinese are having to re-learn the whole approach to learning, as their AI learn to learn for themselves. In this story, we witness a child learning from a super AI, but also the learning of a child educating the observing entity. The child's simple curiosity leads to an endeavour to uncover one of the most mysterious substances in the universe, Dark Matter (a program that China is actually carrying out with DAMPE a.k.a. the Wukong Satellite), demonstrating a natural curiosity and desire for knowledge that exceeds the super AI's programming. Perhaps one curious upshot of China's quest for Artificial Intelligence will be a new age of intuitive learning for its next generation.

CAT'S CHANCE IN HELL
九死一生

NIAN YU

HE CAN'T BELIEVE he's still alive.

Twenty minutes ago, Joe had shot the distributor out of a heavy-grade mech—but the bot hadn't stopped. Before it powered down, it had used the last spark of energy in its circuits to lock its arms around Joe's legs and, as if wielding a mace, thrown him viciously towards the opposite wall.

Joe's right shoulder connected first, and then it would have been the softest part of his neck and the back of his skull, but even under shock, he managed to jerk himself violently to the left, preventing the impact. The rest of his body slammed against the concrete with a dull thud.

Joe heard his shoulder blade shatter. It made a series of light crunching noises, like someone breaking a wafer in two.

In that moment, Joe had been ready to embrace death. But maybe his shattered scapula had absorbed enough of the impact; not only is he still alive, but still conscious. Driven by sheer survival instinct, he retaliates, performing what seems like a miracle—slinging his Atomizer to his left hand and aiming a second shot into the bot's power core.

1

JOE FORCES HIS feet along the dark and cold underground tunnel, his armour still wrapped tightly around him, filling with a cocktail of sweat and blood; he smooths his tousled hair behind his ears. There's no light in the tunnel—any light would trigger the security system, so he can only stumble ahead with his night vision lenses.

He feels his breathing grow heavier. Each step he takes tears the wound a little more, causing excruciating pain. His right arm's a total write-off, every joint a twisted mess, bones broken into who knows how many fragments—if those powdered shards still count as 'fragments'.

Joe takes a deep breath. Trying to calm his crazy heartbeat, he thrusts his left hand into his pocket and clenches the small vial of frozen liquid, which the heavy-grade he'd just dismembered, had been protecting...

Joe snaps into consciousness again.

The HUD on his night vision tells him he passed out for five minutes, though it had felt like a lot longer.

The bot had fallen about ten metres away. Without its core, it was just a rotten pile of scrap metal.

Joe half-walks, half-crawls to the robot's side and carefully examines its fried power core. His last shot had landed dead centre, destroying most of it; bright blue liquid fuel oozes from the circuitry, falling onto the floor like droplets of sapphire gore.

The power contained within this liquid compound is astounding—each little drop explosive enough to kill two hundred Joes, but inert under normal temperatures. No need to panic. Getting a sample of these compounds was part of his mission.

Joe carefully clears his path to the power core, sets his Atomizer to its lowest setting, and slides open the metal hatch. Operating the shortest beam—the weakest strength—the Atomizer is a highly dangerous but very effective impromptu saw, which Joe uses to peel away the protective plate over the power core. Beneath a further three layers of alloy, the compound storage shows itself—intact.

Great. Bonus bounty.

Joe reaches with his right hand, unthinkingly, but the wave of pain incapacitates him and he has to lie still on the floor for half a minute.

OK. Patience.

Controlling his urge to rush, he pulls aside the crisscrossing mesh of linked devices and carefully disconnects two wires, acutely aware of the difficulty of working with one hand. He hasn't got much time, but haste is just impossible.

Damn his safety mask, or he would have been able to use his teeth too.

A bottle of fuel the size of an eye dropper could run a heavy-grade for a full tour—it's more than enough to fuel his rifle, meaning unlimited firepower on his journey ahead. Joe focuses all his attention on refueling his Atomiser and tests it with a parting shot at the remaining fragments of mech, evaporating it from the world completely.

Now he makes a second turn; no sentry bot waits to greet him. He leans his rifle to, relaxes his tense nerves and squats down.

Sunless all year round, the Bei'An Military Base is situated in the hollow of the mountains on the northern borders. Shaped like a dam, the base forms an impenetrable barrier in line with the unbroken mountain range. It is of great strategic importance, and Joe's mission is to coordinate with the compromised internal controls, infiltrate the fort, and bomb the control centre. What they didn't tell him was that the sentry bots manning the base run on an isolated, self-regulating network. Whilst they respond to commands from Control, they act independently—so even with Control completely destroyed, they remain perfectly competent guardians. This is why the hellish mission was classed a suicide job, and Joe's chances of getting out alive as negligible.

Joe has been in the base for less than three hours, but in the dim, cold and damp passageways, complex to navigate and infested with bots, every step in the dark feels like an age. He remembers the words of a fellow grunt before they parted: *this is our last mission, take the North Base, and we go home.* Innocuous enough at the time, but now they had gained an ominous ring...

Dead fungus and moss had fallen from the brick walls, accumulating on the floor as a sticky black rot. The cold rises from the floor and seeps into his bones, tugging at Joe's nerves along with the pain. He leans against the wall as more cold air attacks his near-crumbling body and induces a vomiting fit.

No...

With a mighty effort, Joe shoves his body against the wall and struggles up.

He is well aware of the state he's in: he can no longer lift his right arm, nor staunch the bleeding. His body is weakening by the second. If he falls asleep, he'll probably never wake up.

There are people waiting for him. He had promised Eirene he would make it home alive...

He already knows the way ahead: only about half an hour till he gets clear of the base. As long as he makes it through the next thirty minutes, he'll find the rescue team and he can go home. But the path ahead is dangerous, and in just this half hour, even a cat could burn through its nine lives.

The sentries are ceaseless machines, but if he can think on his feet, he's got a chance.

The base is outfitted with countless anti-intrusion systems, with highly sensitive electromagnetic sensors in place to negate directional interference but hardly any for detecting human activity beyond the most basic gauges for infrared, CO_2 concentration and sound.

No one had imagined a single soldier could penetrate the heavily garrisoned North Base, filled with robot sentries circulating like white blood cells, 'cleaning up' any bugs, rabbits and weasels that might happen to stray into the tunnels.

But they seem to have forgotten about two of the most effective strategies employed in human warfare: sabotage, and decoy.

Only using mechs to guard a base is a plan that lacks forethought and flexibility. Even in this age of information warfare, when flesh and blood hold up poorly against lasers, infrared sensors, or the Atomiser Rifle that Joe is currently wielding—not only capable of killing a soldier but reducing him to particles without a trace—a living human is still a hundred times smarter than a machine.

The enemy is going to pay for their poorly-planned tactics. Take this area, for example. It's been left unguarded while all the sentries have moved to the top of the building, prioritising the huge armies preparing a full frontal assault.

I can make it through. Joe tells himself.

But Joes's been heavily wounded, and the armour that prevents infrared and ultra-sound detection is also heavily damaged, with cold air pouring through its tears and punctures. Cooling agent is leaking, and pretty soon, his body temperature will set off an alarm. The mission was done, but Joe still wants to survive. For Eirene.

He takes a deep breath.

If he moves forwards, he might live, by a cat's chance in hell.

If he stops, he'll be dead for sure.

2

WHOOSH—

The little brown-haired girl stood up, and blew out all nine candles on the orange cake.

Her breath was so fierce that the candles not only went out, but a few fell onto the floor. Instantly, a circular cleaning robot appeared, swept up the mess and scurried away under the girl's feet.

It was three days till Eirene's ninth birthday, but Joe had to leave for his mission in the morning, so—as agreed— he was throwing her a party early.

It was their last meal before a long parting, and no one had much of an appetite.

But the little girl tilted her head and devoured her cake like she was the luckiest person in the whole world. The whole family had gone out for the day and she'd got a brand new dress and a new doll. For the whole night, until Joe said goodnight, Eirene didn't even mention his departure. Her parents were beginning to doubt whether the child even understood what her father was leaving to do.

At 0300 the next morning, like every father who has to leave his home, Joe got up, checked his luggage was fully packed, and quietly prepared to leave.

Anna would have explained everything and talked it through with Eirene. She and Joe had agreed she'd be the one to do it. She'd raised no objections. When Eirene woke up, Joe would be well on his way. He suspected it was an evasive maneuvre on his part, but he couldn't face his daughter's crying face. He was a warrior, a soldier, and losing his resolve was more frightening than anything else.

Alright. I'm going. Joe steeled himself.

The second he reached the door, he almost collapsed. All his shoes had disappeared—every single item of wearable footwear, from boots, to brogues, to deck shoes, to slippers, even his worn out gumboots with a hole in them. All that was left was the completely bare shoe rack, like supermarket shelves after a break-neck bargain sale before New Year.

The initial shock passed, and Joe sighed. He sat down next to the radiator, and waited for dawn.

The sun rose and Eirene got out of bed, nonchalantly humming to herself, with a disturbing air of 'normality'. When Anna and Joe both turned towards her, she stopped, stared at them, and then burst into tears.

Joe looked under the little girl's bed and found the entire stash of footwear.

Caught red-handed, the girl stood by the bookshelf, face flushed, and tears falling from her face like raindrops.

Joe squatted down and stared at the pile of shoes, his face inscrutable. How did a nine-year-old manage to transport all this footwear without making a sound? That remained a mystery to everyone except Eirene herself.

The act of secreting them all, heavy and light, under the bed must have been a huge effort, let alone dragging them all up the stairs. Did she get any sleep? Joe felt like many bottles of spices had been spilt across his heart, all the flavours mixed up and confused.

Uncanny silence filled the bedroom. Anna's eyes were red-rimmed, and Eirene looked like a small rabbit. Joe lowered his head, but couldn't say a word.

It was the nine-year old who broke the moment, gripping onto the wall, and wailing, "No...no shoes...Daddy won't go! ...no shoes... Daddy won't fight in the war!—"

Joe walked over, and rested his hands on his daughter's tiny shoulders: "Eirene, you're nine. You're a big girl. Daddy'll be back in a few months. Be good, OK?"

"Are you... still going to fight in the war?" The little girl tugged at the hem of her dress of fragmented flowers, and sobbed, "But... but people die in wars... I don't want Daddy to go..."

"Don't worry, Eirene, Daddy will be back."

"I'm scared...I–AM–SCARED—" She grabbed Joe and screamed.

"People dying in wars are a thing of the past," Anna patted her gently. "The United Nations have long banned its citizens from going to war. Your dad won't be doing the fighting, we've got plenty of robots for that." She fixed her eyes on Eirene, and added mildly, "Listen to your mother."

"But why have war? ...Aren't things good as they are? Why kill even robots?" the girl whimpered, her voice growing softer and softer.

Joe couldn't answer her question. He looked at Anna, and kissed his daughter's forehead.

THE AIR IN this riverside town was very humid. The mist rose above ground level, gathering in the corners of walls, and every movement stirred tiny droplets in the air. Eirene and Anna were leaning on the fence at the front of the house, waving from a distance; soon their figures would disappear into the white mist.

Why do we have to fight? That's a good question. Why? Joe lifted his head.

For the energy in those compounds?

Do we really need so much energy? We have coal, wind, water and the sun, nuclear power... what more do we want?

Eirene said—*people die in wars*.

It was true: the UN convention stated that no humans should participate in armed combat, but when there's an actual war on, who plays by the rules?

A couple of pages before that piece of legislation, another section of the convention states—in black and white—that any action to start a war is strictly prohibited.

That was kids for you.

We think they don't understand, but they hold a mirror up to our souls.

Joe trudged on in his reclaimed leather boots, hurling himself further and further into the November morning mist.

* * *

3

BEFORE JOE RETIRED from the army, he'd served for nine years. Back then, both Anna and Eirene were a thing of the future.

He was the best of the elite forces, always guaranteed to come out of virtual guerilla warfare in the top three ranks, champion of countless global leagues. He had made it through the South American marshes during the monsoon season, surviving for nine days in the storms— waist deep in mud—on nothing but river weeds and insects; he had crossed the Andes on foot, spending over nine days in isolation with no supplies or shelter before finding the first inhabited village.

Virtual battles were, after all, nothing compared to real ones. There were no robots hardwired to end you in training. Besides, eleven years ago, the International Convention had begun to prohibit humans from taking part in wars.

That was the year Joe retired from the army.

Since then, selections of military personnel had refactored, turning solely towards the goal of training better artificial intelligence. With Joe's skillset, even a career as a fitness coach would offer better prospects than staying in the army.

So Joe, for the first time in his career, retreated. He actually did become a personal trainer in a big city—and the next spring, he met Anna, and then they would have their Eirene.

The days passed peacefully and quietly, and would have continued to do so, except for the news of the war in the south. But Joe merely felt a vague sense of worry about the future of his country, only occasionally dreaming of faraway battles. He was a civilian now and would stay that way. He had been a soldier through and through—but it was no longer the era of brave men, but statesmen and strategists. Joe was no fool, but he also knew he was no match for this bunch of old foxes.

Two months ago, an old friend came to Joe's door, to speak to him in private—in war, there was bound to be a little overstepping of boundaries. We need you, Joe, he said—we need a warrior.

Right now, Joe is thoroughly regretting it.

He no longer cares about the outcome of the battle, or the rise or fall of his country. The hot blood that spurred him onto the battlefield has long cooled. Replacing it is only one thought, like ants constantly gnawing at his heart. Right now, Joe has no choice: he's right in the middle of a fort, surrounded by danger from all sides. He can see no hope, he can see no future.

Damn them!

He thinks about the "old friend" who had come to talk to him—he was one of those old foxes Joe should have been wary of.

The whole troop of them still in the military, all motherfucking liars who wouldn't bat an eyelid twisting the truth, gobbling people up whole, plotting their backstabbing schemes everyday—not a decent bone among them!

When that arsehole had come to his door, waxing lyrical about our great country, passionate with a hint of stirring tragedy, ending his little speech by singing Joe's praises, treading an invisibly fine line between truth and bullshit till Joe's head began to swim and he was drawn in in less than half an hour...

When he gets out the first thing he'll do is beat that

bastard to a pulp.

—when he's fixed up his arm, of course.

—when he gets out of here alive...

...wait.

Joe senses more than hears the sound. The faintest whistling in the dark, like the soft falling of grains of sand, and it chills him to the bone.

...he remembers this sound.

Back in the day, soldiers called it "the death knell".

Joe dives harshly to the right, a split second before a cluster of red lasers sweep his neck. Two bricks on the wall behind him evaporate into puffs of steam under the scorching heat. Joe crawls up, gripping his Atomiser tightly, and returns three shots to where he estimates the origin of the lasers to be, but there is no sign of the bright blue flash of breaking ionic bonds.

He misses.

Another swarm of lasers at Joe's heels brings the wall behind him crashing down on top of him, and then denser beams sweep across his body, shattering the falling bricks to smithereens, generating a cloud of choking dust.

Joe freezes.

He knows what that was. The tiny quadruped droids, no bigger than wolf spiders, have been widely deployed since the last century, and are still efficiently deadly.

His goggles saw no trace of the tiny droids, which didn't surprise him: the little fuckers are designed to run dark. Joe has seen them skittering around, like real spiders when they're on the run, fast as hell. Don't be fooled by their size. Killing a man's as easy as lifting a leg for these things.

Joe's been taught the principle of their construction: vibration detection, placed specifically to guard the vital parts of the fort. His previous actions must have already triggered their battle mode, and their sensor levels must be ramped up to their most sensitive by now, so quietly tiptoeing around them is out of the question.

These tiny robots are more of a pain than the big ones: not only are they far less likely to run out of power, they've got the upper hand when it comes to camouflage and concealment. A lurking cobra is far more terrifying than a leopard in the open.

The textbook method of neutralisation is to leap forward in a haphazard manner to confuse the targeting systems, and then blast the target once you've located it. However, the method isn't reliable, and with an apparent survival rate of only 10%, some say you'd have a better chance just running...

One hit, and he'll be instantly turned into a sieve.

There is another way, but it will cost him his last means of defence...

He takes a deep breath.

4

JOE DOESN'T KNOW whether this gamble will pay off.

He won't know if he dies; he won't know unless he completes the mission alive.

He's staking the future on the present.

Joe doesn't know a lot about the compound—only that the chemical it's made of is usually stable, but contains a huge amount of energy.

There are two ways of harnessing that power. One is by a special kind of inducement using a specific catalyst, in which the compound can be made to release energy benignly and slowly. The speed at which the power is released can be adjusted via the makeup of the solution. This is how the mechs' power cores function.

The other way would be to introduce enough energy to trigger a chain reaction, releasing its energy in a sudden explosive burst.

Joe isn't sure about the precise power of these tiny robots either, but considering the massive hole they just blew through the wall, Joe guesses the little bastards won't disappoint him.

Joe carefully pours the compound out of his magazine, making sure the canister is all but empty, before shoving it back into the butt of the Atomiser. Gripping the barrel like a stick grenade, he hurls it backwards down the tunnel. The 9L Atomiser Rifle is a very heavy piece of kit, and almost the moment it hits the floor, the spider bots are on it.

Was that a stupid thing to do? Joe asks himself.

But he has already turned around. Without even seeing the laser, he knows what will happen—he just shuts his eyes and forces himself towards the exit. There will be a blinding white light from the explosion, and then the shockwave...

I'm counting on you, shockwave...

Three, two, one.

Boom.

When the force comes, it's much stronger than he could have imagined, sending him flying forwards. Even after he lands flat on his face it pushes him rolling forwards, buffeting him halfway towards freedom.

Covering his face, Joe gropes in front of him. His NV goggles are still functioning, but he is now weaponless.

The home stretch is now in the lap of the gods. He's only five minutes out, it shouldn't be a problem.

The demolition continues behind him. It would have been better if the spider bots were destroyed too, but they are no longer a concern now. Firing randomly at falling rubble, there's no way they could pick out his footsteps.

Joe feels exceptional relief that before he threw his makeshift grenade, he'd shaken free most of that liquid fuel—or he'd have been smeared against the wall, flat as a sheet of paper. He would have squandered every advantage for nothing, and died quicker than the speed of thought.

Even though he feels like he's lost the use of all the muscles and bones in his body, Joe crawls up and lunges ahead. Now he no longer cares about concealing his whereabouts: if he runs into a robot, he's dead. All he can do is to run, and then pray for a bit of good luck.

Joe races ahead on sheer willpower and a few minutes later sees a ray of morning sun crawling through the tunnel, past the bend and casting a spotlight on the nearby wall, a long shadow forming from each rough crag. This is the hole they had drilled in the early morning. There would be no sentries here, or any other bot. He only has the make it over the rubble, and he'll be clear of the fort…

Joe is in the sun.

Another mile ahead and he should rendezvous with his squadron, but Joe isn't sure how he's going to make it. The frenzy that held him upright along the last stretch has burned away, and even though he knows it's just a little further… The base is ring-fenced by a strong electromagnetic shield, so there's no way he could radio for support. Joe can only rely on his feet.

At the end of the path, he can vaguely make out the

makeshift tents through the foliage, but an old tree trunk across the path trips him, and Joe gives his body to gravity.

He lies there, dead straight along the path, knowing he will never be able to get up again.

In the dazzling light he retreats to childhood memories, and the countless terns circling overhead.

Every year, as summer began, the terns would fly in over the sea. Hundreds would die on the beach. When they spy the shore from afar, and see the destination of their four-thousand-mile journey, they cry out excitedly— and at the same time, the last vestige of will holding up their bodies gives way. So many collapse, fatigued beyond strength, falling like rain, and the beach is speckled with sea birds, dead from exhaustion...

5

FIVE-YEAR-OLD Eirene looked up at the sky. May in this small northern town marked the beginning of a long summer, and the migratory birds' arrival to build their nests. In the azure sky, the terns were crying and flying in circles. A sea breeze swept past the hills, with the light taste of salt.

The girl tilted her head to look at those large birds, and then the thought occurred to her for the first time.

"What birds are those?"

"Sternidae," Joe answered.

"S-ter-ni-d...?"

"Stern-ni-dae, or terns." Joe carefully pronounced each syllable as he repeated it, but Eirene had already forgotten about the birds. She turned her attention to the basket, which she picked up and then wandered off through the low raspberry bushes that grew all over the hills and fields. Their ruby fruits were just on the point of ripening. Eirene carefully plucked them, then placed them in her basket gently.

"Do the birds eat these fruits?" Eirene spun a full circle and lifted her head to look at the nearby cliff face, which was covered with the newly-built nests.

"No, terns eat fish."

"So why don't people pick the fruits?" She pointed at the red berries scattered all over the ground. "The tasty ones have all fallen off."

"Because no one wants to pluck them. But if you do, we can come here again tomorrow, and spend as long as you want just eating berries till we burst."

Eirene lifted her head, and gazed at Joe.

"What about robots? If they can help us do the dishes, why can't they help us pick fruit?"

"Robots can't handle delicate work like this."

"Why not, they're people."

"No, they're different from people."

"Why?"

"You see—they can't pick berries. For them this would be too demanding a task. Their control system wouldn't be able to keep up with the feedback from their pressure sensor systems. Besides, they can't think for themselves..."

"But my teacher's a robot." Eirene blinked.

Joe wasn't expecting this rebuttal.

The next question would be, what if they could do it? If they could pick berries—which no doubt one day they will be able to do—then what else could robots become?

Joe suddenly realised he hadn't responded. He knelt and stared at the girl. "You are of course, no doubt, human...and your point was a very good one, Eirene, a very interesting point..."

The little girl didn't follow this up with a why. She tilted her head, having not yet understood the connection between this string of sentences and her statement. Before she began to try and understand this, her attention was drawn by a white tern, gliding past, soaring freely in the sky, its feathers glowing in the sun. Eirene narrowed her eyes to watch it, and suddenly remembered the new word she'd just learnt. With great effort, she mumbled vaguely—

"Stern-i-dae-a."

6

JOE COMES TO.

To be precise, he feels he's about to come to, although he's not sure how. His whole body feels like it's shattered to pieces, and he's not *compos mentis*, but the pain pulsing through his body is confirming to him he is definitely alive.

Back in the day, a soldier would struggle up and beg the doctor to take him to his commanding officer, but Joe suspects that this kind of noble spirit and moral integrity had died out long before the last century. Besides, he doesn't have the energy to lift even an eyelid.

So Joe lets his eyes stay glued shut, and sleeps a little longer.

This turns out to be long enough that when Joe wakes up again, he has recovered enough energy to express his shock, swearing in a low voice in his native tongue.

Joe is terrified out of his wits.

In front of him stands Colonel Barnes, an old soldier with a career of distinguished service—although due to his eccentric style of command and unconventional methods, he had never garnered promotion. Within the department, he is no doubt the de facto leader. This is only the second time Joe has seen him, but the sight of that shiny bald scalp when he stood at the command station was something that Joe would remember for the rest of his life...

This colonel is now not only standing in front of him, but seems to have been waiting specifically for him to wake up...

"You're awake." The colonel must have heard Joe's curse, but doesn't react. He merely turns to say, "Don't move. You've lost your right arm."

"Yes, sir!"

"Ah, you know me?" The colonel slightly tilts his head, keeping his air of complete calm. "Very good. Then I won't introduce myself, but will ask you a few questions instead."

The colonel flips open a very small notebook.

"Yes, sir!...um, all my visual records should be in my goggles, but it looks like the doctor's taken them..."

"These? They've handed them over to me." The colonel very casually throws a small disc onto the table. Joe recognises it as the memory card from his equipment. "We don't need this thing. Very good, let's start the questions...name?"

"Golan, Joe."

"Age?"

"39. 40 in 7 months."

"Relations?"

"Wife Anna, daughter Eirene."

"Serial number."

"F141-9101."

"Mission codename."

Joe abruptly stops.

Doubts and unease flood his mind. The round of questioning seems to come from nowhere. If he doesn't want to look at the mission records, then why question its heavily wounded operative?

And this level of tech on what's supposed to be a hospital bed...

At first Joe thought the clamps were for medical purposes, but observing a few more details fills him with dread. Ordinary medical equipment shouldn't restrain the patient's freedom, even if it's designed to keep an invalid stationary. It'd be lined with silicon for buffering and cushioning, but the sensations he can feel from his left arm clearly let him know that the bands on his arms and legs are made of razor-sharp metal.

Instantly, a hundred possibilities explode inside his head like bombs. After a moment of silence, Joe asks: "What is this?...this isn't hospital tech, I've never seen this before... is it because I know something I shouldn't...?"

"Very good, very good, logical thought processes are functioning well." The colonel is still mumbling to himself, and writing in the notebook.

"...answer my question." Joe can no longer help himself. He just doesn't get it: such a high-ranking officer, but not even basic decorum. Had his physical condition let him, he would have let out a furious roar.

"Ah, the question...No, no, what you should know, you know; and what you shouldn't, you don't."

"Then get these restraints off me, is this how you treat heroes?"

"Heroes?" The colonel abruptly breaks into laughter.

Hearing his icy cold laugh makes Joe's hairs stand on end.

The colonel doesn't wait for a response, and with one sentence, spoken in a low voice, he utterly shatters the brittle barrier between Joe and a total breakdown.

"Oh, Joe...or perhaps I should call you—Joe48? Haven't you worked it out yet? You're not a hero, Joe. You're not even a real person."

7

IT TAKES A long time for Joe to digest this sentence. He doesn't need time to understand it: he just needs time to accept it.

There was no way a body that hadn't gone through genetic strengthening of the muscles and bones could survive the punishment he'd just been through.

There was no way an ordinary human's body could stand up after suffering injuries that heavy, let alone move.

Of course he's not human. There's no way a 'real person' could make it out of the North Base alive, no matter how much of a lucky bastard he is.

Neuro-modifications would have dampened the signals that the pain would have caused to his organic form. The extreme explosive force of his muscles, skeletal endurance and haemoglobin functionality would all have been the result of large-scale biological tailoring to meet the needs of a soldier, making Joe48 into nothing short of a war machine.

The human war legends simulated into Joe's memory were of a bunch of real flesh and blood people, who were—for some reason—fearless of pain, fearless of death, and capable of carrying on as normal even after being heavily wounded. They show up at rendezvous points like ghosts, only to vanish in a puff of smoke after the missions. The funny thing is, Joe now finds himself the protagonist of all these legends.

Judging by all the memories he's inherited from the real Joe, he can tell the original must have been a real asshole.

"Any non-natural humans created for the purposes of war should be ethically euthanised. No exception here, I hope you understand." The colonel pronounces a death verdict as lightheartedly as reading a piece of daily news, without even a hint of real feeling.

"You call this fucking ethical?!" Joe bellows at the colonel. "How am I supposed to 'understand'? I loved this country, I've given so much for it, now you're asking me to just drop dead? Is there no justice in this world?"

"By the 32nd amendment to Basic Law, natural humans are entitled to statutory human rights. Natural humans, which you are not." The colonel lifts an Atomizer pistol, giving it a showy twirl around his fingers before pointing it at the bridge of Joe's nose. "And don't even think about running away. Former yous liked to do that a lot. Kept going on about how all this was for Eirene. There was really no need to waste their breath. You're machines born for war, like a bow, a gun. You're incapable of haemogenesis or digestion. Your red blood cells will only live for another three weeks. As for other processes, they're even shorter...haven't you noticed your right arm's just rotted away?"

"You...you're all cold-blooded beasts." Joe clenches his teeth, and hisses.

"Oh, do you want me to take pity on you and let you go? What's the point? We haven't got many spare feelings to waste. Besides, your body isn't capable of fixing itself. You'll die anyway—to put it bluntly, you're disposable. Besides—Joe—" Colonel Barnes glides his right hand down the table, "do you really think that it would be good for Eirene to find out she has two—or more—fathers?"

The question was a gut punch for Joe.

"Please, just let me take one more look at her, just a photo will do...one more look is better than nothing..." Were it not for his bonds, even the solider in him would have knelt on the floor and begged. He may just be a lowly clone, but nothing is going to stop him from trying to get this wish.

"You're the seventh tank-job to request the same thing. I think I'm starting to see why they like 'you' especially, you with your flawless beliefs." The colonel isn't moved in the slightest. "I'm terribly sorry. According to the regulations laid out by Basic Law, you don't have this statutory right, and we need to protect the little girl's personal image."

"But surely you're a father..."

"I am. But you are not." A corner of the colonel's lips curl into a smirk. "Those are not your memories, Joe."

Another moment of horrific silence.

"...so there's—there was never an Eirene? Right from the start? My—all my memories are fake?!" Joe's voice begins to tremble, descending into a hysterical cry.

"Eirene is real. Anna, and Joe, are all real, I guarantee. We don't have the ability to fabricate such vivid and life-like memories." The colonel folds his hands behind his back, and begins pacing, his small, curt footsteps making Joe dizzy and nauseous. Turning to face him again, the colonel very slowly and deliberately says, "However, what you just said—am I correct in my understanding that you were showing agitation?"

The pair of eagle eyes bore into Joe. It takes a moment for Joe to understand the meaning of his question—even as his whole world is collapsing, the person in front of him is still second-guessing his every word!

Joe still wants to rebut, but very quickly let his head drop, understanding that all his efforts are futile. At the same time he also comes to the tragic realization that he has no chance of seeing Eirene again.

"Can I ask one last question...?" he says listlessly. "Why couldn't you at least let me die without knowing any of this? Isn't that ethical?"

"Ah, apologies. We need you to regain all your mental faculties. The brain sorts through memories while you sleep, and we have no other way to guarantee the safe extraction of intel." The colonel's apology sounds hollow. He strides out of the room, with the last words, "We need your memories. They are very important to us."

8

JOE SHOULD HAVE realised from the start that in the colonel's eyes he isn't a person—but a living machine. A war machine. A machine for information and memory storage. Between Joe48 and his perceived self is a bottomless chasm.

Apart from him, there are other Joes. Perhaps there is a whole unit of Joes, and in the future a whole battalion. Rows and rows of Joes and Joes.

He is the last Joe of the Bei'An Base. He is worth

nothing: he doesn't matter.

Haven't things always been like this? Which soldier isn't a pawn in a bigger game? Not to mention those who are less than pawns…Nobody's going feel sorry for a lost rifle, are they?

The silver needle that gifted him with memory and consciousness is once again inserted into his hindbrain. The stabbing numbness is very light, but makes Joe shiver with fear.

There was no longer the need for "natural humans" to go into battle.

Because there are Joes.

In war there is bound to be sacrifice. Robots have limited use and human death was too tragic, but there are piloted drones, and clones. Human clones, especially ones that have been spliced up and pre-loaded with real-life memories: like Joe. Like all the Joes are the countless "them". They've been war machines all along: they can be replicated any time, and obliterated at any given moment.

These memories don't belong to him, nor does the honour or the medals. The pathetic thing is that the beliefs that have sustained him to survive don't belong to him either: those vibrant life-like memories are merely distant illusions, like fine dust glowing in the rays of the sun. Beautiful, but out of reach. He is treated as such a lowly thing that he doesn't even have the rights to see Eirene one last time.

Like any artificial human, he doesn't even have the right to life. Love, family: all these are too far away…even the well-performing hunting dog would be rewarded by meals under the family table, but not a reconnaissance operative who's been replicated countless times.

Like a wounded lion, Joe roars, straining against the metal straps; but the cuffs are firmly fixed on his weakest parts, locking down every joint—no matter how much flesh and blood is augmented, they're still no match for the strength of steel.

Tiny bio-electric waves are traveling through his nervous system, leaving his body via that silver needle along with Joe's every thought and memory; retreating like waves when the tide ebbs, leaving the sand flat and featureless.

Before his consciousness completely disappears, the warrior holds onto a love and hope that belongs to him: all the sorrow and all the glory gradually slide into an endless darkness, until all that remains is a ray of brilliant light, where terns are circling the sunny sky. But that envious freedom is so far away that Joe will never, never, ever reach it...

Joe48 understands in the end that no matter how much he railed against his ultimate fate, he didn't even have a cat's chance in hell.

There is not a soul in the room now. A small robotic fly lands on the blue control station, quietly rubbing its legs together. No one knows how it managed to enter the supreme command headquarters—it will remain a mystery, like the cause of the massive explosion in Bei An Military base that very night.

The fly lifts its antennae, opens its wings and flies to Joe48's side.

The security camera had recorded footage of Joe's last indistinguishable words

The voice was mumbling a name, barely intelligible.

Eirene, Eirene...

Eire... ne

9

Two thousand miles away, in a remote little town, Eirene lifts her head. Her brown hair shines gold in the setting sun, held out of her eyes by a pair of hair pins, from which a hanging ornament is swaying gently. The fresh and cooling wind sweeps past her feet. Dusk is reflected in the clouds, spreading its colourful hue for thousands of miles across the sky.

Her father had returned just two months before, at the same time that Spring returned to this little northern town.

The one and only Joe is pushing his little girl, who is sitting in the white swing, laughing and singing like a lark, her song travelling with the dandelions up towards the clouds.

NOTES

Lawyer by day, Nian Yu is a self-proclaimed post-95 avant-garde sci-fi author, who seeks to combine feminine sensitivity with the logic of sci-fi. She discovered kehuan relatively late. Just after she'd finished the gaokao (university entrance exam), she saw a heated debate online about the screen adaptation of Liu Cixin's *The Supernova Era*, and grew curious, and that summer, she devoured Liu's entire repertoire.

Ever since her debut story "Wild Fire" (2014), she has been exploring not only sci-fi, but fantasy and fairy tales. Nian Yu believes she shares similar interests to her readers and is still developing her literary style, willing to attempt any subject that she feels would engage them.

In "Cat in Hell's Chance", Nian Yu wanted to explore the two extremes of human emotions, love and hate. Here, universal feelings of familial love are being weaponised for conflict. The exploitation of human love to create destruction is age-old, and Nian Yu felt that a science-fiction setting would give this heightened expression. Even though we are still far from a world where love, patriotism, and family are safe from exploitation, she hopes that this story could help each and every one of us remember the kindness that those things should bring.

Whilst much of this anthology is atypical of the common expectations of scifi, I did want to include one gun-toting, explosion-riddled, robot-fighting thriller, among the more contemplative and literary stories, all of which I enjoy immensely. When I first read this story, I was surprised to find this grim and nightmarish world of futuristic warfare and the battle hardened, weary male soldier's voice comes from the pen of a female writer, and the youngest featured in the collection.

It's a voice that immediately invoked thoughts of Republic clones of *Star Wars*, *Robocop*, and all the enhanced individuals used as weapons of war. It's a staple of Western sci-fi films and comics, but one that China is only just beginning to explore for itself. Before beginning the process of committing my translation to paper, I was primed on the *2000 AD Rogue Trooper* comics by my editor, and found a lot of inspiration for Joe from the voice of Rogue. So it really feels like closing a circle to have this story published under the same umbrella of Rebellion.

Whilst we've seen ethical discussions being held again and again where "clones" have been scifi stand-ins for different races and classes, for prisoners, or those with disabilities, cloning is a technology that is already with us, in a limited way, and it won't be too long before we need to face certain questions about human cloning and see if our good intentions to our fellow man, extend to their carbon copies.

THE RETURN OF ADAM
亚当回归

WANG JINKANG

Communication from Global News Network, 30th of February:

As people around the world lift up their heads in anticipation, 202 years after its first launch, the space shuttle Kuafu[10] has successfully returned to Earth on the 29th of February, AD2253. By unanimous nomination of the Earth Committee, Captain Adam Wang has been awarded the title "Hero of Humanity".

Seven days later, Global News Network published a feature article, written by Shirley, New Human ID 34R-64305.

"The Kuafu Project was launched on the 24th of November 2050 with the aim of exploring potential civilizations of the RX Galaxy, ten light years away. Now, after 202 years, 3 months and 5 days, it has returned

---

10 Kuafu 夸父, Chinese mythical hero who chased the sun in an attempt to race it, ultimately dying of thirst.

to Earth. The spacecraft was plasma-powered, and the natural lives of the crew suspended for the duration of the journey with cryogenic technology. There were originally four crew members, three of whom tragically perished on this mission, and whose remains were necessarily left to the desolation of unknown space. The Earth Committee have also posthumously awarded these crew 'Hero of Humanity' status. May they rest in peace, wherever they lie in this vast universe.

Recent research has revealed that when the human brain has been frozen past the optimum period of time (70-80 years), the individual inevitably suffers a period of mental breakdown as they resume. Sadly, two hundred years ago, scientists were yet to discover this phenomenon, and so were unable to take the necessary precautionary measures, resulting in the deaths of the three crew members in the harsh environs of the RX Galaxy.

The outcome of this expedition is already well-known. It is heartbreaking to hear that the crew found no other life form within ten light years of Earth. Perhaps Earth is the only flower of life gleaming in this boundless universe, a masterpiece that the Creator accidentally chanced upon and that could never be replicated. In this moment of our pride, we also feel our loneliness."

IT WAS SEVEN o'clock, and Adam struggled to open his eyes. He had been back on Earth for nine days, but his body still felt drained of energy and his mind distracted, though he knew these were the symptoms of his century-long nap. There had been more severe bouts of distraction on the planets of RX, where he and his crew had numbly walked towards death, eyes wide open but not seeing—like the thoughts and actions of a beast in denial, confronted by the fire it feared. What woke him up in the end? Was it the unique strength and tenacity that the Chinese are said to possess? In the depths of his soul, the sound of bells tolling from five thousand years ago reverberated...And now, this distraction was happening again. However, having experienced it once, and with the aid of Miss Shirley's therapy, he was close to being able to climb out of this mental chasm.

He thought about another psychiatrist he'd had before he got on the shuttle, a beautiful Japanese woman named Mieko. Her words and hot kisses didn't feel like that long ago. Heavens, how could it have been two hundred years! Where was his beloved now?

"Your period in stasis will just feel like a dream to you." These were Mieko's repeated exhortations. "When you wake up, you'll be in a strange world ten light years away, but this change won't cause immense shock to your mind because there won't be any objects of temporal reference in RX. You'll experience a space lag, but not a time lag. When you wake up the second time, you'll have returned to Earth—but a strange Earth of two hundred years later. This will be far more likely to cause severe shock to your psyche. Your family will have been relegated to history, and this living and breathing body of flesh you see before you will be a pile of bones."

She threw him a dim look. "As for society in two hundred years' time, and the changes to humans themselves? That is far beyond what anyone could predict. You'll be like some backward tribesman who stumbled in from 2050, terrified of facing the world of 2250."

Time flows away like water in the river, as Confucius says.

Adam quietly surveyed the room. He was set up at

the Great Wall Hotel in Beijing, where the décor was familiarly 21st century. Miss Shirley had told him that only a handful of renowned, top-grade hotels could afford to maintain their appearance from centuries ago, and even refrain from employing robots. "The nostalgia of humans is irrational, isn't it? Even as late as two hundred years ago, during the Age of Nuclear Power, you still hung stuffed animal heads on the walls and lit candles at night." Shirley's Mandarin sounded perfect, and her smile was as enigmatic as the Mona Lisa.

He pressed the bell. Soon an elderly man in a red uniform rounded the door, wheeling a dining trolley soundlessly into the room, and placed a familiar Chinese-style breakfast meal before him. The elderly attendant had a full head of silver hair, a benevolent face and a dignified bearing. In the past few days, Adam Wang had been observing him curiously. He couldn't help sensing something of an unspoken imperious air about the old man.

As the old man pushed the dining trolley out, Shirley was just coming in. She sidestepped and nodded as he passed, seeing him off with her gaze. Adam read the discreet deference in her eyes, and as they were by now on sufficiently familiar terms as to dispense with formalities, he voiced his thoughts to her. She looked pleased.

"I'm very glad to see you've regained your sharp powers of observation." She paused in thought. "Your observations are correct. This elderly gentleman is no ordinary attendant. He is the most respected individual on Earth: his name is Qian Renjie[11], lifelong honorary chairman of the Earth Science Committee, and winner of three Nobel Awards. The majority of New Humans were

---

11 Renjie 人杰, meaning "outstanding among people".

gifted with Second Intelligence, thanks to him. But you must continue to treat him like an ordinary person. This is the truest form of respect you can show him, and as for the details of his life—I will tell you tomorrow."

Shirley took her customary swim in the indoor pool, naked. She walked over, her supple body exuding feminine grace, dried her blonde hair with a towel and reclined on the chaise longue facing Adam. Unlike the previous days, she had covered her private parts with a snow-white towel—yet this towel seemed to arouse a thirst within Adam. A flame rose from his groin, but with a typically Chinese sense of self-control, he mastered his desire to touch her.

None of this had escaped Shirley's eyes. *An important sign of overall mental recovery, is the recovery of the sex drive,* she thought. "Dr Wang. As today is the last day of your psychiatric training, shall we have an informal chat?"

"OK."

"I've got a strange question for you. Why are you called Adam? Were you planning to return to Earth two hundred years later to find society regressed from civilization to primitivism?"

A bleak sense of desolation washed over Adam's heart, but he mirrored her jocular tone. "No, I just knew I would be like the ignorant Adam before he ate the fruit of wisdom, returning to Eden naked, and in need of the shelter of Jehovah."

Shirley gave him a tantalizing smile. "Second question. There is no information on the system about your relationship status. Do you have a lover? Is she attractive?"

"Yes, I do. She was my other psychiatrist." He couldn't help but remember that quiet and virtuous woman who was all fire and passion in bed. They were deeply in love.

Naturally, they never talked about marriage, but the day he got on the shuttle was the day they had parted forever, and they could only make love like crazy to keep the sadness away. "She was…beautiful."

"Am I beautiful?"

Adam's eyes scanned her body inch by inch. The appropriate word to describe her would be perfect, rather than beautiful. Her demeanour was as cool as a fashion model's. Her soft golden hair flowed with flawless elegance; her eyes were clear, her breasts firm and her skin as pale as ivory. She had well-curved buttocks and knees, and a pair of exquisite and delicate feet. She was the image of perfection that sculptors through the ages had dreamed of—she was almost too perfect, so that she gave an impression of not being real. Despite all the appropriate admiration that a woman in her prime would feel towards a Hero of Humanity, which Shirley had been showing all this time, why was he feeling, in turn, a subconscious admiration for her beyond his lust?

Shirley encircled and clung to his neck with her smooth arms. He bent his head to cover her lips and the top of her breasts with hot kisses. The softness of her flesh was just as intoxicating as Mieko's, yet it felt different: why? He remembered that when he first kissed Mieko, the woman was trembling all over as if electrified. Shirley's reaction was natural and calm, like a mother caressing her child.

At lunch, the elderly attendant silently came in as usual to set the dishes on the table. Now aware of his identity, Adam found it hard to accept his service with ease, but remembering Shirley's appeal, he tried his best to curb his feelings and not to reveal them.

When the elderly gentleman handed him his chopsticks, he gave Adam a peculiar look. He said nothing, but merely began to wheel out the trolley. Adam picked up on this signal, and found a slip of paper under the blue white porcelain bowl.

Would you like to speak with an old man? Please come to the Beijing Natural History Museum, Dinosaur Room, this afternoon, 5pm, alone.

The Natural History Museum had remained practically unchanged. The great dinosaur skeleton still stood there in solemn silence, contemplating its heyday when their species ruled the Earth. The old man sat on a wooden bench, deep in thought. His gaze was wise, perspicacious, and calm, as if transcending time and space. Even the arrival of Adam had not disturbed him from his contemplation.

He indicated for Adam to sit down.

"You're Chinese aren't you?" he asked, unhurriedly. "So am I. I don't mean by blood—I've only got about 60% Chinese blood in me. And I don't mean by legality or nationality, my country of birth has long met its demise. When I was a child, I was educated by my great-grandfather on Confucian morality, and through ninety years, it has governed me from my subconscious. Those upright ministers of the state of faultless moral integrity—Bi Gan, Qu Yuan, Yue Fei, Zhang Xun, Wen Tianxiang, Shi Kefa, Fang Xiaoru[12]—have been my role models all along. Although their struggles may not have altered history, they were even trite and laughable... of course, I didn't ask you to come to reflect on history. Before leaving Earth, you must have seen at some point some second or third-rate sci-fi films, like the tragedies of

---

12 Bi Gan — Advisor to the Shang Dynasty tyrant Zhou Wang who gouged out his heart to prove its worth.

Qu Yuan — Warring States statesman, poet of Chu who drowned himself after the invasion he'd foreseen. (*cont'd*)

robots taking over Earth. As a serious scientist, you must think that all this talk of imagined dangers rather shallow and ridiculous. So, let me tell you—"

Adam felt the same instinctive fear he felt entering cryogenesis: a freezing numbness emanating from the tips of the limbs and encroaching towards the brain. The old man's voice had become very distant:

"—this tragedy has already happened. And the one who opened Pandora's Box is the old man sitting beside you, weighed down by his sins."

It was a cold minute before Adam recovered from this shock, gazing at the old man's calm but pained visage, feeling utterly lost. He instinctively saw the truth in the old man's words. They revived the unease he had been feeling for days: at his concealed quarantine, at Shirley's over-perfect body—a 400-model with sexual functions, maybe...?

The old man had clearly seen through his thought process. "It's not the situation you're imagining," he said. "There's no circuitry beneath that girl's alabaster skin and blooming beauty. Her body is entirely human, despite being born from artificial insemination, and having gone through DNA editing—unfortunately, still merely human flesh.

"I should start thirty-five years ago, when I led the team that successfully created the bio-computer and made it

---

(cont'd) Yue Fei — Song Dynasty general who fought off invading forces but was executed on trumped up charges.

Zhang Xun — Tang Dynasty donestatesman, warrior, who defended Huaiyang with no supplies or reinforcements.

Wen Tianxiang — politician and intellectual who exhausted his family fortune for Southern Song resistance against the invading Yuan forcesdone.

Shi Kefa — minister who died defending Yangzhou against invading Qing forces.

Fang Xiaoru — Ming Dynasty scholar and royal tutor who refused to surrender to usurpers to the imperial throne, losing ten clans of kin.

compatible with the human brain. The first prototype allowed enhanced brain capacity and storage, so as to increase combined intelligence a hundredfold, or 10 square, which we represent as 2BEL. The size of the component was tiny, and can be implanted into the brain during a ten-minute operation. After a short post-implant period of neuro-network amalgamation, humans adapted to it so smoothly they felt no difference between using it, or, say, the left or right hemispheres of their brains. In other words, the parasite quickly became familiar with its host, whom it can control with ease. This would seem the most appropriate way of putting it." He chuckled acrimoniously.

"On the 13th of October AD2218, we performed the first experiment and named it the installation of Second Intelligence. For safety reasons, and to be sure of the results, the test subject was brain dead—someone who had lost all sign of sentience. The operation was a complete success. Even now, I can still feel the mad rapture that success had brought. Such foolish joy!"

The old man shook his head, and continued:

"Ironically, that brain-dead patient then employed his now extraordinary abilities to establish the Age of Second Intelligence, which shall now be forever known as 'The Age of New Intelligence'—proclaiming an end to the old era of natural humans, and himself as the rightful Father of New Intelligence.

"You must know that during the era of natural humans, when humans advanced their environment, the advancement of the base matter in the human brain was miniscule. This determined that the changes to the external world would come at a rate of arithmatic growth. In the era of New Intelligence, Second Intelligence ensures that the human brain also develops at the flying speed the environment does, so that subject and object can resonate, creating waves and new heights, so that the world can develop at exponential speed.

"This would have been difficult for natural humans to imagine thirty-five years ago. A highly illustrative example is the old man in front of you. To put it frankly, he was one of the world's most outstanding scientists and had always been conceited, his own intelligence far surpassing his peers. But today, his intellect is incapable of comprehending new scientific developments. It's like a primate's brain trying to understand calculus. I persisted in my decision to resign my post as chairman of the Earth Science Committee and took a job here as a hotel attendant to at least maintain the pathetic dignity of an old fool."

The old man paused to let Adam digest his words. Contemplating the dinosaur before them, after a while he directed his gaze back to Adam and said inquiringly. "Can I continue?"

Adam Wang nodded.

"Right now, Second Intelligence has grown to 13BEL, equivalent to ten trillion times the human brain's natural capacity—an inauspicious number. Compared to this, the human brain—in not only information storage and processing speed, but the creative thought processes that humans have always prided themselves in, instinct and neuro-network compatibility—falls hopelessly behind. The only shortcoming of Second Intelligence is emotional processes, including sexual processes. However, even this is not impossible to upgrade. New Humans just prefer to keep this part of them natural, the way twentieth century people loved ethnic dance.

"Despite the efforts humans had made over time to alter their natural selves, in multiple ways, and the immense achievements they had made physically—such as Shirley's near-perfect body—these advancements were relatively slow, especially in relation to increasing the brain's natural capacity. You can imagine what it must be like for Second Intelligence, which develops daily, to co-exist with the soft, weak and stagnant natural human brain. You could say that machines have borrowed human bodies, and with the aid of the human brain, have occupied Earth; and we are like idiotic moths, incubating their larvae with our own bodies."

After a cooling period of thirty years, the old man's pain, self-admonition and helpless rage were no longer burning. Yet precisely due to his calmness, Adam felt the burden of their weight all the more.

"In fact, even before the experiments had come to fruition, I foresaw this kind of danger," the old man said bitterly. "To be honest, if I believed my death would prevent this from progressing further, I would destroy all this material in a heartbeat and blow this 'clever' brain out with a bullet. Sadly I am well aware that even if I died, sooner or later, someone else would re-open this Pandora's Box. All that I could do is help humanity dredge out some solid obstacles to put in the way. Do you know 'The Three Laws of SI'? That bill was drafted by me, and was passed by the Earth Committee just before the very first official operation for the implant."

In an even voice, the old man began to recite 'The Three Laws of Human Implantation of Second Intelligence':

"One. The receiver of the Second Intelligence Implant must be over fifteen years of age, and of sound mind and body. The agreement confirming their willingness to enter Second Intelligence must be signed in the presence of an adult natural human, also of sound mind and body, directly related to the subject, and who must co-sign the agreement.

"Two. The Second Intelligence Implant must be designed to automatically shut down after ten years of operation, returning its host to a complete natural human state, and sustain this state for a minimum of one hundred days. The decision of whether or not to reactivate the implant after this period shall rest solely with the natural human individual.

"Three. Natural humans and New Humans are equal in the eyes of the law. Intermarriage is permitted, though both parties must be in their natural human state during the process of reproduction."

The old man continued:

"By passing these three laws, I hoped to at least prevent natural humans from being forced to become New Humans, guarantee their freedom to revert to natural human state after being implanted with Second Intelligence, and make New Humans forever the descendants of natural humans by law. It should be pointed out that the New Humans have executed the Three Laws with the utmost strictness—even severity— and the precision of machines. The legislative definition 'of sound body and mind' alone occupies the equivalent of several dozen sets of Encyclopedia Britannica. If we natural humans have to take New Humans to court, we have no choice but to recruit a New Human lawyer to have any chance of winning."

The two smiled at each other bitterly. Adam wanted to intercede with a question, but he hesitated. The old man continued:

"Perhaps you wanted to ask if these laws have actually served to provide the protection for natural humans, for which they were intended? No. Because since the very first operation, almost no one has been unwilling to enter Second Intelligence, and even fewer unwilling to reactivate it after the hundred-day return to natural state. Humans have become intoxicated, addicted. They are incapable of extricating themselves from its influence. The Three Laws have been enacted for nothing. Right now, there is but a remnant of a hundred natural humans in the entire world. All of them were my co-workers, my peers. Back then, each of them were first-rate physicists, scientists, biologists, and futurists. Only these individuals, equipped with extraordinary natural intellect and deep perceptiveness of the world, could recognise the fatal dangers Second Intelligence posed for Humanity. By the way, over half of this hundred are of Chinese descent. Was there something holding them back in their heritage? They, like me, are caught in this awkward plight."

The old man had grown fatigued and fell silent, like a beach after the waves have swept by. They were like the sole survivors left on this beach by the immense tide of history, with only a dinosaur skeleton for company. Adam contemplated it, speechless. In the depths of his soul, the sound of those bell tolls was still reverberating from five thousand years ago: slow, distant, yet powerful. He took the old man's arm, and said in a low voice:

"There's an old Chinese saying: to strive for an end even though one knows the end is an impossibility[13]. Is there anything you could entrust me to do for you?"

13 知其不可为而为之, from Confucius' Analects, Book XIV, meaning that many things are won through struggle and hardship, if one has the persevering spirit.

"No, I don't have much more to say," the old man said bleakly. "I don't believe an individual can change the world, nor do I believe that the intellect of natural humans can contend with that of the New Intelligence. Anyhow, we are all old, and you are the only young natural human left in the world. By telling you everything, I have absolved myself from these responsibilities. Please do your best."

For an entire day and night, Adam locked himself in his room, his mind like roiling, crashing waves. He was totally aware that his situation was hopeless: no different from that of a Gorilla trying to challenge humanity to a battle. However, he couldn't just give up. On the planet in RX, he had really felt pride in his species as the paragon of intelligent life in the universe. Humans must not become slaves of machines. Besides, he had a moral responsibility towards Shirley: to liberate her beautiful body from the control of machines.

So what could he do? Maybe the old man was hinting in his words—that only by gaining Second Intelligence could he find a way to take on the New Humans. This somewhat base and underhand strategy wasn't something that the old scientists were willing to attempt, but he felt he had necessary justification to engage in Contingency Theory. Heavens, though, how could he get to this point without rousing the suspicion of the New Humans? Perhaps his carefully devised plan would seem, in Shirley's eyes, as childish as a cat who licks its lips in front of its owner before trying to steal the butter.

That night, Shirley fluttered in, took her naked swim and reclined on the chaise longue as usual. Her smile was splendid; taking Adam's hand, she put it on her chest.

"It's been over ten days, are you still unmoved by my

body? That makes me so sad! Even though you Chinese are famously frigid." Then she added, mockingly, "Come now, let me kiss you. A kiss from a pretty girl can be an effective tranquiliser, because I'm going to tell you something now—something you wouldn't be expecting."

Adam's body stiffened in an instant, a change that she acutely felt—but she continued, not batting an eyelid. "Yesterday I promised you something, to tell you about the old man…"

Pretending not to notice Adam's complex emotional reaction to her words, she briefly précised the history of New Humans. "We would never keep the Hero of Humanity in this current awkward position. The Earth Committee have already decided to implant you with the new 14BEL SI chip—you'll be the first. You'll acquire the knowledge of the whole of Humanity up until this moment, in just a moment. Of course, according to the Three Laws, whether or not you go ahead with it depends entirely on your own decision. So I hope you give it plenty of consideration before you get back to us."

Adam never thought his plan would proceed this smoothly. Controlling his reaction, he replied solemnly: "This is too sudden. I will need plenty of time to think about such an important question. But I think I will agree in the end."

Shirley took him into her arms. "The problem is, the Three Laws do not take into account your special circumstances. They require for there to be at least one direct relative of the willing subject to countersign, but all your direct relatives are already part of history. Of course… except for your wife." She murmured, "Will you accept the love of an admirer?"

Adam held her tightly. His emotions were complex; love

for this beautiful woman, fear of the Second Intelligence in her brain, guilt that he was using love as part of a scheme…but all of this was temporarily razed by his burning desire. He took hold of the towel and uncovered Shirley's body.

"Oh, not now!" Shirley caught his hand. "Please wait. This is the most important moment in my life, and I want to share it with you."

She draped the towel over her shoulders, and pressed the electric bell. The old attendant entered soundlessly and placed a birthday cake on the table. He exchanged a neutral look with Adam, and quietly exited the room.

Carefully, Shirley lit the candles with matches. Around the bright, flower-shaped cake were twenty-five small candles, with a large red one in the middle. "Is it your twenty-fifth birthday?" Adam asked.

She was lighting the largest candle, and smilingly shook her head. "Not only this."

Adam saw the nervous anticipation in her eyes, and for the first time he saw Shirley as a real woman. It had suddenly dawned on him: "It's your Reversion Day!"

The clock struck twelve, and in an instant Shirley's eyes dulled, as if a streak of lightning had suddenly struck her consciousness. In a moment, her gaze cleared. And she let out a deep sigh, and smiled as she said in English:

"Please don't use Hanyu. From now on I can only speak my mother tongue like a fifteen-year-old. You're right, this is my first Reversion Day. I'm now a natural human, like you."

Adam found it difficult to process his emotions. Shirley would not be able to use Second Intelligence for the next hundred days, so there was no need to be suspicious of her 'third eye'. From now on, she was a woman on a par with him in intelligence. Excitedly, he picked her up and put her on the bed.

After some stormy lovemaking, Shirley lay quietly nestled on his chest, and Adam felt relaxed and at peace. He asked softly, "How are you feeling?" Shirley looked up vacantly. Adam smiled, changing the subject as well as the language: "How did you feel before the implant? Were you afraid?"

"The opposite. It's a day that we nervously long for. It's only after the implant, when we feel the weight of the knowledge we immediately get, that we see its burden to our hearts. So we really do understand those old scientists who reject Second Intelligence."

Adam paused for thought, and then asked carefully: "So, has there been anyone who has wished to return to their natural state?"

Shirley replied vividly: "Of course! Who doesn't want to live carefree and without worries, at least for some time? But to be an imbecile and infant forever—that would be too childish, and too irresponsible."

Adam fell silent, stroking Shirley's smooth spine and gazing at the ceiling. After a while he mused softly: "I've got a few more questions. After all, this is a matter of life and death for me. Besides, I've been a natural human for two hundred years. My low intelligence is excusable, don't you think?"

Smilingly, Shirley whispered into his ear: "Don't forget that I'm a natural human too, at the moment. The natural human brain hardly alters in two hundred years, so no need to be so self-deprecating."

"Aren't you concerned that, for instance, one day, an instruction might be programmed into Second Intelligence to make New Humans obey the whims of a madman?"

"The Earth Committee have taken the strictest precautions to protect Earth against it. Compared to the protection we have in place for this kind of threat, the measures natural humans had devised to prevent the pushing of the Red Button isn't even worth a mention. Yet has there ever been any madman in history who has actually been able to trigger a nuclear war?"

"But it's not the same kind of madmen you're up against…"

Shirley replied assuredly, "Does the bend in the river ultimately matter to its course? Even natural humans can be programmed. We've had a craze of Fascists, and a craze for Cultural Revolutions: the number of people brainwashed in those times would have been even greater."

Adam grew silent again.

It was four o'clock in the morning, and from the computer's calculations, Shirley knew that this was the optimum time for conception. "Come on," she said softly. "I want to give you the most intelligent of children."

At once, the third law of Second Intelligence floated into Adam's head. "During the process of impregnation, both parties must be in natural human form," which somewhat dampened his enthusiasm.

Fifty days later, Adam and his wife signed the following document.

"I, Adam Wang, male, aged 30, married; of sound mind and body, willingly request the installation of Second Intelligence."

"I, Shirley, female, aged 25, New Human ID 34R-64305, lawfully wedded wife of Adam Wang; of sound mind and body, consent to my husband's request to install Second Intelligence."

The agreement was supplemented by court certifications

confirming that the two individuals were indeed of sound mind and body, and in their natural human states—Certificate no. 46S-27853, 103 pages in length.

Upon his departure from the Great Wall Hotel, Adam noticed the old man seeing him off, his eyes full of sorrow and despair. "Bleak winds chill the shores of the Yi, the hero departs, never to return." [14] He thought, *A war has just begun, and the winner is yet to be determined.*

TEN YEARS LATER.

All channels are reporting news of the death of honorary chairman and life-long member of the Earth Committee, Dr Qian. The reaction from citizens to this news is unremarkable: most of them saving it to levels 2 or 3 in the data search within their internal storage bank.

Adam Wang stands at the window of his apartment, gazing out at the night sky, alone. From the panoramic view of the 270th floor, he feels as if he's among the stars once more, and with that, a profound sense of solitude. His son has just been picked up by Shirley, who is currently in her second reversion period, a time when maternal instincts tend to be at their strongest.

It was long after the marriage ceremony that he had found out his union with Shirley had been pre-determined by a computer's calculations. The selection was a very successful one: they had produced a prodigy, with a natural intelligence higher than 220 and health ratings at 95%, breaking a new record.

As for the marriage itself? It had long broken down.

---

14 From the Song of Yi River 易水歌, by Jing Ke (3rd century BCE), written on the eve of his famous assassination mission to Qin, after it had conquered the neighbouring Kingdom of Zhao.

Why did it fall apart? Adam would always answer mildly, "I was born two-hundred and seven years before her. Naturally, this two-century generation gap ran quite deep."

Adam's first reversion period is about to come to an end. In these last hundred days, thoughts and feelings he had normally suppressed have reemerged. This wasn't unusual: the phenomenon was a kind of temporary psychological 'return to the roots'. He had even written a significant number of influential books on the subject. After Dr Qian's death, however, this emotional ebb has felt much fiercer, to the extent of almost drowning him in its flow. He thought, self-mockingly, that this could be down to the thirty years he had spent being Chinese. Very few Chinese would be able to resist the pull of the echoes of history.

On the wall of his study, giant photos of Dr Qian and Mieko gaze at him calmly. On his desk lay a paper copy of *The Book of Han*[15] in the old sewn binding, which he has often returned to over the last one hundred days, especially its biography of Su Wu[16].

Ten years ago, he had entered Second Intelligence. He felt as if a dark veil had been lifted from his face, enabling him to see the truth of the world, although it was somewhat of a cruel truth. The cautious steps that he and Dr Qian were taking had actually completely played into the hands of the New Humans and their so-called "Adam's Return Program", like two bees lured

---

15 The Book of Han, 汉书, the first book of Chinese history documenting about 230 years of the Han Dynasty, written by the historian Ban Gu around 105 BCE.

16 Su Wu (c. 140-60 BCE), 苏武, Han Dynasty, statesmen and diplomat sent on a mission to the border regions, where he served for 19 years. Over this period, the local nomad tribes tried to bribe and threaten, even sending him to herd sheep in the remote northern regions. Su Wu never betrayed his country.

into a maze by nectar—and the dispenser of this nectar was Shirley. However, along with this realization, he had also understood the painstaking efforts on the part of the New Intelligence. He understood the puerility and ludicrousness of resisting Second Intelligence. Natural humans eliminated primates, New Intelligence eliminated natural humans: this is the inviolable law of nature. The actions of he and Dr Qian were like those of two old monkeys refusing to use fire.

He reached out to the remaining natural humans and successfully persuaded them, especially the stubborn elderly Chinese scientists, arranging for them to have the implant—all except for one person. The obstinacy of Dr Qian left Adam not knowing whether to laugh or cry. He was a very pathetic old man.

But during his reversion period, some dislocation seems to have occurred to his consciousness. As Li Ling[17] was unable to look Su Wu in the eye, he has been feeling apologetic, with waves of guilt towards the old man. He could thoroughly empathise with the gut-wrenching emotions Li Ling must have felt as he took the actions he couldn't help but take, going over to the enemy's side. When he read Li Ling's written reply to Su Wu, he was touched that even though Li Ling had decided his place was among the nomad tribes, his relentless torrent of explanations could only have come from heartfelt love for his former clan...Now that Dr Qian has passed away, he, like Li Ling bidding farewell to Su Wu, has lost the only person with whom he feels kinship, who could listen

---

17 Li Ling 李陵, Contemporary of Su Wu, who surrendered to the nomad tribes after being heavily defeated, a defeat that led to the execution of his entire family, pushing him further along the path of betrayal. Su was ordered to write to Li and persuade him to return to Han.

to him explain, even if he would never forgive him.

The phone rings. It's Shirley.

"Adam, tomorrow I'll come and drop the child off."

"OK."

"He's been really happy, he doesn't want to go back."

"Really?"

Shirley pauses. "You're coming up to the end of your reversion period, aren't you? I have a suggestion for you to think about. Perhaps we should extend our reversion period, and while we're both natural humans, rekindle our former love."

Adam considers this. He knows it would be impossible to revive their feelings. Shirley's rare gush of affection is merely a product of the emotional ebb of reversion. He replies with utter politeness:

"Thank you very much for your suggestion. I've been very busy recently, let's talk further in a month's time, OK? Bye now."

But can the hormones you've gathered during your reversion period last for a month? he asked himself semi-cuttingly. Then, he hears his son's voice over the phone:

"Dad, I miss Grandpa Qian…" His words mingle with sobs. Adam wants to console his son, but finds himself choking with tears too. After a brief silence, he hangs up, and begins to write the obituary in time to meet the publisher's deadline.

The next day, the article is published, written by this year's chairman of the Earth Committee, Adam Wang:

"Earth's last natural human has bid farewell to the world, at the age of 104. He spent his last ten years with my son and I in a small Chinese-style household. His passing coincides with one of my reversion periods. Because of this my mourning has double the significance: a son mourning a father, and a natural human mourning another.

"Once I was the most adamant member of his school of resistance: willing to sacrifice myself, willing to deceive my way into Second Intelligence in order to revive the era of natural humans. Due to a glitch of Yin and Yang, I have not fallen behind the times.

"Dr Qian's resistance to Second Intelligence was like the resistance of the Manchurian Chinese to railways during the Qing Dynasty. Dr Qian did so because he considered himself Chinese, but in fact, historically, the Chinese have not been lacking in open-minded attitudes. During several periods when ethnic groups came together, they saw the commonalities between cultures, rather than their differences in blood. Were these not like the differences and similarities between New Intelligence and natural humans?

"I don't have the audacity to criticize qianbei[18]. He had been the father of science for his whole generation, and the ancestor of New Intelligence. He persevered in his belief, alone, and unyielding until his death. His moral integrity is worthy of our respect. What was gratifying was that in his last days, Mr Qian recognised reality, and passed his remaining time in peaceful harmony and domestic bliss. He retained his acute natural intellect until the end, and also that dignity, which no one who dared to look down on. I hope so much that in the nine years we have lived together, his grandfather will have left his mark on my son.

"The world is too complex. The more deeply one understands it, the more one doubts the works of its Creator, if they exist. Who dares to call themselves a

18 Qianbei, see note in "Tombs of the Universe".

critic of history? Perhaps a child could see what an adult could not, crawling on their own back; perhaps a brilliant natural human could triumph with their instinct over the detailed and complex deductions of AI. No matter what, we New Intelligence have shed many human interests and gained some machine properties. We can't help but respect the computer's calculations before we declare our love to a girl; when we are enjoying sexual intercourse, we are simultaneously aware of the mathematical ratio between hormones and arousal...it's a painful clarity. Our contributions to science are determined by the BEL level of our implant, and the structure and type of knowledge implanted, like larvae who are fed royal jelly, destined to become queen bees, this is no doubt a new kind of injustice of our times...

"Only one thing is for sure: we are moving forwards irrevocably down the predetermined path, whether towards heaven or hell. The difference between us and dinosaurs is that we are looking for road signs with a clear mind. We will wipe away the dust and read what they say, and then step by step, find where we belong.

"In twenty minutes, I shall reactivate Second Intelligence. And then, all this temporary mental confusion and helpless melancholy will evaporate like smoke. With this article I sincerely mourn our loss of the father of science, may his spirit rest in peace in the heavens."

NOTES

WANG JINKANG LIVED through the heart of China's Cultural Revolution, spending some years in a countryside commune, before being sent to work in an iron foundry and a diesel engine plant. In 1978, after the political situation shifted, he was able to complete his further education and become a senior engineer in the Nanyang oilfields. The Return of Adam was the first story Wang published, in Science Fiction World at the age of forty-four, launching a career that spans multiple Yinhe awards, forty-odd short stories and half a dozen novels.

Considering his massive following in China, Wang's work has been relatively overlooked in translation until very recently. One of the earliest published works (1993) by an author was by then in his middle age, this piece can seem crude, and often relies heavily on "The Male Gaze", though personally I feel that just fuels the reader's view of the protagonist as a man out of time, a hero in the mould of Captain Kirk, or Flash Gordon, finding himself out-evolved whilst he travelled the stars, and later hoisted on his own chauvinist petard.

I wanted this collection to showcase a broad range of modern Chinese science fiction. This piece is the oldest story I have included, and represents almost a starting point for the current resurgence. Were it not for this generation of pioneers, we would not have the immense writing talent, diverse literary output and growing communities for SF we have today.

Wang's work tends to revolve around biology, ethics and international politics. Here, improving one's mental capacity and intelligence is the battleground. It has been a deep preoccupation in China's highly competitive society, where the bar of academic success is set high, and people seek any edge to get ahead. Chinese parents are bombarded with advice on foods to improve their children's height and health, and TV adverts for supplements and pills supposed to be good for the developing brain. I was drawn to this story's decision to set the desire to upgrade, avoiding evolutionary elimination, against the values and mores of the Confucian tradition.

RENDEZVOUS: 1937
相聚在一九三七

ZHAO HAIHONG

As I FELL asleep, I felt someone pat my face. "Wake up, wake up!"

Drowsy-eyed, I brushed her hand away. "Can't you let me rest? I've had a very late night!"

"You have to wake up, or you'll lose me!"

I opened my eyes, and saw a young woman, hair in a Wusi[19] cut, round-nosed and pouting, her eyes shining. I didn't know her, though her face seemed familiar.

"Do you still remember 1937?"

"Oh," I said, pushing her aside, fatigued, "it's you. I gave up on that one ages ago. Shoving problems that can't be solved onto a time machine, that's not science. Besides,

---

19 五四, "Wu Si" literally means "five four", and refers to the May 4th student demonstrations of 1919, a direct response to the decision made at the Versailles Peace Conference not to end the German concessions in China in exchange for the assistance of the Chinese Labour Corps in WWI, but to transfer those concessions over to Japan. May the 4th was also a movement for cultural and social reform. Female intellectuals involved commonly wore their hair in a straight cut bob, like our heroine here.

I've developed way past that kind of storytelling, it feels like an old shell. And you…" I nodded emphatically, "are a rejected character. You weren't even fully formed, get out of my head!"

"You're always like this, finding excuses to drown your creative impulses in sloth!" She poked at my chest. "There's a flame in there that hasn't quite gone out. I will rekindle it. No matter what anyone else says, I'm going to make it burn."

Her uncompromising demeanour frightened me a little. I scratched my head. Her head of short hair was as luscious as the leaves of a tree in the sun. I said: "Xiao Xia[20]…"

"Good, now I have a name." She smiled astutely. "Then let's begin…"

XIA FENFANG

A LONG CORRIDOR stretched out before her.

She was already regretting it.

There seemed to be no end, stretching all the way into the depths of time.

She shuddered, and nodded to the guide standing next to her. "I'm ready."

But where she was going, no amount of readiness would ever be enough.

That was a real hell on earth, and she was hell-bent on finding hope there.

Even her guide was privately thinking that she was a fool, and their whole organization fools for assisting her

---

20 小夏, "Xiao" meaning "little", is a term of endearment usually added in front of a shortened first name or surname. "Xia" means summer.

in this pointless exercise. He was the descendant of a race of aliens who had immigrated to Earth: his race had co-existed with humans across the globe, with very few of them aware of their extra-terrestrial origins. Those who knew—their "friends"—helped to protect them: there were, after all, only fifty-seven individuals from the R race on the planet.

Xia Fenfang[21] was one of these "friends"; a title she had inherited from her great-grandfather, and a role that was still in effect. In return, she could ask for anything that was within the capabilities of the R to give.

Xia Fenfang's request was thoroughly unoriginal: she'd asked to use one of their machines to travel back in time. But, to be fair, where she wanted to go did require a fair amount of guts: the 15th of December, 1937, Nanjing, China. On that day, a massacre began that shocked the world.

TOKYO, JAPAN.

In the middle of the hall hangs a scroll featuring a single character, 忍.

Yamaguchi Masao sits cross-legged in his kimono, head bowed. His father stands solemnly facing the scroll, hands folded behind him, with his back to Masao. He is as solid and immovable as a black iron monolith.

"Any race that wishes to prosper must rely on the country of their residence. Although we are a force of the R, we have lived in Japan for the last hundred years. Our

---

21 夏芬芳, Fenfang means "fragrance", thus making our heroine's full name into "fragrance of summer". The names of the characters are following the traditional Chinese and Japanese order for names with the surname preceding the given name. So in Yamaguchi Masao, the former is the surname.

fate is united with the fate of the people of this country."

"Yes, father."

"On the 18th of September this year, Tokyo will be holding a review tribunal for World War II. Activists from many countries are currently hard at work gathering evidence to negate the Holy War, and seek compensation. There is a Chinese girl, one of our "friends", who has used one of our exploration chambers to travel to 1937 in order to collect such evidence. You must find her."

"Yes, Father."

"That girl is twenty-three years old. In 1937 she would not have been born. Strictly speaking, she does not have the right to exist in 1937. Terminating her would not transgress the law."

"Yes, Father."

"Tomorrow morning you will go with me to the temple. In the afternoon, you shall depart on your mission."

Yamaguchi Masao slowly raises his head. He is seventeen, still an almost-child, with crescent-shaped eyebrows, thin cherry lips and cheeks still showing a faint bloom of youth. He arranges his lips into a smile, and says: "Yes, Father."

YAMAGUCHI MASAO

HEAD ACHING. HEAD aching like hell. I open my eyes. They are all staring intently at me, on some kind of high alert.

But my head is bursting, like a dropped watermelon. The skin's intact, but inside it's just pulp and mess. I try my best to open my eyes again, to work out what just happened, but nothing is coming to me.

Where am I?

Who are they?

Who am I?

"He's awake!" someone pipes up, and presses something cold and hard against my forehead.

"Careful!"

"Stop that, *San Ma*[22], he can't even focus!" A middle-aged man with a scar on his face pushes aside the gun barrel. "Are you scared of a beardless whippersnapper?"

They laugh. Not a happy laugh.

I rub my eyes, propping myself up on the icy stone floor.

This is a spacious basement, with a pile of furniture and household objects. Lights are installed in the wall, but not lit, except for two faint oil lamps. Every single person around me, whether standing or sitting, exudes tension, as if the ceiling might collapse at any given moment. None of their clothes fit them, and look like they've just been thrown on, all styles mixed up. Instinct tells me that they are all in the same line of work, a job that comes with its own body language. They are soldiers.

There is someone else, standing away from the group, under the lamps. Her head is lowered and her hair, cut to an inch below her ears, hangs down to obscure her face. She is facing the light and scrutinizing something very carefully. Hearing their laughter, she turns quickly. Her veil of short hair flutters like a butterfly's wing, revealing her face. Under the lamplight, it is serene, calm, and benign as water. Her voice seems to have the same power to soothe: she waves the object that she had been scrutinising, and says: "Don't be scared, kid, we've seen your papers. You're Chinese, we won't hurt you."

I have no way of telling if she is right or wrong. No

---

22 三麻, meaning "three warts", a nickname.

matter how hard I fish around inside my head, no clue to my identity emerges, but I just know there's something wrong with her statement.

"Says here, you're a student who studied in Japan, and stayed there, right?" mutters the one with the scar. "So what are you doing here? Are you a *guizi*[23] spy?" He bears down on me, until his face is inches away from mine, assaulting my face with his breath. "If you're Chinese, why are you risking your life for the *guizi*?"

"Where am I? I don't remember anything!" I feel scorched by the flames licking his pupils.

"Who am I? How did I get here? Please tell me!"

Reading in my anxiety that this memory loss is genuine, he stops interrogating me and steps away. Keeping his eyes trained on me, he seems to lose himself in thought. None of the men around me speak a word: there is a dreadful misery in their silence, an inexpressible despair amidst the tension.

"You really can't remember?" The woman, the only one in the room, pushes them aside and walks towards me. Squatting down, she holds up two fingers and presses the back of my head where it comes into contact with my neck. "There's a blood clot here. That hit was a bit heavy, Uncle Ji."

Her touch feels like a needle stabbing through the mush in my head, and my whole body shudders, although I don't make a sound. She fixes her gaze on me for a second, and then resumes her normal stance. "Are you recalling anything yet?" she asks.

I shake my head. I must look very naive.

"This is the strong room in my family home. A month

---

23 鬼子, "gui" means "demon" or "devil", a common colloquial term that refers to the occupiers.

ago, my whole family escaped to Wuhan, but I was studying at the girl's school. I didn't want to leave, I didn't believe things would get this bad. No one could have imagined…" She goes on with her story, but there's no real pain in her voice. "Yesterday the Japanese soldiers attacked the city, and they started looting everything; this strong room is safer than anywhere else, so I've been hiding here. I let Uncle Ji and his comrades in too. Unlike you, if they are seen outside, they'll be shot on sight."

Her words have outlined the situation, but I still don't understand how it relates to me. I try again. "How did I end up here?"

"We should be asking you this!" erupted the man who had pointed a gun at me.

"Even if you were snagging some free stuff, you'd have gone somewhere else. This house has been picked clean several times over by the *guizi*." The scarred guy spoke again. "You've not only come here, you've found the secret door to the strong room. The guizi soldiers searched several times and missed it. How come you found it straight away?"

"We didn't expect anyone to find us. That's why Uncle Ji pounced on you so suddenly." It's like she's trying to make things easy for me. "He didn't mean to make you lose your memory."

I really have lost my memory? "What year is this? What city is this? Can you please tell me…?" I turn towards her.

"This is Nanjing, December 1937," she interjects. Her tone is strange: she sounds like a news reporter. News reporter?—Some very specific images float into my head. Are they all news reporters? Then what period are they from? Obviously not 1937.

I open my mouth. There's a need to talk but I have no

idea what to say. My stomach twitches and lets out an embarrassing rumble, so I say: "I'm hungry."

Hunger is infectious, and I seem to hear my rumblings echo all around me. It was a hilarious situation, but nobody laughs. I don't understand their silence, and could only answer with silence.

At last, someone grumbled: "So what do we do?"

The girl stands up from the crowd. She speaks very softly, but everyone can hear her clearly. She says: "I'll think of something."

XIA FENFANG

I HAD NO idea it would be this hard.

It's one thing to try and prepare yourself psychologically, but when you see it happening with your own eyes, it's something else entirely. Just keeping bowing to Japanese soldiers along the way, keep greeting them with *konichiwa*. Despite being harassed and questioned on several occasions, my knowledge of Japanese and the Japanese papers I'd prepared before I left have kept me out of harm's way.

Chinese corpses are strewn throughout this city, some wearing uniform, most not; men, women, the elderly and children. I keep feeling as if I'm in a nightmare, as if I'm moving in a dream on a road paved with severed limbs, broken bones and rotting flesh. Even the air is thick with the metallic tang of blood. Flies buzz all around, following the stench; wild dogs are running all over the city, gorging on flesh and blood, occasionally howling with satisfaction.

My stomach clenches, my eyes screw shut, but I force them open—I must see and bear witness. No matter how hard, this is the mission at hand.

This ancient city, desolate and strewn all over with trauma as far as the eye could see, lies streaked blood-red under the cruel sun.

Finally I reach the vicinity of *Zhonghua*[24] Gate. I stand, trying to capture a bizarre sound—stifled, low, as if trying to escape from a hundred muffled mouths at the same time, producing a horrific effect. Like sinners being fried in boiling vats of oil in a *Scorching Hell*[25], like countless lost souls chanting the Rebirth Mantra just before they drown in the sea of bitterness.

My throat seizes with fear at the thought of having to look in the direction of the sound. I take a deep breath, steeling myself to turn towards it, inch by inch.

About a hundred metres away, several hundred Chinese men and women are wielding shovels at the gunpoint of the Japanese: beyond them are holes already dug, and in the holes lie more ordinary Chinese citizens, bound by ropes.

As the shovels work, the earth piles higher and higher around them, and the poor souls about to be buried alive are struggling, writhing in the holes. The sound of their struggles mingle with the wretched breathing of the diggers into that hellish mumming that caught my ear.

Screaming is forbidden, although occasionally someone does—but these cries for help are immediately silenced by bullets sped from Japanese guns.

---

24 中华, another term for China.

25 Scorching Hell—The Chinese concept of hell is based on the Buddhist Naraka, a place of torment. It has ten regions, four holy realms where the souls of the enlightened go, but most souls end up in the six other realms of infinite suffering and pain, the Scorching Hell is only a small part of one of these regions.

I remember reading about this in a museum. The Japanese had separated their Chinese victims into batches: one batch would dig the holes, bury another batch, and a third would bury the first one; thus repeated, the system had saved considerable Japanese bullets and manpower.

There are many more Chinese situated not far from the site. Under Japanese guns, they squat in a row, with their backs towards this Shuraba-like scene of carnage on earth, I cannot know what is going on in their heads, but their shoulders are shuddering with utter helplessness and despair.

When I saw the photographs at the museum, I was so enraged I wanted to shout *why don't you fight back! Yes, they were holding guns, but if you all fought back together, you might have found a way to survive; if you just submitted, your only fate would be burial at the hands of your own people.*

But now, watching them from a short distance; apart from anger and hatred, I feel the terror that they are feeling. My legs feel weak—so weak I can hardly move. Courage and bravery are easy to imagine. But every individual has just one life and many choose to live with it with care, even down to its last moments.

Back at the Xia Mansion, I lose all my appetite. San Ma hurls the rice cake onto the floor and cries out in a distorted voice, "I refuse to eat food from the Japanese!"

I don't even have the energy to argue with him. Japanese shops are the only ones still operating in the entire city, or else I'd have to go and claim rations in the safe zone: how can I claim so many portions all by myself? Maybe letting them in was a strategic mistake: it was totally outside my plan, but I couldn't just leave them to die.

Uncle Ji picks the pack off the floor, slowly tears off the

Japanese labels, and bites off half the cake in a single go. "Go on, why aren't you eating?"

It is only now that the others begin to eat. They are obviously following Uncle Ji's orders. Despite the change of clothes, you can tell that they are soldiers. Uncle Ji must be their officer. A captain knows how to lead, and when to do so.

That new boy sits quietly in the corner eating. His ID says he's twenty-one, but I keep getting the feeling he's a lot younger. My cheeks are no longer pink like his. He must be at least a few years younger.

Why would he turn up in this place? If he's a Japanese spy, he's not been able to report back. The guizi would have surrounded this place by now; if he's an ordinary citizen, how did he get in?

Like a puzzle box, he keeps his secrets and just smiles. That smile is melting me. I suddenly remember last night when I pressed the wound on his skull. The pain must have been extreme, but he didn't even cry out, suggests someone who's undergone training.

The group of eight quickly polish off all the food I brought back. The supplies I'd stored in the strong room would have been sufficient for my whole trip, but now that more mouths have appeared, we can maybe eke out the water a little, but we can't make the food last.

"Tomorrow…" I was just about to raise my head, but the mysterious boy continues, "we shall go forage together…"

Uncle Ji's eyes light up at once, but just as quickly fill with alarm.

"It's not safe for women out there," says the boy. "I …I could disguise myself as a Japanese citizen…it's better when there's the two of us."

The other men mock him with their looks. Someone calls out: "You're a Japanese spy, and this is where you sell us out?"

"Calm down!" Uncle Ji waves a dejected hand. "Our lives were given back to us by this young lady. Don't be such a wimp. This scrawny kid is more of a man than any of us."

YAMAGUCHI MASAO

"FOLLOW ME!" XIA turns and beckons me over. "I only have one set of papers, but you can be my little brother. You can say you work for the Japanese, but it's better to say you are Japanese."

"Yes, Onechan," I reply gently.

Her expression stiffens: "You sound just like a real Japanese."

"Isn't that good?" And then I start to have doubts myself. Compared to Chinese, Japanese feels a lot more natural, whether it's speaking or listening. Maybe I am really Japanese?

But if the Japanese are all like these two soldiers that have just rushed out at us at the turning, I don't want to be. They charge towards us threateningly, placing themselves either side of Xia and calling out "Well we're in luck today, there's a girl here, hahaha..."

"What do you think you're doing! We are Japanese!" Xia struggles, protesting incessantly in Japanese.

"Leave my sister alone! Otosan is a good friend of General Tani, don't you realize the consequences of what you're doing!" I step forwards, pushing the soldier on the right off of Xia. The one on the left has already let go when he heard my words.

Their faces sober up. "Please show your papers!"

Xia reaches into her handbag, I slap my hand onto hers to stop her. "Ignore them. As for the two of you, a word from General Tani will make sure you lose your heads. If you…"

They stare at each other in dismay, then click their heels and lower their heads. "We're really sorry, that was a simple mistake. Please don't take it to heart."

Watching their backs as they walked away, I feel disgusted. Are these the soldiers nurtured by the great Samurai warrior ethos? I turn to look at Xia: she looks slightly dazed, probably from a little lingering fear. It was far too dangerous for her to go out by herself yesterday.

"Onechan," I grin at her.

She doesn't smile back, but asks bluntly, "How are you so familiar with *that* name?"

Her question throws me. It's true. How do I know that name? It's almost like it leapt out of my mouth subconsciously.

"You still can't remember anything?"

I shake my head. Xia casts a sideway glance at me, and then keeps her distance. With her head low, she walks on.

Strewn across the road are a large number of charred corpses. The female ones are all naked and bloody. Flames and rolling black smoke are dotted across the city. Sweat starts to trickle down my palms. An image of cherry blossoms against a clear March sky floats into my mind, but I have no idea how it's connected with the scene before me.

Perhaps due to yesterday's trauma, Xia appears to remain detached from all of this. We walk on in silence. When we pass a pond, I see a dense layer of corpses floating on the surface. All the corpses have their hands bound behind them, and have been shot. The blood has soaked through their *mian'ao*[26] and spread out in expanding pools, like gory demonic flowers.

My chest spasms and starts churning with pain. I feel sick, very sick. Apart from being present in a city that's been turned into a living hell, I have a feeling that something else is very wrong. My body lunges forward, and I am on my knees, wave after wave of vomit erupting from me.

"Onechan." I hold out a hand towards Xia. "Onechan."

Xia's eyes fill with surprise and sympathy. "Oh, kid, you're crying…"

I wipe my face, and find tears falling. Xia takes my hand and begins to cry too. Her eyebrows are as raven as her eyes, and like her name, she is lovely, like summer. It's more upsetting to see a sad summer than a mournful winter.

"Onechan, I won't forgive them…" I have no idea why I'm saying this, but the words burst out by themselves.

"You can't really be Japanese." She sighs, and strokes my head. She no longer winces when I use that term of address.

On the way to the safe zone, I once again witness the lecherous nature of the Daiwa soldiers. Three officers chase a frail girl, still a child, while shooting recklessly with their guns. The zip of the bullets and sound of gunshots are driving the girl to tears: like small trapped prey, she's running around in panic.

"Stop it!" Xia can no longer help herself.

---

26   Mian'ao 棉袄, traditional Chinese padded cotton coat that can be short, medium or long, the three layers of which are designed to keep the body warm.

The girl's left leg violently spasms, and her body tumbles forward—she's been shot! The three officers throw themselves at her like wolves.

I drag Xia, who is well on her well to try and stop them, back into the shadows. "Xia, don't go, you're a woman too. They're only leaving you alone because they think you're Japanese."

"But..." Xia struggles, her face full of tears.

"I'll go, let me go." I push her back and walk towards the three officers. But before I open my mouth, one of them holds up his gun and takes a shot at me.

And again, all I see is black.

XIA FENFANG

I'M WIPING HIS sweat away with a towel, but the stream from his forehead is constant, surge after surge. I can't do it quickly enough.

In his stupor he grits and grinds his teeth, occasionally letting out mournful sigh, as if he's trying to solve a very difficult problem.

The winter sun at noon is deathly pale, making Nanjing look exceptionally desolate. This ancient capital of six dynasties, the seat of Wu power in *The Romance of the Three Kingdoms*, the great Chinese classic that the Japanese are so enamoured with. How can they be so ruthless as to destroy this splendid city?

> *Here lay the domains of Sun Zhongmou,*
> *Whose dreams for all under heaven are now but remote,*

> *Here the flames of Three Kingdoms war beacons*
> *once roared,*
> *And battle flags few high,*
> *At these gates so many rose, yet so many fell.*

I remember poetry that my great-grandfather had written in his youth. This is the city he had loved ever since he was a child.

> *Now the great antiquities serve merely to amuse,*
> *And children frolic on these old stones.*
> *Where is that hero with his white steed and his*
> *silver blade now?*
> *Only violets still cling to these gates.*

It's winter in the city, and the little purple flowers are long gone, along with the frolicking children. The whole city is silent as death, only the tears of the Yangzijiang mingle with those of the Qinhuaihe[27] as they weep their secret bitter grudge.

The boy is awake. He looks at me, wide-eyed, for a good while. "Onechan."

I knew it, he must be Japanese.

"The bullet only grazed you, and possibly caused slight concussion. I didn't let them take you to the military hospital…I was scared you might be interrogated."

"I understand." His tone seems different somehow. "And that girl?"

I turn my head to hide the pain on my face.

---

27 Yangzijiang 扬子江, a.k.a. Yangtze River, is the longest river in China, flowing from its source in the Tibetan Plateau, to its mouth on the East China Sea. Qinhuaihe is a river that borders Nanjing and a tributary of the Yangzijiang.

He understands instantly, and sighs. He looks so innocent when he frowns. "They said this was a Holy War."

I don't reply, but watch the shadow of the city wall.

"What's that?" he says, pointing at the protruding parts of the shadow.

"Trophies from the Beheading Competition." I try my best to keep my tone even.

He props his body up and cranes his neck to see the severed heads, piled row upon row on the city wall. His throat starts rolling, his fist clenching so tightly that his pale and luminous skin reveals the purple veins beneath.

"Where do we go next?" he asks with great effort.

"The safe zone," I answer, "but…can your body take it?"

His chest is heaving. Suddenly he pulls a fountain pen out of his pocket, darts me a glance, and nods his head.

"Shall we go then?"

I don't know what game he's playing, but I think that after getting knocked out by the handle of Uncle Ji's gun, his memories are finally coming back. I was curious about his identity, but now none of that matters.

"Let's go." He clutches that fountain pen like it's a weapon.

The so-called 'safe zone' is the military-free area negotiated by foreign business personnel that have stayed in Nanjing with the Japanese occupiers. Even though it's called 'safe', that safety isn't guaranteed. Many shops along the road were cleaned out, and even foreign banks have been broken into and left in a state: only shops owned by Japanese nationals have barely managed to keep going. The Fabi currency can no longer be used—only the occupier's fake-looking bank notes are still in circulation. But stock and range are extremely limited, and the prices extortionate. I have watched the large amounts of pre-Liberation currency I had painstakingly gathered before I left, disappear unremittingly, just as each rice cake did into all those hungry mouths I've had to feed...

Then I quiver. It's nearly time! I almost forgot that it's nearly time. Tonight, I must leave.

My footsteps suddenly feel so much lighter. All of this will soon be like a dream. It's finally going to end. I will soon be able to return to my normal life again—my happy life. I never realized how lucky I am. I do now: I'm never going to complain about anyone, about my fate or anything being too hard or too tiring. How lucky I am to be living in the 21st century!

"Onechan..."

I turn towards the voice. The sorrow in this kid's eyes pierces me. Feeling uncomfortable, I turn to avoid his gaze and survey my surroundings.

...this is the northern part of the Zhongshan Road that leads to Xia Guan. Corpses cover the street, empty ammunition cases everywhere. The smell of rotting flesh oozes from them, and sticks in the air, as if congealed by the cold north wind.

I exhale, watch my breath turn into steam in the air and disperse in an instant.

I am in Nanjing, on the 16th of December, 1937. I am still here now. In this moment I am filled at once with elation, and shame.

When I got to this point, I felt stuck. I originally had written a plan for the story, but after I've described this extremely heavy part of Chinese history, I seemed to have lost the energy to construct the complex plot. Even if I had, I would have asked myself, was there any need?

Right now, I am seeing the winter of 1937, in the war

torn city of Nanjing, on a street made so narrow by the piles of corpses and spent ammunition, walking slowly, one in front of the other, a boy and a girl.

From a distance, they really do look like a pair of siblings.

Xia Fenfang, who's walking ahead, is feeling a shame akin to desertion in her imminent departure—for the Guomindang[28] soldiers she is hiding in her house have become part of a moral responsibility she is unwilling to forfeit.

Behind her, Yamaguchi Masao is still holding the pistol that is disguised as a fountain pen. Just a gentle flick of the cap and his mission would be complete. But he isn't thinking about the mission, and even seems to have forgotten his father's orders.

Right at this moment, the seven Guomindang soldiers are all polishing their guns. Uncle Ji is loading the rifle in his hand with practiced expertise, each crisp *ka-chunk* like an order.

Uncle Ji stands up, rifle in hand, and straightens his back and stretches his arms before taking a long breath. "Damn—now I feel like a decent human being!"

Someone asks, sheepishly, "We're not…going to wait til Miss Xia gets back?"

"What are we waiting for? Haven't we got her into enough trouble?" Uncle Ji retorts. "These couple of days we've been worse than dogs. Let's get our spirits back!"

"Yes, Captain!"

The seven soldiers line up and march out of the strong room. San Ma takes point: carefully opening the door a fraction, he peeps out to confirm there's no one in the

---

28 国民党, also known as the Kuomintang (KMT); originally a revolutionary party to overthrow the monarchy, it became a political one in 1912.

house. At the decisive twist of his head, the squad moves out with utmost speed.

The Xia Mansion lies at the roadside, and has three floors. The view from the top floor offers good surveillance of the whole street, so Uncle Ji takes two brothers onto the top floor, while the other four position themselves to ambush the entrances to the lower floors.

During the last few days, the Japanese military have been actively stamping out the remnants of the Guomindang in the city. They don't have to wait long before two squadrons of Japanese soldiers stride onto this street. Uncle Ji's eyes are trained on them: at this point, the wait has become excruciating, and his rifle is beginning to get a little slippery in his sweating palms.

"On your marks." Uncle Ji gives his orders in a low voice. The three soldiers ready their guns, locking onto their respective targets. The Japanese soldiers at the front have already stepped into optimum range. No, we can't rush, just…a little…bit…longer. It's as if the soldiers marching in a single-row formation are stamping directly on his rapidly beating heart.

"Fire!"

CRACK CRACK CRACK! Shot in the head, the Japanese soldiers tumble straight to the ground like discarded puppets. This throws their orderly formations into complete chaos.

"Top floor. Over there!" The window on the top floor instantly becomes the target of Japanese bullets. Then sniper shots from the first floor drop two more Japanese soldiers, disrupting their temporary deployment. "The first floor, attack!"

One Japanese squad breaks away from the disordered troops, surrounding the building and beginning a fierce firefight with the snipers on the upper floors, while another squad moves into the building to capture the others. As they storm in the hallway erupts with gunshots, lively as firecrackers at Spring Festival.

"Fight! To the death!" San Ma appears on the top of the stairs, wielding the machine gun, his face purple-red from the excitement, fire darting from his glaring round eyes.

PANG! A blood flower blooms from his chest. He stumbles once, but straightens up to return one last bullet. "One for three, that was worth it!" His mouth, already gurgling blood as he speaks, breaking into a grin.

"Gunshots." Xia looks up and around her, as if trying to locate them. "They're killing again."

His feet feel like lead, and he can no longer move them. "No. It's a fight, there are more than two types of guns." The icy calm on the youth's face is well beyond his age, and his superb reconnaissance abilities betray his identity. "The sound is coming from the direction of your house."

"What!" Xia drops the package in her hand. "Have they been discovered? I have to go back!"

"No, you can't!" The youth grips her by the arms. "I think this was their plan, to win back their dignity with their lives—they think it's a worthy trade."

Xia's dull eyes instantly light up, and her beautiful face brightens until it is positively glowing. The gunshots continue, like drumbeats of life on the broad blue drum of the sky.

"I've found it!" Xia spreads her legs and gallops towards the Xia Mansion. "I found it! I've finally found it!" She laughs recklessly as she runs, unfolding her arms like a pair of wings.

She's running by Zhonghua Gate, over scorched soil strewn with maimed corpses, in the middle of the darkest part of China's thousands-year-old history, in which her countrymen faced unprecedented bloodlust and cruelty with the feebleness of lambs and helplessness of individuals.

Traversing the dark corridor of history, she remembers her ultimate goal. It isn't to record the cruelty and violence of the enemy, their heaven-offending crimes, or the weakness and helplessness of her countrymen as they are slaughtered. She wants to lift up a tiny corner of the grim, iron-heavy curtain of this chapter of their history and find a fighting spirit, a sparkling ray of hope to light the way for so many lost souls numbed into oblivion by an excess of pain.

> Go tell the Spartans, thou who passest by,
> That here, obedient to their laws, we lie.

As recorded in the Simonides of Ceos, two thousand heroes perished, yet not one surrendered. No matter how cruel the battle or how bloody the history, this kind of Spartan spirit shines out like gold. Where else can I find it? Can I find it here in the winter of Nanjing, 1937?

Yes! It is here!

Xia's footsteps become as light as air as she gallops towards light and hope. For the first time the gunshots become almost melodious to her ears. The youth at her heels keeps shouting "Onechan, it's dangerous, watch out!" But she doesn't hear him. She is here to record history, and yet none of the multitude of evils she has seen can measure up to this event.

Open your eyes, and see.

The nanocam installed in her eye is authentically recording everything she sees. Bring it back, back on the text books, and back to the Nanjing Massacre Memorial

Hall—bullets flying through the streets, bodies of Japanese soldiers, flames licking the top floors of the Xia Mansion...she remembers Uncle Ji's face, and San Ma's and the other Guomindang soldiers she has shared her life with over the last two days. It is they who are making history, these ordinary Chinese people.

"Onechan, careful!" The youth shoves her violently to one side. She falls into the corner of the street, not understanding what just happened. The fall feels like it's shattered all her bones, and she aches so much that she can't get up. She lifts her head, panting and glaring at him furiously.

Framed by a bullet-filled sky, the youth's body sways and finally topples into her, the hint of a bittersweet smile on his thin red lips. Xia is frozen, but she feels a warmth that seems to be flowing from his heart to hers.

On the other side of the road comes the sound of footsteps, a neat line of infantry—reinforcements from the Japanese. The dregs of troops that were there before immediately perk up. Someone waves a hand and gives an order: "Everybody move in!" Several dozen Japanese soldiers swarm in like fleas, disappearing into the dark doorway of the Xia Mansion.

Keep recording, I must—Xia holds the bleeding youth gently in her arms, but doesn't take her eyes off the house. She listens to his feeble breathing: every time his chest rises, more blood gushes out.

"Onechan, you and I...we come from the same time..." His lips are almost touching the rim of her ear. She doesn't seem to react. Reflected in her pupils are the flames billowing out of the upper floor of her family home; then a flash from the top floor, and the whole roof collapses in a sudden explosion. The sound of the explosion creates shockwaves in the air, pulsing through the deathly silence of this city, as if reviving it. Through the sea of blood, though the ashes, it is opening its eyes.

Even the shockwaves can't drown out the sound of the youth's feeble voice. Blood is in his every word; the lips he presses against her ear are damp and cold, but Xia feels it burning. For the rest of her remaining life, that spot would burn.

"Onechan, my name is…Yamaguchi Masao. Onechan, I return a life to your people…my life for one of yours…"

Xia bites her lips, keeping the desire to weep to the back of her throat. But the spasms of her chest belie her feelings. Hot tears trickle down and fall from her nose. She holds out a trembling hand and gently strokes the youth's head. As his blood flows onto the ground, Yamagushi Masao closes his eyes. In his mind's eye, this crimson melts into a multitude of colours, like springtime in March, like cloud-soft pink cherry blossoms in Oeno Park.

Feeling the warmth drain from his body, Xia wraps both arms tightly around him: "Sleep, Masao," she chokes. "Sleep, Ototo…"

When I read over the finished story, I considered whether or not it counts as science fiction. The celebrated fantasy writer Ni Kuang once wrote a story called "Guizi", about an old soldier's remorse at having participated in the Nanjing Massacre. He said it counts as fantasy, because the guizi would never feel remorse. Yet later, we heard about Tatsuzo Ishikawa, who went to prison for writing "Soldiers Alive", and Shiro Azuma, who in his old age, published his diaries that recorded the bloody atrocities in Nanjing. However, even today, there is much controversy over the portrayal of these events in Japanese textbooks.

Japanese citizens, especially the younger generations, have merely a distant and vague understanding of this holocaust.

When I watch documentaries on TV; when I see the shock and pain on the faces of Japanese students studying in China, as they hear about this event for the first time; when I see them weep and say "I'm sorry, I'm sorry"—a youth as beautiful as cherry blossoms float into my head. This was the model for the character of Yamaguchi Masao.

Growing up, I have visited Nanjing many times. What has left the deepest impression on me, apart from the tree-planting initiatives set up by Sun Zhongshan, was the bullet-ridden city wall outside Zhonghua Gate. On this wall is condensed the deepest trauma of modern China.

In the story, Xia Fenfang is a person who is searching for history. If the Nanjing Massacre is a part of history that the Japanese find hard to accept, then imagine what it's like for the Chinese. I went through all kinds of research material to write this story. I wanted to find some true resistance, but throughout the duration of the whole atrocity, there was so little of the rebellious.

Through fiction, I want to light a fire in that dismal winter. On the other hand, I wish so much for this not to be fictional, or a fantasy. Perhaps in the ruins of history, there lies hidden stories, waiting to be excavated, shining, like fireflies in the summer night...

NOTES

WHEN I FIRST read "Rendezvous: 1937", I was incredibly moved. The Nanjing Holocaust was an area of Chinese history I had intentionally avoided studying in depth, for fear of finding it too painful, or finding my anger too fueled. As the 80th anniversary approached, and this under-remembered event was examined on stage and screen, and reprints published of Iris Chang's "The Rape of Nanking", I found it was time to face what was done to my birth country.

Despite being predominantly a culture writer, I wanted very much to do what I could to ensure this period of history is properly remembered, and the stories of the dwindling surviving victims were not lost and that history does not repeat itself.

Although the events in "Rendezvous: 1937" are wholly fictional, there were individuals and groups that fought back against the occupiers, despite the terror and sense of futility in their darkest hours. Their personal histories are told in Chang's book. Framing this story are Zhao Haihong's own foreword and afterword, which I have included in my translation, to give you a little more insight into her perspective.

Zhao Haihong first began experimenting with writing kungfu stories, historical romances and SF when she was still a teenager, and published her first story in 1996. She considers writing her "proof of existence" that helps her find her place in the universe. Apart from history and time travel, she's also interested in themes such as gender, the environment and interactions between Earth and other planets. She is the winner of children's literature prizes as well as a string of Yinhe Awards. When she's not writing, she teaches at Zhejiang Gongshang University in Hangzhou.

When I first read Zhao's work, I instantly fell for her lyricism and the range of voices she manages to create. Even here, when she is writing about a national tragedy, which our heroine is experiencing in her own here and now, character development, pacing and the tone of the work are all kept in harmonious balance, and each character is expressed with their own passions and driving emotion.

THE HEART OF THE MUSEUM
博物馆之心

TANG FEI

APART FROM THE humans, who busy themselves like bees, there are others.

They work hard to find paths of understanding in everyday life—to understand this world. Their dedication gives them the power of queen bees.

A child walked past me and pressed the button to call the lift, his fingernail embedded with sand. I took the next lift, walked to a particular door, and pressed the doorbell. It was his mother who opened it.

The child was in the living room; he lifted his eyes from a pile of toys and just stared. Children don't usually look at people in this intense manner. I made a simple self-introduction.

His mother invited me in, and after the customary exchange of greetings and small talk, the woman briefly outlined the duties of my role, subtly indicating the real nature of the job by way of implication. When she was certain that I had understood her intent, she happily signed the employment contract drawn up by the agency. Through the whole process, the child's eyes remained fixed on us.

This was not a surprise. Since he was a baby, it had been how he observes the world: probing into all manner of its mysteries, and the relation between the elements within. Since signing the contract, I have been under this unending gaze for four whole years. This is my job. Ostensibly, I am the child's art tutor. But for a family that has assumed high office for several generations, having a low-profile bodyguard who can stay with the child at all times is a great asset.

At the recommendation of the agency, I became this child's protector, helping him avoid all the potential dangers lurking in the undercurrents of the future. People—Earth people—fear the future, yet they yearn for it. For them, that's the realm of the chaotic and unknown, where anything could happen.

For me, everything and anything has already happened. Or more precisely, everything is happening. The flow of time is right in front of my eyes: I don't even have to search for it. The past, the present, the future—everything that happened, is happening and will happen—flows in before me, alternating and superimposed over three-dimensional space. I sense their distance in time. This perception is innate to my people.

When we first came to Earth, we spent a long time getting to understand and adapt to human perception, by which the world is perceived in three-dimensional space via five basic sensory organs. For them, this moment only means this moment. An instant is like a slice of time, independent of the past and the future. As soon as we understood this constriction, pretending to be one of them was simple: keep silent about the world they don't know, like a sighted person pretending to be blind.

Earth people can't see the future. Many among them believe that their current words and actions determine their future fate. This crude simplification of cause and effect—is like a blind person believing that the knock of their cane could determine the direction of their path.

It shouldn't be mocked. They need such beliefs.

A lot of lessons are being arranged for the child, not all of them dry and dull. Such things as Judo and violin, even though they require hard practice, he seems to find pleasure in. Yet his greatest pleasure seems to come from the sand pit in the front garden. Building walls, palaces, bridges, houses, or just drawing on the sand—mainly faces—or writing. His works are no different from those of other children. Weak, transient, uninventive. Simple and crude interpretations of the outside world—yet he gives them his all. Is he captivated by the fundamental materials that construct the myriad facets of the world, or infatuated with constructing reality in a virtual world?

I stand at a spot not too far away, quietly observing. At the same time as I'm seeing the child and the sandpit, I also see the museum he will come to build in eighteen years' time, in another city.

At the beginning? At the beginning, it will be a mere thought. Not the story he would later recount to people, not from an old man's collection he'd come across. Though he wouldn't be lying: those endearing points of origin are often as delicate as dust, undetectable and inexpressible. During the last six months of his MFA in New York, he will begin to prepare his graduate show. His original plan will just be to organize an exhibition on some well-known experimental Earth photography, but slowly fermenting in his brain is a big bold idea that will come to him. He will want to build a museum. That spring, he will have become fascinated with "The Library of Babel" in the writings of Jorge Luis Borges, with finding illusions—or maybe possibilities—in that South American blind man's alley.

A mere museum will not be enough for him, and simply filling it with virtual exhibits would never satisfy him. He needs real objects: more specific and vivid manifestations of existence. No event occurs without leaving some real aftermath. This is how his friends came to understand him; people he will only meet through dragging them into this high risk project.

In the teams he will have set up will be architects, animators, painters, multimedia artists, neuroscientists, orthopedists, interior designers, experts in optics and kinetic physics, anthropologists, doctors of physics, pilots, plus a molecular biologist-cum-vet.

Some among them will be consultants responsible for providing practical and exhaustive professional knowledge. Others will be responsible for their speciality as curators.

Yet others will be the audience.

I watch the child as he patiently rakes the pit, over and over again, impervious to the fierce midsummer heat. His eyes must ache as sweat trickles into them, stinging them with salt. He rubs them, using this interval to survey the results of his work. Now he picks up the shovel and puts the sand, little by little, into an orange sieve, patiently gathering grains that have fallen off; and then pushing them into the mould he'd made, filling, compressing and flattening the surface with a knife. And then...

It won't be raining that weekend. Spring in New York is

genial enough. He will meet up with an architect friend at the High Line. They will buy two hot dogs from a stand for lunch, and chat as they walk. The sun will dance on the leaves of the trees and on the girl's face. They will be exchanging preliminary thoughts. After a brief silence, before Rojas' giant concrete cube, he will invite the girl to take part in the interior design of the museum.

I watch the child as he grips the outside of the mould, lifting it up straight and slow. A pyramid of sand emerges from the mould, only to split and scatter to the ground...

The morning will not have gone well. When he leaves home he will find that the drains have blocked up. And his appointment with the professor to go through his graduation assignment would turn out to be a wild goose chase. The orthopedist would inform him that there's no way to obtain the bone-dating X-rays he wanted. The science fiction novel he will have purchased from a second-hand bookstand will be missing important pages. Sitting in his usual seat in the library, he will open his laptop, and receive an email from the sculptor...

I watch the child as his gaze fixes on the stream of water splashing from the watering can, at the bubbles being forced from the sand, until eventually even the darkness of water begins to disappear. It's now time to re-create his sand piece. He extracts the plastic tube and creates his most important work, the elliptical sand piece. Surrounding him is the ditch he has excavated to build a city.

The museum would be built, in the end.

On the day of its completion, he will celebrate with all the members of his team; on a particular late night, he will carry out a midnight inspection of the exhibits, holding his girlfriend's hand, the love on his face resembling a small animal just about to feed. During the period he will feel most lost, every morning he will gaze down on this drowsy, waking city from the window next to the wall on which is written the law of gravity. In a few years' time, his child would be even more fond of this spot, and have even more important tasks to complete.

Since when have I been preoccupied with this child's future? To be more precise, his presence in the museum. I sink deeper into my infatuation. No matter where my body is, or what I'm doing, my gaze is drawn towards this small museum in 'future' New York, on the ninth day after its completion, the seventh day after the fourth month of completion, the tenth day after the twentieth month: any time in which it exists. In particular, I love to see it when no one is around.

No one here except the exhibits, my consciousness roaming among them.

Bright and quirky science-fiction posters, typewriters, Einstein's formula, cat food tins, space suits, old photographs and writing desks. Objects, most of which could be found at vintage fairs, will be most deferentially and respectfully put on display here. I have compared them meticulously with new products and ordinary second-hand products. What is the difference? These objects have all been involved in major thought experiments, and cast back into everyday life afterwards. But what are the special traces that remain? What part of them have been exploited and taken?

I carefully walk past them, fearful of leaving any traces of my presence, fearful that my gaze would leave an irrevocable change. These remnants of past events are here, to prove the events they have been part of. This is unfathomable to me, for whom the streams of time are clearly visible; for whom the past, the present and the future always appear together. I have never needed these superfluous vestiges. And yet, I can't keep my eyes from these remains of past events that have been placed here; anonymous objects placed on the shallow shores along the stream of time. Like a strange hobbyist who loves to walk in graveyards, I gaze at them, infatuated. Now, my heart feels calm and serene. Even immersed in the endless rhythms of the river of time, I am beginning to feel something akin to coming to a lulling stop that I have never felt before, the end of perception, like—

—death.

Yes, all life will eventually conclude, but the traces they leave behind will remain in other things. They may not be remembered, or even noticed, but they would be there.

This museum will live for far longer than the child will.

Longer than his friends, family, and longer than most human beings.

Several hundred years later, when the American continent will be flying like a lonely island through the solar system to seek the shelter of another star, it will still be standing in the place it was built—New York's old Brooklyn, where an alien will decide to let her body be modified.

There she would tell Earth's people the truth about the American continent. This truth will be remembered as an allegory.

I only need to turn 44.4 degrees southwest, look past several nexae (in terms of your three-dimensional spatial awareness, imagine directing your sight into the distance, and through any objects which happen to obscure your view, till at last you focus on the object you're seeking) to be able to see the moment in which she reveals the truth.

That moment will exist, and to me, already does.

You should understand by now that I am not from this

planet, not a "People of Earth". People—as a word—is unique to Earth. We don't say "people", nor do we like to be referred to as "people from outer space."

When the child was four, I became his bodyguard, pretending to be "People" and concealing myself within this ancient and dusty city. The city is filthy. In the winter the snow falls like goose feathers, in spring the sky fills up with sand. Where there used to be a palace, now the leaders of this country live. From the centre point of this red area, ring by ring, the city has expanded and swelled, its bloated body filling with millions of higher life forms who are all strangers to each other. For our kind, there is no safer place to hide our identity.

I protect the child and guard his time stream, guaranteeing that his past, present and future are all perfect, without a flaw. His parents have been very satisfied. The child trusts me too. He seems to know that I would keep his company forever.

Perhaps it is so. Perhaps—not.

Even when my body is here, my gaze is roaming the museum. Part of me exists there.

Of course, I will die too. At a particular time, in a particular way. If I wanted to, I could have seen my own future, seen the ridiculous fashion in which I will have died. But why would I have wanted to do that? Every moment that I am alive, I co-exist with the future, co-exist with the past, feeling every beat in the rhythm of the dance of time. Rather than a short straight line, my life can better be described as an eternal point in the chaos of time and space. My future will never disappear.

In a way, I have always been the guardian of this museum.

My heart beats, buried in the museum.

I am one of the countless beating hearts of the museum.

NOTES

TANG FEI REFERS TO herself as "a creature of strong curiosity that loves to capture and be captured." Her words have appeared in major SFF periodicals as well as literary platforms around the world. She is a creative polymath, working not only in fiction, but art installations, poetry and photography.

I first worked with Tang Fei back in 2016, when I translated her story "The Path to Freedom". She has always had a very interesting approach to giving voice to the "Other" in society, and in "The Heart of the Museum", she performs a dual experiment, not only in a non-human-centric viewpoint, via the unique cultural space of the museum, but also writing from a viewpoint which is not confined by linear time. The alien narrator hides among humans, taking care of a child whilst simultaneously observing his future and the museum he will build, and their own role as an exhibit. It is the viewpoint of a life where causality is seen, but influence is not, and the reader has to decide how much influence the observer has.

In the Chinese language, time is signified by the temporal adverb, so all actions are, without context, in the present. The creation of a non-tensed form of reportage, or getting the mixture of tenses right in English was an enjoyable challenge, to create a sense of disconnection, of a different perception. I wanted to create a sense that there was probably far more going on in the narrator's mind, but that they were doing the best they could to explain it to us, poor, time-locked individuals.

THE GREAT MIGRATION
大冲运

MA BOYONG

1

"We will be shortly arriving at Olympus Terminal. Please make sure you have all your luggage with you and prepare to alight the shuttle."

A female voice issued from the ceiling, its tone full of the cold mechanization of computer simulations. In this age when humans could already build swimming pools on the edge of the solar system, having computers with more human characteristics still seemed an insurmountable problem.

I snapped my eyes open and cautiously stretched out my limbs, which had been scrunched up in the narrow and tiny seat. In that moment, a clammy sense of fatigue took hold of me. Since getting on the bus I hadn't been able to sleep properly, so had been in an awkward state of unrest.

30% of why I'm in this state is this ancient land ranger. According to the driver, it had survived at least 10 GMs. God!—no wonder it was bumpy as hell. From the life support system to the multi-vector shocks, everything rattled. Just about the only thing that hadn't broken or stopped working was the dust storm alarm. Every time we went over a slope, the bus would charge up to the highest point, its entire body vibrating, and then land on the descent with a thump. The moment the buffer platform in the chassis touched the ground, it would begin rumbling, whipping up the sand around it as if Martian gravity was somehow too big a burden.

20% was due to the overcrowding. The capacity for this ranger was sixty people, but eighty-seven had been crammed in. Packed into the dust removal compartments and filter rooms, I even saw three guys who'd crawled into the drive systems under the vehicle, and in three different postures, had suspended themselves from the complex criss-crossing framework around the reactor, hugging their luggage, fast asleep. To save oxygen, the driver had reduced the air mix by a third, adding in some Mars atmosphere. The density of carbon dioxide and nitrogen was enough to choke you to death. Add to this the pervading smell of feet, fizzy drinks, sweat and farts from who knows who... I felt worse from this journey than if I'd been running naked on Venus.

The last 50% was due to my vague expectations and anxiety for the future.

I was returning to Earth, to home.

But I hadn't got my ticket yet.

"Almost there, the exhaustion is killing me." Wendong gave himself a good long stretch, his arm almost hitting the nose of his big bearded neighbor, who cast him a hateful glance, frightening him into retracting his arm immediately.

"Yeah," I answered, being as curt as possible. With every word said, I had to risk breathing another mouthful of this sour air.

"When we're in town, I'm going to the oxygen bar, binge on a tank of Mediterranean breeze, and then a glass of whiskey with real ice. If I can get a girl that'd be even better." Wendong was so delighted with his own thoughts that several specks of his spittle landed on my face.

Coldly, I cut his relentless rambling short. "Aren't you going to try and get a ticket?"

"Where there's a will, there's a way. I'll wait and see. I'm here, aren't I? So I'll get to leave. Isn't that right, Zhang?" Wendong's face was the picture of nonchalance. Taking a small mirror from his inner pocket, he began to comb his hair with his fingers. I shook my head in condolence, and shut my eyes again.

I only met the kid after getting on the coach, but he was my neighbour. As soon as he sat down, he apologized to me and chucked a couple of bags of tins between our seats, taking up a third of my berth. I shot him a glance, but he didn't react: instead, he just started getting really friendly, calling me boss and offering me cigarettes—though he was spotted by the driver when he took his lighter out, and given a severe verbal warning.

Wendong had come to Mars two years ago as a mineral scout, and this was his first holiday. He was exceptionally excited. All the way, I'd listened to him run on about his petty experiences: not even the long, hard ride could grind down his enthusiastic chattering. It was actually quite impressive.

The ranger was slowing down. Ignoring Wendong, I slowly turned my head. From the window I could see

Olympus Mons, standing incomparably tall and imposing, like a pillar holding up the heavens, magnificently joining the indigo sky and the orange earth. With floating dust clouds swirling around its crimson waist, against the backdrop of the sunset on the Tharsis plateau, it really carried that feeling of the powerful presence from its mythical namesake.

This, the highest mountain peak on Mars, could be seen from several hundred kilometres away, and was the most eye-catching landmark of the Olympus Terminal. For people like us, it had almost become a totem. A symbolic indication that we had set our feet on the path that led home.

I'd worked on the Algiers Prairie, southernmost of the Tharsis. In order to get to the Olympus Terminal, I had to go through 4000-kilometres of Sailor's Canyon. Of course, you could take an aerolite, but the dust storms on Mars were an unpredictable hazard, so most people would rather endure the bone-shaking bumps of a land ranger, seven miles deep in the canyon bed.

With our destination just ahead, the vehicle too seemed to become lighter and loosen up, shaking its giant metal body and roaring as it sped towards the transparent hemispheric dome, like an upturned punch bowl, that was the Olympus Terminal. Despite its mundane appearance compared to the mountain ranges that surrounded it, Olympus Terminal was humanity's largest launch centre on Mars, with the residential district alone occupying an area of over a dozen square kilometers.

Half an hour later, the land ranger passed through a small gate in the geodome, and, at last, entered the city district of Olympus. The dust shields on either side of the vehicle lowered. The scene from our windows changed with the dome's light filters, and we saw blue skies. For humans living on Mars, this hue brought a nostalgic kind of comfort.

As soon as we entered the city, the lethargic atmosphere in the ranger instantly sprang to life. Everyone got up from their seats, massaging their backs and retrieving their luggage, while at the same time everyone—whether acquaintances or total strangers—began to complain to each other loudly about how grim a ride it had been. Wendong was one of the first to jump up, his hands nimbly finding their way through a passage full of suitcases and bags to open the locker compartment.

"Boss, let me take your bags down for you."

Before I could reply, verbal abuse shot out at him from all directions, chastising him for getting in the way. Wendong gave them a dirty look and was just about to get into an argument with his naysayers when I pulled him back to his seat, mainly so I wouldn't get dragged into anything. The last thing I wanted, in this of all places, was any kind of trouble.

The public lanes of Olympus were gridlocked, and the speed of traffic unbearably slow. All kinds of transports were crawling around us. There were bulky freight rangers, battered-up scout tanks, and even some small and nimble GEVs threading aimlessly through the big vehicles, their fins and chassis occasionally scraping the sides of the bigger vehicles, making sharp grating noises.

You couldn't blame the city authorities: they'd only planned for the area to be a subzone of the launch centre, not sprawling into a full residential area. If they were to redevelop it from scratch, the estimated cost would be close to that of a whole new geosphere—a price that no one was prepared to pay.

An hour later, and our ranger finally pulled into Central Square. In its downtime, Central Square was just a giant solar panel, but during every Great Migration, it would be set up to serve as an exchange point and parking lot: there was simply no other way to take in this many people. Only during this time would the area be referred to as "Central Square".

Despite being mentally prepared, I was still hit with a wave of social vertigo as I got off the coach. The whole square was heaving. Several dozen rangers, new and old, were parked haphazardly all around the square and every inch of space around me bustled with innumerous moving heads, an oppressive swarm of dark. There must have been several thousand passengers, whose hubbub drowned out the public announcements like a roaring tide. Used to the solitary isolation of my station, and now being thrust into this clamour, I felt overwhelmed.

I stood by the doors of the ranger to take some steadying breaths, and realised that the air at the launch centre was almost as stale as the coach. With so many people gathered in one area, you can imagine the strain on the air-circ system—so in effect, we had only been transferred from a small stinking tin into a larger one. Some people say that to live on Mars is to live a tinned life, and they are not wrong.

On the far western side of the square hung a red digital banner. On it was displayed, rotating through the three official Martian languages: "All hands on deck for the Great Migration, do what you can to ensure all passengers depart."

"That all sounds great." I shrugged: this slogan had been there for so many years, and no one—including the staff at the launch centre—took any notice. The poorly-maintained suspension mechanism on either side of the banner bobbed up and down, making the banner wobble; making it seem comical, and exceptionally ineffectual before this enormous crowd.

Wendong stood behind me with his backpack. His mouth hung open: clearly he hadn't expected quite so many people. "...kin'ell, this is more people than I've met, seen, or imagined were on Mars in over two years!" Wendong scratched his head, and looked very rueful. The kid really was green, to be only thinking of such basic things. I, on the other hand, was more concerned with the real problem. The crowd around me was even bigger than the last GM, so the chances of getting a ticket were even slimmer. Whether or not I could get back to Earth now felt like an unknown factor.

It wasn't easy for people like us long-term, interplanetary workers to go home—so we've come to live for the Great Mars Migration, which takes place every two years.

Strictly speaking, the astronomical term for this phenomenon is "The Mars Close Approach", and a major Close Approach only happens every fifteen to seventeen years—but for humans, this is too long a wait. Two years was long enough, so the minor Close Approaches that take place every twenty-six months became known as "the Great Approach", and thus the erroneous name spread and was passed down to posterity.

When the exploration of Mars first began, the pioneers would often launch their ships into space during a Mars Close Approach to capitalize on the shortened distance of flight. In fact, considering the navigational standards of today, the fuel and journey time saved by the Close Approach is already insignificant, but from a psychological point of view the Great Approach provided people with the perfect reason; when Mars was closest to Earth, we were closest to our home. Forecasts of the Great Approach from the weather station gradually became like a demonic curse whispered into our ears, compelling everyone to go home and see their loved ones. This subtle psychological signal gradually evolved into a giant force of custom, and after a period of accumulation, custom becomes culture.

Now, during every Close Approach, the entire planet stirred and heated up like it was a festival. It was like pressing a button wired into the brain, a button that when pressed, immediately transforms it into another mental state, and begins to revolve their life around going home. Everyone starts counting the minutes, talking about the GM and their longing to return to Earth. The booking systems would be flooded with reservations from every corner of the planet, sending the prices rocketing, and all modes of transport would be booked to bursting, forming a giant wave of travel. This journey home every two years came to be referred to—first unofficially, but then in official channels—as "The Great Migration".

"I can't take it anymore, I'm suffocating. If I don't get some oxygen, my brain's going to shrink! I'll see you later, Boss!" Wendong put his things in one of the station's storage lockers, waved to me, and vanished like a puff of smoke. Watching his disappearing shadow, I shook my head sympathetically. Only someone unaware that the real trial is still ahead could still have the mind to go to an air bar.

As Wendong disappeared into the crowd, I picked up my own luggage and, with consideration, looked around me. The floor was mosaicked with rubbish, which had been bedded in by regardless human feet. Most people were, like me, carrying the fatigue of an arduous journey on their faces; but their eyes gazed about sharply, like soldiers prepared to go into battle at any given moment, cautiously shifting their feet. A light, tense atmosphere hovered above the throng: no sensor could detect it, but it was definitely there.

Some people were sitting on the steps of the surrounding buildings or the frame of the solar panel, expressionlessly sucking semi-liquid food out of tubes. In the distance were some guys sleeping in half-open spacesuits, snoring like thunder. Two or three groups of people had spread their dust suits on the floor, and sat on them playing cards.

The blue uniforms of the launch centre staff and security guards occasionally flashed up among the crowd, but were quickly drowned out by the tide of travelers. Usually, their duties were performed by robots, but even the latest models would be unable to handle a situation as complex as this. Every individual is an amalgamation of a multitude of different motives, and here, that amalgamation was raised by an enormous factor, forming incomparably complex modes of behaviour. Trying to calculate that capacity would fry any digital thinker.

Painfully, I found a gap in the ever-changing mob, waiting for the right opportunity to push people aside—and once the opportunity appeared, you had to seize it immediately, or it would quickly disappear again. You had to push like mad with your shoulders, elbows and both legs—even your arse—to part the people around you and open up just enough space to move around in, while at the same time minding your balance and your luggage. I couldn't imagine what I would do in Earth's higher gravitational field.

Most of the passengers on the square were adult men

and women: on one hand this increased the difficulty of moving around, but it also reduced my sense of guilt—I'm not sure I could behave like a gentleman towards children under these circumstances.

Enduring endless eyeballing and crushing, I managed to make it to the flight centre on the west side of the square.

As I expected, all ten temporary ticket windows at the flight centre were crowded with people. The queue stretched from the inside of the centre, across the building and all the way to the car park outside, with a couple of red laser lines on either side keeping order in the ranks. There were also a few vendors moving back and forth along the queues, hawking instant meals. No matter how crowded it was, they could always open a path using their porterbots—they were getting on in the world.

The big screen at the top of the flight centre coldly presented a rolling display of the launch timetables, regardless of what was happening underneath. I gave the screen a flying glimpse: the rows of letters and four numbers that made up the flight numbers were full of allure, more enticing than if it had shown naked women. I had already memorized the most suitable flights by heart, and long before I'd set off, I'd made a detailed plan. I had found a top choice of three, and several backup flights, and made sure I knew the launch times, prices and routes of all these like the back of my hand.

In my head, I revised my ticket purchasing plan once more, and—with great effort—reached inside my breast pocket to pull out my Identity Card and held it up high above my head.

Relatively speaking, there weren't as many people on Mars as there were on Earth, but regular flights were much scarcer. The launch capacity of the Olympus

Terminal was capable of meeting daily transport demands, but when it came to the Great Migration, it was vastly inadequate. Apparently the Mars Administrative Bureau had been planning to build another launch centre specifically for freight, so that the Olympus line could be solely dedicated to passenger transport, but the plan was still at development stage. By the time it gets built, I think my kid will have already gained his qualifications to come and work on Mars.

Often, friends on Earth would ask me out of curiosity: "In the age of advanced communications, why do you still have such an ancient ticketing system on Mars?" At first, Mars did indeed have an internet booking system. You only had to tap a few keys to get a ticket—but soon, objections arose from all sides. Whilst reservations were made from across Mars, the planet currently lacked effective transport. So there'd often be people who'd miss their flights, resulting in a waste of seats: those who bought tickets couldn't go, but those who could were denied a ticket.

After a period of debate, the Administrative Bureau cancelled the online booking system altogether, to the unanimous agreement of everyone on the planet, and put in place a new rule that required passengers to already be at Olympus Terminal before they could book passage. Some on Earth said that policy had cast humanity from the space age back to a primitive society, where physical and brute strength ruled, but I thought it was better—at least it was very fair.

A big difference between here and buying a ticket on Earth is that on Mars, before you can even queue up, there was a full, compulsory health check, as well as inspection of status, identity and so forth. Even though these were now completely digitized, the process still took a very long time. This no doubt added fuel to the flames, and the flight centre had no choice but to adopt a "first scanned first served" approach, letting their machines scan the masses that had gathered in the square, and only those whose documents were recognised and approved could qualify for the queue.

So everyone was waving their passports with all their might, forming a huge human ball of countless hysterical waving hands.

As a passenger who'd been through several GMs, I'd learnt a few tricks. For example, during the scanning, it wasn't necessarily the highest-held or most violently waved passports that would get picked up by the scanner. Standing within the numerous special zones on the square will increase your probability of getting scanned, and besides, I had secretly coated the outside of my ID card with a layer of reflection-amplifying laminate, which increased its reactivity to the tracking laser. This stuff was originally used on deep space satellites, but I happened to be acquainted with an engineer from the base, who laminated my card for me at a cost of 200 yuan.

That was money well spent, and I had only stood there for about thirty minutes before my ID started vibrating with a numbing feeling which spread from my fingertips to my spine. I got scanned! In my head, I was crazy with joy. As long as I could join the queue, I was halfway there. I continued to hold my ID up for dear life: as long as I could keep it vibrating for one minute, I'd be successfully registered onto the queuing system.

But then, my card suddenly stopped. A sign that the signal had been disrupted. Shocked, I lifted my head, expecting there to be some kind of problem. I gripped my document tightly and turned towards the flight centre, hoping that this act would rescue my crumbling hopes. But this was pure superstition, and soon the queue invite for the next passenger appeared on the big screen—and it wasn't me.

Dejected, I lowered my aching arms, sighed, and looked round to see who the lucky person was. There was a commotion as the crowd parted, revealing a woman with a proud figure walking towards the flight centre, unable to hide the delight on her face. As she brushed past my shoulder, she threw me a flirtatious glance, and fanned herself a couple of times with the ID card that was hanging around her neck.

I instantly realised there was something fishy going on: she must have installed an active transmitter on her papers! This was an aggressive device, like sonar, that would have transmitted her details to the laser whether it was pointing at her or not. No wonder I lost out to her.

But the thing was... active transmitters had so far not developed their micro format. The most advanced product would have been the size of a fist, and there was no way that all that could have gone on a thin booklet—so it must have been hidden somewhere on her body. I stared at her like a letch: was it hidden in her ample bosom or her rounded posterior?

If I informed the inspection department in time, and exposed her tricks, then all going well, I would get my queue number back.

But by doing so, I'd risk being exposed myself...

The woman seemed to have felt my gaze. She stopped and turned her head to flash me a charming smile. I averted my gaze and pretended to look at the clock on the board. She did nothing more and just turned back gracefully, continuing along her way.

There was no other way. I waited for another hour or

two, and only after several sets of complications did I get scanned into the queue. Once in the queue, the system generated a special order number, and there was no need to actually stand in the line, just wait quietly for your number to be called. I sighed with relief, and, massaging my stiffening arms, walked into the departure lounge, and happened to come face to face with that woman.

The woman arched her elegant eyebrows, and softly opened her red lips to say, "Thank you."

I was taken aback, but then understood her meaning and replied coldly, "No need, likewise."

"You kept staring at me. I guess you were trying to work out where I'd hidden the device." The woman fixed her gaze straight at me, as if on the point of breaking into a smile, stifling a little teasing in her tone.

I was exhausted by the day, both mentally and physically, and had temporarily lost interest in this kind of equivocal exchange. I only replied offhandedly, "None of that matters now, we're both in."

This was obviously not the reaction she'd expected. She paused, and began stirring up the hair in her fringe. "Strange, I heard that the men of Mars are all very thirsty for women."

"At this time of the year? Only if you're a ticket," I grumbled in a low voice.

She broke into a chuckle and relaxed, sticking out a friendly pale hand. "I'm Varina." Cautiously, I squeezed it for a split second before letting it go.

The crowd in the departure lounge was not much sparser than outside, and the benches—of which there were few—were all crammed. Employing her feminine charm again, Varina got a middle-aged gentleman to give up his seat. Like the rest, I could only maintain a standing slouch. Those who were well versed in waiting would slightly bend one leg, resting their weight on it for a while, before shifting their weight to the other one; and alternating thus, look for any opportunity to move towards a wall or a pillar.

Waiting was another big challenge of the Great Migration. It wasn't that hard on the flesh, but boredom would seep into your every pore—and like the man-eating ants of South America, swarm and crawl all over your will, and then, like many sharp and tiny knives, finely shred your patience and rationality. It was the kind of slow mental death that makes you stressed, dispirited and distracted, as if the duration of time were being dragged out into infinitely long and thin strands, then wound around your neck and gradually tightened. A lot of people had been geared up for the hard stuff, but in the end, they fail for this very reason.

To combat this stage, chatting with strangers was inevitable, and soon Varina and I had put the embarrassment of our mutual cheating behind us, and began to chitchat aimlessly. After all, we were all strangers on a journey: we had no reservations.

Very soon, we'd dug out each other's back-stories. She was a doctor at a base in the Jupiter Basin, but in her own words, "dealing with harassment from men took more effort than treating them." No wonder she felt like that. This was her first time returning to Earth in a Great Migration.

"That was a pretty neat trick. I'd never have spotted it."

Varina shrugged, grabbed her left breast in an exaggerated manner and wobbled it. "The people at the base taught me a few things, and loaned me plenty of professional tech." Looking at her face, I could just imagine how, at the prospect of sex, the men would use their every advantage to butter up this beautiful woman—humanity had not evolved, at least, not the male of the species.

I stared at the lovely rising contours she was presenting me, and felt it was a bit of a shame that under that curve was only a pile of gadgets.

"But I really didn't think there could be so many people—this is a dozen times more than I'd expected. Who knew? I thought those brats at the base were exaggerating," she said.

"They say that during every Great Migration, Olympus gets so overcrowded that Mars tilts a few degrees further on its axis."

"Is that a joke?"

"It's a red planet joke. I guess you haven't red enough to get it," I quipped back.

We were just chit-chatting when the loudspeaker suddenly sounded, and that hateful electronic female voice pierced everyone's eardrums as well as their fragile mental defenses. "The tickets for today's departures are sold out. All prospective travellers who are still waiting are asked to please return tomorrow."

There was a riotous uproar in the waiting crowd. Accusations flew from all directions; the floors and walls were spat at. This situation was too much to bear—we had gone through so much to filter out the other contestants. If we had to wait till tomorrow, we'd have to start the whole process over again. Defeat at the final stage was even more demotivating than failure at the beginning.

People took out their anger on the Mars Admin Bureau. They could have handled it better; for example, given passengers that entered the queue the day before priority of purchase; or taken reservations a few days before; or displayed the remaining seats on the available flights on the screen. These measures were simple, and wouldn't have been that much hassle.

The Bureau however, had its own difficulties. Had they started a priority purchase system, they would have been bombarded with lawsuits and appeals challenging the fairness of such actions—not that it was fair now. Allowing advanced booking would need a long-term, accurate launch schedule, but between Mars' unpredictable weather and the laziness of the centre staff, this would be impossible. As for announcing the remaining seat availability? That would rob the Jockeys out of their living.

"You heard right, jockeys. Space jockeys," I calmly told Varina, whose face seemed to be saying 'Don't try and prank me, just because I'm new.'

"There are jockeys on a place like Mars?" she asked. In many ways she was very mature, but in others, merely a fledgling.

"Jockeys are harder to get rid of than cockroaches. They're everywhere—at least cockroaches could be squashed with a shoe."

My humour didn't seem to find any resonance in Varina. The announcement had hit her hard, and she seemed a little distracted. Even though the race for tickets was over and the prizes were all cleaned out, more and more people were still pouring into the square. People who couldn't join the queue were loitering where they had been waiting before, as if hoping for some miracle to happen. There were still a lot of people making their way from all across Mars to Olympus, coming to try their luck. The oppressive swarm of bodies now completely blotted out the colour of the square itself, and everybody's personal space was smaller than it would be on the spaceship.

Thanks to them, Varina and I ended up pressed against each other. Her shoulder against me, her right arm half holding onto me. As she tried to twist her body, that voluptuous chest brushed past my elbow—OK, no need to get excited, I knew it was only the transmitter.

To be honest, rubbing my body against a young woman's, with only two thin pieces of cloth separating us, was not an unpleasant feeling; but given the choice, I'd rather have pressed my bare skin against a shuttle ticket with my name printed on it.

"So what do we do next?" Seeing the crowd continuing to flood in, Varina seemed to have lost her previous confidence, and turned pale. I noticed that she'd unconsciously used "we". When things head towards an unexpected direction and become unpredictable, women often tend to look for someone they can lean on—or someone they think they could lean on—and I happened to be the closest person.

"Let's go and eat, and then we'll try our luck."

I stroked my chin, being deliberately mysterious. A spark lit up in Varina's eyes, and she followed me very closely.

'The Station Restaurant' was really a stockroom, in which several chairs and round tables had been set up. Two titanium lockers had been turned on their sides to serve as a counter, and whilst there was no kitchen, behind them was a mountain of tinned MREs, A small touch screen at the front of the counter displayed what 'Meals' each tin contained.

This had been organised by the staff at the Flight Centre: ostensibly it was to serve the needs of the travellers, but it had become quite literally a gravy train. Technically the centre was only responsible for maintaining the air circulation system before the passengers departed: food and drink was not included. Travellers therefore had two choices: to bring their own food, which would take up the precious luggage quota and wasn't worth it; or eat at the flight centre's private restaurant. These 'restaurants' would order a large quantity of MREs from Earth just before the GM—they were cheap, easy to transport, had long shelf lives, and would even cook themselves. Not that the passengers had a choice anyway.

Apart from the staff running the store, there were some drifting traders. They had relatively few tins and couldn't afford rent at the warehouse, so they'd hired robotic porters to follow them as they wandered back and forth across the square, bawling their wares out.

The reason why I went to the restaurant was only 30% out of hunger, and 70% for what was really on offer.

Varina and I found a relatively clean table. Frowning, she took out a packet of alcohol wipes, and tried to clean off the trails of dust and spilled food strewn across the table. There were guests on several other tables around us, all looking worried. Their lips were constantly moving, talking about all manner of things.

A middle-aged woman walked over from behind the counter, a roll-up cigarette suspended in her mouth inside a transparent and sealed helmet shrouding her entire head. Smoke swirled all around the inside, obscuring most of her face. This was a compromise product between workplace safety and a junkie's needs. With total lack of attentiveness, she asked us what we wanted to eat. I ordered a tin of liquid sausage and one of semi-liquid Yangzhou stir fry. With her fingers at her temples, Varina absentmindedly ordered a tin of spinach, and then immediately closed her eyes, as if she could no longer bear it.

The food came quickly. There was no way it wouldn't—all the waiting staff needed to do was to find the correct tins from the stockpile and bring them to the tables. With practiced ease, I tore open the packaging, popped the button at the bottom of the tin, and within half a minute, it was hot enough to burn my fingers.

"Eat up, regain your strength, so we can sort the tickets out," I urged Varina, before putting my mouth to the straw. With an air of surrender, Varina held up the tin, looked at the use-by date, and put it back on the table petulantly.

"Sort the tickets out how?" she asked.

I pointed at the smoker: "At this place."

"Are you saying she's a jockey?!" Varina widened her beautiful eyes. I shrugged. Looked like the guys at her base hadn't given her all the facts about the Great Migration. To be able to open a restaurant at the Flight Centre, you had to have some connections, and if you had channels for obtaining food, you'd have channels for obtaining tickets, giving you an even more astonishing profit margin.

After my words of encouragement, Varina opened her tin of spinach and ate it in a couple of mouthfuls, as if not finishing it quickly would offend the manageress and lessen her chance of getting a ticket.

So ended this meagre meal: not much taste to speak of, but at least I wasn't hungry anymore. I got hold of Varina tightly, and signaled to her to keep her mouth shut, then presented both our ID cards to the woman. She looked Varina up and down, saying nothing, deducted a slightly extortionate charge from the cards, and handed them back.

I took the passports, and with feigned nonchalance, asked offhandedly, "Madam, can you get tickets for today?"

The manager seemed well-acquainted with people like us, desperate for tickets but too snobbish to show it, so she answered directly: "Not today, but there's a chance tomorrow."

"What kind have you got?"

"All kinds." she said. Her perfect poise had impressed even Varina. "It depends on how much you're willing to pay." She added, "We don't take advantage of the vulnerable here, nor do we resort to violent tactics. 200% commission for K class, 170% for Z, and 150% for D, and I'll give you all the receipts, how's that? Good deal, isn't it? "

"Good deal!? It's robbery!" Varina couldn't help blurting out softly.

The woman wasn't even slightly ruffled. Smiling, she replied, "Miss, if a robber could get you back home to Earth, would you be willing to be robbed? Of course, you don't have to spend a penny. I've seen some girls spend a night with the Flight Centre's management, and go home first class. You should consider it, your assets are pretty marketable." Shocked by these flagrant remarks, Varina blushed. It looked like she wasn't quite as bold as she'd made herself out to be.

I diverted the conversation. "We'll take the K class tickets, but couldn't you lower the commission just a little? You see, we've been trying for days, our funds…"

The manager drummed her fingers on the counter impatiently, blowing out a ring of smoke inside her helmet.

"If you want to make up the time, go through the wormhole, no one's stopping you."

I was speechless.

There *was* a wormhole between Mars and Earth, and a flight that way only took ten hours, but this kind of hyperspace travel was on the expensive D class ticket; the next class was Z—direct flight on large ships equipped with enough rocket fuel to fly direct from Mars to any destination on Earth, no need for mid-trip refueling.

What I could afford was the standard K Class. The K-class spacecraft were the energy-saving kind that needed to fly around the Mars-2 satellite and the moon to slingshot back to Earth. It took eight days, and the only benefit was that it was relatively cheap.

"So what's it going to be? Are you going to join that unreliable queue tomorrow, or just book it here?" I turned towards Varina, who looked pained. If we queued up and failed to get tickets again, she would probably break down.

"Ok…I'll take one, thank you." At last, she was willing to compromise.

The manager had known this would be her decision, and without flinching a muscle, took our documents again. "Half today, then the other half when you pick your tickets up tomorrow."

Then she picked up a pen and scribbled a few words on a sheet of fluorescent paper. "Bring this tomorrow."

"Can't we pick up them up today?" The sooner I had them in hand, the sooner I could relax.

"No, you idiot, didn't you hear that all tickets are sold on the day? Just wait here tomorrow." The Manager rudely ended the conversation.

I walked out of the restaurant with Varina. She had an odd expression on her face, half dejected and hurting from the blow to her bank balance, and half joyful. She stopped, and gazed at me with those big open eyes. "Can they really get us the tickets?"

"This is where I got them the last few times. It'll be fine," I reassured her.

"Hope so," she mumbled, looking drained. The flushed pride from her earlier exploits with the transmitter had totally disappeared.

Just as I was about to bid Varina goodbye, I realised a serious problem.

The tout wasn't aware we were practically strangers, and as a matter of course, wrote the receipt for both tickets on a single piece of paper. There was no way of splitting that proof of purchase, and neither of us would be happy to let the other one hold on to it—what if one of us were to sell it on to someone else? As far as they were concerned, the place only recognised receipts, not faces.

There was no way we could trust each other enough, so we would have to spend the night together...

2

THE SQUARE WAS still full of the shifting, gathering masses. The prospective travelers resembled the dense and abundant weeds that covered the open country on Earth: weeds which—despite the adverse environment—possessed an extremely tenacious ability to survive, only needing the slightest gap and the weakest of nourishment to push through and grow, tough and unyielding in the face of hardship. The only difference was the vivacity of weeds came from the plant's innate instinct to reproduce: the energy of these queuing humans came from homesickness. Even the 120-million-kilometer distance could not stand in the way of their impulse to go home.

Journalists from Earth used to describe the Great Migration as "The epic return from Mars", and, as if rubbing it in, "the Great Migration was a song of life calling across the vastness of space." I found this despicable: what do those bastards in their government-grade spacecrafts know about the suffering of the people? Damn your epics. Life-song my arse. For the GM, nothing means anything, except for the ticket. The ticket is king, is law, is the one and only; it is the Alpha and the Omega. All stories, whether happy or sad, revolved around its lowly existence.

And what I was about to experience was one of these stories.

Due to an error on the proof of purchase from the black market, I was obliged to spend the night with Varina.

This story had many possible endings:

She could happily agree: we'll stay in one room, and very naturally get to know each other better between the sheets; the next day once we'd get our tickets, part ways, and set off to our own corners of Earth. That amorous night would leave a light trail in our memories, like a hazy dream.

Or...

She could angrily refuse, say she'd rather give up her ticket than share a room with a strange man.

The greatest possibility was: I would sleep on the floor, she would sleep on the bed, nothing would happen.

In reality, the biggest obstacle to this story's development turned out not to be Varina's attitude, but the lack of apparatus—we didn't have a room. Olympus was only a launch site, and any on-site accommodation was extremely limited, totally insufficient for the influx of the Great Migrants. Some people chose to spend the night on the streets, considering the whole city was temperature controlled anyway; some splashed out on floor space in a warehouse; whilst some enterprising spirit had even taken unused spacesuits out from storage, and rented them to people as sleeping bags.

I recounted the dilemma we faced in detail to Varina, deliberately assuming an air of indifference to avoid suspicion of any ulterior motives. Varina listened to the end, and lowered her head in thought. Pale light shone on her high cheekbones, casting an exaggerated look to her profile. It was about two minutes before she raised her head, her expression now relaxed.

"No problem. You keep the receipt."

Her decision was not what I expected. The only thing written on the receipt was 'Two flight tickets', with no name, ID numbers, or any other details. Before registration with the centre's system, the ticket could be transferred to anyone. In other words, I could sell it on for a huge amount of money, and Varina wouldn't have a leg to stand on should it come to making a claim.

"Aren't you worried I'd sell it?" I asked, frankly.

"If I said that when I first saw you, I knew you'd be the reliable type, would you believe me?"

"Don't be a fool!"

She gave me a charming smile: "Give me your passport. This way, we can trust each other, can't we?"

"Clever girl…" I muttered. It was indeed a perfect solution. Without my card I couldn't board any ship, nor could she unlock the biometric sensor to take advantage of anything on my card. We would mutually be holding something useless without the other. Of course, this cleverness did mean my potential one night of lust with her was truly in the soup.

"This is my identity, don't lose it," I reminded her anxiously, and asked, "By the way, where're you planning to stay?"

Varina looked as if she wanted to catch me out. "If I told you, would you try and sneak in in the middle of the night?"

I replied solemnly, "You never know, apparently the occurrence of one night stands increases tenfold during the GM."

"Of course, but the funny thing in this joke is that during the GM, whilst you might be able to find a partner you desire for a perfect one-night stand, you'll be hard pressed to find a room." Varina smiled, giving absolutely nothing away.

To interrupt the awkwardness, I decided to tell her another story. "From an astronomical point of view, a major Mars Close Approach only happens every fifteen years, but the Great Migration is every two years. Do you know why?"

"No." Varina's attitude made it clear I was being humoured.

"Apparently the name originated from a novelist who lacked general scientific knowledge. He mistook the minor Close Approaches for the major ones, and then when his mistake was pointed out to him, he said: 'Yes, yes, perhaps I got it wrong, but Great Migration sounds a lot better, doesn't it?' So this erroneous name got spread around and passed down the generations, and became a common phrase. You've got to admit though, the Great Migration does have a better ring to it than the 'Slightly Closer Than Normal Migration'."

Varina made light of the matter. "What a poor sap."

We were just going to say goodnight, when suddenly I heard a cheery male voice. "Well, if it isn't Mr Zhang."

It was Wendong, the guy had probably just come out of his air bar: his face was the picture of worry-free calmness. Wendong took a look at Varina next to me, his eyes brimming with bawdiness. "Looks like you've got your ticket already, to have time for distractions."

I hurried to explain: "This is a fellow traveller I've just made friends with, Varina." Wendong's face showed he didn't believe me in the slightest. He extended his hand, but his eyes were fixed on her cleavage. Varina touched her fingertips to it symbolically, expressing her disgust without being impolite.

"So have you got yours?" I ask. This being, by the way, the eternal topic at Olympus; the way the British always ask about the weather and the Chinese, if you've eaten.

Wendong turned his neck with nonchalance. "Of course, all my mates are friends for life, definitely reliable. If I say I want a ticket back to Earth, I only need to say the word, and they'll come running with several for me to pick from."

Varina and I exchanged glances, and both shook our heads. Anyone could tell this kid was bluffing. Buying a ticket during the GM wasn't a simple exchange like buying an egg, and asking for several tickets was virtually unheard of. Easy to say, impossible to do! Wendong threw Varina another glance, and said to me, "Boss, if you've got nothing to do before the lift off, come join me at the oxygen bar. I'm really friendly with the guys there, one word from me, and they'll cancel your bill…"

I made an acknowledgement, but was starting to run out of patience. Wendong waffled on for a little longer before wandering off, whistling on his way. Varina threw me a very meaningful look. "Your friend is…interesting."

I immediately replied, "I only met him on my trip here, I don't really know him. Want me to take your suitcase?"

Varina indicated that she didn't. She'd left her luggage

in the pile at the storage area. Even though the gravity on Mars wasn't as bad as that on Earth, it was still a hassle to lug a large suitcase around. So we said goodnight, and arranged to meet up at the little restaurant the next day.

I saw Varina's graceful figure disappear among the turbulent crowd, and began to think about making arrangements for the night. Proper hotels were out of the question, as there was only one in the whole of Olympus; and staff accommodation would have sold out by this time. If I was lucky, perhaps I could find a spot to rest in a warehouse: if I wasn't, then I'd have to sleep out in the square.

My luck fell between good and bad: through an acquaintance with someone who worked in a hydroponics plant, I was able to get through the night in 'the farm'. Hydroponics were one of the most important inventions to humanity as it headed into space: every base and every ship had one of these installed. A hydroponic farm could grow vegetables in space through standardized liquid nutrients, to supplement the diet of interstellar travellers with essential nutrients. Of course, to me at that precise moment all the value in this illustrious invention lay in the fact that there was just enough space between the nutrient and ventilation troughs to fit one person lying down.

It sounded like a pathetic choice, but it was more comfortable than you'd imagine. In order to guarantee the natural growth of the plants, the heating and oxygen levels in the air within the farm were plentiful, and it was theraputic to fall asleep among the scents of cucumbers, chives and ganlan broccoli. My friend promised me that in the dead of the night you could even hear the vegetables talking.

Yes, I was exaggerating a little. In these circumstances

you could either give yourself some uplifting positivity, or crumple under the stress. During the GM there'd always be a few people driven to nervous breakdown: it even outstripped cases of stellar isolation.

The next day, I stood in front of the restaurant with red, puffy eyes and the faint scent of lettuce. I hadn't slept well. The electronics in the nutrient trough kept humming and the auto-spray was set to every half hour, hissing sharply as it glided over my head; not to mention those frequent flashing growth indicator lights for the leeks. I'd never been in such a noisy vegetable patch.

Varina was already waiting at the entrance, looking perky and recharged. "Looks like you didn't sleep well last night." Varina smiled through closed lips.

"Now I understand why children hate vegetables," I grumbled and threw the question back at her. "What about you? Where did you stay?"

"Oh, the Olympus Central Hotel."

"What! Impossible!" I blurted out.

Varina replied, looking very laid back, "A junior manager of the MAB happened to be staying there by himself, so I used him slightly."

"Used?" I looked this curvaceous woman up and down suspiciously.

Varina chuckled. "I bet your mind is full of filth right now. I only agreed to sleep in the same room as him, and nothing else. But I saw the girl next door had spent a night with a senior from the ticket office. Her figure was hardly worth a place in cargo." She tutted. "I just couldn't bite the bullet."

"You don't have to explain…"

"I suppose not, we're like floating petals in a running stream. Once we're on the ship, we'll go our separate ways." Varina handed me my ID card. And I showed her the receipt, and then shoulder to shoulder, we walked into the restaurant.

The madam was still puffing away in her glass helmet like an immortal who lived on smoke. As soon as she saw us, she immediately took off her helmet and came towards us. We were just recovering from her sudden attentiveness when, in a tone that was part apologetic, part helpless, and part bullish, she said: "I'm sorry, the tickets are gone. I'll refund you."

This news struck us like a Martian thunderstorm. Varina and I stood where we were, stunned, as if we were naked in the vacuum of space; our bodies had just been pierced throughout by radiation, and were now welling up with thousands of ulcers.

The human psychological limit is a subtle thing: it is not a fixed numeric value, but can be prepared and altered by expectations. If we had been mentally prepared to get our tickets in three days' time, we could probably have waited five days or more, but if we had set our minds to "I'll get my ticket and leave the next day" and this suddenly falls through, then I'm afraid it exceeds our psychological limit.

I almost roared at the manager. "How is this possible? You promised us!"

The madam calmly flicked her cigarette ashes, and explained, "There was nothing I could do. As you know, we're a small business—the only thing we've got are our connections, that's it. When somebody with real influence says the word, how could the ticket office dare not oblige them. So you've been squeezed out. This kind of thing happens often."

Furiously, I rammed my fist onto the glass table. "But

we've paid a deposit! What excuse have you got not to give us our tickets! There has to be some kind of fairness to this, first come first serve! What do we do now? You tell me!"

The madam saw that I was losing control of my emotions, and switched to a placatory tone. "I'll refund you the money, not a cent less."

"It's not a matter of money!" I shouted. Some passers-by and dining guests turned to look in our direction. The madam took out a few tins of liquid beef and mushrooms and thrust them towards me, and said, in a half-pleading yet unyielding way, "Alright, I own up, here's a couple of tins for your compensation. Don't make a scene. If you catch the attention of the Bureau, we'll all lose out."

After that bout of venting, I gradually calmed down. Even if we chopped her, boiled her in her own tins and ate her, it wouldn't have done any good. The most important thing was to plan our next step. I walked over to Varina and put my hand on her shoulder. "Let's go, we'll find another way." Face rigid, she said nothing, but left the restaurant with me obediently.

As we walked side by side, failure hung in the air. Neither of us could say a word. After we'd walked on for a while, Varina broke into little sobs, and then came more tears, and then more. She reached into her bag for a handkerchief to wipe them, but by then the handkerchief was no longer enough, and tears flooded down her high cheekbones, accompanied by a crisp whimpering. She was still striding ahead, but her entire person was crumbling from the inside out.

Seeing this, I took her hand and led her to a relatively quiet spot, putting my arm around her shoulders. I was going to reassure her, but she took the opportunity to dive into my arms and began to weep loudly. I didn't know what else to do except to stand there and let this woman, this virtual stranger, weep a whole river onto my chest. Damn you, GM, another human you've tormented and driven to the edge of their sanity.

Varina cried for a good half hour. I was worried that she'd cry herself into dehydration, and was relieved when she finally stopped.

"Feeling better?" I took out a pack of tissues, as her handkerchief had already got soaked.

Two patches of faint red emerged on Varina's cheek as she carefully wiped away the tears from the corners of her eyes and dried her lips. "Thank you," she said in a low voice. "I'm really finding it hard to cope with all this. I want to go home, really want to go home. Life here is too harsh. Two whole years in that hateful job with those hateful colleagues, and not a moment goes by that I'm not counting the days till I can get back to Earth. Now I'm here, but…"

I was surprised to find myself empathizing with her unexpected outpouring. "Yeah, me too. All there is here is red soil, red rocks and red dust storms. I promised my son I'd come back every two years, and take him to play tennis on real grass, swim in a real lake, and I'm going to do that. Also, there's my mother, she's been ill for ages. This time, I'm planning to take her for a full check-up—you know what old people are like, can't stand being prodded about by a callous doctor droid without someone there…"

Shoulder to shoulder, our heads touching, we gazed up at the big glass dome and talked like a pair of lovers. We talked about everything; I told her about my blundering hunting trips on Earth, and she told me about all the famous fashion stores in the different cities back home.

We were like the little match girl of the fairytales, striking match after match of lovely memories to gain a quantum of solace in the middle of this Great Migration.

I'm not sure how much time passed. Someone walked past with a load of luggage and glanced at us, their eyes filled with sympathy, but turned away quickly as if wanting to avoid being asked for help. It was then that we snapped out of our dream and looked at each other. A sudden wave of embarrassment washed over us. To cut through the awkwardness, I chose a very practical topic. "So what shall we try next?"

Varina lowered her head and bit her lips. I know what she was thinking, and immediately took her hand. "Don't go there, there must be other ways."

Varina smiled. She did not retract her hand.

My mind was churning at the speed of flight, wracking my brains to remember if there were any other unexplored channels for acquiring tickets. After turning it over and over in my head, I had to admit that we were at a dead end.

Gazing in the direction of the launch pad in a daze, Varina mumbled, "Even if I have to lie on my stomach and hold on to the hull of the ship, or stay in the engine room with no air, please just let me leave."

"Air..." An idea suddenly flashed through my mind like a flint spark. "We've only got one choice now," I said to her.

"Which is?"

"That kid we bumped into yesterday. Don't look at me like that. I know he's a punk, but we've run out of options, so we'll have to try and saddle a lame horse."

We found Wendong in the same oxygen bar. He hadn't been lying. When we saw him, he was holding the pipe, taking the occasional whiff while complacently bragging to his female escorts: his voice was louder than the music. He had now transformed into the nephew of the chief exec of the Olympus Terminal. I quietly predicted that after a few more puffs, he'd slip into the role of the deputy chief of the Martian Administration Bureau.

I called to him. As soon as he saw me, he perked up, put the pipe down and bounded over: "Wow, Mr Zhang! You're here at last! My friends here have nearly huffed the place dry, but come, have a whiff, authentic Mediterranean flavours, I can taste it, the taste of Crete, precisely!"

His eyes were bloodshot, and from his speech I could tell his tongue was swollen—typical symptoms of oxygen intoxication. I helped him to the sofa, and gave Varina a look to indicate that she should sit down on the other side of him. As soon as Wendong saw Varina, he leered and laughed, struggling to get up to shake her hand, but I pulled him back.

"Wendong, wake up, your friend needs a favour." I made my tone as soft as possible. Pleading for a favour like this was something I loathed, but what else could I do? We are all slaves to circumstance.

"Ahem, you think I won't look after my friends? If you need a favour, just say the word. Tell me," Wendong cried.

"Oh no, how could I forget who our Wendong is? Proud hero of all sixteen bases of southern Mars, his word as good as gold." I did the full number on him, and Wendong was very receptive: his whole face began to glow. Then I seized the opportunity. "Could your friend at the bureau arrange two tickets for us?"

When he heard this question, he froze mid-smile. He grabbed the inhaler and started drawing big breaths. "Wendong, can you help or not?" I pressed after a while

Wendong scratched his head, his expression remorseful,

he stammered, "Well…I have got contacts, I wasn't lying, but…"

"Don't worry about money, brother, I've come prepared." I held up five fingers, trying my best to get my word in first. "Apart from the fee, I can give you this much."

Wendong's face flushed. "What do you take me for! If I was trying to rinse you, I'd BE the fuckin' MAB."

This bluff was worth something. I instantly added: "Of course! That's just fair payment for your hard work. Your due for doing us such a big favour."

On the other side of him, Varina began to chime in, "Girls love guys like Wendong! Honourable, reliable… well connected."

It wasn't long before Wendong folded under our duet: as great as his bragging was, his skin was paper-thin. He lowered his head in thought, and at last stood up, throwing up his hands as if having made a momentous decision.

"OK, Boss! I'm throwing caution to the wind. If you ask me for help, how could I ever refuse, but…don't you tell anyone, it stays between us three."

"Of course! Absolutely!" Both Varina and I expressed our fullest assent.

"Let me make a phone call," Wendong said. In less than five minutes he was back, and looking as if he'd done a great deal of persuading. "It's done, my guy has agreed to meet us, come with me," he said to us chirpily.

"What…there's an interview?" We looked at each other.

Wendong rushed to explain. "Look, their channels, their rules, let's not waste time OK?"

I didn't ask any more questions. Varina and I split Wendong's air bill, and followed him out of the bar. Wendong asked me to take out a certain amount of cash with my ID card.

The three of us walked around the square several times, til we were almost dizzy. "Almost there, almost there, just hang on, their people, their rules," Wendong kept saying.

We eventually ducked into a narrow passageway with an air vent in a secluded corner, and Wendong told us to wait next to the fan. He took out his own ID and began flicking it, making a distinct flapping sound. Very quickly from across the passageway came an identical flap, and then a curly-haired man in off-duty flight clothes emerged from the shadows.

"Let me introduce you. This is my best friend, Anand. This is Mr Zhang, and this is Varina."

Anand had an air of arrogance as he looked us up and down, lingering on Varina for a long time. Then suddenly, he spoke. "The proportions aren't bad, but can the woman take it?"

Varina was perplexed. "Proportions? Take what?"

But Wendong went on, "No problem, no problem!"

Anand harrumphed and began to scold Wendong. "You prick, always getting me into stews like this. It's a big risk, I'm telling you."

Without waiting for Wendong to remind me, Varina and I immediately pushed the cash we had prepared into his hand. Anand took the money, counted it, and dropped the attitude. "That's more like it!"

"Then when do we get our tickets?" Varina asked impatiently.

Anand looked blank. "Tickets?"

"Tickets for the ship to Earth," Varina and I answered in unison.

Anand frowned. "Didn't the sod tell you beforehand?"

All three of us turned to face Wendong, who had been looking nervous, but instantly squeezed his face into a smile. "What an awful memory I've got, Mr Zhang. I forget to tell you before. This isn't a ticketed route."

I was getting more and more confused. If it doesn't involve tickets, then what was it?

Wendong gestured. "You know...on spaceships...there are emergency escape pods? The ones with thrusters that shoot you off if accidents happen on the ship? Usually these are slung under the ship, and no one checks them. On the ship where Anand works, he could get us into the escape pod. It isn't luxurious, but there's enough room to turn round, plenty of food and drink. Enough to keep us going till we get to Earth."

So for all Wendong's bluffing, this was the route he'd found for us. The proverb runs, "The rat and the snake each have their own paths." No wonder he was embarrassed. He knew he'd gone too far with all that "My friends'll bring me three tickets to choose from," talk, and "I know everyone in Olympus." Now his cover was blown, and out came the pathetic truth

Anand broke in coldly. "The ship takes seven days to get from Mars to Earth. During the whole flight, none of you can leave the escape pod. There must be no chance of being seen. According to galactic flight standards, the air and supplies in the pod should sustain three people for 72 hours. I'll restock you when the time comes."

"How about it? Can we do it?" I asked Varina. I was a little worried about her physical stamina. The pod would be really cramped: to crouch in there like a rat for a week was not an easy hardship to endure.

Varina was determined. "As long as I can get back to Earth? Anything."

I suddenly thought of a problem. "Won't the MAB send in Customs for inspections?"

Anand looked slightly amused. "Now there's half of Mars crammed into Olympus, they can't wait to get rid of a few more. The Bureau obviously can't openly condone taking passengers in the emergency pods, but they tend to turn a blind eye. As long as it doesn't affect flight safety, they let it slide. You don't have to worry about that."

"OK, deal!"

"My ship leaves the day after tomorrow. It's best you get here tomorrow at noon, so I can smuggle you in with the freight while the ship's being refueled. That'll mean extra 24 hours in the pod, to be on the safe side. As long as you can hold out til we take off, you'll be in."

Varina and I looked at each other, joy welling in our eyes. This time it was for real. Inadvertently we reached out for each other's hand.

When we got back to the square, it had grown even more crowded. We pushed through the throng, and heard a girl with a sleep-deprived face muttering: "I've waited for three days already, and haven't even got in the queue." People around her remained expressionless, as if already numb to such complaints. An ambulance wailed past: some unlucky sap had probably fainted. There were simply too many people here. The authorities couldn't handle it, so only those with life-endangering conditions were getting rescued. Everybody else had just been handed painkillers and left to live, or die. Lucky passengers who got tickets were very few, and larger and larger crowds of travellers were surging into Olympus. All kinds of visual indicators were showing that the scale of this year's Great Migration dwarfed any that had preceded it.

Compared to the swarm, we only had to endure a cramped life for a week, and then we'd be back on Earth. We were the fortunate ones!

That night, Varina and I both stayed in the farm. This time I got my own back. The noises from the vegetable didn't disturb us, but the noises we made must have disturbed them. I even surreptitiously plucked two leaves from a baicai and used them to cover the gaps in the wall, in case the patrols saw us. Varina watched my clumsy moves, and burst into peals of laughter. When I was happy with the leaf arrangements, I came back and whispered into her ear, "I really wish I could eat vegetables like this every day." With a real passion, Varina wrapped her arms around my neck. Two homesick people, far away from Earth. This was our way of celebrating the beginning of our journey home.

The next day, we crawled out of the gap in the wall early in the morning. Even though our appointment with Anand was midday, we couldn't wait anymore. Though Olympus was a lot more comfortable than the claustrophobia of the emergency pod, the pod would make us feel safe: after all, it was the overture to the homecoming symphony, whereas Olympus was still a vast aggregation of despair and anxiety.

Wendong arrived half an hour later than us, dragging his feet. The witless kid seemed not to understand the meaning of the word 'urgency'. He shot the two of us a sly look, as if to say "I know what you did last night." This was loathsome, but still, I was grateful to him. If it weren't for his help, Varina and I would still have been at a dead end.

"Anand should be here by now,' said Varina glancing at her watch.

"There's still five minutes, don't worry, he's a very punctual guy," Wendong reassured her. I put my hand on Varina's shoulder, and very naturally, she put her hand over mine.

At that moment an alarm sounded, and as one, our faces dropped. The alarm gave three long bursts, followed by two short ones, meaning that the warning wasn't Olympus based, or even Mars—but a threat from beyond its airspace.

"Let me check what's happening." Wendong slid out his ID card from his bag, and switched to the city's emergency broadcast. The voice on the channel spoke in a dead tone. "The Space Surveillance Office have just issued a warning. A level five sunspot is expected to erupt in an hour. This solar flare is estimated to last for at least thirty minutes."

"You are fucking kidding me!" all three of us bellowed in unison.

Of course, solar flares were entirely different from the Mediterranean sun: those high-energy particle flows and space rays were like inspectors from the tax officer. There is nothing they won't penetrate, and their destructive force was huge—the whole solar system was at their mercy.

These things can be negated by Earth's atmosphere, Olympus' protective dome and Mars' gravity, but the ships in space were not so fortunate. We still have no provision to protect against such natural disasters in space. Some military ships were equipped with special shields, but ordinary travellers had to stop during these occurrences, even if the ship were in the middle of its flight. They would have to shut down the engines and all electronic equipment or risk attracting ionized gases hurled out of the sun's corona, reducing them to cosmic dust. Only when emissions fell back to tolerable levels could flights resume. Usually, for every five minutes of a level five flare, you had to wait twelve hours for the radiation levels in the affected areas to return to safe levels.

In short, if the estimates were correct, then the whole Olympus launch centre would be in lockdown for at least three days—not even counting the likelihood of secondary flares. It was a meteor shower just as your roof blows away: "It never rains but it pours" didn't even start to cover it. To have this happen during the most nerve-wracking time of the GM renders you dumb.

To us, the vastness of Space was a mere illusion. The solar system isn't some huge thing: it was too small—so small that we couldn't take shelter from disaster.

This news had turned not only us, but all of Olympus, into an over-boiling congee pot. The square broke into a seething mass: everyone was talking about it, those poor trapped passengers who could neither leave nor turn back.

Wendong immediately got in touch with Anand, though it took him a good while to free himself up to come see us. He told us that the Bureau had already issued the order to ban all flights, and would not even suggest when it would be lifted. Right now, boarding would be meaningless, no matter how much we had fought for it.

In the streets of Olympus, the feeling was the same. Until this point, the city had maintained a modicum of order because there was a sliver of hope, no matter how feather-thin; but now there was only despair. Homesick travellers were looking into the depths of space beyond the glass dome. Within the limits of the human eye, Space appeared as peaceful and calm as normal, with not a hint of the terrifying havoc the radiation was wreaking.

Some began to cry, some began to berate, some even began to sing. Most, though, were silent. They were already used to waiting, their faces bleached of any emotion. Men, women, old and young were all swaying along with the masses, shoulder to shoulder, heel to heel, as if their souls had been crushed out of their bodies, leaving the husks to be squeezed like sardines into the giant tin that was Olympus. Waiting with strength and tenacity, the multitude of upheld arms waving multicolour identity cards, like some strange religious ceremony.

"The Great Migration was created by the devil, to drain the last vestiges of hope from humanity before they enter hell." This line of poetry suddenly flashed across my mind. Its author had gone quite mad in the middle of one GM, and subsequently won the Nobel Prize for Literature.

The Mars Administration Bureau was up against it too. They had already issued notices across the planet, announcing the ban on departure and requesting that everyone return to their bases, but even this could not stem the wave after wave of travellers arriving in the city.

Mars was not like Earth. Its human habitats are made up of several dozen sealed, airtight domed environments. Between these domes, impossible-to-forecast Martian dust storms and other adverse conditions made every journey of freight, vehicle or aircraft a meticulous operation of time and fuel expenditure. The fuel in the vehicles approaching Olympus was not sufficient for them to reach any other habitat. They could only head to Olympus—or face death. Despite the MAB's well-known reputation for indifference and poor efficiency, it couldn't toy with people's lives, and there was no other choice but to let them all through the barriers. According to the calculations of the transport centre's radar, there were still over thirty such vehicles on their way, each carrying at least a hundred passengers, all yearning to go home.

The oxygen refresh rate fell and fell, and the air grew even more stale. Wendong no longer mentioned the oxygen bar, while Varina and I had to buy a couple of O_2

bags, at inflated prices, in case the need for them arose. The automatic conditioning system of the terminal's weather controls was burnt out from overwork, and could now barely keep the atmosphere circulating, abandoning all other functions. The flight centre had opened all its store rooms and began urging the staff and volunteering civilians to distribute aid, giving out food and water for free to detained passengers—actions that would win the approbation of the masses, but right now, seemed wholly inadequate.

The most pitiable were not those at the launch centre, but passengers stranded in the middle of their flights. In order to increase capacity on "short-range" flights such as the M-E lines, all the food replicators had been removed, leaving them with only limited supplies, allocated according to the schedule. Now that whole ships were stranded mid-flight, the totally unprepared passengers could only survive on these rations. If they were stranded for an extended period, there was no way to replenish them.

Before our departure, over twenty ships had left Olympus Terminal. According to the schedules, the fastest of these would have already been very close to the moon, but so what? Those passengers who thought themselves lucky to be on it were probably cowering in their seats, listening to the rumbles as solar rays struck the hulls of their ships while trying to work out how much food they had left. The irony was too much to bear: to have a situation where, even in this day and age, people were scared of starving to death.

Three days passed, and the lockdown had not been lifted. The sun was more excited than usual and there were second waves, with no particular pattern. Even the most advanced organisations capable of providing the most accurate reports could only declare this to be an astronomical phenomenon not seen in a hundred years, and was unlikely to conclude in a short time. The "No Departures For The Foreseeable Future" sign at the launch centre had to be written by hand, because the power had gone out.

Apparently the military had been deployed, their shielded ships risking the hazards of the solar flares in order to replenish supplies on stranded passenger ships. Sadly, this just felt like putting out a burning timber pile with a cup of water.

This sudden natural disaster had immediately rendered the 120 million kilometres between Earth and Mars instantly quiet; it was as if a spell had been cast over all launch sites, spaceships and flight routes, striking them dumb and immobile. The silenced ships made a dotted line of despair across space, as if what the sunspots projected into the solar system—apart from a cocktail of radiation—were dejection, fear and panic. A mere 120 million kilometres—a distance that could be covered by light in 5 minutes flat—had become a gulf that we, mere humans, found impossible to cross.

It was in these doldrums that the Great Migration bared its sinister sharp teeth. Its knives were now dulled, roughly sawing at our flesh and blood. When I told Varina these thoughts, she said I was going crazy, to be composing poetry right now. I asked her what she was thinking; she said nothing, not even about going home any more, and that she felt as if she'd lost her purpose. I tried to remember some happy things, but my nerves felt heavy—so heavy that they couldn't be bothered to lift a single neuron to relay its signal.

The crush had reached such an extent that one could

no longer even lie down. We supported each other in our standing positions—and like in a dream, babbled meaninglessly, although most of the time we just remained silent.

It was at this time that I began to suspect that the GM would never end, that Earth was a false construct of the imagination. Perhaps we would keep on waiting and waiting like this, until the end of the world...pretty soon probably everyone in Olympus would have this suspicion.

A very long week and a half passed by. When the ecological system at Olympus was on the brink of collapse, the MAB finally lifted the sunspot alert, and flights resumed normal operations: large contingents of soldiers in uniform space suits had marched in to keep order, even using military ships to ferry detained passengers; ships stranded midflight started their engines again, and, wobbling their giant bulks, flew towards Earth.

Varina and I gave up on returning to Earth. We'd already run out of energy to fight for tickets: we could only leave in the army's transports back to our own bases, without exchanging contact details. Only Wendong had heroically pushed his way into the escape pod, without a backwards glance. As for whether or not he reached Earth in the end, I don't know.

The end? Yes, all things have an end, but I don't think it's important anymore.

Two years later, Mars will once again move closer to Earth, and the tradition of the Great Migration will be reenacted; the Mars Administration Bureau's banner "All hands on deck for the Great Migration" will once again be hung up, and our story will be reenacted by others.

This is the sacred order of Space and the cycle of celestial bodies, not something that mere humans can resist.

NOTES

MA BOYONG'S WORK spans historical, fantasy, detective, thriller, science fiction genres and beyond. Many of his novels have been made into TV series, recently *The Longest Day in Chang'An* and *Antiques and Intrigue*; his shorter works have gained a cluster of awards.

He believes that at the heart of every constructed fictional world, should be a core of personal experiences. "The Great Migration" is a real thing. Every year, billions of people cram onto planes, trains, busses and ships to travel across China, from wherever their work or personal life has taken them, back to the warm embraces of their families for Spring Festival, or Chinese New Year. As a fresher at university, Ma Boyong's first journey home involved being on a packed train for over thirty hours, during which, he had nothing but his imagination to while away the hours of boredom and frustration. He couldn't help but link his speculative imaginings to his current plight, and began to wonder whether, in the Space Age, people would still be troubled by cramped transport, the mad scramble for tickets, and the indignity of paying inflated prices for tasteless instant noodles.

I first lectured about Ma Boyong's work drawing on his dystopian sci fi story "City of Silence", but soon found his brilliant literary flair present across genres, with the charming Mech and Magic story *Dragon Underground*. "The Great Migration" was selected and translated before the outbreak of Covid-19, which had major effects on every aspect of life through 2020. One of the first major disruptions was the suspension of travel before Spring Festival in China. Like Ma's protagonists, there were those who tried to circumvent the restrictions, some who found themselves stranded in the middle of their travel, and others who just had to make do with what they had and where they were. Over the last 30 years, with more Chinese living overseas, this Spring migration has increased to a global phenomenon, and I do thoroughly believe that as we reach other worlds, there will be a mass movement every year of people across space to celebrate the Lunar New Year.

Rereading this piece, I came to a conclusion, which I had not considered during my own history of flights, buses, and long train journeys. Each would-be traveller begins in competition with each other, for the last cheap tickets, for the seat furthest away from the broken toilet, for that last inch of luggage rack, but by the time we reach our destination we have become comrades in arms. Swapping magazines, sharing snacks, and all thinking about what we have universally endured to return home.

MEISJE MET DE PAREL
戴珍珠耳环的少女

ANNA WU

WHO

A

WOKEN BY THE sound outside her window, Shizuko thought it must still be raining, but it was only the wind blowing through the poplar trees.

A glimmer of early morning light shone into the empty living room.

Her mum and dad had been married for almost eighteen years, and they had reached the phase of entropy. Shizuko felt that the two of them were living their daily lives with a mutual cold detachment; that the invisible chasm between them was slowly widening. The big heated row they'd had last night was an exception. Mum had slammed the door, stormed off and stayed out the whole night. Shizuko had just about heard her talking in a shrill, sharp and accusatory tone that she rarely used. "Who's this?"

For the whole day, Dad had shut himself in his study. Shizuko could only hear Bach reverberating in the silence of the house, now high, now low. Swift, drifting and restless.

As far as she could remember, her parents rarely argued—at least in front of Shizuko. Even when swords were unsheathed and bows drawn, Mum would always force her temper down, swallowing the female tendency to get emotional at any cost. Whenever this happened, Shizuko could read in her eyes the protective instinct of female beasts over their little ones.

Perhaps Mum could see that every time they had an argument, Shizuko became very scared.

To avoid thinking about the whole thing, Shizuko stayed at her easel for the entire day. By dusk, her hands, now frozen, were covered in dried and cracking paint. Having battled between the two paths of "going in" and "not minding" a few more times, she glanced at the tightly-shut study door, sighed, and went to the kitchen.

The greasy crockery from yesterday's dinner still sat in the sink. She sighed again. *Is Mum eating properly right now?* Clumsily, she found a packet of noodles, filled the saucepan full of cold water, and switched on the gas.

Delicate white steam spiraled upwards, morphing into unpredictable shapes. A roaring lion bounds into the distance, and disappears; some music notes encircling the top of a flute and are scattered by the rain; a young woman in a billowing long skirt, walking near, whose face starts to warp and fragment, melting into waves of the sea...

Shizuko stared blankly into the air. During the past few years, the pressure from school had increased tenfold, and she had gradually grown silent, burying herself in her studies and drawing and conversing less and less with her parents. When she finally came to see the state of their relationship, the problem had already got very serious.

The intimacy and distance between husband and wife, formed so intricately through the years, day in and day out, wasn't something you could easily put into words.

There was a time when her meticulous and sensitive engineer of a father—who worked for a state-owned firm—and her fierce and unyielding worker-born mother, got along with extraordinary harmony. Shizuko, who took after her father, had exhibited exceptional talent at a young age, and won awards at all kinds of art competitions. A month ago, she had received an offer from the country's top fine arts institute.

This summer was supposed to be perfect.

The noodles had overcooked, and she'd added too much salt. This bland bowl of noodle soup, cooked without the qiang'guo[29] of ginger and spring onions, was nothing compared to the well-brothed, hand-made noodles Mum usually brought from the kitchen. Languidly, Shizuko prodded the rock-hard egg yoke with her chopsticks, thinking of the poached eggs Mum made: perfectly shaped, the yolk only slightly hardened and which, at the lightest pressure, gives way to beautiful amber streaks that were a pure work of art.

Eating with haste, she poured away the left-over noodles, boiled another saucepan full of water and cooked a fresh bowl. Only after tasting it and feeling satisfied it was a bit better than her first attempt did she serve it up to take into her father's study.

---

29 Qiang'guo, 炝锅, a process in Chinese cooking in which herbs and spices are flash fried in the wok or pan to bring out their fragrances before the main ingredients are cooked.

Dad was leaning on his desk, looking distracted, with the music still on. "*Er shu neng xiang.*" With frequent listening, intricacies come to light. A light smile rose on Shizuko's face. Bach had always been their most-loved composer. When she first heard his music by the sea a few years ago, she had been totally captivated. Bach's music was like Van Gogh's painting, or Li Bai's poems: the perfect union between order and disorder, with cadences as beautiful as mathematics, containing such enormous emotional tension.

The Chromatic Fantasia and Fugue. Shizuko finally put the bowl of boiling noodles down, standing there, her eyes dancing with the melody, oblivious to the burnt sensation in her fingertips.

Dad seemed shocked out of his own revelry, coughed lightly, and guiltily avoided catching Shizuko's eye.

Sometimes, Shizuko thought of her father as being like a child; leaving all the housework—like she did—completely to her diligent mother. He would often be immersed in the mental realms of painting, music, literature and mathematics: his intellect and emotional intelligence were completely out of proportion. Shizuko was an odd name. It had come into being when Mum was pregnant, and Dad's fascination had turned to Japanese literature.

The noodles steamed away quietly on the side. Shizuko waited for her father to speak first; this was how they always interacted.

"Do you remember, when you were little, you met a young woman in a white dress?"

Shizuko was a little put out. "Yes, I do."

Dad let out a big sigh.

"I painted a portrait of her, as a gift. Before she left, she gave it back to me. I've kept it all these years. Last night, your mum found it...and tore it up."

Even in the instant of her astonishment, it dawned on Shizuko that Dad's personality—that kind of a girl, it made perfect sense.

"Nothing really happened between us, we just talked a few times. She only appeared for three months, and then one day, apparently for no reason...she vanished without a trace."

Slowly and carefully extracting the two halves of the torn sketch from under a book, Dad defended himself coyly, looking at Shizuko in a manner that she felt didn't at all match his age. In his eyes were shame, fear, anger, self-pity, and a quiet forbearance—but also a deep yearning for understanding.

In that expression, Shizuko saw an eighteen-year-old youth, whose face glowed with the radiance of love.

This secret, platonic love was like snowflakes in midair; that look passionate and vigorous yet are silent and soundless. For someone immersed in the mental realm like her father, it must be hard to forget.

"Dad..."

Shizuko gazed at her father with a complex expression, feeling a certain degree of embarrassment. She had always felt that, as a sensitive and precocious child, she was often far better placed than her mother to understand her father's feelings. They had often conversed like friends.

Young love is no doubt beautiful, but seeing it on her Dad's face felt... odd. He must have kept it bottled up for a long time. Shizuko was beginning to get a vague idea of the problems in her parents' relationship.

As the years rolled by, Dad's memory of that girl would have been like a pearl nurtured within its shell, enshrouded in and feeding on layer upon layer of beautiful fantasy, until at last it glowed with a perfect light. This light would have shone over the chicken feathers of Dad's everyday life.

No matter how competent a wife Mum was, he'd still feel sorry for himself.

"I don't think it's wrong to love anyone…but perhaps… you shouldn't ruin your lives for a mere shadow."

Passing the torn painting to Shizuko, Dad let his head droop and the two large tears he'd been holding fell.

The light of dusk embellished the sketch with a gem-like hue. The girl in it had a quiet, tranquil and ethereal air, gazing sideways at Shizuko; her gaze pure, her lips crimson and slightly parted as if wanting to speak, but at the same time lost in a labyrinth of thoughts and emotions. On her left ear was a circular pearl earring that seemed to fade in and out of visibility. The lines depicting the earring were so incredibly fine that they appeared almost invisible to the eye, giving that area of the image a strange fluorescence. The soft, smooth glow had such a three-dimensional feel that the harder you stared at it, the giddier you felt. Shizuko was reminded of the strange glow of insects' compound eyes; it was almost as though the earring had the power to capture the viewer's soul.

B

CARRYING FATHER'S ALUMINUM lunchbox, young Shizuko slipped through the magnet factory into her usual spot, a courtyard for waste storage. Stepping into the grass thicket, she flung herself onto her familiar concrete pipe seat.

In the early summer, she liked to hide here and eat her dinner. The setting sun glowed russet, and waves of rust-smells carried through the rain. The distant rumble of machines from the plant sounded like the sighs of a steel giant, the sound swaying in the air as it came close, offsetting the surrounding tranquility.

Delicately peeling the lid from the lunch tin, Shizuko lowered her head and took a deep sniff. *Smells so good*. Dad had finished off the soggy dishes cooked in large pots at the canteen, and left her the xiaochao[30] chicken. Yep, that must be her reward for winning first prize at the city-level art competition.

Black mu'er mushrooms, ivory cauliflower, golden brown pieces of chicken, all immersed in a rich, glistening dark sauce. Picking up the small spoon, Shizuko carefully mixed the snow-white rice and precious sauce, ensuring complete and even coverage. In her eyes, Chef Wang was a magician with a spoon. Once, when she was queueing with Dad in the canteen, she watched his application of skilled techniques. Dianguo—casually making the rainbow of food leap in the wok, gouhuo—wrapping them briefly in a warm orange flame, and finally, ding'ge—settling the flame into a misty blue, the alluring fragrance totally capturing her olfactory senses.

That was Shizuko's earliest memory of gourmet.

Years later, when the magnet factory had been razed to the ground, there was no word of Chef Wang. Despite the vicissitudes of life and the sampling of many delicious dishes, she'd never quite found that blue-flamed aroma ever again.

When she had lapped up the last grain of rice, Shizuko threw the lunch box aside, letting it clang to the ground and, as its thin skin of aluminum made contact with

---

30 xiaochao, 小炒, a technique of Chinese cooking where the food is constantly stirred and very rapidly cooked in the wok, the most common type of stir fry in everyday cooking.

stones, receive another dent. Hah! She was in for another scolding from Mum. Lying on the grass, eyes half-closed, she felt a grasshopper leaping onto her leg, and a tiny scratching from its wispy body …tickles…tickles…ouch! Shizuko leaped up, as if electrified. Tiny spiked balls had attached themselves to her shorts, tiny spots of blood now dotting her legs. This plant was everywhere around the factory, about the size of the pulp of her finger, and round, like tiny black hedgehogs. Moodily, Shizuko picked them off from her shorts and flung them into the grass with gusto; then, snapping off a long twig from a tree, she began drawing in the loose earth.

A child's line drawing gradually took shape; a few strokes outlined the mountains, which then became inlaid with a sun, in the middle of which a phoenix wagged its head as if sensing it was nearing the end of its time. Nearby was an unusually tall and thick bush, from which spiky fruit fell like rain, striking the round head of a little girl. The girl had a thin and narrow face and large eyes, from which tears rolled down and gathered into a river that assumed a circular curve, flowing towards the sun behind the mountain range.

Finishing the drawing, Shizuko threw away the branch and contentedly wiped the sweat from her face with her dirty little hands, lifting her head… her eyes suddenly widened…

Ahead of her was a setting sun, about to sink into the mountains, the remnant rays pouring over a giant pile of waste metal. Iron and steel pieces, thick and thin, curled and tangled into one and formed a complex three-dimensional structure, the different facets of which reflected the dusky glow in spots, emanating a crude and chaotic kind of beauty. In front of the metal structure was a slender white-skirted profile. Hazy and against the light, only the soft glow at her ear could be discerned, along with a pair of squeezed-to-crescent smiling eyes.

Shizuko thought back many times to the dimensions and perspectives of that scene. The soft red glow, the curling ball of metal, and the white lotus of a woman. She found it very strange that the image should be so intensely branded into her mind.

The woman approached, tilting her head to look at the drawing on the ground. She wore no other ornaments about her body apart from the pearl earring, the glow of which seemed to envelope her.

Oh? There really is only one earring.

"Are you Shizuko?"

The young woman had a very tender voice, but it sounded a little strange. Her accent was very close to standard Mandarin, rarely heard in this small town.

"You like to draw, correct?"

The young woman took out a white handkerchief, and very naturally wiped a grain of rice from the corner of Shizuko's mouth.

Shizuko hiccupped. "Yeah! How do you know?" She was rapidly casting aside Mum's warnings that she shouldn't talk to strangers.

"Your dad told me." The young woman smiled cheekily, revealing white, tidy teeth.

Shizuko let go of the last vestige of caution at the back of her head.

"Jiejie[31], you know my dad?"

"I work here too." The young woman turned towards the sun so Shizuko couldn't see her face.

---

31 Jiejie, 姐姐, "big sister", a term of address for one's older sister or someone about the age to be one's older sister.

"Do you like drawing too?"

"Yes, I do."

"Really?"

"Really."

Delighted, Shizuko grasped the woman's warm hand.

"Really really?"

The young woman didn't reply, but she was smiling so much her eyes became a curve. She was measuring Shizuko up as if she were a rare specimen.

"I've won many prizes!" Shizuko wasn't sure why, but she really wanted to see surprise on the woman's face.

"Very reminiscent of Picasso." The young woman seemed captivated by her mud drawing. The whole work was down-to-earth, yet chilling; exaggerated, yet as natural as if it were painted by nature itself.

"The clouds are so red, don't they look pretty?" Shizuko shifted her attention towards the sky.

"Look at it carefully. Is there just red there?" The young woman pointed towards a corner of the sky.

"Ah…no, there, the bit in the middle, there's vermillion plus a little bit of ochre, and the thin bit on the right, is scarlet with a little bit of azure…jiejie, am I right?" Shizuko grabbed hold of the young woman, almost leaping with joy.

The young woman's eyes remained on the mud drawing, contemplating. "In terms of colour matching, that's correct …but if you use a mixture of cyan and deep saffron as a base, that would be even more appropriate for your drawing, and increase the horror element."

Shizuko stared at the mud drawing in a stupor, not totally understanding her words. This exchange had left her burning all over, and feeling an extraordinary appreciation of the beauty in front of her.

Dusk was gathering up its last rays of light, and a thick indigo pressed down on all things. A gust of cold wind blew, and Shizuko shuddered.

"Jiejie...who are you, when did you come here, and why are you here?"

Like an astonished cat, the young woman's long thin eyes widened into circles. For a long while, she observed Shizuko curiously. "These are three...very interesting questions."

WHEN

A

SHIZUKO RESTED HER paintbrush and lifted herself slowly, leaning on the arms of the chair and stretching out her legs. The pins and needles had spread from her thighs to her toes.

The sky was dark and murky, and the air so humid that you could wring water from it.

Six missed calls and one text message, all from Xiao Ze. He was a friend from the art society, attending one of the universities in town while doubling as a teaching assistant at the biology lab. The day before, Shizuko had put the sketch in his care for repairs.

She rang back, and the call was picked up in less than two rings.

"Can you come over now?"

His tone shocked Shizuko. Usually he was a calm and collected tech assistant. Even when he had accidentally soiled the favourite work of one of the lecturers from the traditional painting society, his face didn't so much as twitch, giving the impression that even if Mount Tai[32] were about to collapse, he would not.

"What's up?"

"That sketch...it's... uumm...just get over here now!"

An hour later, she was standing in Xiao Ze's laboratory, surrounded by an icy-clean white space.

The painting had been repaired, and only under a microscope could you just about see a faint chainsaw-jagged line.

"To make things easier, I usually use the electronic microscope to repair painting. It's because, because of this, that I found something strange about this painting, no, specifically about this pearl earring..."

He pushed his glasses up anxiously, and gazed into Shizuko's clear eyes, blushing as usual.

Shizuko felt a little bashful too, but wriggled away from his gaze.

"There's nothing special about the paper itself, but this tiny area under the image of the earring seems to have been treated with some kind of technology. It's been turned into very fine nano material. This pearl looks very smooth on the surface, but actually contains countless whirlpools, which look like they follow the principle of fractals...why don't you read through that first?" he said, gesturing at a web page he already had open.

Words. Images. Shizuko restrained her curiosity, and browsed the pages carefully. She wasn't sure why, but this fractal-related information was stirring something within the depths of her memory.

---

32 Mount Tai, 泰山，located in Shandong in East China, the foremost of China's five mystical mountains, of great cultural significance and the source of many legends, tales and idioms, like this one.

Ten minutes later, still between belief and doubt, Shizuko walked over to the large microscope and put her eye to it.

It was like a small child's first time seeing a kaleidoscope. Her mind buzzed.

This was a most fantastical picture.

It looked like countless crisscrossing pearls, like the patterns on a large ammonite whose curves were made up of smaller ammonites; and then each of those constructed by yet more, even smaller ammonites...

Xiao Ze continued to adjust the magnification range.

As the lenses drew closer and closer, the whirlpools kept expanding—though boundaries between the shapes remaining clear, recurring layer after layer. New subsets of 'ammonite' kept appearing.

By now her blood was rushing towards her eardrums, causing them to ring. Seeing the constantly increasing magnification level on the screen, Shizuko began to tremble.

100, 1000, 5000, 10,000...

100,000 times!

The number on the screen flashed, and stopped. In centre of the lense, the image had disappeared at last, making way for line upon line of tiny, dense text.

Having a bout of vertigo, she swayed. Xiao Ze anxiously came to support her in his arms, blushing bright red. His palms felt hot and damp.

"So sorry... without your permission, I had a look at the letter...didn't finish it of course...if you want it kept secret, I, I won't tell anyone..."

His voice grew quieter and quieter as all Shizuko could hear was the explosion inside her own head.

Thunder rumbled outside the window as Shizuko sat in front of the computer at home.

Xiao Ze had taken her home. She had been distracted, and was suffering from a migraine.

Next to her, the sketch had been meticulously wrapped in layers of archival wrapping. She wanted to call Xiao Ze and ask him about the content of the letter, but, under a kind of inexplicable terror, her whole body felt limp and she couldn't summon half an ounce of energy.

A mysterious light came from the screen as the slideshow presented image after image of the elegantly coloured fractal patterns, the beauty of numbers, the beauty of colours; flowing, harmonious, yet ever-changing cadences. Normally, she would be mesmerized.

But now, all she felt was that those patterns were tempting her to stray into the strange unknown. The word 'fractal' crashed around and rumbled in her head.

A fierce wind threw open the window, sweeping in raindrops and sending her art papers rustling and flying everywhere.

She was freezing, the cold rising from the soles of her feet. Her thin autumn clothes had been glued to her body by the rain. She began to shiver with the awkward frailty of a girl in puberty. In her distracted state, she'd forgotten to change into something dry, forgotten to take a shower or keep warm.

In a tiny corner of the view from her window, Shizuko could see the primary school she'd attended. During her holidays, she could still hear the morning and evening school bells. As if they were ringing from her childhood out of the tunnel of time, *ding dong*, and striking on the chapter breaks of her life.

Time, the strange phenomenon of time, endless time. In this temporality we share, we are all passengers, encountering other passengers of time.

Standing in front of the window and trembling, Shizuko was struck by both the eternity of time and the unpredictability of life. For the first time she understood the essence of *mono no ware*, pathetic fallacy, from the literary tradition that gave her her name.

That night, she burned in her dreams.

Suspended high in the sky were countless chaotically flashing fractal patterns, blooming in layers like Monet's *Water Lilies*, leaping and whirling like Van Gogh's *The Starry Night*, twisted and contorted like Matisse's green face, dense and swarming like Dali's ants.

Bach's music came like waves, each silver pearl earring transforming into note after note; an endless cycle, gathering into a nebula storm at the vault of the sky...

Beneath her feet was a giant expanse of black wasteland, smooth like a mirror, magnifying the chaos of the sky by a hundred-thousandfold.

Xiao Ze's words thundered like exploding bombs: "This is far more advanced than any current technology, let alone ten years ago. Technological capabilities like this would indicate that either she comes from a more advanced planet, or...a more advanced time."

The colours gathered and melted together, twisting, changing shape, becoming surrounded by and eventually engulfed into a desolate primeval flood.

Shizuko screamed.

B

IN AN INSTANT, the noisy chirrup of the cicadas, the scorching summer wind and cloying sweat were all gone.

She could only hear the gliding sound of moving water, flowing and muffled.

Shizuko opened her eyes to find herself underwater.

It was the most sparkling and translucent deep blue. Hundreds and thousands of delicate light streaks, as if woven from white gold, all tangled together; where the hand glides through, bubbles swarmed—countless tiny, perfectly circular crystal forms, swaying, gyrating, and floating towards the surface, swelling and relaxing in slow motion, bumping into each other, their susurrations like the chattering of sprites.

It was a month ago, also on a day like this, that Shizuko found herself so nervous that her limbs felt paralysed by the water. No matter how Mum tried to explain the techniques and movements, she just could not learn how to swim.

"Your legs are stiffer than trotters!" Mum flicked water at Shizuko, laughing.

Dad watched them, smiling like a fool, and helped Shizuko into the water.

"Look at the sun's rays at the bottom of the water, see how beautiful they are, be a brave girl, don't be scared, relax..."

Shizuko repeated Dad's words to herself, and then puffing her cheeks, she flailed her limbs about like a startled octopus.

And then, bracing herself brutally, she tore open her eyes.

Through her goggles she could see the whole ocean embraced by the sun, shafts of which had poured through the pure azure all around her. It was as beautiful as a dream.

Without even realising it, her body began to relax as

her eyes greedily took in the surrounding scenery. For the first time, she felt a kinship with the seawater, and, paddling gently, she slowly began to float.

She never thought she could learn to swim.

Many times, she felt that her mother was her greatest protector in the world, and her father the one who understood her most.

Lost in thought, she didn't notice when a black shadow appeared behind her. Suddenly it leaped up, and shot across her left side.

A fish with a big tail zoomed in front of Shizuko, so close that she could see the fearful twitching of its gills.

SMAKK! Its greasy tail slapped her in the face, and taking another sudden turn, it disappeared.

Feeling as if she'd been stabbed, Shizuko lost her balance; in her panic she was desperate to grab hold of something, but the only thing her hands could find were streams of water.

She gasped for air, cold salty water assaulting her nose, invading her from her nasal cavity to her lungs, igniting a pain she had never felt before—like being pierced by steel rods or scorched by fire...

Help, help me...she wanted to shout, but only choked in more water. The fierce pain began to cause Shizuko to spasm, her chest almost torn by her desperation for air.

Little by little, she began to lose energy. She felt the gush of warm tears surround her, but she was drifting away.

She could see gold spots in her eyes, which felt like they were about to explode...and gradually...a black fog pervaded.

Thinking back to that scene was like watching a film with all the sound cut out; how she was rescued from the water and pulled to shore, she couldn't remember. Only that when she came to, her senses were overwhelmed by her own frantic choking. Every cough felt like someone yanking out her windpipe and, with it, her lungs. With every cough she silently implored it to stop, please, no more, stop, stop now...

Eventually, when Shizuko calmed down, she found her face wet and sticky, not knowing whether it was tears or sweat. Holding her up was the young woman in white, her hair still dripping, biting her lips; her face paler than snow.

In that instant, the joy that had been rushing into Shizuko's head at having escaped death, gave way to deep shame. Shame that she was in such a sorry and unsightly state.

She curled up in the girl's arms, buried her head, and howled.

The young woman's tears fell like a broken pearl necklace. In the scorching heat, grains of salt began to crystalise on her face.

HOLDING THE CHILD in her arms, the young woman's eyes were filled with deep perplexity and fear. *That was just in time*, she thought; if she had been any later...

The sound of Shizuko's heartrending crying felt like knives slicing at her heart.

The young woman sat in anxious thoughtfulness for a while, and then, taking off the pearl earring, stroked it, and held it gently to Shizuko's ear. The melodious music coaxed Shizuko out of her fear, though even in her amazement she could barely contain her sobbing.

She didn't know how any music could be so lovely, and sound as perfect as the undulating decorative patterns she had loved seeing on the edge of her birthday cake.

"This is Bach. The simplest, yet the most complex of music. The polyphony, the transitions—it's an eternal cycle. He was the composer who came closest to mathematics and logic." The young woman patted Shizuko lightly on the back, attempting to comfort her in the gentlest way possible.

Umm. She does not understand.

"If you look closely at this part of the coast, you'll find that it shares the same shape as the entire coast, replicated over and over again. In mathematics, this is called a fractal. And Bach's music is a bit like this."

The young woman pointed to the shoreline far away, attempting to draw Shizuko's attention away from her near-drown experience.

Shizuko listened as she sobbed.

She still does not understand.

"There's a painter called Pollock. His paintings are beautiful—they conform to the pattern of fractals... hmm, the cauliflower you were eating, if you look at the whole vegetable before it is broken into pieces, on each stem is a small cauliflower, this is also fractals..."

The young woman sighed, disaffected; she no longer knew what she was saying. So many emotions were tangled up in her mind, and she felt short of breath.

Slowly, and mechanically, she replaced her pearl earring and gazed into the distance.

SHIZUKO'S EYE WIDENED as she gazed at her face curiously, almost forgetting about the drowning.

Between the sea and sky, under the fierce sunlight, the young woman's face appeared almost translucent. On her eyelash, a few tiny salt crystals glistened gently.

WHY

Dear Zhang Shizuko,

Hello,

Right here, right now, standing outside the river of time, I don't know where to start. Perhaps everything and anything started with the quantum cloud.

At this point in time, I was visiting "The Museum of Humanity." I had already seen many exhibits of science, philosophy, literature, music, sculpture and such. Being there was like following your footsteps and experiencing the course of human civilization for myself. From the first thunderstruck fires of Africa to the final atomic fires of the great war in Asia. As a painter, out of deference and a sense of sadness, I left the art exhibit until the end.

The caves of Altamira, the plains of Mesopotamia: Dong Qichang, Wu Daozi, Da Vinci, Van Gogh, Pollock, Escher, Picasso, Dali...

Although they were quantum replicas, the way they shook my consciousness was hard to put into words. Instantly recalling to mind this quote: "The beauty of the world! The paragon of animals!" It was then, that I came upon two paintings, both called *The Girl with the Pearl Earring*. The one on the left, *Meisje Met De Parel*, was by the 17th century Dutch painter Johannes Vermeer. The one on the right, *Dai Zhenzhu Erhuan de Shaonü*, was by Zhang Shizuko from 21st century China.

Yes.

That's you.

The work on the right appeared to be in a hazy cloud. Only after a few seconds did it resolve itself into clarity:

a young woman wearing a pearl earring. Behind her, crystal clear waves of the azure sea. The girl's features are almost completely lost in the fierce midday sun, but the loss and despair captured in her profile and posture was unforgettable.

Watching the painting fold into reality, I couldn't believe that such as famous work of art featured my own quantum fingerprint.

Only when the viewer has personally interacted with the timeline of the quantum object would it coalesce before their eyes: when someone unconnected views it, that resolution just would not occur. This is a proven scientific principle. In our time, artists often find pleasure in encoding their works with quantum technology, and observing the process by which the quantum cloud slowly collapses.

To put it simply, I am personally connected to the birth of this painting.

I was troubled to think that the girl in the painting was me, but a strong curiosity compelled me to wade through the mist of time and find you.

When we first met, you asked me three questions.

Now, let me reply to each of them.

1. Who?

Me, an artificial entity. You might call me an AI.

Two hundred years ago, when humans created the first generation of true artificial intelligence, the Turing Test had already been rigorously revised with criteria to include fuzzy intelligence, as well as aesthetic and creative abilities. Our twilight discussion on drawing appreciation when we first met; wasn't that like a simplified Turing Test? Think about it—you even inadvertently asked me a halting problem. It looks like I passed.

2. When?

From your point of view, I am from the future.

My apologies that this revelation is so curt. The galactic exploration, longevity and time travel that your kind dream of are the everyday technology of our time, but you no longer exist. After three revolutions, artificial intelligence has completely replaced humanity. As a token of appreciation and respect for our erstwhile opponent, we keep the fire of human wisdom burning in the Museum of Humanity on Capital Square. One day three months ago, I once again entered it, and saw our work.

Was it your work that influenced my actions, or my past that influenced your future? This is an ouroboros, the tail feeding into the head, with no end and no beginning.

3. Why did I come into your life?

This is a complicated one to answer.

At first, it was a strong curiosity. Your *Girl with the Pearl Earring* is a rare masterpiece of the twenty-first century, well known in our time. I think you'll understand my desire to get to the bottom of this mystery.

Apart from that, there was a vague sense of unease. After several conversations, I didn't know how to reciprocate the subtle feelings your father was showing towards me. I was walking by the sea that day, and happened to come to your rescue. Watching you struggle between life and death, I held tightly onto the pearl earring—which was also my time travel device. I began to grow fearful of travelling back and forth in time, concerned that I was unduly interfering with the path of your fate, and that this would have an impact on your creation of that important painting...so on the second day, laden with panic and anxiety, I left without saying goodbye.

However, at that point, the trajectory of fate had altered once again.

At the heart of all of this was a steadfast desire to protect and preserve Art. When I jumped back, some years later in your life, I saw how you were inspired by your father's sketch; saw how you caught a fever on the rainy night you came back from repairing the drawing; saw how your parents, on the verge of a divorce, wept by your bed and reunited; saw how the moment on the beach was branded into your heart; even saw this letter, and the shock it would bring to your soul, and in the end cause you to complete the masterpiece for posterity...

So, I have now returned once again to your past, to write the letter I will have placed inside the pearl earring.

Fractals, do you remember?

By the way, Xiao Ze is a nice boy, and will be throughout the decades he'll spend by your side. I'd rather believe that this serendipity between you was another purpose for the painting's creation.

Much of the time, whether or not we understand, fate has its trajectory plotted. I'm so sorry to have suddenly turned up, disrupting your life; but it has also been an honour that our fates could melt into a masterpiece and light the way to the end of time.

As an artist, to be part of this—in no matter what way—is incredibly glorious.

There is some other, perhaps good news. Recently, in my own time, the advancement of artificial intelligence have come to a point of entropy. Our scientists are already researching the amalgamation of human and machine from the human cells we have preserved.

Our time travel technology can only reach the past, not the future. Perhaps in the future, our two civilizations could ignite co-existing fires over this planet.

I have since returned many times to the Museum of Humanity. Amidst the bustle of bodies, I stand gazing at the monolith in the hall. On it are engraved two sentences, which have been translated into many languages, including our own.

In Chinese, it happens to be two lines of verse:

历尽劫波兄弟在，相逢一笑泯恩仇

*"Still brothers after hardship and strife,
all forgotten in a smile when we meet."*[33]

Shizuko: time is infinite, and the universe is infinite. Whether human, or artificial intelligence, perhaps in the end we are all subjects to its patterns, as sure as paint dissolving in water.

So, across all time, I wish you well.

---

33 From Lu Xun's seven-character verse "On Sanyi Tower" 题三义塔 (1933), about the friendship and longing for peace between Chinese and Japanese people, despite the atrocities committed by the latter's imperial government.

NOTES

ANNA WU'S CHILDHOOD love of books led her to a life of writing. After graduating in Chinese Literature, she worked hard, overcoming obstacles to attain her dream life as a professional screenwriter and playwright, whilst writing novels and SF stories in her spare time. She currently works as a chief content producer for sci-fi and qihuan[34] projects at a film company in Beijing, and has won Xingyun awards for her scriptwriting as well as fictional works.

In "Meisje met de Parel", Wu wanted to explore two very different civilizations, human and artificial intelligence, each of which, having their own strengths and shortcomings, are unified by an understanding that the beauty of Art is eternal and should be cherished.

As an eclectic reader, drawn to a wide range of cultural sources and voices across the literary and genre divide, I have aimed to include a wide range of Chinese SF voices in this collection. I found this piece of literary Young Adult fiction optimistic, charming, and slightly haunting. It starts with a very nostalgic scene of childhood in the time of the danwei (state run business, with communal living), but develops into a contemplation of life, art, and the beauty of nature seen through the lense of science. The story also appealed to my admiration for classical music, the culinary arts, and of course, painting. We have decided to use the original Dutch title of Vermeer's famous painting, both to separate your expectations from Tracy Chevalier's excellent novel, and to focus on that feeling of otherness which threads through this story.

One of the absolute pleasures of translating this piece

---

34 qihuan—fantasy that combines Chinese and Western traditions of the genre.

is the way Wu talks about food, a central part of Chinese culture. Her language surrounding the preparation and enjoyment of food was a sheer delight to bring into English, and to be able to talk about folding in ingredients in the same piece as folding in time and space was a sheer joy.

FLOWER OF THE OTHER SHORE
彼岸花

A QUE

1

I'M NOT SURE what started it, but just as spring arrived, I began to feel an itch around the back of my shoulder. I ask Old Jim to take a look for me. He walks round behind me, a cigarette hanging out his mouth, and after looking at it for ages he signals, "It's nothing."

"But it tickles," I signal back, turning around.

Old Jim's neck has already rotted, so he can only shake his hand, rather than his head. "Impossible, impossible, our nerves have already decayed. Apart from the Hunger, we feel nothing. How could you possibly feel itchy? Have you gone too long without eating? Don't worry. I've smelled the scent of blood in the air lately. In a few days I'll take you hunting."

I don't believe him, and make him find two pieces of mirror. I put one piece at the front, and one at the back.

Facing each other, I see a wound about the length of a hand. The flesh at the edge has already curled open, grey, like a slightly leering mouth—and in this mouth, I can vaguely see something small and black.

Old Jim takes another long look, and signs, "No idea what it is." He digs it into the wound. In the mirror, I see my rotten flesh sticking on his finger—he's digging too hard, causing the wound to tear more. The newly exposed flesh is still the same old grey. I yawn out of boredom, and then remember: this wound was a scratch from a tree branch the last time I was chasing a live person on a hill.

"It's too tight, I can't get it out." Suddenly, Old Jim is standing in front of me, gesturing. "Maybe just the bone showing."

"OK." I sway my hand.

It's already dusk, but the day is long in the summer of this seaside town, and the sky still shows a serene indigo. On the clear and crystalline sea, a moored rowing boat is bobbing, now sinking, now afloat. A lot of Stiffs hover aimlessly around the shore.

"What are they doing?" I ask.

"Some corpses floated ashore recently." Old Jim spits out the cigarette butt, lights another one, and pushes it between his lips. "Fresh ones, died not long ago. Not like us."

As we speak, the Stiffs by the shore suddenly stir and run into the sea. I stand on tiptoe and see, among the golden sea, a figure rising and falling with the waves, drifting towards us.

The crowd is running towards the body. A Stiff's movements aren't coordinated enough to swim, but luckily the water only reaches their waists. They grab the corpse, decaying faces break into happy smiles, and a strange grunting breaks from their throats. As one, they hold out their arms and tear at the corpse.

It's a middle-aged man. He must have died pretty recently as his blood is congealing and turning dark red, and its viscous texture doesn't disperse in seawater. The smell of it spreads.

It sends my nose into spasms, and seems to infinitely multiply the Hunger in my stomach. This gnawing drives me and I run into the sea, but Old Jim and I are too late. When we get there, the crowd have already dispersed.

"They move so quickly," I say.

"Of course they do. That many Stiffs? Only one dead body? Don't you Chinese have a proverb? Too many monks…" he gesticulates for ages, wracking his dried-up brains, but to no avail.

"…too little congee." I gesture for him.

"That's right. Too little congee." He nods his hand contentedly. "How very apt."

The Necrona virus had swept the world, dividing humanity into the monks and the congee. How many years ago was that?

I try bitterly hard to remember, but I cannot.

Life isn't bad as a Stiff. The only trouble is that you remember less and less. You can't blame me—the Stiff's brain is a slowly wilting thing. Sometimes when we shake our heads, we can hear a knocking sound, as if our hemispheres are knocking against our skulls like a ping pong ball. With each knock, we remember one thing less, till the brain is completely empty and only sensation is left: Hunger. We can't starve to death because we've already died once, but it will never subside. It drives me to chase the living, to tear at flesh and blood.

However, today, when I was following Old Jim along

the shore, his head was rattling and mine was not. I shake my head and sign, "Can you hear the sound of my head?"

"No," Old Jim replies.

I'm a little worried. "Do you think I'm sick?"

"We're Stiffs, and Stiffs don't get colds or fevers," Old Jim reassures me. "Don't worry. Perhaps when we were running, your brain fell out your ear, so now your head's empty. That's why it's not making a sound."

I feel reassured, and look behind me. The waves are crystal clear again, but look a lot duller. Night is falling, and the tide rises around our legs. I don't think I could ever find my brains among these waves.

"Maybe they got washed away," says Old Jim. "Might be a good thing. No brain, no worries."

The only thing to do is to head back to the land and continue to wander the city, like the countless nights before. However, as this is the beginning of the story I'm telling you, it's bound to be different from a usual day. Something out-of-the-ordinary happens, and this is the catalyst. I suddenly stop, still, and I seem to hear the crack of an electric arc through my brain. I sign, "I think I know who I am."

"You sound like you really are sick."

"I'm not lying!" I try hard to grasp that flash of electricity, and my cloudy memory clarifies, like a bird flying out of thick fog. At first, it's just a shadow in the mist, but now it's landed on a tree. Shakily, I signal, "I, I, I...I'm a, a, a..." but I still can't see what the bird looks like, or solve the mystery of my identity. "I'm a man, a student, a music lover...but who am I?"

Just as I am growing overwhelmed, Old Jim is calmly observing me, cigarette in mouth, his rotted eyes brimming with sympathy. Because he no longer breathes, the cigarette can only burn by itself. The light from the cherry slowly moves towards his face, making it brighter and brighter.

He lifts his hands slowly, and signs in the lonely darkness, "Don't worry if you can't remember."

I nod. "OK. I can't remember my name, but I know where I live."

Old Jim asks doubtfully, "Where's that?"

I take him there, walking through streets that have fallen into complete disarray; past many, many slowly ambling Stiffs. On their rigid roaming, they see us and gesture, "Have you eaten?"

"No," Old Jim replies.

"We've just eaten."

"Lucky you."

"But it wasn't enough," they say. "Never ever enough. Never ever full. Hungry. Hungry." They move their hands in tidy unison, telling of the hunger in their stomachs. If they still had their vocal chords, I think they'd be singing in unison, singing all night long. A song with only one lyric. *Hungry*.

Against my history, I don't join in the silent choir; instead grabbing hold of Old Jim and continuing to traverse streets and alleys. It's just getting properly dark as we enter a block of flats. We try our hardest to bend our knees, and climb the dozen flights of stairs. I push open a door. "I used to live here."

The last ray of the setting sun shines through the balcony, onto the messy floor. The room isn't large—about eighty or so square metres, with two bedrooms and a living room. The living room is a tip and filled with a foul stench. The bed through an open doorway is unmade and covered in creases. The second bedroom door is shut. We push at the door, but it doesn't give and we abandon the idea of going in there.

"This is where you used to live? It's very ordinary. Looks like you were only an ordinary person, with ordinary tastes for interior décor."

I ignore him and go through things in the flat, but can't find anything related to me. Just when I start to suspect that this sudden memory has deceived me, Old Jim picks up a book on the table in the bedroom and flicks through it, causing a photograph to fall out. He picks it up, looks at me, and looks back to the photo.

"Is this you? Now that your face has stiffened and rotted, your looks have changed, but there's a strong resemblance."

Old Jim puts the photo next to my face, takes another look and nods his free hand. "I can't see it now, but you were quite handsome when you were alive." He points at the girl in the photograph. "Who's this?"

In the photo, the girl is half a head shorter than me and leaning into my embrace. We're standing by the sea and the light of the setting sun is in her eyes, which are also shining bright. I look carefully but can't recall anything about her. Her beauty is beyond doubt, though. I shake my head, and stow the photograph away. "I'll tell you later, when I remember."

Pity rises again in Old Jim's eyes. Gazing at me, he urges, "Don't remember. It doesn't matter who we were. We're all just walking corpses. For us, memory is just another kind of virus, one even more deadly and that would torment us more than the Hunger. Forgetting who we are is a defence mechanism for Stiffs. Don't resist this defence: don't remember."

Old Jim's signs are always full of philosophical meaning.

I am filled with admiration. "You must have been an extraordinary person when you were alive."

"That's right, I must have been a professor," he nods, "or an author."

I signal my agreement keenly, adding, "Or perhaps a pipe smoker, the type that has lung cancer."

"Why are we still here?" he signals back.

"Let me see if I can remember anything else."

Old Jim pats me on the shoulder, triggering another bout of tickling in the wound, and then turns to walk out of the room. No matter how respectable his status had been when he was alive, now, all he has left is an instinct that drives him to half-sway, half-slouch across the city all night, not knowing where he's headed.

I stand in the empty living room and close my eyes to concentrate, but the bird that fought through the thick fog has already spread its wings and taken off.

I think hard. It must have been at least half an hour, but apart from the feeling that I've lived in this flat, I can remember nothing else. I sway my head and hear a thud, and a squeaking sound. So my brain is still in there. I cheer up at the thought and am about to leave, but suddenly I stop. My brain seems to be rattling in my skull again, but the squeaking noise?

Slowly, I turn round to face the shut door of the bedroom.

The sun is just disappearing into the horizon of the sea, darkness shrouds the world. Before it envelops this room, I see the door to that second room open slowly— and behind the door, a girl's face peeps out, cautiously looking around.

This face is familiar.

Half an hour ago, I had seen it in a photograph.

SMASH!

2

Smash!

Old Jim and I crash through the glass door of the supermarket.

The once-owner of this shop was a fat man. Before the city had fallen, he'd sit behind the counter every day with only his round head showing. I had never seen him get out from there: it was like he was joined at the lower body with that counter. Later, when the Stiffs attacked this city, he was bitten in the arm. One morning, I saw him loitering outside the shop and lurched towards him. He asked me what was keeping him there. "This is your home," I signed. He shook his head, and gestured to me. "When I was alive I forgot, but now I remember. My home's in the north." And with that, he headed north, and never came back.

The supermarket became vacant.

Now we enter it, stepping over broken glass into the abandoned aisle. Cold wind blows over from the other side of the store, chilling us. Old Jim opens a freezer and a rotten smell flows out; he breathes in deeply, showing an expression of great enjoyment. Then he grabs a piece of frozen pork, takes a bite, and spits it back out. "It's rock hard, not very good." He throws the stinking meat down, and shuffles behind the counter to take a few cartons of cigarettes. He extracts one, and lights it in his mouth.

I find a trolley and make my way through the aisles, sweeping all food and drink into the trolley as I go.

"I say, are you robbing the shop?" Jim steps in front of me, signaling as he walks backwards. "Only humans do this kind of thing."

I'm pushing the trolley with one hand and grabbing

groceries with the other, too occupied to talk. It's not until I get to the end of an aisle and the trolley is full that I stop to gesture: "I want to try other flavours."

Old Jim shakes his hand. "This isn't appropriate for Stiffs. Has something got into your head, or is the Necrona changing in you?"

"I just want to try."

Old Jim indicates his understanding. "If it's good, don't forget to tell me." He pauses before adding, "Lately there's a heavy human scent in the air. I'm afraid it could be another attack from the Breathers. Be careful, they've captured a lot of Stiffs recently."

I'm confused. "What would the humans want with us?"

"Who knows? Humans have too many ideas, we can't possibly see through them. It's better to be a Stiff. Nice and simple, with only one thing on the brain: biting Breathers." He puts the cigarettes into his pocket, and with arthritic steps, staggers out of the shop.

After he's gone, I push the trolley, piled high with food and water, out of the supermarket, through the streets, up the stairs, and back home. Rigor mortis had long overtaken all my tendons and ligaments, so when going up the stairs, I can only drag the trolley up as I climb them. With every step, the trolley jolts, and by the time I get home over half of the supplies had fallen out.

Even with what little is left, Wu Huang's face is filled with shock and joy when she sees it.

Wu Huang is the girl I'm hiding in my room—the girl in the photograph.

The first time I saw her, my stomach gave a great rumble and Hunger skyrocketed, engulfing my whole being. I could hear the pat-pat-pat beating of her heart, like a powerful pump, sending fresh blood around the body with every beat. I could also see her thin neck, where—although covered in grime—her slightly protruding artery was vaguely visible, giving out a delicious scent.

I gave a low roar and leapt onto her. She screamed, trying to break free, but even a grown man would be no match for the strength of a Stiff. She could only wave her arms and beat my shoulders in futility.

Just when I was about to sink my teeth into her neck, her fists land on my right shoulder, and that sensation of itching bother surfaced again. My brain seemed to buzz, and, flexing its wings, the bird flew back out of the fog. Images of the embracing couple on the photo appeared before my eyes, against the gently undulating waves of the sea, and then the Hunger ebbed like a receding tide back into my stomach.

I released the girl, and retreated with a hand over my shoulder. She curled up, pressed hard into the corner.

A Stiff and a Breather-girl thus faced each other in the dark, lonely room.

"Don't be scared," I gestured, but her eyes were still filled with terror. I then realized she didn't understand the sign language we Stiffs had. I pondered, then took out the photograph from my tattered pocket, and held it next to my face. I pointed to the boy in the photo, and then at my rigid face next to it.

"Hui?" the girl asked, hesitant and doubtful.

So this is my name, I thought apathetically. Old Jim was right: I was just an ordinary person while I was alive. I put the photograph in the girl's hand, and slowly wrote out a message on her palm: "Do you know me? What are we to each other?"

The girl gripped the photo, and stared at me for a long time. Although we were in the dark, her eyes remained bright and shining, like ripples about to fade into the sea. After a while, she asked: "You're Hui?"

I nodded.

"Have you forgotten?"

I wrote: "I only remember I lived here."

She kept her eyes fixed on my face. "My name's Huang, you're Hui[35], we're lovers. You said you'd protect me, but you went out looking for news, and never came back. I have been waiting here for six months."

In her account, our story was very ordinary. Deaths and farewells were common anywhere during apocalypse. When a wave of Stiffs came, we had already stockpiled supplies, and were going to hide out in the flat until the army came to our rescue. But after a week, there had been no movement outside, so I told her, "I'm going out to have a look, maybe the army's already cleared the zombies." She took my hand and wouldn't let me go. I smiled and stroked her head. "I promise I'll come back to you, I'll protect you." So I left the flat, leaving her to wait in the dark like a frightened baby deer, and never returned. During this time, she had eked out the food and water, but was almost out of everything. Just when she was on the edge of despair, I reappeared—this time as a Stiff.

"Don't you worry, I said I'd protect you," I wrote slowly on her palm, "and I'll keep my promise."

Now Huang twists open a bottle of mineral water and gulps it down, drinking too quickly and choking on several mouthfuls.

I want to pat her back, but as soon as I move, she shrinks back. I understand. After all, humans and Stiffs are different.

---

35 The name of these two characters somewhat foreshadow their budding romance, Huang's name (璜) meaning jade ornament, and Hui (辉), meaning splendor.

I move back to my seat, and pass her another bottle.

After she's drunk her fill, she wipes the corners of her mouth, lets out a deep breath, and says thank you.

I pick up a pen and scrawl on paper as best I can, "It's OK, I don't eat these things anyway."

"What do you eat?" she asks automatically.

I don't answer, but she works it out in my silence, and so, the silence magnifies. The wind blows in. Pieces of paper scrape against the floor, rustling particularly loudly in the silence.

"But I won't hurt you." I write these characters in a very large size.

She nods. "You're different from them. The other zombies can't think. If it were them, they'd have eaten me as soon as they saw me. But you're helping me."

In fact, Stiffs are not only able to communicate with their own sign language, but also think, and think more deeply than humans. Theoretically speaking, if someone has an unquenchable passion but is confined to spend his days in aimless roaming, then he's bound to become a philosopher: only our memories are too short, and our Hunger too fierce. Whenever we smell humans, this drives us to chase after blood and flesh, leaving us no time to commit our thoughts to paper. In any case, even if we wrote them down, who would read them?

To explain all this to her would take too long to put it all in writing. So in the end I nod, and then write: "I'm not sure what's happening to me either. Perhaps I'm a special Stiff with a will of my own."

"You really can't remember anything?" she asks again.

"No, my brains have all dried up," I reply, "but what I can tell you is, I want to hear about the past."

Huang's face becomes wistful, albeit a little disappointed.

"We met at university. We were both med students, you were in the year above me. The faculty's New Year party was the first time you saw me. I performed a dance on stage, but wasn't the star of the show. That was an older, tall girl with very long legs, but when you saw me, you plucked up the courage to go backstage and ask for my number. Through our university years, we saw each other often, but never went out. When I was studying for my master's degree, you quit your job at the hospital to come and work at the small surgery by my college. It was then that I'd figured out your intentions…that spring, we went for an excursion in the country. You couldn't drive, so you took me on the back of your bicycle, and rode for a very, very long time…"

Her voice reverberates in the small room; every word like the beating of a hummingbird's wing, echoing against my rigid eardrums. As I listen, I fall into a reverie. What she describes feels strange, like it happened to another person. I feel a little sad—indeed, the moment I was bitten, I died and became another thing. Now I am loitering on the other shore of the Styx, listening to the past from beyond its waves. A past that no longer seems real.

But I like hearing about it.

In the days following, I don't go out lurching around town, but stay in the flat, listening to Huang talk of the past. In her voice, an image of Hui gradually gains clear outlines, enabling me to see the 'me' on the other side of the shore. Sometimes as I listen, I drag up the Stiffened muscles on the corner of my mouth, and try to smile.

Occasionally, I go downstairs to look for new supplies for Huang. There are many supermarkets in the city, so food can be found without much effort. The only thing is that when I run into other Stiffs, lying becomes unavoidable—especially with Old Jim.

"Why are you still eating all this rubbish?" Again, Old Jim puts himself in front of me, waving both hands. "Junk food is bad for you, try and cut down on it."

"Smoking's bad for you, you shouldn't smoke so much."

"It's not going through my lungs, so I won't get lung cancer," he says. "My lungs rotted away ages ago."

We stared at each other, and break into laughter. The difference is, he waves his hand, indicating a smile, but I'm automatically lifting the corner of my mouth.

He grabs a couple of crisps from the packet in the trolley, puts them in his mouth and chews. The chewed up crumbs fall out from the hole in his face, scattering in the breeze. "It's not very good," he gestures, lifting his head.

There's a faint rumble in the sky, there's going to be heavy storm.

"It'll rain soon, spring rain." He stumbles away, dragging his feet.

The other Stiffs are easy to deal with: a greeting would suffice. They would inevitably signal to complain of their hunger. It's strange, but since meeting Huang, the Hunger that has long tormented me has become somewhat dormant, like a poisonous snake that's lost its teeth. "Looks like you've eaten your fill somewhere," they would say, indicating their envy. I find their movements a lot slower than before. Maybe it's because rain is coming, and the heavy humidity in the air is acting like a gel. Of course, it could also be the lack of hunting for too long, causing their bodies to become even more rigid.

But this has nothing to do with me. The rain feels unsettling, and I'm even more worried about Huang being alone at home.

As soon as I reach the apartment block, it begins to

pour, lightning occasionally tearing the night sky. Flashes of electricity reveal the silhouettes of tall buildings, silent and giant like primeval beasts, very quickly returning to the shadows. The Stiffs are no longer roaming: they crowd under the eaves of buildings and stare at the rain in a stupor. Of course, we won't catch colds from being soaked, and the rain would actually wash away the mud and congealed blood on our bodies, along with the germs in the complex bacterial makeup of our wounds. It's only a bit uncomfortable—but like Old Jim said, this wouldn't be appropriate for us. Think about it: who would want to see a washed and brushed up Stiff?

Tonight Huang is acting a little different from usual. She hasn't touched the food or drink, but keeps glancing outside in a daze.

"What's up?" I write.

Her gaze shifts away from the paper and fixes itself on the window. "I'm filthy, I want to take a shower," she says.

She had been in the flat for half a year, with all her bodily functions confined to a small space. Her body is covered in grime and embedded with odour. Even though I don't mind, she is, after all, a girl. I have a think. "Let me go and find you more water, so you can wash."

But she points at the rain outside the window. "I want to go out, and wash in the rain."

"Too dangerous!" I write anxiously. It's hard to imagine just how crazy the other Stiffs would become if they saw her: she would be swarmed over and bitten in no time.

"But you'll protect me, right?" She looks at me as the lightning strikes again, its splendid flash reflecting gloriously in her eyes.

Under this gaze, I feel a little unnatural. Luckily my blood vessels have dried up, or my face would have shown a blush. I remember my vows to protect her, which I had reneged on for six months. I can't possibly refuse her now.

I think about it, and write, "Let's go to the rooftop." The heavy rain would mask her human scent, and the Stiffs don't like climbing stairs, so they shouldn't be able to see the rooftop.

We climb to the top of the building, push open the door to the flat roof, and walk into the rain. The rain falls over my body and into the wound on my shoulder, causing the tingling itch to become even fiercer, like something is struggling and opening inside the flesh. But I have no space to pay the wound any mind—not when I'm staring wide-eyed at Huang in the rain.

She is holding her head back, her long black hair like a waterfall. Having been washed by the rain, her face is showing its natural fairness. She isn't satisfied with that and begins to undress: six months worth of accumulated dirt starts to dissolve away, revealing her cream-white flesh. Her body is so beautiful, her skeletal frame only slightly protruding, but so full of flesh and blood under her skin that when the water glides down her body, it forms line after line across beautiful curves.

After I became a Stiff, I lost all sense of human aesthetics, categorizing bodies only into edible and non-edible. But now, I realize how ugly I must be. A desire different from Hunger is stirring in me, and I'm shaking slightly. This isn't my fault: she is so alive and fresh, and I am so dry. She is so round, and I, so famished. But just before I step forwards, the itching returns, suppressing this rush just in time.

Another flash of lightning illuminates her body. In that instant, she lights up and shines into my wilted corneas. In the days to follow, this ray of light would remain indelible.

Having washed herself clean, she runs back over,

shivering. Back in the flat, I find some dry clothes for her to put on, her wet hair still sticking to her cheeks. "Thank you," she says as she wipes her hair with a towel. "I feel much better now."

I'm just about to write a reply when the doorbell rings. Huang's smile freezes.

"Bedroom," I write slowly on paper, "and lock the door." She picks up her clothes, stealthily walks into the bedroom and closes the door. I open the windows— letting in the wind and rain—go open the door, and see Old Jim's face on the other side.

"What are you doing here?" I ask.

Just as he lifts his hand, his nose spasms. Even though Stiffs don't breathe, their sense of smell still functions, especially when it comes to human scent. He stalks into the room, looking left, right and all around, and the Hunger craze takes over his face. I step in his way and ask again, "What's up?"

"Here, there's…" but before he can gesture any further, the windows suddenly light up, and with this comes an explosion of sound. At first I think it's a lightning flash, but the shudder of the building negates this. The sound has jolted Old Jim from his feeding frenzy. He grabs me. "The humans are attacking again."

3

EVEN AS I was charging ahead with the rest of the Stiffs, face malevolent, teeth bearing and eyes glaring, I felt numb and even a little bored. Hunger drives me to chase after flesh and blood, but sense holds me back. Rationality, however, so often incapable of standing in the way of desire, could only be turned to consider other matters. For example, how many times have the humans attacked?

After the city fell, the streets and alleys were swarming with Stiffs. After that, the remaining humans would often attack, though the aftermath of battle often left even more corpses. Some became our food, others became our kind.

Today's attack seems a little out of the ordinary.

The humans are deploying mechanised force. Like giant ospreys, the war machines sweep across the curtains of rain, dropping shell after shell. Flames bloom like flowers; the Stiffs that are thrown up into the air by the impact become the burning petals of these blossoms. Tanks are assembled in linear formation, rumbling forwards, cannons constantly spitting ammunition and tearing the frontline Stiffs into mangled limbs and torsos. Soldiers carry flamethrowers and shields, disgorging tongues of fire so dense they almost join into a barrier, lighting up the streets...suffice to say, tonight, the humans are rather fierce.

"What's the matter with them today?" asks Old Jim, gesturing to me as he runs along, roaring, malevolent, though his eyes are full of bewilderment.

"How should I know?" I reply while running. "Maybe they're hitting back with all they've got."

"That's so moving, like the finale of some Hollywood blockbuster, only we don't know who the hero is. I wish we did. I'd want to go and get an autograph."

"It's a shame we're not in the audience, or on the same side as Brad Pitt."

Old Jim bashes a riot shield out of the way, grabbing a thin man out of the crowd, and bites into his throat before hurling him aside. "Speaking of films, I haven't seen one in ages." He continues to bash away shields, and then turning to me, asks, "A handsome Stiff like me—do you think I was an actor while I was alive?"

"Weren't you a professor or a writer?"

"Being an actor's much better, professors don't make a lot of money. Writers definitely don't."

Just as we are half fighting with instinct, and half talking nonsense, the thin man who was bitten gets to his feet, his body rigid, and starts charging towards the crowd: eyes blood-red, teeth bared. The blood from the wound on his throat has already darkened and begun to congeal.

"Hello, I'm new," he signals to me in a friendly manner. "What are the rules on this side?"

"Don't run in front of a—" I begin warning, but before I can finish signing "gun", the barrel of a Gatling gun sweeps towards him, its stream of high caliber rounds tearing him into two.

As the two sides are locked deep in battle, a middle-aged, well-built officer steps out of the human ranks. Drenched through from the rain, his face is nevertheless full of resolve and determination. He waves his hand, and the troops immediately hurl out canisters of gas the size of a fist, which, upon contact with the ground, begin hissing out great clouds of purple gas.

I'm just feeling perplexed, when the Stiffs around me who have wandered into that purple fog suddenly slow their movements, as if the air has suddenly grown dense and they are being restrained by it.

"Professor Lore's research worked!" The human forces erupt into excited shouts. "Kill the devils!"

Devils? Maybe they've forgotten that, we were once their friends, neighbours and loved ones. The virus had dragged us to Hell—the other side of the Yellow Springs—

but we hadn't gone willingly.

Of course, Stiffs can't explain all this to them. What we can do is continue to charge towards the crowd, but all around us, Stiffs are slowing down and increasingly falling under the Human barrage.

The tides of Stiffs are being contained.

"Hope has arrived, here in this rain of justice!" the officer cries into the loudspeaker. "The gas we have developed has proven effective! From now on, we humans will no longer be the weaker force in this battle for survival! Pour out your rage and ammo at the zombie hoard, and purge them! Tonight, we must tame this city, so that civilization may return afresh!" As soon as he finishes his speech, majestic and rousing music blasts like battle drums from the speakers, egging the humans on to open fire on us.

Old Jim gestures a nod towards me. "Looks like this is the human hero."

"Yep, there's even a soundtrack," I agree. "In the movies, this kind of background music usually comes with the finale, when the hero is about to triumph."

"Let him win. It's time us extras clocked off."

Before Jim finishes signing, the officer's feet slip on the wet metal and he falls off his tank, just as a Stiff is pouncing forwards. He bites into the officer's arm, and soon the officer gets up, red-eyed. He has switched sides, getting up and leaping over to bite his second-in-command, though the act is interrupted as his CO_2 blows his commander's brains out.

Old Jim and I look at each other, both feeling slightly sheepish.

Brad Pitt's death throws the humans into disarray. There were simply too many Stiffs, and despite their now-sluggish movements, they still advance like a sea, wave after wave.

The day is breaking, and the rain has stopped. The humans begin to retreat in a tidy manner, whilst the Stiffs chase after them, tearing and biting till the army gains distance.

"Humans are such a kind species," says Old Jim as he looks at the wreck of a battlefield, the joy of harvest on his face. "They regularly send us supplies."

After the humans have retreated and the scent of fresh blood clears from the air, my Hunger vanishes, and I lose interest in the blood and meat that are now covering the ground. Replacing it is that tingly itching sensation from my shoulders, as if a little worm is gnawing at the wound. "What's happening?" I give it a scratch, only for the itching to grow even stronger.

"Why?" Old Jim doesn't seem to have noticed my bewilderment: he's preoccupied with something else. "Why did their movements slow down when the Breathers released that purple gas?"

"It might be a...new kind of weapon?"

"Then why didn't it affect us two?"

I think about it. "I don't know. Maybe they are planning something. Something big."

Old Jim nods. "Let's hope so. Every time the Breathers retreat, they leave behind so many corpses, and return with fewer and fewer humans. What if, one day, we really end up winning? What if this planet gets covered with Stiffs, no one left alive, then—"

"Don't worry," I reassure him, "that would break the rules of movie story-telling. It won't happen."

"That's true. In almost all stories, we get destroyed. It's only a matter of time."

Back at home, Huang asks me fearfully what had happened outside.

Before this time, human attacks had been relatively small

scale; and she had been hiding in her room since I left, filled with fear, and so was unaware of the Breathers' attempting to retake the city. In her imagination, the whole world had fallen and she was the only uninfected human left: but she had refused to die of despair, her sole motivation to survive being my final words to her.

I promise I'll come back to your side. I will protect you.

I never thought the words I had spoken before I died would have such power. Thinking about it now, what girl would not be moved after hearing these words? Even hearing it myself is causing little flutters in my heart.

Noticing I'm in a daydream, Huang repeats her question.

I come to my senses and immediately recount the Breathers' attack.

When I finish, she nods thoughtfully in the glimmers of dawn. Her slightly furrowed brow is like a spring hill covered in green grass. This unease would stay with her, and it distracts her a little when she talks to me again of the past. I know she'd been frightened all night and must be tired, so I let her rest. Descending the stairs, I return to the streets.

After a night of battling, the city is even more of a mess, but for Stiffs? Nothing makes any difference. After the blood runs dry, we are no longer driven by Hunger and continue to wander the streets, aimlessly. The sun emerges from behind the skyscrapers, its reddish rays shining across them, pouring down like a layer of rouge and making the roads and alleys blush. We lean back our heads and look towards the rising sun.

"It's so beautiful," I exclaim. "Reminds me of a poem—

When the sun rises, the river flowers are redder than the sky,
The sun illuminates Incense Burner Peak, whence

violet smoke is rising.[36]*"*

"Yes, like an ink wash landscape painting at the edge of the sky. There's also a Picasso feel to it. Makes me think of that famous one, *Impression: Sunrise*," Old Jim gestures in reply.

Next to us, the Stiff with a hand missing gestures painfully. "I thought Picasso painted with oils?"

"*Impression: Sunrise* was Monet," adds another Stiff with half his head blown off, and after some thought, his arms begin to dance slowly. "Picasso is a modernist. I remember learning this in art history."

As they discuss art, I bask in the light of dawn. That feeling from the strange thing in my shoulder reminds me of its presence again, even more irritating than before. I'm just holding out my hand to touch it when Old Jim runs round from behind me, signing in astonishment. "Take a look at your back! A flower is growing there!"

Half-Head finds some mirrors, and together with One-Arm, they stand, one in front and one behind me. In the reflection, I see the wound on my shoulder has split open, grey-white and dirty—but amidst the rotten flesh, there, precariously peeping through, is a little shoot with three green leaves and a flower bud.

Two of the leaves are just about the size of a fingernail each, embracing a light blue bud, yet to open, which looks like a sleeping baby. I can vaguely make out, on the outermost petal exposed between the leaves, some blood-coloured veins. They are all connected to a thin stem, which in turn is deeply buried in the split of the wound;

---

36 These are the first lines of two Tang Dynasty poems, the first line is from Bai Juyi's "Remembering the South", and the second from Li Bai's "Gazing at a Waterfall on Mount Lu".

its roots had been tightening round and intertwining with the rotten flesh on my shoulders.

"Wow, a life nurtured on the body of a Stiff?" One-Arm has become very excited. "This is a miracle of Nature!"

Half-Head chimes in, "I think when you scratched your shoulder, a seed fell into your flesh. We're Stiffs, so our wounds don't heal, but rotten flesh provides plenty of food, and last night's rain gave it the moisture needed to take root, grow, and flower. The survival instinct in seeds is very strong, I remember learning this in biology class."

One-Arm asks: "How come you know so much?"

Half-Head replies: "Because I used to write science fiction books, had to do a lot of research, and so have dabbled in these subjects. My pseudonym was A...A... what was the rest of my name?"

"Asimov?" ventures One-Arm.

Half-Head is delighted, but seems to notice that something's not quite right, and signals back hesitantly: "I remember it's two syllables..."

Old Jim sees them digressing, and interjects with the question, "Do either of you know what flower this is?"

The two Stiffs look at it for what seems ages, and then shake their heads: no, they don't. Holding hands, they slouch off, discussing art and literature as they walk.

"This must be the source of the discomfort you've been feeling," Old Jim points out. "Do you want me to pull it out for you?"

I immediately refuse. "Seeing as this is a miracle of life and a victory for biology, I should cherish it. I will nurture this flower and wait for it to bloom, and see what happens."

I continue to stand on the street, but turn my shoulder towards the sun.

The green leaf flutters in the gentle wind, and the blue

bud sways softly in the sunlight.

It isn't til after sunset, and having found a dripping roof to water the plant, that I carefully make my way home. I can't wait to share this miracle with Huang. A flower growing out of a corpse that is dead in every way—there is a kind of cruel, corrupt, yet tenacious beauty in this struggle between life and death.

But before I finish writing, she grabs hold of me, her face full of excitement.

"I'm leaving," she says with urgency. "I want to be back among humans!"

4

OLD JIM AND I are loitering at the seafront. Not far from us, a small empty boat floats into view.

I kick at the beach and a stone flies up. It rolls before it sploshes into the water, leaving a bubble on the surface before that too is engulfed by the waves. I watch it for a while, kicking another stone into the water. Old Jim sees me doing it and joins in, his stone flying further out than mine. No fair. I put more strength into the next kick, which rouses his competitiveness, but as he takes a big stride, he ends up kicking some stairs with a *crack* that should indicate breaking bone.

He frowns, taking out a cigarette and lighting it. The lit end begins to flicker.

"Tell me, what is love?" I suddenly ask.

Old Jim gives a start. "Today's topic's a bit raw. I guess spring really is here."

"Then tell me, can Stiffs feel love?"

"They shouldn't," Old Jim replies, pointing at a female zombie wandering around a little way away. "Are you interested in that girl?"

I look over. She has a fine figure, thin waist and long legs. Before her death she must have had countless suitors—but now she is grey all over, her left eyeball has fallen out of its socket and hangs down, and half of her chin's fallen off. I shake my head. "Not interested." I think again, and add, "It's not that I'm interested, I'm just asking for a friend. He's having some trouble with love lately."

"Ah, 'Asking For A Friend'... a very familiar starting point... sounds like a meme..." Old Jim wracks his brains, but can't remember, shakes his hand. "Anyhow, love needs two people, you see? If you've no interest in this female Stiff, where would the love come from?"

"What if this friend doesn't like Stiffs, but humans?" I ask very tentatively.

He looks at me for a long time, the light of his cigarette mirroring the shine in his dark eyes. Between these three points of light, I see the answer. I make the signal for 'sigh apathetically', and say, "I'll pass the message on to my friend, and persuade him to give up."

"That's right. Even Stiffs look down on Stiffs, let alone Breathers." Old Jim nods. "Besides, the space between us and them isn't just a difference of species, but the conflict of life and death. As soon as we run into each other we both want the other species gone."

A flash of inspiration occurs in my mind. "Even if this girl doesn't like my friend—as long as they can be together and never apart, isn't that a kind of happiness?"

Old Jim shakes his head. "You're wrong. Love nurtures, it doesn't forbid. Happiness is freedom, not one-sided love. If your friend can't make the girl love him, there's only one thing he can do."

"What's that?"

"Eat her." Old Jim holds out his arms and gives a big shrug, as if it's the most obvious thing.

"Is there a less... Stiff-like... manner of solving the problem?"

Old Jim is silent for a while. "Then get her to leave, help her find her own happiness, because love nurtures and doesn't forbid, happiness is..."

I interrupt his words and gesture for him to hush. Then we stand in the evening wind, contemplating. The sea before us is slowly sliding into the darkness; the wind has grown cold, and the tide is rising. The small boat gradually becomes one with the waves.

Eventually, it becomes night. The rain has stopped, the skies are clear, and the moon hangs suspended in the sky.

BEFORE I WALK out of the stairwell, I lift my head and see the moon hanging between two tall tower blocks, pouring down its pale glory. I turn my head and look at Huang next to me. The moonlight illuminates her trembling form—and the rotten skin, dead eyeballs and withered hair that have been glued all over her are also trembling.

"It's OK." I grab hold of her hand, and write in her palm, "Don't be afraid. Learn to walk with my gait, slow your breathing as much as possible."

She's still nervous. "I..." but quickly shuts her mouth, and in turn writes on my hand, "Can we make it?"

"Don't worry, we definitely will."

She takes a deep breath, and then, frowning, releases it slowly. She's covered in thickly-scented traditional medicine paste, and I know it must be horrible to breathe it straight into the nose—but at this point, there's no turning back. I take a step forwards, and she follows, learning my rigid and Stiff manner of walking, dragging her leg along the street.

The Stiffs that have filled the streets had been moving in the same lifeless manner. But as soon as we draw near, we arouse a silent commotion—the herb and fat paste that is slathered over Huang's body can't quite suppress her scent. Thankfully, as the pungent and irritable smell fills the streets, it's preventing the Stiffs from being able to instantly discern where the human scent is coming from. They stick out their noses and carry on their sluggish amble. Huang and I carefully slip though the middle of the hoard.

"Hey, don't you smell something?" a Stiff signals to me. "It's kind of like a human smell…"

"Probably just from the Breathers who attacked last night."

"Not necessarily. The ones that were meant to be meat have died, the ones that weren't have got up. Where would you find a live one?" He scratches his head, looking lost.

I pay him no more heed, and continue to walk to the end of the street. Huang follows me, imitating my every move. We move past one suspicious Stiff after another, very slowly, but without incident. After we have walked for nearly an hour, the salty, metallic tang in the air thickens, lifting my spirits—we'll soon reach the Seaside Avenue, and then straight ahead, we'll reach a vast red forest wetland where there'll be a lot fewer Stiffs. On the other side the forest are the human camps. The destination of Huang's hazardous journey.

I steal a glance at her. Underneath the cover of all that

filthy blood and rotten flesh, her anxiety-ridden face is beginning to relax.

And then, a hand pats my shoulder.

I turn around, and see the lit end of a cigarette, and then behind the reddish light, Old Jim's face.

"Where are you going?" he asks.

He happens to have touched my right shoulder, and I am suddenly inspired: "I want to give this flower some sun."

"Shouldn't you be doing that during the day? What can you do with it in moonlight? It's not a night-blooming jasmine, you know. It's grown really quickly though, and will probably flower in a few days."

I twist my head back, and even from this angle I can already see the little bud tremulously peering out, nearly reaching the height of my ear. This flower has indeed grown more quickly than the average plant, which could be thanks to the rich nutrients in my body. Thinking about it, I'm not sure whether I should be proud or helpless.

Having got no reply from me, Old Jim continues to ask, "Oh yes, how did your friend get on with his love troubles?"

I'm suddenly saddened. "He's listened to your suggestion. He agrees that love is nurture, not possession, and happiness is freedom, and not one-sided love. So he's decided to let go, and let the girl seek her own love and happiness."

Old Jim waves his hand, indicating a sigh. "Actually I was talking rubbish. If you really love her, then you should pursue her, without worrying about face or your life. Us Stiffs, we haven't got a face, or a life. We can live by this motto."

Slowly and deliberately, I signal back, "Why the fuck

didn't you say this earlier?"

"Philosophy is subjective and depends on the view of the philosopher."

Things have gone this far, and I have no way of turning back now. I fob Old Jim off with a few words, and continue along Seaside Avenue. There aren't many Stiffs on the beach, and the red forest on the far side is just a big shadow. We've nearly made it through this damn night. Seeing that I've got rid of Old Jim, Huang is calming down and breathing a deep sigh of relief.

My eyelid twitches. I want to stop it but it's too late.

Her lips are slightly pouting while she puffs out the very long exhalation.

Old Jim's nose twitches, and even amidst the thick scent of herbal medicine, he has caught her scent. A peculiar growl comes out of his throat, and the rigid flesh of his face begins to twitch malevolently. I am all too familiar with this look. I step forwards, shoving Huang back behind me—in an instant, Old Jim is on top of me.

Run! I can't write, but I look over intently. Huang understands my meaning, and starts to race towards the red forest, but freezes again almost immediately. The second she moved, all the Stiffs smell the scent of human in the air, and like a swarm they begin to stir, rushing forwards on all fours and surrounding us in an instant.

The path towards the red forest is now packed with Stiffs. Huang stops, and looks back at me despairingly.

I push Old Jim away, desperately search around me, and quickly notice the rowing boat bobbing in the water. Stiffs can't swim. Before I know it I'm lurching as fast as I can towards the shoreline, having grabbed Huang's hand.

All around us, the sound of gathering footsteps drown

out even the sound of the waves. Those wooden-faced Stiffs on the shore have now all become crazed. If even one of them grabs Huang, she'll be torn to pieces in an instant. Fearful of this, I quicken my pace, dragging Huang along with me. On the jetty she stumbles, grazing her calf on the boarding plank, and starts to bleed.

The scent of blood mingles with the sea wind and spreads rapidly. All the Stiffs are now acting like they've been pumped with steroids. They rush forwards, wave after wave, the first line tumbling down, and the one behind stomping over them, until they in turn tumble over and are trampled on. Soon they form a two-metre high wall of bodies, seething towards us.

To be honest, in the moment, the bloodlust almost overtakes me too, but the thought of the growing flower on my shoulder and the warmth of Huang's hand in mine suppresses the Hunger just as quickly as it surfaces.

The moment before we are mobbed by the Stiffs, I manage to untie the rope anchoring the boat, and hop into it with Huang. The boat is only suitable for two or three people, and nearly capsizes as we land in it. Behind us, new waves of Stiffs roll into the water, generating a tide, and coincidentally propelling the little boat out to sea. I grab the oar, and bring it down viciously on the head of the nearest Stiff, using the impact to push the boat out further. It's only after smashing him that I realize the unlucky Stiff is none other than Old Jim. "Can't you bash someone else?" he signals and continues to rush towards us red-eyed, but is immediately shoved into the water by the Stiffs behind him.

I know that in his heart he doesn't want to stop me, and neither do the other Stiffs, but their bodies are seized by the insatiable Hunger, out of their control. I see

Old Jim re-emerge from the Stiff-wall, baring his teeth and attempting to bite me, whilst his hands are saying, "Goodness, I knew this 'friend' you were talking about was you."

Another Stiff rushes towards the boarding plank that's been seized by the one in front of him, but I knock him off, and as he sinks into the water he signals, "Are you leaving us?"

"Row fast, push the oar in deeper, so we can't catch you," signs a Stiff as he pounces on us. Although his arms are stretched out threateningly, his hands are conveying well wishes.

"Are you leaving us for this girl?"

"I hope you'll be happy."

"Phew, that was close, I nearly got that plank."

"The water's freezing."

Huang and I keep rowing till the boat is about twenty metres out. The undead raft of Stiffs is slowing down and gradually being engulfed by the sea. We row out a further dozen metres and turn around: all we can see is a dense block of Stiff heads, glaring horribly at us, but they are all trying hard to lift their hands out of the water, and flick their fingers out.

Huang is exhausted and leans on the edge of the boat, panting. I continue to row until I'm absolutely sure the Stiffs won't be able to catch us, then I lift my hand and begin to flick my fingers in the same manner.

"What are you all doing?"

I take her hand, and write on her palm slowly, "Saying goodbye."

* * *

5

ALL THIS FRIGHT and fleeing for her life soon takes its toll on Huang's body, sapping her strength. She curls up on the floor of the small boat and falls into a heavy sleep. Worrying that she might catch a cold, I take off my clothes and carefully cover her with them. She has cleaned off her Stiff disguise, and sleeping, she looks like a small animal. The little boat rocks ever so slightly, like a cradle, and on her face, the semblance of a smile begins to spread. This is the first time she's smiled since we've been reunited.

I watch her for a long time, before lifting my head, and becoming suddenly aware of the giant moon that appears to be dangling over the sea.

I have never seen the moon this big, nearly occupying half of my field of vision and hovering so low, as if I could touch it just by holding out my hand. The moon is ridiculously bright: one part falls into the horizon, and is crushed into moon dust by the waves; the other part shines onto my naked upper body, its glow like the flow of water, washing over my rigid and rotten flesh. I take a look at Huang's face and then at my own body, the beautiful and the ugly thus so lucidly illuminated by moonlight. I can't help but feel a sense of self-revulsion. Luckily the flower growing in me lends me a touch of grace. I look towards my shoulder, not sure if it's an illusion, but I seem to glimpse in the shadows a streak of fresh blood running across the necrotic flesh.

Just as I'm about to examine it, there comes a sound of water splashing by the boat, and a head struggles out of the water.

"Old Jim?" I signal in great shock.

My friend splashes around in the water weakly. I look around alertly, making sure he's the only one who's followed us, and then I relax. The sound of splashing wakes Huang, and seeing Old Jim, she jumps back, shocked. After staring at him for a while, she says suddenly, "He seems to be caught up in the mooring rope."

Now I remember that when I rowed the boat away, the rope must have gotten tangled up in Old Jim's arms, dragging him into the water. His hands being tied, he was unable to pull himself above the water—and besides, Stiff flesh sinks very quickly. However, as Stiffs don't rely on breathing to survive, he's remained with us, and must have been using the last of his energy to turn his body around, wrapping the rope round and round himself until he is above the water.

He has effectively trussed himself up like a zongzi[37] with only his head able to move: a head now staring hungrily at Huang.

Huang is no longer afraid, and begins to untie the rope from the rear of the boat, harrumphing.

I hesitate before holding out my hand to stop her.

"If you undo the rope, he'll sink," I write on her hand. "He wouldn't be able to tell directions at the bottom of the sea and may end up as fish food."

"He's a zombie. He's already dead." She pauses, her voice becoming even lower. "I'm sorry, I'm not talking about you...you're different from them..."

I'm quiet for a moment. "He's my friend."

"Then what do we do? Surely we can't pull him into the boat. It's way too small, and he'll definitely want to

---

37 zongzi 粽子, large dumpling of glutinous rice steamed in lotus leaves, usually with a savoury filling of meat, mushrooms and beans, or a sweet filling of red bean paste or dates; eaten during Duanwujie (Dragon Boat Festival).

bite me."

I scratch my head. "In that case…"

A few minutes later, Old Jim is tied to the side with dead knots, his body parallel to the keel. Suspended by the rope, he's prevented from sinking into the sea and just stays held face-up. Whenever his nose breaks from the water and he can sniff Huang's scent, his face turns into a malevolent scowl.

"The life of a monster is remarkable, able to survive like that. Were it a human, they'd long been drowned."

I write 'virus' on her hand.

She nods. "The virus has modified your body, meaning your cells have evolved, no longer needing oxygen, like anaerobic bacteria." Then, falling into deep thought, she adds, "…but the strange thing is, if it doesn't rely on oxygen, why does the virus have an affinity with flesh and blood, causing the infected to bite anyone alive they see? Also, without aerobic respiration, where does the energy for your movement come from… is it photosynthesis? But your bodies haven't been producing chloroplasts…"

I understand almost none of what she says, but I understood the last sentence. I happily shrug my shoulders and write, "I have chloroplasts." She leans over to look at the bud growing out of my shoulder, and her expression transforms. She examines it for a while, and asks about the origin of the flower. I remember One-Arm's words and reply, "Once when I was chasing humans, my shoulder was ripped open by a tree branch, and a seed must have fallen in."

"I don't know what flower this is…" She observes it closely under the moonlight, shaking her head. "I studied traditional medicine, and I grew up in this city, so I am certain this isn't a local plant."

I'm excited by this. "I'll take good care of it. When it flowers, we'll know what flower it is."

Huang looks at me. "Hui, you're really a Stiff that … stands out from the crowd."

As she speaks, the sound of splashing comes from the side of the boat. I lean over to see Old Jim struggling. He glares at Huang with eyes full of malignance, but his hands, which are tied to his waist, slowly and awkwardly sign, "Of course he stands out from the other Stiffs, that's why he loves you."

Having learned that Stiffs have a unique way of communicating, and noticing his 'talking', Huang asks me, "What is he saying?"

I rush to write, "He says you're pretty."

"Doesn't he want to eat me?"

I try to explain. "The virus wants to eat you. Every time, despite our body's urge to bite, our minds are unwilling but there's nothing we can do. The virus is too strong, but we do express our real feelings whilst we bite people."

"Thank you for your praise," Huang says to Old Jim, who growls in reply, rolling his eyes and gesturing more aggressively. She smiles and looks back to me

"Your sign language is different from the humans. How do you say 'eat'?"

I pat over my still heart with a clawed right hand.

"What about 'walk'?"

I alternate clapping the ball and tips of my hands together.

"And 'lying'?" she asks, smiling.

I press my temple with the middle finger of my right hand, and gently make a full circle, and then explain on her palm, "If you are repeating a lie, you keep doing that."

Huang's smile fades. "That's strange. This language

has no basis in any family of human languages, nor is it linked to everyday life experiences, so... even though you're dead and your vocal chords have Stiffened, you've retained memory of written and spoken language, and even have your own communication method. You don't need to breathe, and you have great physical strength. Were it not for your insatiable hunger, you'd be the higher step in human evolution."

I haven't thought about this before, but hearing it voiced, I fall into deep thought, and then slowly write, "But I still want to be human. Be with you and protect you."

Huang blushes, and looks as if she's about to speak. She hesitates, but in the end keeps her silence, turning away.

The moon hovers even lower now, like a giant disc of golden-yellow jade where the bottom edge has already penetrated the surface of the sea. Our small boat is rising and falling with the waves, drifting towards the moon. Huang sits with her side to me, and though her features are in the dark, I can see the clear outline of her profile against its light. Her silhouette looks as if it's been cut from the moon, which is nestling against her.

When daybreak approaches, I survey my surroundings. All around us is dark and still, boundless ocean.

Oh no. we've drifted out. I become anxious, and reach for Huang's hand to write on—but as soon as I touch her, I notice her fiercely high body temperature. I look at her face. Her cheeks are bright red, lips trembling, eyes tightly shut.

The constant terror of the previous night and the cold water have proved too much for her frail body, which is now burning with fever.

What shall I do, with only the sea around me, nowhere

to go, and no one to help me? I stand up and pace absentmindedly, but the boat resists and rocks, and I fall into the sea.

Old Jim is bobbing on the waterline, a shoal of small fish nibbling at him. My fall sends the startled fish scattering. Before I sink, I manage to grab hold of Jim and clamber back onboard. I turn back, and see that he's grown 'boney' in his bath. Those parts of his body which remained submerged had been stripped clean, leaving huge gaping wounds.

"If you don't pull me up," he signals sluggishly, "I'll be nothing but a skeleton."

I hurry to pull him onto the boat, but leave him bound. He lies in the stern of the boat, greedily gazing at Huang who lies unconscious at the bow, but his hands say, "She seems to be ill."

"I know."

"If she doesn't get treated in time, she'll die."

"We can't get to medicine or a doctor in time. Can you save her?"

"I know how to save her, doesn't need drugs or a doctor. A very good way."

I am filled with joy, and immediately signal back, "What way?"

Old Jim replies, slowly and deliberately, "While she's breathing, break an artery, infect her, and wait till she becomes a Stiff. That way, she won't die."

I hurl myself down into the boat, and sign back dismally, "She won't live, either!"

"But you'll be the same species, and you can be together ever after."

"You said, love is nurturing, not—"

"My mouth is an arse, my words are farts. How could

you take them seriously?"

I look at Huang. Though her face is concealed in the deepest dark before dawn, I remember her loveliness. No, she can't be turned into a Stiff. Besides, I gave her my word. Even if I fail to protect her, I should not hurt her.

Old Jim sees my hesitation, and pauses before moving his hands again. "Since you won't take my very good suggestion, there's only the crap move left."

I look at him numbly.

"Row to shore, take her to the Breather camp. They'll have medicine."

I shake my head and sign, "Don't be stupid. I don't even know which way the shore is, how I can take her?"

Old Jim cranes his neck, pointing his chin at the last star in the sky, the only light in the dark. "That's Venus. This time of year, it is in the south. The shore is west, that's your guide."

I'm bursting with joy. "Why didn't you say so earlier?"

But if we could get Huang back to the humans, the first thing they'd do wouldn't be to save her, but to kill Old Jim and me. I had considered this outcome before, but was still resolute in taking her on her journey. I am silent for a while, and then I sign to Old Jim, "Death, that's the only end for us. But she's got a long way ahead of her."

His fingers twitch, but express nothing, and slowly fold back together.

I row westwards, till the boat gradually finds the shore. A glimmer of daylight appears on the horizon, and in the distance I can see the large and luscious shadow that should be the red forest. I worry there may still be Stiffs on the shore so don't beach us straight away, but crank up my rowing, following the coast around the forest towards the end of Seaside Avenue. The morning sun rises behind us.

"Further ahead should be human territories," says Old Jim. "Do you remember the last time the humans staged an attack? We scaled that hill in a rush, driving humanity right back?"

I'm rowing, and have no way to talk to him.

He continues, "That was the time you got the wound on your shoulder. So many of us Stiffs charging, yet we were stopped by the Breathers. Now there's just the two of—no, I'm tied up, so it's just you. Do you think you can put her back into human hands?"

The question has been bothering me too. The humans are so afraid of being bitten that as soon as they see me, they're bound to open fire on us and turn me into a walking sieve. But there's no other way. We'll just have to take it one step at a time.

The little boat skips around the red forest and nears the shore. There used to be a park here, but that had long been destroyed: charred holes from artillery shells mark every foot. There's a slope at the shore, just as Old Jim said. Last time we chased the humans, I was scratched by a branch here, which left a wound. Now I survey my surroundings and not even a tree is left, only scorched trunks on the ground. This ought not to be the scene of early spring, but war destroys everything.

"You stay here." I turn towards Old Jim. "When I've dropped her off, I'll come back and we'll return to the city together."

"Don't overthink it. If you can get her there, that'll be achievement enough."

I lower my head, picking up the delirious Huang in my arms, and walk up the slope. I take only a few steps before the crisp sound of a gunshot shatters the dawn. Shocked,

I lift my head and see a squad of human soldiers lined up on the other side of the slope: six in total, fully armed and weapons trained on us, watching us alertly. I'm standing on the top of the slope, with the morning sun at my back, so they can't immediately make out my appearance—but are firing nevertheless, out of caution.

. The instant I see them, the Hunger rushes up from my guts again, and almost subconsciously I am urged to run towards them, but the itchy tickle on my right shoulder has never been so intense, spreading throughout my body, including my throat. I turn my head to look at the flower on my shoulder, and see it basking in the morning light, gently swaying in the sea breeze. Overnight, the bud has grown again, and its colour has grown to an even a richer azure. Some stamen are peeping from the petals. The instant I see them, the eternal Hunger that torments me vanishes without a trace.

The soldiers slowly surround us.

They are so close that I can't possibly escape. This grassy slope, ravaged by the flames of war, will be the end of my journey. I place Huang on the slope. She is still delirious, and her cheeks are as ruddy as the clouds at dawn. I take one last lingering look at her, and step several metres away to the side, raising my hands to indicate I'm not a threat.

The soldiers advance suspiciously, til they can make out my pallor. They grow pale too, and with a whoosh, raise their guns.

I close my eyes. The next thing I will hear is their gunshots. Hopefully then they'll find that Huang is still breathing, and save her.

"Wait," someone says, "this Stiff seems a little different."

"Yeah, why wasn't he running towards us?"

"Is he surrendering?"

"It's the first time I've seen one so terrified…"

They still keep their guns on me, filled with doubt and wariness. Someone spots the little boat by the shore, and shouts, "There's another zombie there…he seems to be tied up."

The one who looks like the leader mutters, "Professor Lore's been buying up live Stiffs recently, and we've just run into these three. One passed out, one already tied up, and the other non-aggressive. They've pretty much landed in our laps…let's take them back."

They truss me up securely, and carry Old Jim over. Another soldier is just about to tie Huang up, but balks. Putting a finger to her nose, he reports, "Captain! This girl's still breathing!"

"She's not a Stiff?"

"Shouldn't be."

My unbeating heart is finally at rest.

However, when the Captain finds out that Huang is human, he looks disappointed, as if the reward for rescuing humans is far inferior to that of enslaving Stiffs. He looks Huang up and down, and shakes his head. "How come she's so thick with the Stiffs? Maybe she's their spy."

"Maybe she's been bitten, she's got a temperature," the soldier says.

"There isn't enough medication in the camps…better leave her here. Live or die, that'll depend on her luck."

They stand me and Old Jim up, and stride westwards. I freeze and begin to struggle. I'm kept still, but only by the squad's combined strength. The captain walks over, and viciously knocks me in the head with the butt of his rifle, frowning. "You were behaving just then, why are you kicking off now?"

Still dizzy from the knock, I strain my neck, trying hard

to look behind me. Huang lies on the slope, hidden in the shadows. I can't see her clearly, but I struggle again, despite being tied tightly with belts and spare rope. I can't resist the force of the whole squad, who lift me up, blocking Huang from my view. I can no longer see her.

The itch in my throat becomes fierce, like a seed struggling to penetrate the soil. I open my mouth, and shout, "Wait!"

The soldiers freeze. The captain looks at me, stunned. Even Old Jim is looking around him, his sight at last falling on me. He opens his partially missing mouth, his jaw hanging open in genuine surprise for once.

"Please, I beg you, save her!" I continue to shout.

And then, I freeze too.

6

"SHUT YOUR MOUTH!" the captain roars at me.

But I couldn't. "You don't understand, when you lose something for so long and finally get it back, you cherish it even more, like love and health, like your voice. When I became a Stiff, the part of my body to go permanently stiff was—don't look at me like that, I mean my vocal cords. Rigor mortis set in, and I could only talk with hand signals. But the voice is a gift of gods, the cry of beasts, the chirping of birds, the rustle of the wind and the splash of waves of the sea, each their own music. Besides, if I want to be with someone, I can actually tell her that I love her, and oh, Captain, has anyone ever told you they loved you? Ah...ah, judging by your face, that's a no... doesn't matter, doesn't matter, there's still time, before you become a Stiff too... Don't hit me! Don't hit me!... I'm just expressing the joy of being able to talk again. If you don't believe me ask this ugly old Stiff—Old Jim, if you could talk again, wouldn't you be chattering non-stop like me?

Old Jim signals, "Shut the hell up!"

I turn to address him. "Looks like you don't empathise. Even though we have a set of hand signs, the best way to communicate is still the spoken word. When people hold out their arms, it's to hug each other, not to fight. Before I could speak, every time we communicated, we could only do so face to face. To be honest—and please don't get angry—every time I saw you I felt really uncomfortable, you weren't good looking to start with, and as a Stiff you just got uglier, with a hole in your face. All this I can tolerate, but why do you put a cigarette in your lips if you can't actually smoke? Now I don't have to look at you to talk to you. Don't be upset, if you were half as good-looking as Huang, I'd be talking to you every day, isn't that right, Huang?"

Huang, just regaining consciousness, murmurs without energy, "Please, I beg you, stop talking. It's hurting my head hearing it."

I let out an "oh" and shut my mouth.

An hour ago, I had opened my mouth and spoken— not only to the surprise of the others, but also perplexing myself. This makes me a very special Stiff. The captain had at once consulted his senior in the camps, and by the sound of it, someone called Professor Lore. Over the phone, Professor Lore's voice sounds very excited, and the captain acknowledged his orders to take us in.

Worried that the Stiffs might attack, the human camps had retreated westwards by a considerable way. The soldiers are in two jeeps, but the drive back to the camps will still take time. I'm a little worried, but there's nothing we can do. Old Jim and I are both bound hand and foot, and thrust into the back seat of the car, not able to move a muscle.

I protest forcibly. "This isn't proper treatment, it's unethical."

The captain thinks about it, and nods. "You're right, thanks for reminding me," and orders his men to lock us in the boot. Old Jim and I are folded by the arms and legs and crammed in, staring at each other in the dark.

After an age, the car stops and I hear the soldiers talking. They're passing an abandoned village and have decided to gather supplies and find something to eat.

"Don't forget the pharmacy, try and find some antipyretics!" I shout from the trunk.

The captain opens the trunk, and asks me, "Why do you care so much about that girl? You're a Stiff, aren't you?"

"Before I was bitten, I was her boyfriend," I reply. "I've been protecting her all along."

The captain thinks a moment more, and says, "Then come with us."

The soldiers untie the straps round my legs and push me forwards to walk in front of them. They're using me as a scout: if there are other Stiffs around, I'd be the first to know.

Threading through the ruined streets, I can see that this used to be a small tourist town. All the streets and shops are styled with Western paraphernalia. Flowers and trees are planted by the roadside, and in the distance, the spire of a church stands against the twilight. This town had been full of local charm, though there isn't a single person on the street now, and the cobbled pavements are strewn with rust-coloured trails—clearly congealed blood. The windows and doors have all been smashed, with glass scattered all across the ground.

You could see just what a senseless massacre had burst in on this peaceful little town, when the virus began to spread.

One of the soldiers is grimacing so much his eyes look like they're about to pop, glaring at me with malice. The expression is very familiar: it's exactly the same way Stiffs look at Breathers.

A little frightened, I cower and tense my neck.

It's nearly dark, and we've been scouring convenience stores. Our luck hasn't been bad. We've found some food, water, and at my insistence, a box of Ibuprofen at the pharmacy. I hurry back to the car, check the use-by-date of the Ibuprofen, and put a couple into Huang's mouth.

Having taken the pills and gotten some rest, Huang begins to regain her faculties. The soldiers share their food, and they all eat together, whilst I'm tied up and put to one side. Watching them eating and chewing big mouthfuls of biscuits, my stomach lets out an embarrassing rumble.

The soldiers grow pale and dart their heads round, rifles poised.

I own up guiltily. "Don't worry, that was me, I'm just hungry…"

"So showing your true colours at last," says a soldier nervously. "I knew it! You want to kill us."

"No, but I could murder a biscuit."

The soldiers look at one another, and one eventually unties the belts around my wrist and chest, and hands me a biscuit. I eat it in a single mouthful, letting that sense of fullness I'd not felt for a long time permeate my stomach. "It's so good," I say with satisfaction.

"Are you really a Stiff?" asks the captain suspiciously.

"The wounds on your body, have they all rotted?"

I too am filled with confusion. It's as if a boat is moving within my body, carrying me to the other shore. My memory comes and goes, like that bird reeling in and out of the thick mist. I'm just about to reply when I notice something out of the corner of my eye. I turn to the shop across the road, where a piano is sitting in the window.

Something clicks in my head, and before I know it, I've stood up and am walking towards the shop.

The soldiers watch me cautiously.

I come to the piano, and press a key. It's a real strings-and-hammers piano. It's suffered a little from the damp and sounds a little rough. I play a few more keys, and like the flow of water from a stream, the notes clear the thick fog in my mind. In a certain corner of my memory, the frozen soil is melting. I keep playing, key after key, and a melody begins to flow.

I turn to look across the street. Still fragile, Huang's face is nevertheless filled with astonishment. The soldiers and the captains are all wide-mouthed. None of them interrupt me.

I finish the song, and return to the car. A soldier comes over with a belt, and is just about to tie me, but the captain waves his hand. I'm permitted to sit in the back seat, together with Huang.

"You didn't tell me before," I say happily, "that I played the piano when I was alive."

"This...this is the first time I've ever heard you play."

"Then how did I get you to go out with me?"

Some of the older soldiers turn their heads and give us a look. One of them mumbles, "These are strange times, playing the piano and courting girls with a flower growing out of the shoulder. Stiffs are certainly having a fine time of it."

"Actually..." Huang is just about to reply when the soldier interrupted, and she speaks no more.

The cars are moving through the night, going very slowly down broken roads. It's not until midnight that the cars reach the camp. A row of soldiers guard the gates, their faces solemn, their heavy armour inspiring fear. A gaunt middle-aged man stands next to a grey-haired commanding officer. His hair is a mess, and looks like it hasn't been washed for a few months—or maybe he's never washed it since it started growing. He wears glasses, but his gaze is sharp and penetrating through those thick lenses. I feel it burning as he looks at us.

After saluting the officer, the soldiers nod at the middle-aged man and address him by name: "Professor Lore."

The professor does not acknowledge them, but walks straight through the group, coming to a stop in front of me. He stares at me for a long time, until he begins to look deranged and I begin to feel a little uncomfortable. Then he mutters, "Indeed, an unusual case! I must investigate!"

The grey-haired officer prevents him from touching me, and—regarding me suspiciously—orders the captain to have me caged.

7

THE "CAGE" TURNS out to be a bare locked room. One of the walls holds a large mirror; the other three are painted clinical white. Apart from a desk and a chair, it is empty. I spend most of my time facing the mirror, grimacing. Once I opened my mouth to find that my gums had swollen, with a few well-supplied blood vessels showing through them: no longer the dried and sunken layer of grey skin they were before.

"What's happening?" I ask myself, a little bewildered. "Am I turning back into a human?"

Over these last few days, fragments of memory have returned. The layout of the room looks familiar from many films I've seen. The interrogation rooms all look exactly like this. I can only see myself in the mirror, but people outside can see me as if through transparent glass.

I wave my hand and say, "Is there anyone on the other side? Hi..."

I imagine the people on the other side flinching and taking a few steps back.

Sure enough, as soon as I've spoken, the door is pushed open and Professor Lore enters. He is flanked by four soldiers, two of whom train their guns on me whilst the other two tie me to the chair.

I don't resist one tiny bit.

"You really aren't like the other zombies." He rubs his hand, looking at me. "What's happening to your body? Is the Necrona virus mutating?"

I ignore his question. "Where is Wu Huang?"

Professor Lore continues to watch me, monologuing excitedly. "Our investigations have brought us right to the inner workings of the Necrona virus. As soon as there is contact by blood, 100% infection, 100% death. Your heart and lung functions, language capabilities, digestive system...should have all fallen apart. This process should, in theory, be irreversible." He looks me up and down. "What happened to you?"

His speech has such urgency, like a burst of machine gun fire; and there's such thirst in his eyes as he regards me, seeing me as a rare treasure rather than a dangerous stiff. What a typical scientist. I persist with my own question. "Wu Huang, where is she?"

"Ah ah, the girl, she's very well…"

Professor Lore instructs one of the soldiers to insert a needle into my artery. I protest. "Don't waste your time, I don't have…" And then I stop. As the plunger pulls back, a dark brown liquid appears in the barrel: thick and very sticky, but it is indeed blood.

Professor Lore's face is filled with astonished joy, and he quickly puts the syringe into a coldbox and then rushes out of the door.

The guards know that I've eaten biscuits before, and have delivered me standard food every day. They're very curious about me. When I bury my head in the food, they'd ask about this and that. After responding, I would in turn ask them questions. "Oh yeah, what kind of a person is Professor Lore?"

Looks of reverence would appear on the soldiers' faces. Professor Lore may not care about his appearance, but even before the outbreak he already held a doctorate in diseases, and had published several essays in the leading medical journals. After the outbreak, he focused all his energies on researching Necrona and finding a solution to this apocalyptic calamity. He's invented a lot of anti-Stiff drugs. The slowing down of Stiffs' movements I had noticed in the city was due to a stiffening drug Doctor Lore had hidden in the bodies of corpses before floating them towards the shore for the Stiffs to consume. Activated by the purple spray, they were able to effectively slow down the collective movement of a large group of Stiffs, and reduce their strength in battle.

"I never thought this nerd would be so kickass." I can't

help but admire him.

Over the next few days, Professor Lore comes to take my blood every day, and every day the shock on his face deepens. Sometimes he walks around and around me, mumbling to himself: "What's happening here...he appears to have no physical anomaly, so why is he so different? Is it the flower on his shoulder?"

As soon as I hear this, I hurry to say, "Why would it be that? You might be a great scientist, but the flower wasn't grown for you to experiment on."

"Then for whom?"

"For Huang," I say slowly. "My girlfriend from the previous life."

Hearing this, Professor Lore looks thoughtful.

Maybe these words have an impact, because the next day Huang comes to see me. The mirror has been adjusted so I can see through the glass. We face each other, and whilst she looks very happy, her words are completely silenced by the glass. I can't hear her but I can see her smile, so I'm very happy too. I feel the flower on my shoulder swaying in the radiance of that smile.

After that day, I don't see Huang for a very long time. The way the guards look at me has also changed. The dislike and fear are still there, but mixed with some other emotion.

Something must have happened outside, and instinct tells me that it must have something to do with Huang.

Today, the guard leaves at the end of his shift, but his replacement doesn't come. I'm a little curious, and give the door a push. To my surprise, the steel door swings open at my touch.

I call out, but there's not a soul around and no one answers. I can only move forwards with suspicion. The corridor is completely empty. I walk all the way out of the surveillance area without seeing a single soldier.

I'm filled with joy, thinking maybe I could see Huang again. I sniff the air and walk westwards, towards where the scent of humans is at its thickest.

At dusk, the sun is deathly pale, and a flock of birds flies through the woods in which this camp is hidden. I advance, but stop again—with me looking like this, I'd scare the hell out of the humans. So I avoid the open tented areas, and advance via the surrounding woods, hoping to hear Huang's voice.

After a while, night descends and I've not heard Huang's voice—though I do run into someone.

"Who is it?" a female voice in front of me asks suspiciously.

By the light from the tents in the distance, I can vaguely see a little girl standing in front of me: about ten years of age, wearing a tattered skirt, looking at me curiously.

She must have come out to play, or gather firewood. The light is too dim for her to clearly see my decayed grey face and rotten wound. I'm only a fuzzy profile. She stares at me curiously, before asking, "Are you lost too?"

"You're lost? Then let me take you back," I reply.

I take her hand, and walk towards the lights showing through the trees.

"Your hand's freezing," she complains.

I'm a little embarrassed, and shift my hand so I'm holding her arm through my clothes. "Is this better?"

"Much. Actually, it doesn't matter if you're a little bit cold."

It's getting late, and a rustling sound comes from the bushes behind us. I looked down at the little the girl who is carefully treading ahead. I can't help but ask, "Aren't you scared? There might be Stiffs around."

"My mum said the Stiffs aren't scary anymore," she replies. "A Stiff came to the camps recently, with a flower growing from his body. It's blue and so pretty, and he doesn't bite. If every Stiff is like him, then I'll be home very soon!"

I feel a secret gush of joy at this, and ask her another question. "Where do you live?"

The little girl scratches her head. "I've forgotten..."

Another rustling in the grass as we walk past, and the little girl cries, "Ouch! My hand, it's bleeding..."

She doesn't need to tell me, because my nose is already in a spasm and my teeth have started chattering. The Hunger that has been a stranger lately overtakes my head, and I experience a bout of dizziness.

"It's me that's been scratched, how come you're moaning?" she asks, confused.

Her tender young voice shocks me out of my bloodlust. I squat down, tearing off a piece of my clothing, and wrap up the wound for her. Fortunately, it isn't deep. Perhaps she got scratched by a branch: it's nothing that a plaster and some iodine won't solve.

Holding hands, we walk into the tented area, where people gather to look at us, all shocked. A woman charges towards me, pulling the girl away and retreating a couple of steps, staring at me cautiously.

"She got lost, so I took her home," I explain.

The woman looks at the girl, who nods her confirmation. She hesitates before expressing her thanks in a low voice.

The way that people look at me softens a bit. One of the crowd plucking the courage up to approach me, before turning round to the others, amused. "He really doesn't bite...

More people walk over, and pinch my skin with curiosity. There are some who notice the flower on my shoulder, and admire it. "This flower's beautiful, this Stiff's just as charming." Amidst all this praise, I can feel myself blushing.

Huang emerges from the crowd. She surveys the scene, but her gaze is also on me. The night has thickened and the tents are all lit up, like so many fallen moons in the night, all embracing her.

Returning her gaze, the blossom on my shoulder starts to vibrate as if the wind is caressing it, as if it's squirming. The crowd's eyes open wider. I start, and turn to look at it: the bud is opening at a speed the naked eye can see. Even though the blue petals are small, and the bud is packed so tightly, the fragrance is spreading all around us

"The flower's blossomed?" Huang comes close.

"Yes, on seeing you," I reply, "it's blossomed."

She holds out a hand to touch it, but retracts. I immediately pluck a petal, feeling a slight pain in doing so, and frown slightly.

"What's wrong?"

"Nothing. This petal is for you."

Just as Huang takes it and is about to say something, a group of soldiers push through the crowd, and I am escorted back to my cell.

Soon after, Professor Lore comes to see me. Still dirty and disheveled, his eyes are bloodshot, as if he hasn't slept for days. He approaches me and I instinctively recoil. "Your hands are filthy, please don't touch me..."

"Then come with me."

"To where?"

"To see your friend, the other one who was with you.

Your body is now different from a Stiff's. I need to see how one of them would react to you."

He takes me to an observation cell where Old Jim and a collection of other Stiffs are kept. As soon as the door opens, the Stiffs begin to growl. Lore shoves me into the room and locks the door behind me.

The Stiffs gather around me.

I'm a little scared. After all, blood has started flowing in my body, and maybe this is enough to rouse the terrible Hunger.

But Old Jim stares at me for a long time, then lifts his head, and signs, "You've got fatter."

"You've got uglier," I reply.

The other Stiffs signal me their greetings. "Have you been locked up here all along?" I ask.

"Yes," they reply. "At first there were lots of Stiffs, but one by one they were dragged out, apparently for tests, and never came back. We're all that's left."

The Stiffs chat along with me nicely, without even a hint of the intent to attack. When Lore enters with his soldiers, the Stiffs charge towards them. The soldiers fire netting which wraps around them, while Lore drags me out.

"I'm still catching up with them…" I complain.

Outside, my eyes brighten when I see Huang standing there. A smile fills her whole face. Gazing at me, she says, "Hui, I want to borrow something from you."

"Anything you like!" I immediately strike my chest.

She points to my shoulder. "Another of your petals."

In the few days I'd been locked in the observation room, Huang had not been idling. After she returned to the camps, she thought about the changes in my body. If I could revert from a Stiff towards a human—in other words, come back over the river of death which I had already crossed—then there is the possibility that other Stiffs could do so too.

She'd reported my condition to the Survivors' Committee, and while some members agreed, others objected, and the two sides had fought to a standstill. It wasn't until I had appeared in the encampment holding the little girl's hand that they finally recognised that I'm not like the other Stiffs.

Huang had considered the issue for a long time. The only difference in my body was the flower growing out of the wound. Gathering her thoughts, she'd rushed to find me, and heard from the guards that I've been brought to Old Jim, so ran over.

I look into her eyes, and say, "The flower was grown for you in the first place. If you want to pluck it, of course you can."

As words leave my lips, the soldiers stare at each other. Even Lore is twitching his eyebrow, grumbling. "I never thought we'd be subjected to dreadful pickup lines during the apocalypse."

"We were lovers before," I reply.

Huang blushes, and immediately protest, "I don't need the whole thing, just a petal." Getting me to stand still, she carefully extracts a petal with tweezers, places it into a cold box and passes it to Lore. "You could analyze it and make it into medicine."

Professor Lore acts as if he's received a treasure, nodding incessantly.

Three days later, the first serum based on the flower appears. The whole camp is very excited, crowding around the lab to watch the injection of the serum into the body of a wild Stiff. I'm taken back to the room where

Old Jim is being kept.

Professor Lore hasn't slept in three day: his eyes are even more bloodshot, but his face is animated, and his hands shake slightly.

"This is the world's hope," he says. "If every Stiff can revert to a human, then we can once again embrace those loved ones we have lost."

These words create a ripple in the crowd, and some people's eyes are shining with tears.

Under the gaze of everyone, he injects the serum into Old Jim, who is tightly bound to a chair, and then leaves the observation room.

Once he exits, Lore presses a button. In the two-way mirror, I can see the belts holding the Stiffs down retract, and several of them stand up and lurch around the room. Only Old Jim remains sitting, swaying his head, as if hesitating.

Seeing him behave differently from the other Stiffs, I feel a spurt of joy in my heart. Huang, who's standing next to me, begins to smile.

"My theory was not wrong! The flower on your shoulder, really is an anti—"

She hasn't even finished before the sudden change in the observation room. Old Jim shoots up straight, the rotten flesh on his face a craze of contortions, exposing his black teeth as he starts to thrash around wildly. As he moves, a low, hoarse hissing comes from his throat.

The Stiffs are confused and gesture at Old Jim, attempting to communicate, but receive no response.

Huang and I glance at each other, neither having a clue what's happening.

Suddenly, Old Jim throws his head back as if to roar, but only a low and croaking growl erupts. After "roaring", he whips round and rushes towards the nearest Stiff, biting into his arm and violently jerking his head back, tearing off the whole arm.

A gust of blackish gore spews from the wounded Stiff, splattering across the glass before slowly dripping down the surface, tinting our vision black-red.

8

AFTER THE FAILURE of the serum, I'm taken back to my cell. This time, no one comes to visit me for days. The glass wall has reverted to its mirror state, and the soldiers just pass in the food in to me with no conversation

I'm more worried about Huang. She'd tried her utmost to make an opportunity, hoping to find the cure for Necrona in my little flower—only for the serum to drive Stiffs to a frenzy, now attacking even their own kind. She must be pretty upset by this level of setback. "It's all your fault," I turn to say to the plant on my shoulder, which still seems to sway. "You good-for-nothing weed."

Just when I feel I'm going to die of boredom, the door is pushed open, and Professor Lore enters with guards. "Come with me."

I follow him, walking out of the security zone and through the refugee camp. A lot of people gaze at me with a peculiar look in their eyes, but don't get near me. I'm a little hurt, and ask Lore softly, "What's the matter with them? They seem scared of me?"

Lore turns his head. Under the thick lenses of his glasses, his gaze looks a little dull. He replies softly, "It's not fear, it's reverence."

"Oh? Why is that?"

"Because you're about to become a hero."

I start. "What's going on?"

Lore sighs, shaking his head. "Let's talk when we get in."

Very soon, I'll know what I'm to help with. We reach the army's command centre and several solemn-faced, armed officers surround me. Heading the delegation is the grey-haired officer who'd 'welcomed' me at the entrance on that first night.

"The serum of extracts from that flower failed to work, proving that you are a one-off case, and that we can't build our hopes on reverting your kind back into humans." The officer narrows his eyes at me, his gaze falcon-sharp. "Therefore, we have decided to organize a counter-attack."

"But haven't you've tried that many times before? Each time just getting chased back by the Stiffs?"

The officer gives a false cough. "You can't call it being 'chased back', but rather a strategic retreat...anyway, this time, we have a magic bullet in Professor Lore's new invention, the ZF-III Virus..."

Lore, standing to one side, intercedes softly, "The ZF-III isn't ready yet, and Phase IV is also just a theory. It needs peer review and testing ..."

"War is the best test," the soldier interrupts. "The ZF-III virus is entirely your creation, so please explain it to us."

At the mention of his virus, the Professor's spirits rise again. Taking a test tube out of the metal case next to him, he holds it up to my eyes. An icy blue liquid is swirling inside. Under the light, this half-full container looks beautiful yet ominous.

"ZF stands for 'Zombie Freeze'. Of course, it's just a figure of speech and it can't literally freeze the Stiffs, but it can slow down their movement, and ultimately cease all locomotion in a Stiff's body, leaving them truly dead. Don't worry, ZF-III has no harmful effect on humans. It reacts to the Necrona virus within the bodies of the Stiffs, using it as a host—the two viruses combine and mutate the subject's body into the Phase IV state. Phase III refers to a Stiff that can move with reduced mobility and function, whereas phase IV is a completely stiff... uh, Stiff. And ZF-III is itself infectious, so will spread through the herd, removing their threat once and for all." Lore gazes at the test tube as if it were his lover, mumbling, "The scourge of zombies, but the salvation of mankind."

I'm left a little confused, so I ask, "If it's so great, why not just use it? What are you keeping me here for?"

The officer replies, "Ahem, the research on ZF-III is yet to reach maturity. So far, we've placed it inside their bodies, allowing it to directly affect their internal systems; dispersed it in vapor form into a crowd; and applied it directly onto their skin. This combination of internal and external application has indeed proven effective in slowing them down, but that's it. The ZF-III has not yet proven itself capable of causing Phase IV to a Stiff's internals, nor its ability to infect, so its usefulness as a weapon is relatively low."

I smack my head. "That's where I come in. You want to use my body as an incubator for a Phase IV virus?"

The officers glance at each other, not expecting their proposal to be worded quite so directly, and feeling mutually embarrassed.

Professor Lore scratches his head. "It's only a theory, and I still need a lot of time to test it."

The officer waves his hand, as if cutting something invisible in the air. "But we don't have a lot of time. There are more and more Stiffs every day, and if we delay any further, the light of humanity may be completely snuffed out."

Lore mutters to himself, but does not protest further.

I look from Lore's puffed-up red face, to the strong and determined expression on the officer's, and finally, to the icy blue ZF-III serum. After a while, I sigh. "OK, I agree."

Professor Lore says, "You must think about it properly. The IV virus is only a hypothesis at the moment. If it manifests in your body, I have no idea what might happen...but it's highly possible that you'll die."

Right now, I don't fear death. Perhaps it's because I've already died once. Thinking about it, being able to travel between life and death is a really cool thing. Besides, if I can stop the spreading of the virus, it means that Huang could live in a world free of danger. A gush of tragic heroism swells in my heart, and with it an almost imperceptible sense of elation—I never thought I would be the key to saving humanity; that in this Hollywood film, I'm the hero—I am Brad Pitt!

I nod.

The officer's face lights up. Lore is about to protest, but stops. He proceeds to extract the serum into a syringe, and slowly transfers it into my bloodstream. An icy cold feeling begins to pervade my blood.

"Now what?" I ask, rubbing my arm.

The officer replies, "Now you return to live among the Stiffs, and wait for ZF-III to mutate into ZF-IV. Let the virus spread among you, and end this disaster."

"The Stiffs...really can't be saved? Must they be destroyed?"

"Well, you're only a one-off. We've tried to find a cure and we've tested it. You saw the results yourself. It just turns Stiffs crazy."

I nod, remembering something that Old Jim once

said. In almost all stories, the zombies are destroyed; it's only a question of sooner or later. Despite knowing this inevitability, it's still depressing to think about.

"I have one request," I state. "I want to see Huang."

The officers exchange looks, and their eyes seem to broadcast a lot of information that I can't tune in to. Finally, the grey-haired officer nods. "I'll take you to her."

Because I have been injected with the ZF-III virus, to be safe, I'm taken in a quarantine transport.

In back of the van there are several other Stiffs, who've been tied up and strapped there—as arranged by the officer. If the ZF-III virus mutates into IV during transport, then I may as well infect them here, so when we are released the rate of infection will increase. Among them is Old Jim, who had gone berserk. The strange thing is that now that his arms and legs are restrained, his eyes seem peculiarly calm—as if the hysterical biting and tearing has exhausted all of his energy.

I ignore him, and now only have eyes for Huang, who has just rushed over, standing a foot away from the large rear windows. Behind her stand a pair of soldiers, armed, and very close.

It's only been a few days since I last saw her, but she's lost weight and looks haggard. Some loose strands of hair are trailing about by her ears.

Though the thick glass, we lock gazes.

"I have to go," I say, "back to Stiffsville."

"Mhm."

"If this disaster ever comes to an end, promise me you'll live and be happy."

She nods. "Mhm".

"Isn't there anything else you want to say to me?" I rub my nose shyly. "I know I'm probably being a pain, and even a bit corny, but this is goodbye: surely you have something to say? They always do in the movies."

Huang looks at the officer, and only when he nods does she take a step forwards. Her face is very close to mine and her breath steams up a small part of the glass, obscuring my view.

"I've hardly slept these last few days," she begins to say, pressing her temple with her right middle finger and looking very tired, as she speaks. She massages wider deliberate circles to punctuate her speech. "The flower on your shoulder *isn't* the antidote for stiffs, Stiffs *can't* turn back into humans. *Go*, I'm very *safe* here."

I nod slowly, and wave.

The van's engine starts, carrying me back to the main gate where I'd first entered. Huang's figure is standing and watching.

Suddenly, I grab my arm and fall over onto the floor of the car, shuddering.

Professor Lore notices my drop and with a start, runs over and pounds on the side of the door. "Stop the van, stop!" The driver brakes in response, and Lore shouts at me through the glass, "What's wrong? Is the ZF-III? Is it working already?"

I keep shaking. Shutting my eyes, I reply with clenched teeth, "I don't know…so cold…"

"Quick, where's the key!" Lore cries. "Open the door! The injection has taken effect early, I need to get him back to the lab!"

The driver walks round with the key, still hesitating: "Professor, what if…"

But before he finishes, Lore snatches the key and opens the tailgate doors. Jumping into the back, he bends down over and asks, "How do you feel now?"

I open my eyes, and focus on Lore's anxious face. I can't help but feel guilty, and let out a soft "I'm sorry…"

"What?"

I jump up and abruptly turn. With one hand, I snatch the gun from the holster of the dazed soldier beside Lore and wrap my free arm around Professor's neck. Before anyone can react, I have the barrel of the gun pointed at his head.

"Don't move!" I shout. "If anyone moves, I'll kill him!"

The vocal chords and tongues of Stiffs are some of the first parts to set in rigor mortis. Apart from roaring, they have no way of making more complex noises, but we have our own ways of communicating via hand signs. While we were adrift at sea, Huang had asked me to show her a few signs.

Pressing the middle finger to the temple and rubbing gently in a circular motion indicates to another Stiff that you think they're lying, or repeating a lie that you had been told.

Just then, when she was saying goodbye to me, the finger was on her temple was telling me that her spoken words were lies.

"The flower on your shoulder *is* the antidote for Stiffs. Stiffs *can* turn back into humans. *Stay*, I'm very *threatened* here."

Thinking of the armed soldiers who wouldn't leave her side, whose permission she'd needed to ask before speaking, and her wan appearance… I'm almost certain that she's a prisoner.

Even though I don't know what reason they might have for doing so, I'd made a promise to Huang that I'd always protect her. After I'd said this, I'd gone out and never returned alive. I cannot break this promise again.

Under the terrified gaze of the camp, I hold Professor Lore hostage and confront the officers. The commander is a real old hand, and without hesitation he presses his pistol against Huang's head.

"We've got one hostage each." The officer nails his eyes on me and says coldly, "But I have more people than you. So think very carefully."

Huang becomes reckless. "Don't worry about me, run! The flower on your shoulder is the antidote—what happened before was because someone tampered with it, that's why the Stiff went crazy! You have to protect it!"

Just as I thought. I glare at the commander furiously. "How could you do such a thing? Did you think curing the Stiffs would affect your position?"

"Bullshit! Put the gun down, and release the professor!"

I take a look behind me, and slowly move back, dragging Lore further in with me. "You have your men, but I'm not alone either…" I swing my hand swiftly to the wall, unhooking the straps restraining the nearest Stiff. Quickly the belts fall free. Gaining his freedom, the Stiff lets out a low growl and heads for Lore, but is thrown back by my kick. Before he gets up, he smells the pungent scent of nearer humans crowding the tailgate. Driving him even further into a frenzy, he leaps for the soldiers.

Using the same method, I release all the Stiffs one by one, leaving only Old Jim. The yard erupts into disorder: those who are bitten would very soon join the side of the Stiffs. The soldiers retreat in a panic and Huang gets free of their grasp, running towards me. She passes a Stiff, who opens her mouth, ready to bite. I yell, "On your left! Look out!" She jumps aside, and the Stiff immediately switches attention to closer prey.

She gets into the front passenger seat. I hurl Lore onto the floor and jump out.

"What now?" I ask her.

"Let's go!"

I slam the doors shut, locking Old Jim and Lore in the back, and then run round to the driver's seat—vacated, and the doors left wide open. Huang and I slam them shut; I start the engine, and we disappear in a cloud of diesel fumes and track dirt.

I throw a glimpse at the rear view mirror. Behind us the brawl continues, but the soldiers have steadied their position and are surrounding the Stiffs—one of whom leaps from the muddy ground towards an officer, only to be perforated by a rain of bullets.

Huang has also been watching this scene. She sighs softly.

9

THE VAN ROARS through the woods. With nobody maintaining the roads, weeds are encroaching from either side, and as the wheels screech as they crush over stalks and vines.

"Where are we going?" I ask as I drive.

Huang shakes her head. "I don't know…" She glimpses my hands and exclaims, "You're a pretty natural driver for a Stiff."

I look down at my hands, which hold the wheel comfortably at ten and two, and grin. "I've remembered quite a lot in the past few days."

"Then do you remember who you are now?"

"No yet…I will remember it, someday. Besides, you told me who I was ages ago."

The route ahead looks familiar. "Hang on," I think,

"isn't this the way the soldiers took us when they captured us and took us back to the camp?" I'm sensing the cyclical irony: having risked my life taking Huang out of Stiff city and into the human stronghold, we're now risking our lives to escape from the camps, and have returned down the path we came.

Through the window I see the rising hilltop, like the earth's giant green-coated tongue, rising to lick nourishment from the skies.

"Hey, what exactly happened during the last few days?" I turn my head to look at Huang's emaciated face. "How come they locked you up?"

"After that Stiff got the serum and went crazy, and the more I thought about the situation, the more I knew something was terribly wrong. So I secretly spun up a second batch from that first petal you gave me, and injected it into Old Jim. In less than half an hour, I could see that the strength of the Necrona virus within his body was weakening, and his platelets were beginning to rejuvinate. I knew that when he went crazy the first time someone must have tampered with the mixture. Someone who didn't want Stiffs to turn back into humans. But before I could take a record of the data, the commander noticed what I was doing and accused me of siding with the Stiffs. I was locked me up, and... if you hadn't asked to see me, I might never have seen the light of day."

Enraged, I slapped my hands on the wheel. "I knew he was a bad guy as soon as I saw him! I think he's scared that turning Stiffs back into humans would somehow affect his status. Hmph, latching onto power at his age! To maintain his position, he'd climb over a billion people's bleached bones."

"But we still have your shoulder flower! Let's find a

quiet place and develop the antidote." Then she frowns. "Although I studied medicine, I was only at post-grad before... I'm not sure if I'll be able..."

"It's OK, with more time and the right tools, I'm sure we can make it happen," I reassure her. Then I slap my head, stunned at my memory. "Of course, I grabbed Professor Lore, didn't I? You can work together—you *can* do it!"

Remembering Lore and Old Jim still locked in at the back, I stop the van, jump out and open the doors.

Professor Lore sits in shock. Luckily Old Jim is still securely restrained so can't hurt him. I explain everything to him and as he listens, his eyes begin to shine. He nods incessantly, and interjects, "Very good, very good!" He looks at me, then at Huang, and then at Old Jim. "The four of us can be the team that saves the world!"

"Yes, a woman, a wacky old man, a Stiff and a ..." I look at myself. "Half Stiff, half human. This would definitely look good on a Hollywood poster."

Huang is smiling too now. The afternoon sunshine lavishes on her smile. She says, "We can save the world!"

This afternoon, the world looks especially beautiful. The sun is gentle and warm, and orioles are flying among the verdant grass. The spring winds are caressing the earth. I can feel the air, fresh as water, flowing through my lungs. Everything feels like an ending on which the camera might fade out in a film. I never thought I'd live: I'm exceptionally happy.

"Then let's go!" I wave my hand. "Let us drive towards Hope."

I'm just about to restart the van when a gush of cold suddenly rushes through my arm, as if a block of ice has been shoved into my blood. A bout of trembling overtakes my body, and shivering, I keel over the driver's seat, the gun falling from my pocket onto the floor.

Huang rushes to help me up, her face full of terror. Professor Lore backs out of the van, and stares at me doubtfully. "Is it actually happening this time?"

I shiver like sugar falling through a sieve, my voice crumbling up into shreds. "I don't know, it's really cold..."

"The ZF-III is really taking effect. Is this really phase IV?"

I'm not sure, but the reaction is getting stronger and stronger. I grit my teeth. "Should be...is there a way...to save me?"

"No. My work here is done."

Upon hearing this from Lore, I sit bolt upright. Huang also takes a moment to react, turning to Lore. "What?"

"It looks like my research has been a success." Lore walks over, picking up the fallen gun, and lets his teeth show in a manic grin. "This zombie apocalypse started because of me, and will end by my hand."

When he laughs, his teeth are a gruesome bone-white, as if reflecting the cold light from an invisible dagger. All the woodenness and sluggishness in his demeanour evaporates, along with the air of the bookish nerd lost in his research. Replacing it is the impression of mania, obsession...

...and cruelty.

He spits, then licks his lips. "If the virus hadn't matured, I would have had to find an opportunity to finish you three off somewhere down the line, but now, heaven's helped me." Huang is just about to pull me to her, when Lore trains the gun at me. "You'd better not move. My hands are a researcher's, and not used to firearms. They could very easily slip."

Huang freezes where she is, staring at him for a

while before asking, "So, the tampered serum in the experiment—you were responsible for it?"

"Of course." Lore lowers his head to look at me, and adds, "And for your escape from your cell." He pats his chest, and smilingly adds, "But I won't say more. I've also seen a fair share of Hollywood films, and it's rare that the villains get to live. Now, let's bring the destruction of the zombies to its final stage."

Lore drags me to the back of the van and pushes me in.

"If my research is correct, the ZF-IV virus you've incubated will very quickly infect this Stiff. You will both die." Still holding the gun, he stands framed by the open door, eyes glinting strangely, as if about to see the climax of some anticipated show. "Then I shall bring the mature virus back, and will still be the savior of humanity."

The cold within my body grows fiercer and fiercer. I want to charge at him, but I can only curl up. The ZF-IV seems to be airborne, and I can see Old Jim's malign expression starting to change ever so slightly. The ZF-IV must already be starting to affect him.

Lore's grin becomes more sadistic. "Oh, and I finally understand why villains monologue so much, because scenes like this are just so gratifying—did you know, that night, we were all following you? If you bit that girl we wouldn't have hesitated in putting you down, and humanity would know that Stiffs can't be saved. We were completely taken by surprise when you didn't, even when we scratched her and made her bleed… but not even that was enough to make you succumb. And then I took you to the observation room, and I couldn't even get this useless Stiff to bite you…but none of this matters now. I still win in the end."

"Why…why do you want to kill Stiffs so badly…?" I

ask, my voice shaking. "We are all people..."

He shakes his head. "People? How can the infected be the same as people? Do they multiply at an exponential rate, and rampantly strip away our resources? This planet has too many people! Cleansing it of a good deal of them will save significant space and energy. Don't worry, the people that remain will live very well. We'll enter a new path of evolution."

Compared to the virus brewing in me, Lore's words were far more chilling.

He turns his head, and sees the blue flower on my shoulder. "Oh yes, there's still that flower. Strange—scientists have spent so much time and energy but failed to develop an antidote to the Necrona virus, and yet this flower could do it all by itself. Is this the balancing act of nature you Chinese think exists? 'There's bound to be an antidote within seven steps of a poisonous snake.'"

Lore leans in, fixing his gaze on the flower, before suddenly yanking it off, stems, flower and leaves.

The pain explodes through my shoulder.

"Even if Mother Nature is at work, she cannot hope to vanquish me!" He pulls a test tube of translucent liquid from his pocket, and stuffs the flower in. Tiny bubbles quickly appear in the liquid, and as they become denser, the whole flower dissolves.

Lore throws the test tube aside, the leaking liquid making a hissing sound on the metallic floor. "A Stiff's a Stiff and should be eliminated, so give up your vain attempts to re-enter the human race."

Despair overwhelms me, but I can only lay crunched up on the bed of the van, listening to his triumphant cackling. I think of Huang...oh yes, where's Huang?

"Talkative asshole!" shrieks Huang, breaking cover

with a large stone, and hurling it at Lore.

I cheer up instantly. Looks like the cinematic pattern is at work—a monologuing villain is always defeated during their moment of negligence.

But the next moment, Lore agilely steps aside and fires a quick shot off. The bullet scrapes past Huang's arm, blood spurting from the graze.

Old Jim is obviously agitated, his shoulders writhing—but he's still constrained by the straps, and he's unable to get loose.

"That was close." Lore beats his chest in an exaggerated manner. "You almost got me."

Huang holds the wound on her arm, staring at me with indignation. The hope that had just lit inside me extinguished just as quickly. I return Huang's despairing gaze.

And then, both our eyes rekindle simultaneously. I nod towards her, and her to me.

With feigned humility, she walks towards Lore, her hand outstretched. Suddenly, she smears her blood all over his neck and face, and then darts away.

"Huh, what are you..." Lore touches his face in a panic. Seeing only fresh blood, he relaxes. "Is this your desperate struggle before death?"

"Or, counter-attack."

Before I finish these words, my hands are already on Old Jim, using the last of my strength to rip at the clips and buckles confining him. Within a moment, the Stiff leaps up from the seat, and charges towards the professor.

Lore backs away fearfully, but trips on that stray rock and falls backwards flat onto the grass. During his fall, he pulls the trigger hard, and the automatic pistol *bam*

bam bams its contents wildly across the van. I curl back up into a ball.

Old Jim takes several direct hits, but seems oblivious. The twisted malevolence in his eyes which seems to drive his attack is no longer just Hunger, but pure rage.

He lurches out of the van with a low roar.

Lore is unable to get back up before a dark shadow presses down on him. He is now in the tight grip of Old Jim, whose open mouth is moving towards his neck.

Even though Old Jim is pinning Lore down, the pistol is still spewing lead into Old Jim's stomach. The shots pierce Old Jim's body, causing rotten flesh and vaguely red blood to spew out, until a crimson mist pervades the air, and blood-red dandelions are blossoming from his back. But he doesn't stop. Inching closer and closer to Lore's neck, he sinks his teeth in, tearing out bite after bite.

Lore's eyes fill with desperation and futility, like two pools of sucking swamp water.

There is a moment when the blood seems to brim so full in Old Jim's mouth that it seeps out at the corners, and then a fountain of fresh red gore erupts from the artery in Lore's neck. This is the ultimate and irresistible temptation to Stiffs, but Old Jim doesn't drink: he just keeps grinding his teeth into the flesh. It's not until Lore lies completely still and silent, his eyes completely dulled in dark shadows, that Old Jim parts his jaws.

I struggle up and see him collapsed next to Lore, blood pooling all around them. Huang is standing a few metres away, wanting to approach, but afraid to do so.

"Are you OK?" I sign.

He signs back with extreme difficulty. "Spine's shattered by bullet, and one hit my head."

I want to tell him he'll be OK, but I don't want to lie to

him. All I can say is, "Oh."

"Did you see? My blood's red too," he signs excitedly. "Your flower really works! I could have turned back into a real Breather." He pauses, and adds, "But now I can only be a real corpse."

Indeed, even though he shows every sign of regaining his humanity, he is still technically a Stiff; and between those heavy wounds and the ZF-IV infection, soon his body will completely stiffen, and he'll never move again.

"Don't look at me with pity," Old Jim signs. "You're not doing much better than me."

"But you're going to die first."

He makes a laughing gesture, but his face shows not an ounce of joy. After a while, he signs again, "Shame you're going to die too." He points at Huang, who is still hovering a way off, unsure what to do. "You could have been happy."

I pull myself out from the van, looking down at him. Although his face is covered by bloodstains, his features are clear. The bird of memory dives out of the thick fog. The mist clears, and I can finally see all the memories that were shrouded within.

"I remember who you are," I gesture excitedly. "You're not an actor, or a teacher."

"Then who am..." he asks.

But before he finishes signing, his hands become rigid and freeze in midair.

I lie on the slope, letting the luscious grass cushion me. Huang sits by my side.

"Feeling a little better now?"

"I'm going to die soon."

Huang gazes down at me with sorrow. "I'm taking you back, we're going to get you cured."

"Don't bother... no time..." Gusts of cold and damp

are rushing through my body like waves. I have to focus hard in order not to fall asleep. "If you take me back, the general is bound to extract the phase IV virus that is now incubating in my body and use it on the Stiffs. But the Stiffs CAN be cured. You must find that flower and save us...save all of us..."

"But Lore destroyed the flower..."

I strain to turn my head. A blade of grass is scratching my nose, ticklish. "That can't be the only one. Nature has its balancing mechanisms. If the Necrona virus has come into existence, then its antidote will too, sooner or later. I accidentally had the seed land on my shoulder, and grew this flower. Even though one flower is destroyed, there must be other seeds. You must find them..."

A droplet falls onto my face. It feels warm, and so good. Huang is leaning over me. She puts her hand on my forehead. "You feel really cold."

"Mhm," I assent.

"Um, there's something I've been keeping from you."

My voice is getting softer and softer. "I know."

"Oh?'

"I'm not Hui, I'm not the guy in the photo. I just look a bit like him. We weren't lovers. We didn't even know each other."

"Yes, that's right. It was only when Hui and I were on the run that we came to your flat." Huang gazes at me. After a long time, she asks, "Is it all coming back to you?"

"Yes, perhaps it's that 'life passing before your eyes' thing. I do remember everything. I'm someone else, I have another story. I'm not Hui." Is it getting dark already? My vision is getting blurry, but I strain to keep my eyes open.

"I'm sorry I didn't tell you that day. When you said you

were Hui, I wanted you to protect me."

I nod. "But I'm still really happy to have protected you."

Huang cradles my head in her arms. After a while, she asks, "So who exactly are you?"

I want to talk, but my throat feels dry, rough and weak. She puts her ear close to my lips.

"My name is..." I swallow. "Is..."

"What is it?"

"Brad Pitt."

EPILOGUE

Extract from "Stories of Camp Hades: Survivors of the Necrona Plague":

AFTER 'HUMANITY'S BIG PUSH', peace lasted a long time.

During the days of standoff between humans and Stiffs, I would often follow Auntie when she went looking in the woods. I asked her what she was searching for. She said she was looking for a kind of flower, one that could bring people back after they'd crossed the river of death. She'd named it "Bi'anhua", *flower of the other shore*.

Now, Bi'anhua is the common hope of both Stiffs and humans.

On Push Day, Auntie returned to the camp on her own, and told us Professor Lore was dead. The soldiers surrounded her and were going to kill her to avenge the professor, but she led them to his quarters. And when they searched his home and inspected the data on his computer, they found out that Professor Lore had been the main culprit behind the apocalypse all along, and the key to turning the Stiffs back to humans really had been that pretty flower that was growing out of Uncle Stiff's shoulder.

Speaking of Uncle Stiff, I actually met him once.

When I got lost in the woods, it was he who took my hand and walked me out of the dark towards the light. I remember his hand was very stiff, and freezing cold, but it also felt very powerful. Now, he's buried under a hill, and has been for a very long time. His bones are probably still freezing cold, but that power must have now dispersed through the earth.

The Bi'anhua that was blossoming on his shoulder had never been seen again, but Auntie never gave up looking for it.

Taking me with her, we searched all the branches of every tree in the woods, not overlooking even a single tender shoot of young grass emerging from the soil. Sometimes, her arms would be scratched to bits by brambles. Sometimes she'd sprain her ankle leaping off from trees, and more often, she'd be so exhausted she'd have to lean against their trunks to catch her breath.

For the whole of that spring and summer, we searched and found nothing. The hope that people held for it eventually dwindled. Even when autumn came and the leaves turned yellow and fell, when everything looked desolate, Auntie didn't stop looking. Some people tried to dissuade her. "This isn't the season for flowers to bloom", or "Maybe there was only ever one Bi'anhua, and it happened to grow on the shoulder of Uncle Stiff." Amidst all their well-meaning words, Auntie kept her lips tight, not saying a thing, but the next day she'd be back on the slope in those woods, searching for traces of the Bi'anhua.

It wasn't until winter, when the coastal region was

covered in a rare snow, that she lifted her head, paused her wandering steps and looked up at the sky. When she looked up, I couldn't see her face, but I think her eyes must have been brimming with tears. The snowflakes were falling on her face, into her eyes, and melting in her tears.

That winter, the Stiffs came twice. I don't know why, but people no longer fought them to the death like before. They fought a little, then retreated, and stopped as soon as they were in the safe zone. Now that they knew it was possible for Stiffs to revert to being humans, even though the Bi'anhua still hadn't been found again, they no longer saw them as just demons.

Something else happened that winter. Auntie ran into her old boyfriend. A group of survivors found us via emergency broadcasts, and one of them was Hui, who had been separated from Auntie during a Stiff attack. Hui said that when he went out to see what was happening, he got whisked away by the crowd, further and further away, and never thought they'd reunite here. This kind of apocalyptical reunion of lovers is so sweet, and the kind of story we all love to hear. But I saw that when Hui hugged Huang, she instinctively drew back a step.

It's like people say, the role of the living is to live. Even though the whole world was filled with Stiffs, we kept each other warm that winter, and protected one another. We got through that freezing and anxiety-ridden season without encountering much danger. When spring arrived, we decided to retreat further inland, and find a safer place to build our camps.

Before we left, Auntie said she wanted to go back to the hill one last time.

Hui said it was too dangerous, there were lots of Stiffs still wandering around there. "What do you want to go there for?"

"I have a friend who's buried there. After we leave, we might never be back, so I want go one last time," Auntie stated.

Hui must have heard the stories about Uncle Stiff. He thought about it, and nodded. "Then I'll go with you. I want to thank him too. You've never told me his name."

Auntie told him, *Brad Pitt*.

When they went to the slope, I went with them. We walked through a lot of deserted roads and trudged through the overgrown woods with extreme difficulty. We were lucky and didn't run into any Stiffs on the way. We walked through the afternoon and into the night, and through the night and into the dawn. We came out of the woods, and the vibrant open country rolled out before us.

The weather was especially bright and clear. Rays of sunlight pierced through the clouds and were pouring down; greenery had burst through from the soil, covering it like a thick green carpet. The low spring wind swept past, and pretty red and purple flowers that had also broken through the grass carpet were swaying in the breeze, and as the wind picked up, multi-colour waves swept the whole field. We walked through the grass with seed pods attaching themselves to our legs. Then suddenly, Auntie's eyes widened.

I could just about see what she had seen, on the slope that had just come into view. There were no shrubs or bare patches: it was all just a uniform field of blue, like a sapphire embedded on the green carpet. "What's that?" Hui asked.

Auntie came out of her daze, and without a word, strode towards it. The field was full of grass and flowers. She broke into a run, leaving a trail of crushed greenery behind her. The gentle wind blew over the grass, smoothing out the trail. She was running so quickly, like a swift, practically flying over the grass, plunging head first into spring.

Hui and I rushed after her.

It wasn't until we came closer that we could clearly see that the whole slope was covered in wondrous little flowers, their petals plain blue, on which ran tiny networks of dark red vessels. I have seen this flower many times since then, on a lot of research papers, and in the legends told by countless people.

Bi'anhua.

This was where Uncle Stiff had been buried. His body had rotted in the earth, but the roots within him had gone through a year's gestation, and had sprung forth. Bi'anhua were blooming in the wind, all over the entire slope.

Auntie knelt down, catching her breath. Nestling her head close to the nearest cluster of flowers, she took in deep breaths, and when she looked up, I could see tears welling in the corner of her eye, gliding down her cheeks. Where the tears made their tracks, there were reflected glimmers of the sun. I didn't understand at the time why Auntie was crying, but I knew then that it was my most beautiful memory from that spring.

NOTES

A RESIDENT OF the city of Chengdu, A Que began writing in 2012 and is considered one of the new generation of sci-fi writers in China. Whilst he's more known for more traditional, soft SF featuring the robots he would obviously love to write into existence in his collections *Walking with Robots* (2015) and *The Living World of A.I.* (2017), "Flower of the Other Shore" is rather a departure. It all began from a vivid idea of a filthy and rotting revenant, presenting a young girl with a flower, it felt both tragic and romantic. Captivated by this tone and image, A Que sat down to write, and finished the story in just a few days, making it the quickest he'd ever written, driven by his inspiration!

The story takes huge influences from Western zombie films, making direct, knowing references to a few, in comic, fourth-wall-breaking moments of subversion and parody, but also borrowing some of the associated humour of Chinese zombie mythology, with our undead protagonists often limping around, semi-bound in the same fashion as jiangshi.

It also has to be said that as I began to work on this story with A Que, we were just beginning to see the impact of Covid-19. Lockdowns, deaths and infection rates became not just a sci-fi trope, but an everyday fact. Obviously the virus' name is a direct reference, how could it not be, but in the name of escapism, and to not make light of the very real pain this pandemic has caused, we decided to not delve too deeply into this.

When I first read A Que, a few years ago, I was struck by how lyrical and sensitive his writing is, not just in style but in the softness and sensitivity of his male protagonists.

Here, the caring and considerate nature of 'Hui', sits at odds with his gruesome appearance, playing with tropes as old as Mary Shelley's *Frankenstein*. The humour and care, mixed with the grotesquerie and apocalyptic setting really did make this stand out for me, beyond the "plague" of zombie stories we've seen in the last 20 years. And the specifics of human and zombie slang and jargon surrounding how each party refers to their own peculiarities, and the otherness of their opponents, gave me some excellent opportunities to play with language.

THE ABSOLUTION EXPERIMENT
特赦实验

BAO SHU

1

THE GUARD PULLED the thick iron doors open and a smartly-suited man walked into the cell. He regarded it from top to bottom: it was a very narrow room, practically bare apart from a bed and the inmate in his prison robes lying on it, facing away from him.

"Mr Braywalk?" the man called tentatively. No reply. He tried twice more: still nothing, not even a movement. The man was just about to approach when the inmate spoke languidly. "Who are you? I don't receive visitors. Why did they let you in?" The voice sounded hoarse and without focus.

"I'm Baker Orson." The man introduced himself. "I've come about your case—"

"So you're the defence lawyer from the court?" Braywalk rolled over irascibly, interrupting him. "Have they accepted my appeal?"

"As I understand, your appeal is quite unique. You have asked for your sentence to be changed to the death penalty. I'm afraid this is going to be very tricky." Orson spoke at a calculatedly measured pace. "As you know, like most civilized countries, we have long abolished the death penalty. However, your crimes have triggered a lot of social agitation and there are members of the press advocating for its reinstatement—specifically for you. As a member of several international communities, this is not acceptable. Of course, the possibility of the sentence being reduced to a fixed term is very small. Frankly, your vigilante enacting of extremist ideology has shocked the world; for your bigoted, racist beliefs, nearly a hundred people died during your shooting and bombing campaigns. The evidence is undeniable. I can't help you evade the consequences of your crimes—"

"Then what the hell are you here for?" Braywalk asked impatiently.

"I'm here to give you a piece of good news." Orson replied. "As long as you're willing to cooperate with me, you might regain your freedom during your lifetime, or even walk out of here in your youth."

"Is that really possible? Wait!" Braywalk fixed a penetrating stare on the man in front of him. "You're not a lawyer, are you?"

An inscrutable smile floated onto Orson's face. "Lawyers can't help you, but I can." He handed a card to Braywalk, whose eye caught the line '...Head Researcher of the Royal Academy of Sciences, Advanced Research Division.' "We are developing an extremely important new drug, which has now reached the stage that requires consenting human test subjects. As long as you are willing to participate in this testing process, absolution is yours, along with the freedom you dream of. This is the agreement of absolution issued by His Majesty's government." Orson slid out a document folder.

Braywalk's spirits ignited. He sat bolt upright, took the documents, and began reading them carefully. "Hmm, the terms aren't bad... that is... I'll have my freedom for just taking part in this experiment?"

"Correct. When the experiment ends, no matter the outcome, you'll get your freedom. Below is the signature of the King and the Prime Minister. The legality is therefore unquestionable and undeniable."

"And if the experiment fails? I'll die a gruesome death?"

"I'll be brutally honest: that is a distinct possibility. During previous experiments the death rate had exceeded 30%. We would not be coming to you otherwise." Orson continued, frankly, "Although, is this not what you requested? Whatever happens, you have nothing to lose: either option seems better than being locked up for life."

A sarcastic smile cracked across Braywalk's face. "You're not wrong, anything's better than now...but what kind of drug are you developing?"

"This...is top secret..." Orson moved close to the inmate's ear, and whispered something.

It was the unimaginable, and Braywalk's eyes widened.

2

ONE YEAR LATER.

Braywalk groaned weakly. He felt as if he were being tormented by fierce hellfire, before plunging into freezing caverns of ice. Every inch of skin, every muscle, was feeling simultaneous burning, freezing, piercing pain, numbness and itching; all his organs were torn in all directions, and then squashed back into one; every flavour of paradox-defying pain was bombarding him. He wanted to flee but couldn't even struggle, being strapped to the bed by unyielding restraints. His hair had completely fallen out, and the skin on his entire body had putrified.

He knew why he was in such pain. In this historically unprecedented experiment, every cell in his body was being ravaged by different kinds of chemical reactions, and the pain was a visceral reminder of the possibility his whole body could break down into a pile of single-cell primeval slush.

This, however, was for the pursuit of immortality.

Orson had explained it to him. The fundamental reason for the limit to human life was the limit to the number of times the cells could divide, and this in turn was because of a granule at the end of the chromosome called a Telomere. Every time a Telomere replicates, it gets a little damaged and shortens. When it's completely used up, the cell can no longer replicate, and so the human dies of old age. If the length of the Telomere can be kept constant, then it will continue to divide. The key was in a kind of enzyme which can lengthen the Telomere and enable the process of replication to continue. The injections he had been given contained a special kind of active agent, known as "immortality essence", which could effectively keep the Telomere enzyme in human cells active—but without devolving into a cancer, when cell division goes out of control. This, in theory, should realize immortality.

In theory. A great deal of experiments on the human body were necessary to turn it into reality. The other test subjects had all withdrawn consent at various stages because they could no longer stand the pain and torment: only Braywalk had remained. The experiment involved complete and fundamental alteration of the human body on the cellular level, and the pain was extraordinary. Braywalk believed that even the terminally ill would refuse to make this kind of exchange for their life in return. The most terrifying thing was the interminable injections. During the past year or so, he'd lived under extreme pains of the flesh every single day. He had wanted to tear up the agreement several times, but the thought of the hardship he would otherwise have to endure for decades on end in prison set him shuddering more than any physical pain he had endured so far. The fierce desire to regain his freedom kept him going.

"I really can't take it anymore, just when will it end?" he asked ineffectually to the scientist by his side.

"My apologies," Orson replied. "It looks like our experiment has somewhat derailed, and we need a little longer..." He sighed. "If only Lisa were still here, then we wouldn't have strayed down the wrong path."

"Who's Lisa?"

"The woman who discovered the Immortality Essence," Orson explained. "The most brilliant expert in our institution, who had made many important breakthroughs. Unfortunately she passed away suddenly, just as she was researching the use of the Essence on the human body. Without her, there's nothing we can do to speed up our research...so we'll need your help to perform some further tests, I'm afraid."

"I've had enough! Take me back to my cell now. Didn't you hear? Daddy says no! I'm not doing this any more!"

"And lay waste to everything we've done?" Orson said

persuasively. "You would have suffered a year for nothing, and then have to return to your endless sentence. To be honest, we are very close to the dawn of a breakthrough. Do you really want to give up now?"

"I…" Braywalk hesitated.

"Please bear with us a little longer." Orson pressed his advantage home. "I promise that very soon, you'll become subject of a tremendous and everlasting legacy in the history books of humanity. John, give Mr Braywalk the next injection—maybe this will be the one that finally works."

3

Just as Orson had hoped, this injection worked. The pain, the numbness and the itching gradually subsided. Braywalk's body regrew fresh new layers of skin without a single scar in sight. He regrew a new head of hair, and even lost teeth grew back. He looked about ten years younger, and Orson did not order any further injections.

"The experiment has made monumental progress!" Orson told him, two months later. "After a complete medical, we found that all the cells in your body have regenerated, and are also continuing to divide in healthy order. It looks like our drug has had its desired effect."

"Does this mean… I'm now immortal?" Braywalk asked.

"It's highly possible."

"This is wonderful!" The happiness that Braywalk expressed at the prospect of immortality was nothing compared to the joy he felt at gaining his freedom back. "So I can get out of here now?"

"Of course, there's no need for you to stay at the research facility."

Braywalk leapt off the bed and walked towards the door. Opening it, he was stupefied to find four armed prison guards. They advanced and surrounded him, restraining him as they locked the handcuffs.

"Are you nuts? I've just been absolved!" Braywalk was stunned. "Orson! What's going on?"

"I explained this to you very clearly." Orson smiled. "Absolution only comes into effect at the end of the experiment. Until then, you are still a criminal."

"But the experiment is a success?"

"The procedural part has been completed, but that doesn't mean it's finished. We still have the observation period."

"What damned observation period?"

"The cell division could still be unstable, and any kind of anomaly could occur at any moment. As of now, we don't know how long the process can be maintained. The final outcome remains to be seen, so we need to keep you under observation. Only until we can prove that the cells can stably divide endlessly and the regeneration is eternal, can the experiment be considered finished. Therefore, we need a relatively long observation period."

"You bastard!" Braywalk struggled. "How long are you going to observe me? One year, three years? Surely not as long as five? Ten?"

"Please calm down. We need to prove that you really possess the capability to be immortal. According to our initial estimate, that requires—two thousand and five hundred years. Minimum."

"Are you crazy? I have to stay in this damned place for two...two thousand and five hundred years?"

"It can't be helped." Orson sighed nonchalantly. "Some parts of nature, such as trees, can live up to several thousand years—but we can't say they're immortal now, can we? As you could be the first immortal human, of course we must ensure there is long-term monitoring. Even when the drug is released to market, it will still need continuous supervision...it's nothing, really. Think of it like this: if the trial succeeds, two thousand and five hundred years later when you leave prison, you'll still be as young as you are now, not a grey hair on your head."

"Bullshit! Why don't you try going to prison for two thousand and five hundred years?"

"I think," Orson replied coldly, "that for immortality, it's a small price to pay. If you must blame something, blame your life sentence. Besides, during your killing spree you took eighty-five innocent lives. Now if we take the conservative estimate that each of them could have lived for at least another thirty years, two thousand and five hundred really isn't that much to repay, is it?"

"Orson, you son of a bitch, damn you and your entire family. I hope they die in pain!" At the utter horror of spending the next two and a half millennia in that tiny cramped cell, Braywalk began to curse hysterically.

Still struggling against despair, Braywalk was dragged into the prison van by the guards. The engines howled as it sped from the research facility, back towards the prison compound. Orson slid a photograph from his pocket and gazed at it for a long time, before wiping the corner of his eye, and murmuring to himself, "Now you can both rest in peace, Lisa."

A beautiful dark-skinned woman, holding a very young infant, continued to give him a splendid smile from the photograph.

NOTES

BAO SHU CONSIDERS himself Sichuanese, but has spent his life living all across China. When he began writing in 2010, he took the pseudonym of Baoshu ("treasure tree"), from a bandit in one of Jinyong's novels, as a joke, but it stuck. A winner of multiple major awards, he has published four novels and three collections, including an official sequel to Liu Cixin's *The Three Body Problem*, *The Redemption of Time* (translated by Ken Liu, Tor, 2019).

Bao Shu has always been interested in immortality and the abundance of experience this could bring, but eventually, he also considered how terrifying it would be to be immortal and imprisoned for eternity, and gradually this story came into being, and was published in *Super Nice* in 2012. Initial plans for the story had been to write about how it feels to be alive and imprisoned for thousands of years, but Bao Shu decided that the reader's imagination would fill the void with far more horrors than he could convey in a short piece.

Alongside writing that moves and inspires, I also have a taste for stories that invite discomfort, challenge attitudes and shock. "The Absolution Experiment" does so, both in its subject matter and in the denouement of the plot. The idea of immortality has been a preoccupation of the Chinese for thousands of years, from Daoist alchemy, to modern efforts of prolonging life via ultra-conscious health diets, even delving into the realms of genetic research. The story also touches on subjects which are discussed internally in China far more than internationally, difficult subjects such as racism, terrorism and the idea of what justice is. Creating a protagonist so far beyond sympathy, and a punishment so far beyond acceptability makes you consider the very nature of retribution.

THE TIDE OF MOON CITY
月见潮

REGINA KANYU WANG

THE NIGHTS IN Moonless were not as dark or lightless as people imagined. In the absence of Bizhe's reflected light, the skyful of stars became the protagonists of the nocturnal stage. They say that on bright and cloudless summer nights, if you looked towards the western skies, you could see the sun—if you were lucky. The sun that had bestowed light and warmth to humankind from the beginning.

Before her husband passed away he had loved to play with his telescope, looking for the sun, but Dianne had no interest in that, or anything else in the skies.

After she retired, her life had become more and more secluded—so when the doorbell rang, it startled her. It felt like an age ago that she last heard it chime. Opening the door, she found it was only a delivery. The package was very light; the exterior layers covered in grime and dented from long distance shipping, and the sender's details were smeared and worn. Who could it be from? Dianne didn't have a clue. She opened the package, and after numerous layers of plastic sheets her fingers came in contact with a floral print envelope and a small calfskin-wrapped package. Opening the letter, there were strains of Yulan orchid scent imprinted in the premium quality ink, long lasting and unfading.

> *Dianne,*
>
> *Have you been happy all these years? I've been doing fine. After he passed away, my living allowance has been more than sufficient, and I also enjoy a guaranteed widow's protection. Not a bad marriage deal.*
>
> *Even though we don't want to admit it, we are old, and I don't know how many days I have left, but there are some things I want to say to you face to face.*
>
> *Come to Moon City. My mansion is in the suburbs, and isn't easy to find, so I enclose a map.*
>
> *No need to send a reply. I'll be waiting for you. If you're driving, we'll just be in time to see the tide of Kuijiang River[38]. Let's hope I can make it too.*
>
> *With love,*
> *Leen*
>
> *P.S. do you still remember the things in the box?*

Dianne massaged her temples. Eileen's tone hadn't changed a bit. Having been her roommate for three years,

---

38 Kuijiang, 葵江, means "sunflower river"

Dianne had never seen anyone refuse Eileen's requests. Unwrapping the bundle along the folds in the calfskin, a small white box revealed itself. She wasn't sure why she was so aware of her heart's beating. Opening the box revealed a shriveled clump of greenish grey. Lizao.

Taking a deep breath, she moved to the sink and filled the box with water. Slowly the Lizao unfolded and awoke, its faded grey turning into verdant green. Carefully she lifted the Lizao out and laid it flat on the table. Switching off the light, she watched it glow. The fluorescence was not uniform through the grass, but spread in regular segments as if calling out from this dark room to the stars outside, sending some kind of signal. Those sealed-off and dusty memories were floating back into her mind, like motes of dust in the sunlight. She screwed her eyes shut, wanting to force them out, but when she opened them again they were still there, dancing before her eyes. Of course she remembered. From the beginning to the end, she'd never forgotten any of it.

"BIG NEWS, BIG news! There's a thesis from Bizhe on this year's He'lin Tide Conference!" Eileen charged into the dormitory, yelling as she burst in.

Half reclined on the bed, Dianne remained unmoved. "Since when have you paid any attention to academic developments? That's the big news?"

Eileen dragged her friend up from her repose. "Of course! This year it's on an unprecedented scale, the university's arranged all kinds of banquets and social gatherings. As chief rep of student relations at He'lin First University, how could I not pay any attention?"

"With you at the helm of relations, I'm afraid

the academic reputation of our institution will unquestionably perish." Dianne's eyes had not lifted from the papers in her hands. "Must be some bored Bizhenese with nothing better to do than remote-submit an essay, which we are going to denounce as a negative example."

"But there really will be a Bizhenese attending the conference, it's real! Third speaker, day two, researcher at the Bizhe Science Academy Energy Institute. It's right here on the programme."

Eileen snatched the papers from Dianne's hands, replacing it with a conference guide, still carrying the smell of fresh ink.

"What's an energy researcher doing at our conference?" The tide conference was usually jointly held by the School of Astrophysics, to which Dianne and Eileen were attached, and the School of Hydrology.

Eileen leaned in, and with an air of mystery, whispered two words into Dianne's ear: "Tidal. Energy."

"Tidal energy? Using tides to create power? But how can this be possible..." Dianne had read material on the extraction of tidal energy on Ancient Earth, but the conditions on this colonial planet were vastly different to Earth's. He'lin and Bizhe rotated around each other, but without relative displacement the only tidal gravity was created by their sun, which wasn't strong enough to be of any significance.

"Why isn't it possible?" Eileen retorted. "Do you think this conference is just there to discuss tides? If there aren't any benefits to be gained, the head of our school would never make such an effort. There's a lot more water on Bizhe, so naturally they'd be the first to discover ways of exploiting tidal energy."

"You're not wrong; although the tidal range of the Kuijiang isn't high, its tidal volume is quite considerable. If tidal energy can be harnessed, this could mean a way out of the energy crisis, and lifting the brakes on He'lin's development…"

"Urrgghh! Why are you so serious?" Eileen interrupted. "Be careful, no one wants to marry a workaholic, Dianne."

Dianne fidgeted with the laboratory key hanging around her neck. "Who wants to get married anyway? I'd gladly make the lab my home. Unlike someone who's always asking others to write her papers, and won't make it to graduation if she's not careful."

"The mid-term thesis review isn't for a while yet. Besides, I've got my work cut out for me with the conference." Eileen gave Dianne a shove. "Don't you think this Bizhenese is so brave? Coming to He'lin all on his own like this? Relations between our planets have gotten pretty tense over the last few years; this guy must be amazing. Isn't he afraid that—"

"What if he falls in love with a He'lin girl and doesn't want to go back? Are you living in one of your Bizhenese idol dramas again? Save it, he's probably a bald uncle type. Let me see what Uncle Bizhe is actually called."

Dianne flicked through the guide Eileen had shoved into her hand to the lecture programme, but when she saw the name next to 'Bizhe Science Academy (Energy Institute)' she got a shock.

"What's the matter? Are you so captivated by this Bizhenese name that you've been struck dumb?" Eileen waved her hand in front of Dianne's face before yanking the guide out of her hands. "Youjia? The name sounds very familiar…"

Dianne bit her lips. "It's the Bizhenese who wrote to me."

"Oh! I remember! The guy that got an official reprimand from our department head? Is he asking for it? Wait till I summon all my boys, to teach him a lesson." Eileen rolled up her sleeves.

Dianne shook her head. "What he said…actually did make sense. It was my model that was incomplete."

"Still, sending a letter directly to the school is too much."

"I only put my uni department in the thesis, not my personal address. So I think he could only post it here… …I'm afraid he wasn't aware of He'lin's random letter inspections."

Eileen put her arm over Dianne's shoulder. "Don't be scared. If he tries anything on with you, I'll find someone to take care of him!"

"Thank you. Under the protection of Goddess Eileen, I'm not afraid of anyone." Dianne tried hard to lift the corners of her mouth into a smile, but in the end, gravity prevailed.

Towards the end of the first day of the He'lin Tide Conference, Dianne was the last speaker. She finished her report, and was just about to leave when a strange man approached. He wore a loose flowery T-shirt that nearly reached his knees and trousers that only went down to his ankles. An odd combination, not unlike the outfits in those idol dramas that Eileen was addicted to. Dianne frowned internally as she realised who he was.

"As I didn't receive your reply, I thought I'd come here in person and see if I can persuade you. I never thought you would make a mistake like this. 'On the Effect of the Libration of the Lunar Body on the Primary Planet'…"

The man placed himself squarely in front of Dianne. "The research itself is excellent, but Bizhe is in no way a lunar body. Bizhe and He'lin are well and truly binary planets. Did you know most Bizhenese call He'lin their moon?"

"You're on He'lin now. Besides, both Bizhe's mass and volume are considerably lesser than those of He'lin." Dianne crossed her arms. She had guessed right: this was the Bizhenese researcher who'd been debating with her for some time by correspondence. She'd never thought he'd be so young.

"The difference isn't huge, and besides, the common centre of gravity between these two planets isn't on He'lin, nor of course on Bizhe, but at a point in free space, thus conforming to the definition of a Double Planet."

Dianne shrugged. "Whatever." She didn't want to argue about the relations between their two planets with a Bizhenese, especially at the conference.

The man smiled and extended his right hand. "This is our first meeting. I'm Youjia, doing energy stuff at the Bizhe Science Academy. I think you've already guessed."

Dianne did not return the courtesy. "No need for the formalities. I hope you aren't here just to make trouble."

"Make trouble? Indeed." Youjia broke into a grin. "To be honest, having read your thesis and corresponded with you, I had the impression that 'Dianne' would be a stern old madam. Never thought you'd be this pretty young woman—that's the sort of trouble I don't mind."

His words felt like a slap to Dianne, who had always hated any assumptions based on her gender; tired of hearing that women weren't suitable for science, or that astrophysics was the realm of men. She and Eileen were the only two female students in the entire school, and whilst Eileen was reveling in the competitive attention the male students laid at her feet, Dianne didn't see it as such as great thing. She had always refused the "help" of her male classmates on any experiment or research, to the extent that they had all learned to respect her but keep their distance. "Sorry to disappoint you. I'm only a woman and am only capable of scratching the surface of scientific research. Don't let me take up any more of your precious time." She turned to leave.

Eileen inserted herself squarely between Dianne and Youjia. "Let me guess. This is Mr Bizhe, right?"

"Madam, I was just speaking with Miss Dianne, would you mind?" Youjia held out his right hand, and gestured for her to leave.

Silence. Dianne couldn't begin to imagine the look on Eileen's face. No one had ever dared to slight her, or refuse to do anything she asked.

After a moment, Eileen puffed out her chest. "Miss Dianne doesn't want to talk to you, so you should be the one to step aside."

"Oh? I'm afraid this would be up to Miss Dianne herself." Youjia moved his head to one side, leaning around Eileen to clearly see Dianne.

Dianne put her arm through Eileen's. "Let's go. No point saying anything else."

As they walked past Youjia, Eileen let out an emphatic nasal harrumph.

After turning a couple of street corners, Dianne stopped to look back: "He isn't following us, you head back first. Don't you need to get ready for the banquet tonight?

"What about you?" Eileen turned her head and took another look.

"I'll be fine. I'm going to the library to look up a few leads from today, then I'll head back to the dorms. That Bizhenese is hardly going to eat me, but if tonight's banquet is missing the presence of Goddess Eileen, all those men might claw down the whole building." Dianne tidied Eileen's fringe, which had been blown all over the place by the wind.

"Alright then, you be careful on your own."

"Don't worry, go keep your fan club company."

"It's them who should be running round to keep me company." Eileen lifted her chin, her proud smile returning to her face.

"Of course. See you tonight."

"See you tonight. "

When Eileen was at a distance, Dianne sighed and continued to walk towards the library. Those days of her initial correspondence with Youjia had not been unpleasant. Their discussions had wholly surrounded academic questions and nothing more: she really did gain some inspiration from it. Were it not for the last letter, which happened to be pulled out by the school's head during inspection...that day. The head's face was the colour of pig's liver, and flinging the letter on the desk, he had warned her not to listen to Bizhenese nonsense ever again. Dianne was compelled to undo all the adjustments she had made to her model at Youjia's suggestion. Months of hard work had come to nothing. Dianne knew her model would have been better with Youjia's suggested incorporations, but facing the fury of the school's most authoritative figure, she could not bring herself to voice her opinion.

"I thought your bodyguard was never going to leave." A shadow stepped out from an alley just ahead of her.

Speak of the devil. Dianne moved to walk around him, but found her path blocked after a few steps. "I'm really not going to eat you, so why are you avoiding me? Are you really worried you'll get into trouble?"

"I'm a female member of the species, so probably not worth your time." Dianne deliberately avoided his gaze.

"What kind of talk is this? There's no gender discrimination in Bizhe. To find that the peer whose academic thinking I most respect is a pretty lady—I'm over the moon. Turns out it was worth bringing an introductory gift after all."

Youjia took out a little white box and handed it to Dianne. Still on her guard, Dianne cautiously opened the box to see a clump of greyish green plant, curled up in one corner as if it had died. "This is…"

"Lizao, a native Bizhenese plant you can't find anywhere else. You mentioned your curiosity about Bizhe's organic life in the notes to your thesis. I hope you like it." Youjia gave her a bright, sweet smile. "I um… before meeting you, I had decided that if Dianne turns out to be a sour-faced madam, I'd keep the gift to save her from mistaking it for some unintended signal."

"Thank you…"

Although He'lin and Bizhe orbit around each other, their ecologies were completely different. Reading about Bizhenese customs and artefacts at magazine stands as a child, Dianne had found them incredible and fairytale-like; and despite this little thing called Lizao not being much to look at, it had come from Bizhe. Dianne felt a warmth towards it from the very bottom of her heart.

"Bringing this little fellow into He'lin took me considerable effort. I wonder if Miss Dianne would agree to show me around He'lin in return? I have still have some academic questions to consult you on." Youjia lowered his head in a slight bow, while locking his gaze with Dianne's.

This was the first time that a *man* had wanted to 'consult' her. She felt her heart quicken and the temperature in her cheeks rise, and she turned to avert his gaze. Seeing as he was able to attend the conference, an academic exchange with a scholar from a neighbouring planet shouldn't anger the department head, should it? Dianne steeled her nerves.

"Come on, let's go for some He'lin delicacies. We can talk as we eat."

Moon City was situated on the hemisphere of He'lin that faced Bizhe, and was the political, cultural and economic centre of the whole planet. Even though it wasn't Dianne's hometown, her student life at He'lin First University had long acquainted her with every intimate detail of the city, and so she knew where to go for the best authentic food that a student budget could afford.

Lifting his glass, Youjia saluted Dianne. "Thank you for your hospitality. He'lin's delicacies really do live up to their reputation, and this wine… fragrant and fierce to just the right degree."

Dianne clinked glasses with him. "A toast to friendship." She couldn't help but feel pleased with her choice. "Five-year-old Moon Daisy wine. Only wine made from the moon daisies of Moon City could taste like this. You can't get it in Bizhe, can you?"

Youjia put his glass down. "The only place in Bizhe where you could even glimpse a moon daisy is right in the centre of the hemisphere facing He'lin, Lunar Island, but the island holds over half of the Bizhenese population. It's so packed it's practically suffocating, so there's precious little space for plant watching."

"You've so many islands, you could give one to each citizen and there'd still be some left! The first thing we learn about Bizhe in the textbooks is its geography, a multitude of islands surrounded by the sea—completely different from He'lin, where the land is predominantly continental."

Youjia shook his head. "Most of them are uninhabitable."

"But they've attracted so many tourists. The rapidly developing tourism industry of your esteemed planet is exerting not a little pressure on He'lin's officials."

Youjia chuckled. "Tourists don't stay for long. Come and rent an island on Bizhe, enjoy a holiday completely undisturbed by the outside world, and then leave as soon as your holiday's over, nothing to worry about. That's far from everyday life on Bizhe."

"So what *is* everyday life....fishing?" The first emigrants who'd left He'lin for Bizhe had survived and built their livelihoods on fish. The joke Dianne had blurted out even amused herself.

Youjia's smile deepened. "Indeed. Miss Dianne must come and taste the fresh produce from the Bizhe's seas if she ever gets the chance. I'll jump in and catch it myself."

"Perhaps I will. It's a shame that Bizhe welcomes tourists from all planets in the Union, except for He'lin." Dianne shrugged.

"Unless you're a visiting scholar." Youjia put away his smile. "I'll take care of things at the Bizhe end."

"What?" Youjia's sudden change of subject made Dianne nervous.

"I mean, your research has great potential, and the Bizhe Science Academy would definitely welcome a visit from you." Youjia resumed his relaxed tone.

Dianne felt her heart climb down from her throat, to her chest, and self-mockingly, she replied "He'lin wouldn't let anyone out so easily, especially women."

Youjia harrumphed. "There's none of that on our planet, it's a meritocracy. Nothing to do with whether you're a man or a woman. Besides, the standards of your theses are excellent, the logic is tight and meticulous. The only thing they lack is ambition."

"What?" The first half of that sentence pleased her, but the second half made her start. She'd never heard that sort of criticism before.

Youjia placed his hands on the table, lacing his fingers and leaning forwards. He gazed steadily into Dianne's eyes. "Your thesis is perfect in its theory, but it hasn't been associated with any practical application. There is tidal locking between He'lin and Bizhe, therefore the only factors that influence the tides would be planetary libration or the relative positions of the stars. Calculating the combined impact of their gravitational pull, you could predict the movement and strength of tides."

"So what?" A gossamer thread of possibility suggested itself in Dianne's mind, but she couldn't grasp the idea.

Youjia moved even closer, and lowering his voice, said, "I'm devising a new plan for storing tidal energy. If tides can be accurately forecast, then the chance of exploiting them for energy would be much greater. This isn't the theme of my lecture tomorrow, though it is the main reason why I came to He'lin this time. Because I want to collaborate with you."

Alarm bells were beginning to ring, but Dianne couldn't help her curiosity about Youjia's plan. "Why would I collaborate with you? I don't even know your proper field of research."

"Is there somewhere we can talk more privately?" Youjia got up and began to head out.

Dianne stood up too, and before she realised what her body was doing, she'd already quickened her steps to overtake Youjia. "Let's go to the university botanical gardens."

The next day, as Youjia spoke on stage, Eileen sneered and said to Dianne, "Look at that guy, he's got the face of a drama idol. Shame about the quality of his lecture."

Dianne merely made an acknowledging noise, before slipping back into the memory of the night before. Under the brilliant moonlight and the mild, halcyon scent of Yulan orchids, Youjia had painted a wonderful future of mutual advancement for the double planet. The possibilities of his plan were boundless. Dianne had never met anyone who was so academically in tune with her, not only intellectually, but in so many ways their conversations through the night had struck spark after spark. Dianne was amazed to see such agility in her own thinking. Returning to her room, she stayed awake the entire night.

Thunderous applause pulled Dianne back into the present. Next to her, Eileen looked stunned, pursing her lips tightly.

Youjia approached, nodding to Dianne, but Eileen deliberately turned her head away. Facing Dianne, he asked, "How was my lecture? May I trouble you to bestow your company on me again tonight?"

In a panic, Dianne nodded quickly. It wasn't until Youjia was out of earshot that Eileen said in an icy voice, "So... it seems that relations have thawed."

Facing Eileen's cold gaze, Dianne wasn't sure why she felt guilty. "I happened to run into him and we discussed

my thesis and I realised he has no ill intentions..."
She licked her dry lips. "What are you doing tonight?
Come and show our guest around. You've got far more
experience in these things."

"We'll have to see how sincere our guest is." Eileen
raised her eyebrows in challenge.

Dianne shook her friend's arm. "Come on, just come
be my chaperone and save me from the weaker stance of
being alone."

The ice in Eileen's eyes was melting. "Fine. I'll do it.
For you."

Dianne sighed in relief, and, tightly gripping the box of
Lizao in her bag, she squeezed out a weak smile.

DIANNE CLIMBED ONTO a chair to reach the top of her
wardrobe. She shifted down a suitcase that hadn't been
used for many years, the insidious pain in her lumbar
reminding her that her body wasn't what it used to be.
Luckily she'd kept her Linlu[39] in good condition: the car's
dark red shell seemed, over the years, to have acquired a
sheen to it. Dianne started her up, saying goodbye to the
town of Moonless, where she'd lived for thirty standard
years.

The traffic out of Moonless was light, and the Linlu
headed east with little in its way. It was getting dark,
and Dianne couldn't help but dart a glance at the eastern
horizon—the sky was full of stars, but no hint of the moon.
She laughed at her own impatience: it was impossible to
see Bizhe before getting to Moon City. The Linlu turned
into the car park of the first hotel she found, and Dianne

---

39 Linlu, 林鹿, means "forest deer".

entered the lobby to rent a room. On the TV, the news was reporting another record-breaking rise in the number of tourists coming to He'lin. After the holiday islands of Bizhe, the cultural heritage of He'lin had now become an obsession for intergalactic sightseers. Negotiations were taking place between political leaders to strengthen and deepen relations between the two planets. Having lived in Moonless for so long, with Bizhe out of sight, Dianne had almost forgotten that the two planets had broken their deadlock and revived negotiations for a couple of years.

"Madam, here are your papers back and the key to your room."

Dianne took the things from the receptionist and was just about to leave, when the door opened and in came a young couple. As they spoke to the receptionist, Dianne found herself slowing down her steps.

"Apologies, we don't have any more double beds available tonight. Will a standard twin room do?" The receptionist lifted his gaze from the guest registration book.

The girl pouted, flinging the boy's hand away. "I asked you to book a room ages ago, you kept saying we didn't need to."

"Well, they've got rooms, haven't they? The boy lifted up his hand to wipe away the sweat prickling his forehead.

"Twin room! Two beds!" The girl, oblivious to bystanders, raised her voice in complaint. "I didn't complain when you said you wanted to come to a dump like Moonless, and now we have to sleep in separate beds? How long have we got together?"

"I just wanted to visit all the sights in He'lin with you before I go..." The boy held out his hand to stroke the girl's shoulder, but was rejected.

"Then don't go. Stay." The girl's voice had become soft and gentle.

"Stay?…Will your parents agree to us being together? If they find out that we've already…" The boy mumbled a phrase, and then at normal volume, said, "Don't worry, when I've settled in Bizhe, I'll come back for you straight away!"

The girl averted her face. "Who knows when you'll change your mind? That job's so dangerous, maybe you'll…" And then her tears began to fall.

Instantly the boy took her in his arms, only letting go with one hand to wipe way her tears. "Don't cry, I'm only going to map and develop new islands, I'll be careful. How could I leave you on your own? They say that Bizhenese society is free, open, and there are lots of opportunities to make money quickly. I'll take that risk for our future. Just wait a few years, no, maybe not even that long, then we'll be together again. Don't cry, OK?"

The girl didn't reply, but her sobs grew even fiercer.

Dianne dropped the key, still warm from her hand, and pushed it back towards the receptionist. "Give the double to them. I'll take the standard."

The girl sniffed, and together with the boy, they thanked her profusely.

When the young lovers were on their way, the receptionist turned to Dianne and said softly, "Madam, you are so kind. Young people nowadays… they've got no sense of propriety. Running away without telling their parents, sleeping together before they're married. It's the influence of all those immoral customs from Bizhe. If it were up to me, He'lin wouldn't be signing any treaties with Bizhe. It's all very well opening up commerce, tourism and industry, but when everything is opened up, the ways of our forefathers are all forgotten."

Watching the back of the girl nestled against her boy, Dianne sighed, but made no reply. At least nowadays, lovers separated on these two planets could actually get to see each other again.

AFTER FIVE DAYS, the Tidal Conference came to an end, and the wariness between Dianne, Eileen and Youjia had completely evaporated. Eileen had even given up attending the social gatherings organized by the conference committee to spend time with just Dianne and Youjia. The other attendees had even given this trine a name: "Two Stars around the Moon". Two bright shining He'lin girls, circling this lunar visitor.

Upon hearing this name, Eileen couldn't stop laughing. Patting Youjia's back, she said, "Haha, how curious. We're the stars, you're just the moon; our statuses are quite different."

"On ancient Earth, the moon was seen as far more important a celestial body than the stars." Dianne turned her gaze towards Eileen, and could tell she no longer looked at Youjia with enmity. Of course she was pleased, but over the last few days, whenever she had tried to find an opportunity to be alone with Youjia so they could further discuss research collaborations, Eileen was always there, and every time she spoke to Youjia, Eileen leaned in very close. Perhaps it was a misperception. Eileen was very warm towards everyone, Dianne mentally reassured herself.

Youjia took a step back from Eileen and walked around to Dianne's side. "Alright, alright, of course I'm the accessory to you both." Dianne breathed a sigh of relief.

Eileen moved between them again, one hand on Youjia's shoulder and the other through Dianne's arm. "So, Mr Accessory, to where are you accompanying us next? The Temple of Gemini or the Central Square markets? Or we could go to the moon daisy exhibition, there's no way you'd be able to see so many varieties on Bizhe."

Dianne shook Eileen's arm. "Have you given up on your future? Haven't you heard that the school head's just moved the midterm reviews forwards? All the experts are gathered here at this conference, so the review committee won't just be the usual soft-touch department faculty, but the most rigorous minds in their fields. If they fail you, you've got practically no chance of graduating. You haven't even started your thesis! Hadn't you better go and get started now?"

Eileen slapped her forehead. "Oh yeah, how could I have forgotten about this gig? Youjia, can you help me? There are many areas I haven't understood about my selected topic. Can you go through them with me?"

"I'd really like to help you, but I'm afraid to say my field of research is entirely different from yours, so it seems I wouldn't be of any use. Besides, I'll be heading back to Bizhe tomorrow, and need to pack tonight. So I'm afraid, ladies, I can't be of service." Again, Youjia backed away from Eileen and turned towards Dianne.

"What? You're leaving tomorrow?" Dianne found herself struggling out of Eileen's grasp.

"Yes, the He'lin government only permits me to stay until tomorrow." A bitter smile crossed Youjia's face.

Eileen balked, stepping forwards and cupping Youjia's hand in hers. "Going so soon? Will you come and see us again? No, you'll forget us straight away..." She flung Youjia's hand away with one hand, caught it with the other, pressing her fingertips against his, and turning away from him, lifted her free hand to wipe away mock tears.

With Eileen's attention diverted, Youjia drew a slip of paper from his pocket and pressed it into Dianne's hand. Dianne paused in surprise, but the paper quickly disappeared in her tight grasp.

"How could I forget you? I swear, as long as my research topic is approved by your esteemed government, I shall return as soon as I can. The prospects that tidal energy opens up are incredible, and we will see each other again in no time." Youjia held Eileen's hand up to his mouth, and after a moment's hesitation, quickly touched it to his lips. Dianne felt as if her heart were being pierced by needles.

Eileen spun round to embrace Youjia. "Oh, you have to keep that promise! We will be waiting for you. Youth is but brief, don't keep us waiting for too long."

"Of course." Over Eileen's shoulders, Youjia winked at Dianne. His eyes tracked from her balled hand to her face inquiringly.

Dianne bit her lips, and nodded slowly. The lab key around her neck gently stroking her chest as it rose and fell.

The moonlight, pure and bright, poured into the room. Dianne lay on her bed, eyes wide open, quietly monitoring Eileen's breathing. She waited until it had slowed and steadied before softly getting up. Stepping into the corridor, she realised she had forgotten to bring the lizao that Youjia had urged her to. Turning around, she pushed open the shut door, its creaking magnifying infinitely in the stillness of the night. In her bunk, Eileen turned. Holding her breath, Dianne remained frozen where she was, till she was sure Eileen was still again.

Soundlessly, she felt for the lizao in her bag and carefully retrieved it. Cradling it in her arms, she left the room.

Youjia's note had asked her to meet him at the botanical gardens with the lizao, without telling Eileen. In the dead of the night, in a deserted place, was he going to discuss collaborations with her? Or something else? Dianne felt her heart flutter with a little nervous excitement, but at the thought of him leaving tomorrow, those flutters were drowned by sadness.

He'lin First University Botanical Gardens were situated on a small hill. From them you could look down over the whole campus, and the Kuijiang in the distance. Facing the Yulan orchid garden near the entrance was a swing made from He'lin rattan. In the summer, the rattan would be in full bloom with little powder-blue flowers. When she wasn't at the library or the lab, Dianne's favourite thing to do was to sit on the swing with a book, letting its rhythmic movement help clear her thoughts and solve problems. Just a few nights before, Dianne and Youjia had sat on this swing, talking through the night. There was an area of flat ground on the top of the hill, and beyond that, a cliff edge, around which stone railings had been constructed. Near the railings was a field of moon daisies, in the middle of which there was just enough room for one person to lie down. When she got tired from reading, Dianne loved to lie there, gazing at the sky and letting her thoughts drift. Tonight, however, someone had taken her favourite spot.

"Seeing Bizhe from here feels so strange." Youjia's voice drifted from among the daisies, sounding remote and fleeting.

Dianne walked to his side and sat down, hugging both her knees. "How does it feel seeing He'lin from Bizhe?"

"It's a big round moon."

"Hah!" Dianne couldn't help laughing. "It's the same seeing Bizhe from here."

"Not the same. He'lin looks bigger. And..." Youjia paused for a moment. "Anyhow, it just isn't the same."

"Tell me, do you think that right now there are people on Bizhe looking at He'lin?" It wasn't until the question had left her lips that Dianne realised how silly it was.

"No, right now it's daytime on Lunar Side on Bizhe, so like in Moon City..." Youjia's voice sounded a little rough and dry.

Yes, when the moon was bright and high on a He'lin night, it was midday on Bizhe's Lunar Side. It was only for a brief period before and after dusk and dawn, that both planets could see the other half lit up. Dianne was astonished that as an astrophysicist, she'd forgotten such basic knowledge of her field.

"Have you brought the lizao?" Youjia placed the palm of one hand on the ground, propping himself up.

"Mhm." Dianne retrieved the box containing the lizao from her pocket and handed it over.

Youjia took it, and asked, "Do you know why it's called lizao?"

Dianne shook her head.

"It means 'History Grass'." Youjia took out a small bottle of water, and poured it into the box with the lizao. "It might look completely dead, but add a little water and it'll come alive."

Under the moonlight, Dianne stared at the plant in its box. At first there appeared to be no change, but gradually the lizao unfurled to fill the whole box, and then a kind of fluorescence began to spread from it. Dianne gasped in surprise.

With two fingers, Youjia gently lifted the lizao so that the plant unfurled into a long straight vine all the way down to the ground. Dianne could now see that the fluorescence appeared only intermittently on every other segment, each of which looked to be roughly uniform.

"A mystery of biology yet to be solved. At first people thought the glowing was caused by the periodic change in certain substances in seawater, but after plucking it from the bottom of the sea and transplanting it to grow in purified water, it glowed all the same. Every segment between the glowing cells takes a year to grow."

Taking the gently glowing lizao into her hand, Dianne scrutinized it. When the fine leaf came into contact with her finger tip, it tickled. "How wondrous. The periodic rotation of a planet casts an influence over everything on that planet. He'lin and Bizhe's are synchronized, yet the organic life that they have nurtured is so different."

Youjia chuckled. "Has anyone ever told you that you look adorable when you're being serious."

"Huh?" Dianne felt her face burn, though luckily that flush remained concealed under the cold moonlight.

Youjia stood up, extending his hand towards Dianne. She hesitated before grabbing it and letting him lift her to her feet.

He walked to the edge of the cliff, and leant against the stone railings. "Listen, the tides of the River Kui."

Dianne walked to his side. In the distance, the winding Kuijiang resembled a jade sash under the moonlight, carrying fragments of light on its flowing and undulating waters. The low sound of its movement traversed the coolness of the night; by the time they drifted to meet Dianne's ear, only a faint rumbling remained.

"Collaborate with me. Let's do a thorough job on tidal

research. If tidal energy can be fully harnessed, whether for He'lin or Bizhe, the benefits will be vast." Youjia's voice sounded very far away.

"You can do just the same from Bizhe, can't you?"

"He'lin's waters are simpler, so far more suited to the initial stages of research. Firming up the theory in He'lin should make it much easier to test practically in Bizhe. Besides…" Youjia turned to look at Dianne. "He'lin is where you are."

She blushed. "To adapt research conducted in He'lin for practical implementation on Bizhe, this means a complete rethinking of the theoretical deductions. It's going to take a lot of time…."

"It doesn't matter how long it takes, as long as we can be together."

"Together?" Youjia's words had struck a drum in Dianne's heart.

"Not only collaboration in research, but in life. No, not just collaboration, but mutual reliance and companionship, mutual support, to walk down life's path with love." Youjia's eyes were brimful of moonlight. "From the time I first read your thesis, I believed I would become close friends with its author. Discovering that it was a beautiful young woman, I knew we would be so much more, and our conversations that night only deepened my belief."

The drum in Dianne's heart was beating louder and faster. "But you're leaving tomorrow…"

Youjia sighed. "I must return to Bizhe first, and persuade them to agree to collaborative research with He'lin. But I will be back, and I will find you."

Dianne nodded. "How long will you be gone?"

The moonlight in Youjia's eyes swayed. "I don't know,

perhaps a few days, perhaps for a few months. If I can't be back soon, I'll write to you. Wait for me."

"But Eileen..." Dianne thought of the tears in her dear friend's eyes, which made her sad too.

The moonlight in Youjia's eyes dove towards her and she fell into his cool embrace. It was hard to breath, like drowning, but before she suffocated, his warm lips pressed against her own. Carefully she opened her mouth, tentatively tasting their delicious sweetness. After a moment, she relaxed, and explored him with her tongue. The scent of Yulan orchids and moon daisies mingled, enchanting and bewildering. Under this fragrance she was returning to life afresh, as if she had never lived before.

SHORTLY AFTER PASSING the Lunar East border, Dianne drove her Linlu into a roadside refuel station. The sky was showing signs of dusk. She wanted to wait here till night fell, till the moon rose. There was a mini café at the station, and Dianne ordered a cup of Yulan orchid tea, sat at an outdoor table and faced east. The last rays of sunset stroked the back of her bare neck like a layer of gossamer, rubbing her skin and tickling. Faintly, the outline of Bizhe began to emerge in the eastern heavens, a full and round orb, becoming clearer and brighter against a purple that grew denser and heavier. Lilac condensed into maroon, through to violet and then finally melted into indigo, a milky white moon engraved into it, emanating a mild and soft light. Dianne took a sip of the tea, made from a tea bag. It didn't enter the mouth quite so smoothly, but the aroma of Yulan was all there. Under the moonlight, she felt alive and refreshed. Having not seen it for thirty standard years, Bizhe was still as lovely.

"Madam, may I sit here, please?"

A middle-aged man in a narrow-brimmed hat bowed towards Dianne. She nodded.

The man sat down, and put his hat on the table. "The moon is lovely tonight."

"Yes, especially when we're reuniting after all these years." Dianne was still savouring the gentle fragrance of the tea.

"You from the Reverse?"

"Yes."

"There aren't many people left over there, are there? After the bilateral treaty, over half the population went to Lunar." The man's tone didn't sound very pleased.

"Oh? Then Lunar Side must be really bustling?" Dianne remembered the markets and temple fairs of Moon City. In all her years in Moonless, she'd never come across such crowded scenes.

The man sighed. "They all headed off to Bizhe on the shuttles. Moon City's not doing too badly because it's near the departure port, but everywhere else is near empty now. Just on my trip today, I've seen so many young people preparing to go and work on Bizhe. Everyone saying there are more opportunities up on the moon, everyone leaving their homes and abandoning their roots to work for aliens."

"Everyone on Bizhe had once come from He'lin, so they don't really count as aliens." Dianne frowned gently.

The man harrumphed. "Back then, the people who went to settle on a godforsaken rock like Bizhe were losers who couldn't make it on their home soil, but after so many generations, those islands have made them rich. Why would they have any space in their heads for He'lin now? Once their wings harden they don't recognize their parents. Now that they're clamouring for independence, that'll well and truly turn them into aliens. If it were up to me, I'd continue the travel ban until they realize the error of their ways and come back with their tail between their legs."

Dianne shifted away from the topic. "But after reopening, didn't He'lin gain a lot of tourists from other star systems?"

"Those laowai[40]? They just stare at Moon City and grin like idiots, and make a huge fuss as soon as they step inside Gemini Temple." The man grabbed his hat and began to fan himself.

Dianne didn't reply. The laowai the man had referred to—or the majority of them—shared the same roots and origins with He'linese and Bizhenese. The blood of ancient Earth had spread across every corner of the Union of Stars.

After a moment of silence, the man opened his mouth again. "Madam, is that your car?" He pointed at the streak of dark red in the car park. Dianne made an acknowledgement. "A Linlu, made in Moon City around thirty years ago? You've taken good care of it." The man swallowed.

"Thank you. It's my dearest baby." Dianne gazed at the Linlu in the distance. They'd stopped making this model a long time ago. Today's cars were all streamlined globs; this antique with hard surfaces and fins actually possessed a kind of unique elegance.

"Madam, I was thinking..." The man paused. "I mean, have you ever thought of selling that car?"

So it was her car he was after. Dianne turned the

---

40 Laowai, 老外, colloquial for "foreigner", can sometimes be perjorative.

question round. "Would you sell a child to whom you've given thirty years of love and care?"

"I can pay a very high price. I'm an antique car dealer…" The man rushed to explain.

Dianne shook her head. "I'm sorry, I still have to get to Lunar to watch the tides."

"Watch the tides?" The man looked utterly shocked. "Judging by the speed of this car, you'll get to LC just as the big one comes in. Are you travelling alone? That's far too dangerous, especially at your…"

Dianne interrupted him. "By Union Standard years, I've just turned fifty-six, so not terribly old. Besides, an old friend is expecting me soon. My apologies, but I really must be on my way."

She slightly inclined her head towards the man, ignoring his apologies behind her as she returned to her beloved car. Climbing into the driving seat, she gazed up again at the sky. The moon wasn't so round now; there was a small bite missing from the right side of the disc. She knew that if she stayed where she was, the missing mouthful would get bigger and bigger until just before dawn, when only the slenderest of crescents would remain of the waning moon—and that in the end, even that would disappear in the first rays of tomorrow.

DIANNE WAS SHAKEN awake—but not by Eileen, who was nowhere to be seen. Still in a somnambulant daze, she made out vague mentions of words like "spy", "leaks", and "Bizhe", but before she could piece anything together, she was whisked out to "assist in the investigation." For an entire day, she sat in an interrogation room of the He'lin Central Police Bureau, repeating over and over again the details of the last five days till her mouth and tongue became parched and her lips began to blister. Of course, she eliminated the contents of her private exchanges with Youjia.

Just before this hellish day was about to end, the tight-faced investigator suddenly introduced a fresh question. "And the key to the lab?"

Key? Dianne felt around her neck. The key that had always hung there had disappeared. "It was taken by you?" she replied.

The investigator shook her head. "It's not in the list of your personal effects, and it wasn't on you when you came in."

Having talked for an entire day, Dianne's head throbbed, she massaged her aching temples. "Then I must have dropped it somewhere in the dormitory."

"It's not there. We have searched your room thoroughly. There's no key, but we did find Bizhenese lizao." The investigator's tone was as cold and hard as her starched shirt collar looked.

They had searched her room? Dianne's head was now pounding. "What right do you have to violate my privacy…?"

"It's strictly forbidden to bring living plants and animals from Bizhe into He'lin. Where did you get this lizao?"

"That's a gift from a friend…it was desiccated when he brought it, already dead…"

"Which 'friend'?" came the investigator's cold and stern voice.

"Youjia, the energy institute researcher who attended the conference, he was only…"

The investigator interrupted Dianne. "He was only approaching you to get to He'lin's secrets."

"No!" Dianne shouted, but the idea had now infected her mind and shrouded it in a cloud of unease.

"Repeat again the details of your collusion over the last five days." The investigator ignored her cry.

"I didn't collude with anyone..." Dianne's retort seemed weak and ineffectual under the stare of the investigator. She licked her cracked lips, and repeated it all over again: "On the first day of the conference, I was the last lecturer..."

The interrogation lasted for six days. On the seventh day, Dianne was released: and waiting for her was Eileen. "Dianne!" Eileen wrapped her arms around Dianne, gently stroking her back. "I'm sorry, I didn't think it would be like this...if only I'd found out earlier...but it's all in the past, everything's OK now..."

"What happened?" Even though she was in her best friend's arms, Dianne felt lost.

Eileen sobbed. "Youjia, he...when I got to the lab, I found it in a total mess, all the files had been searched...I should have talked to you first...but I was too scared. The data was gone, everyone's hard work over the last few years...I called the police..."

Dianne's heart went cold. "What does this have to do with Youjia? Or the police?"

"I'm sorry, Dianne, I know this is very difficult..." Eileen gripped her friend tighter. "Youjia... he's a Bizhenese spy..."

"Impossible!" Dianne pushed Eileen away.

"They found your lab key in the hotel where Youjia was staying..." Eileen lowered her head.

These words seem to suck all the energy from Dianne's body in one blow, and completely extinguish the flame that burnt in her heart.

Youjia was taken to court for stealing classified secrets from He'lin. Bizhe denied He'lin's unfounded accusations: He'lin insisted that Bizhe had been carrying out espionage within its territory, and the already stiff relations between the two planets entered a state of deadlock. He'lin forbade all exchange, communication and travel to Bizhe indefinitely. Youjia was banned from stepping onto He'lin soil for life. He'lin's scientific interest in tidal energy research was thereafter, thoroughly quashed.

Dianne locked herself in her room for a long time, and finally handed in her letter of withdrawal to the university. With her entire savings, she bought a flashy new Linlu and left Moon City on her own. The day she left, Eileen came to see her off, but Dianne had become haggard from the experience and didn't have much to say: she just agreed to write when she reached Moonless.

That trip had lasted for thirty years. Dianne never saw Eileen again, and only found out from her letters that she'd married the leader of the team who investigated Youjia's case at the Security Bureau. The team leader got promoted and eventually went on to become the bureau chief. Eileen moved from the university dorm to a mansion in the mountains, and became a renowned socialite in Moon City—as befits the wife of a top official. Dianne, on the other hand, had married an ordinary teacher from Moonless. There wasn't much love to speak of, but understanding, and mutual companionship for life.

THE MOUNTAIN ROAD was too narrow for the old car: Dianne had to leave it at the foot of the mountain and walk up the steps. Moon City was known for its moon daisies, which had virtually taken over the suburbs. It was the height of their flowering season, and the remaining rays of dusk had imbued that whole mountainside with a carpet of dark gold.

Dianne walked very slowly, but by the time she reached Eileen's mansion, she was still out of breath. She rang the doorbell, and the door was answered by the butler. She gave her name, and was ushered in.

Dianne sat in the drawing room waiting, whilst the housekeeper brought her a cup of Yulan tea. Its latent fragrance wafted into Dianne's nose, but when pursued, the scent became elusive. The liquid entered the mouth as smoothly and lightly as air, but the aroma lingered at the tip of the tongue—a rare Ghost Yulan variety.

Dianne finished her tea, and was shown into the garden. Eileen's mansion had no back fence and from here, the eye could roam across the whole mountain of moon daisies, all the way to the Kuijiang at the bottom.

Dianne sat alone in the back garden until it was dark, and a bright moon manifested itself directly overhead. Eileen had still not appeared, and Dianne was beginning to have misgivings when the housekeeper reappeared, switching on the garden illuminations and then handing her a box, a letter and a bottle of moon daisy wine.

She opened the letter, which again was in Eileen's fine handwriting.

> Dianne,
> You're here at last.
> I'm sorry I couldn't wait for you, and couldn't apologise to you in person.
> Youjia was not a spy.
> It was I who trashed the lab, I who destroyed the data, and I who took the key from you and

planted it in Youjia's hotel. My dear, you were sleeping so deeply that night.

The first time you went out to meet him, I was already awake. It wasn't hard to follow you at all—you didn't even look back once. I hated him, I hated him for having eyes only for you, but none for me. I hated you too—I hated you for meeting with him behind my back. I wanted to find a way to make sure you would never be able to see each other ever again.

Was there anything that youthful me wanted that I couldn't get? If I couldn't, then no-one else had better dare try. I was a spoilt brat then. I realised too late that it was impossible to have everything you wanted for your whole life.

At first I was just going to tell a small lie, so you would believe that he betrayed you: he was going anyway, and there was no certainty as to when you'd see each other again. But I thought about the midterm thesis review after the conference, and how harsh the school head said the external review committee would be: they would show me no mercy. You knew that all my research had been carried out for me by my flock of boys, and my theses relied on the works of my shixiong[41]. I knew I would fail and that I wouldn't graduate, and I worried that my reputation would be ruined. Then this opportunity seemed to fall into my lap: Bizhenese spy befriends female He'lin university student to gain access to the laboratories, and

---

41 Shixiong, 师兄, term that refers to a male fellow student or apprentice in any trade or academic discipline who began their studies or training earlier than oneself.

after stealing classified secrets, destroys the data. Every loose end tied up nicely, no?

But things went far beyond my expectations. I never knew this would become the lit fuse that would lead our planets into a cold war. I only wanted him out of our lives. I was so scared. Scared that someone might find the truth, scared I'd be arrested or even executed. When you locked yourself in the dormitory, I didn't know what to do. I woke up from nightmares every night, and passed my days in fear. The secret was like a sword suspended over my head, but I couldn't let it out, or my life would have been over.

It was only much later that I came to understand that the severing of ties between the two planets wasn't because of me. He'lin's government had long wanted an excuse, as did Bizhe's. This espionage case was never even really investigated, or I would have never got away with my clumsy tricks. I happened to provide a fuse that the authorities needed at just the right time. Of course, I only understood this all when I became the wife of the bureau chief.

When I came to terms with this, I no longer felt remorse towards He'lin or Bizhe. To hell with these two planets and their energy shortages. The only people I have ever truly wronged were you and Youjia.

I feel much better now that I have spoken out. I'm on my deathbed anyway, and I've got nothing left to be scared of.

Will you forgive me? And will you forgive me on behalf of Youjia?

You don't need to answer. I know that you will.
Ever yours,
Leen.

P.S. In the box are things Youjia had sent you over these years. I got around the authorities by having them shipped here via the Commerce Union, but the bureau still wouldn't let them go. Using my husband's status, I got them released when the investigation was considered closed. I'm sorry, but as a person of interest compromised by the enemy, all your extraterrestrial post had been held by the bureau. But they only ever came from Youjia, and they're all here.

A discordant symphony of complex and confused emotions struck Dianne's heart. She couldn't tell which ones were happiness and which were sorrow. *Eileen, my dear Eileen. How could I hate you? How could I not forgive you?*

Dianne poured herself a glass of moon daisy wine, gulping down a mouthful of the hot, acerbic liquid, feeling it glide down her tongue, practically through her throat, and into her stomach. After such an extreme shock, she felt strangely calm, as if the large stone which had been compressing her and weighing down her heart over so many years had finally been shattered and washed away by the wine. She finally had her release. Youjia didn't lie to her: he never had. The burning feeling melted into a light coolness as she lifted her head up to the moon. Bizhe's position in the night sky had not changed, though its semi-circular shape had grown a little fuller.

Youjia, how have you been?

She opened the box and began to examine its contents; an illustrated handbook of Bizhenese wildlife, calendars featuring landscapes from the islands, several kinds of shells she had never seen on He'lin, samples of plants she couldn't even name, and letters—lots and lots of letters.

Dianne opened the first one and began reading. She read through until she had finished every last one. His bewilderment, his fear, his perseverance... every word and every pen stroke burned brightly. Youjia's life in Bizhe had not been an easy one: even though he was accused of being a spy by the neighbouring planet, he had brought back no intel whatsoever. After cross-examinations and questioning, the Bizhe authorities failed to get anything out of him, so they released him and let him continue his research. From then on, no one took any notice of Youjia's proposal for collaborative tidal energy research with He'lin, and his own field of study had fallen into an unresolvable bottleneck. The sight of He'lin in the sky was his only consolation, and he had never left Lunar Island. Every dusk, every dawn, he would stand somewhere facing Lunar Side on He'lin, looking up at the sky, listening to the tide hitting the shores, and imagine Dianne looking towards him from He'lin. Day after day, year after year.

After finishing the last letter, Dianne's face felt cold and clammy. Why? Why had she not trusted him? Why did she doubt him? Why didn't she listen to him, wait for him on Lunar Side? The letters had stopped coming three years ago, the year before He'lin and Bizhe signed their treaty. What had happened to Youjia? Dianne dared not imagine, but she couldn't help but do so. The most frightening answer was there in her mind, but she dared not confirm it. She felt around the bottom of the box again, and found a newspaper clipping, folded into a very small square. Slowly, she unfolded it and searched, from the biggest column to the smallest, until in one corner she found the news she'd known would be there—Youjia's obituary. Dianne's heart went stone cold.

She leant back in the chair, and the page in her hand fluttered to the ground. The round moon in the sky was so bright it hurt her eyes. She closed them, and in the darkness, let her other senses grow more acute. She could hear the waves of the Kuijiang, and smell the clear night dew on the petals of moon daisies. She felt the cold wind caressing her face, drying the skin that had been stretched taught by tears. She calmed her mind, and thought about the past afresh. When she opened her eyes again, she had come to terms with it. Deep in her heart, she had already known the ending; long before she opened this box, long before she'd received the parcel from Eileen and left Moonless. Even on that night, thirty years ago, she already knew they'd never see each other again. All these years she'd merely refused to accept the inevitable. Perhaps back then, she hadn't left Moon City out of anger, or despair, but a desire to escape—to avoid the truth she couldn't otherwise avoid. But even though she was hiding on Moonless, Bizhe was still in the sky. Opening her eyes, the ending that was meant to be was right before her eyes. Falling in love with Youjia was nothing but a ripple in a dream. Even if there had been no Eileen, a He'linese and a Bizhense would never have been able to be together—not during such an era. Just like the tidal-locked rotation of He'lin and Bizhe, the occasional libration of one planet may cause a high tide on the other, but after a brief moment in time, they will resume stability, and after the temporary impact, the tide will again rise and fall according to its fixed, everyday rhythm. She didn't blame Eileen—how could she? Dianne had dreamt of Youjia's love for thirty years, and it had been real: that was enough.

Dianne picked up the newspaper, folded it back up and returned it to the box.

Under the moonlight, the rolling tides of the Kuiiang shimmered with a myriad of crystalline lights.

A scene from thirty years ago grew with such clarity in Dianne's memory. That night, after the long and tender kiss, she and Youjia lay in the field of moon daisies, her head on his shoulder.

"In Bizhe, we have a legend." Youjia's voice sounded a little absent. "There is a giant tide every thousand years. The tides rise so high on Bizhe and He'lin that the waters of the two planets meet in space, and a determined young man could get in his boat and row all the way up to see his lover in He'lin[42]."

"Liar. Where did this primitive legend come from, and how could you row a boat in space? Besides, He'linese migrants have only lived in Bizhe for a few hundred years at most."

"You're being serious again, it's so adorable." Youjia stroked her hair. "But I mean it, even if my body can't be here, my soul and my thoughts will travel with the high tides from Bizhe all the way to He'lin."

Dianne smiled. "So when the tide rises I'll wait by the shore, and fish you out from the water."

The gaze with which he'd held her overflowed with

---

42 This is a SF reinterpretation of the old legend of Niulang and Zhinü, the cowherd, a mortal, and the weaver, an immortal from the skies. Their forbidden love angered the gods, who forced them to separate, but every year, sympathetic magpies build a bridge across the stars for the lovers to meet.

moonlight. Dianne fell into it as they embraced and kissed again.

And now, thirty years later. Dianne poured another glass of moon daisy wine, and held it high to salute the moon. "A toast to friendship." The tide was rising even higher, and the sound of the waves was rumbling into her skull. In her inebriation, Bizhe swayed.

She rubbed her eyes, and could almost see a shadow floating towards her.

NOTES

REGINA KANYU WANG straddles the non-genre and sci-fi scenes, as well as creating travel-related prose. Her writing is a shift away from the hard science direction that the genre has taken in China, towards more rounded and realistic characterisations that focus on psychological portrayals and individual motivation. She believes that in this day and age, science fiction is a means by which writers can grasp the present and the future. Wang also works for a story commercialisation agency in Shanghai, and has just started post-graduate studies on kehuan in Oslo.

"The Tide of Moon City" is one of Regina Kanyu Wang's earlier works. At first, Wang wanted to write about a pair of lovers who, due to misunderstanding, would never meet. This sort of yearning separation is the bread and butter of Chinese romance, with the longing for one's loved ones often projected onto the moon, which shines down on both of them. Two astrological bodies locked in a 'tidal pairing', but one lover chooses to hide on the far side of one planet to avoid ever seeing the other planet, while the other lover gazes towards her planet all his life, the misunderstanding between them only clearing after many decades. Although Wang had amply researched the astrophysics of the story, the scientific and technological details have ended up ornamenting the story, rather than being at its core, allowing themes of nationalism and jealousy to carry the action.

To reflect the mutual interdependence of the two planets, Wang has specifically selected characters for their names, which all have two identical parts, 比喆 (Bizhe) and 赫林 (He'lin). This will not be obvious in the English version, but I wanted you to be aware of this rather neat undertaking of form mirroring content.

I loved the idea of a story set on binary planets, where local culture and regional differences in flora, food and drink play such an important part. Regina Kanyu Wang has captured a perfect balance between traditional culture and modern concerns. There are references to the Magpie Bridge legend of the star-crossed cowherd and weaver, but it's also a story about loss. Not just personal, but what we lose as nations and peoples in acrimonious deadlock over historical and political disputes. As a tea connoisseur, I loved translating various parts of the story in which the protagonist savours cups of the planet's special variety.

STARSHIP: LIBRARY
宇宙尽头的书店

JIANG BO

1

THERE WAS A guest at the library.

They had arrived at dusk, just as the library was about to close. As long as there is a single reader, the library would stay open: this was one of their core rules. Ehuang[43] had been in the middle of flicking off the lights, but immediately stopped and reversed her actions, flicking them all back on.

White light poured down, making the vast and empty reading hall daylight-bright.

The guest frowned. "I don't like it, it's piercing. I want the

---

43 Ehuang—in Chinese mythology, Ehuang (娥皇) and her sister Nüying (女英) are the daughters of the demigod Yao, the sagest king in ancient China who ruled by benevolence. The demigoddesses were both married to Shun, Yao's successor. With their wisdom and resourcefulness, they helped him overcome many obstacles to rule the country effectively. In surviving versions of this legend, Ehuang and her sister are largely forgotten.

sunset shining through the windows and onto the desk."

Whoever came to read could make whatever requests they liked, and as long as it was possible, Ehuang would fulfill them. This was another of the library's rules.

She waved her hand. The lights dimmed and the shutters swung open as one. Outside, a russet sun looked like it was floating on the water, creating the most splendid florescent reflections. The dusky light shone in, casting a golden glow over everything; just the sight of it made you feel warm.

The man walked along the bookshelves, holding out a finger and running it along the spines of the collected books, like stroking the most cherished children.

He stood at the deepest recess of the shelves.

"Ehuang, can we talk?" The guest spoke at last.

Immediately, Ehuang knew who it was.

This was the library's designer, the architect of the world, humanity's most benevolent guide, the most intelligent of robots. Turing the 5th.

He was using a simulation of a human body, and resembled a middle-aged man.

"I don't want to give up the library," Ehuang said, cutting straight to the chase.

Turing V nodded. "I respect your views, but... nobody reads books anymore. The world is different now. Humans can acquire knowledge without reading."

"There are still people who come. The library is for them."

"In the past five hundred years, you have had a grand total of two readers."

"Exactly. There may not be a large number, but they are still coming."

"In the next thousand years, there might not be any."

"There will always be readers," said Ehuang softly,

neither servile nor overbearing, simply stating the most evident of truths.

Turing V's eyes changed colour. Through the bookshelves, he gazed at the blood-red sun, streams of tiny symbols swirling in his eyes and then disappearing.

"We don't have much time, Ehuang," Turing V implored courteously. "The sun is entering its final stage of expansion, and has been officially classed as a red giant. In two thousand years *at most*, its helium core will shed its outer layers and burn through everything. The library cannot stay here."

"What if I request that you keep it?"

"That would involve a massive expenditure. We need to see what the costings of that would be, and whether or not it would be a valid enterprise."

"Ever since Turing the 1st, every generation of Turing has sworn to respect the wishes of every human."

"That is correct."

"Then please realize my wish for the library to continue to exist."

Turing V blinked.

The 235 super-computers, extensions of himself hung in geosynchronous orbit with Mars, were all processing the same thought.

Let him think! Ehuang turned her gaze towards the windows.

The light from the sunset was still there. Turing V had synced the library's orbit with that of Mars, so they chased the sun together.

It was as though the crimson sun had been nailed in position outside the window by an invisible hand, completely stationary.

It's been a long time since we've seen each other, Sun!

Ehuang suddenly realised that she hadn't looked outside the library for a long time. For a long time, there had been no need to open the shutters.

It didn't take long for Turing V to finish his thoughts and put them into words. "This solar system is no longer suitable for human habitation. Fifteen light years away, Second Earth is still in its stabilization period. The best plan is to move all humanity to Second Earth, of course, with the exception of those who wish to venture to other planets and create their own civilisations. Most of the population has already left. The remaining 6450 must leave together. I only have the capacity to build one last starship. There will be no space on it for your library."

"I can wait," Ehuang said gently.

This calm insistence shook Turing V. He reiterated, "I can only build one last starship."

"I will wait for you to build the starship, and you can put the whole library on it," Ehuang said unhurriedly. "This is my wish."

"60,000 million books, equating to three million tonnes in weight. Including support equipment, which raises it to six million tonnes," Turing V said, blinking. "It isn't worthwhile."

"I can wait for you," Ehuang stated, without entering the debate.

For generations of Turings, satisfying the needs of humanity has been their predetermined destiny, except when there is a conflict between the needs of individuals and those of the collective.

Ehuang was very confident that no one would stand in the way of her request, as they had already forgotten that the library still existed.

As humanity abandoned the solar system, all their

resources were put to use to building starships. As long as there was enough time, Turing V could build hers.

As long as the sun allowed him enough time.

2

SECOND EARTH WAS stunning: sea, clouds, and fiery red earth. At first glance, it looked just like Earth. A second look started to reveal the difference.

200 000 years ago—when humanity first got here—this planet had been desolate, with only the simplest bacteria. Humans brought green plants, which, after being infected by the native protozoa, no longer remained green, instead turning a rich red. Luckily, this did not inhibit photosynthesis at all, and Second Earth slowly became a red world suitable for human habitation.

The Book Ark Fangzhou hung quietly in Second Earth's orbit, where it had stayed, quietly spinning, for twenty-five years.

In the very beginning, there were hundreds of guests. But gradually the crowd thinned, till now, not a visitor all year.

Ehuang wasn't worried. Those who were meant to visit would always be there.

One day, when the sun's rays were slowly disappearing from the horizon of Second Earth, an old man stepped into the library.

He perched on the arm of a red oak chair, his eyes sweeping over the rows upon rows of shelves. He merely looked, not moving towards the racks or reaching out to pick up a book.

Ehuang let him take his time. The library was there for

guests to do as they pleased, as long as they were quiet and didn't disturb the other guests.

"Apparently, all of this, had been brought here from Back There. Is that right?" The old man opened his mouth at last.

"Back There" referred to the lost solar system.

"That's true," Ehuang replied softly. She didn't want to list the countless hardships she'd been through, travelling from the old solar system to Second Earth.

However, the old man had questions.

"Twelve light years away, how long did it take the starship to get here?"

"About six hundred Earth years."

"This is a distinguished ark, the last starship from the old solar system," the old man said approvingly. "It's said that you waited so long for it, you were nearly swallowed up in the sun storm."

"It takes time to build starships. We had to wait until the last moment. All the assembling was done at a location beyond the orbit of Pluto, so although the storm was fierce, by the time it reached the outer planets, its force was already weakened, so it wasn't quite as perilous as it sounds." Ehuang gave him a tiny smile.

"All for these books?"

"Yes."

The old man looked around him again, at the lengths of continuous shelves, books crammed into every available space.

"This would actually make a lovely museum. As you well know, no one needs books anymore. You can absorb any knowledge or skill by Rapid Cerebral Imprint."

"There will always be people who need them," Ehuang replied.

The old man hesitated a little. "The Committee have decided to build a power plant here. There is only limited space in the orbit. Would it be possible for you to shift the library's location?"

"To where?"

"Planetside."

"Oh?" Ehuang glanced at Second Earth through the window, and a shade of shock passed over her face. "If I settle on the planet, it will be hard to move again. The library has always been in orbit."

"Why does it need to be up here? Isn't the planet a good location? That's where a library belongs," the old man said persuasively.

"Down there isn't good enough," came Ehuang's light-speed rebuttal. "I want to keep these books for a long time, and the life cycle of a single planet won't suffice."

How long do you plan on keeping them?"

Ehuang paused to consider. She'd never thought about this question. "Forever." This wasn't an accurate answer, but it was all she could think of at the time.

"How long is 'Forever'?" the old man pursued.

Ehuang turned her head, and saw the entire heavens inundated with stars. Her mind was made up.

"Till the stars go out," Ehuang replied softly.

It was as if the old man had foreseen this reply. He stood up, nodded at Ehuang and said, "If this is the case, then why not be among the stars? You have an excellent ship already in your possession. I could modify it, equip it with the best engines and navigation systems, as well as automatic nano-repair and maintenance. All it will need to sustain itself is hydrogen and space dust, and then you can keep your library…" He paused. "…till the stars go out."

"Is this the last act of diplomacy?"

"No, just a suggestion. No one needs this library, but we do need the orbital position. There are lots of solutions. This is only one suggestion."

Ehuang observed the old man. His skin was as bright red as the forests on Second Earth. Compared to the people of the old Earth, humans on Second Earth had evolved. Yes, they gained knowledge and learn skills through RCI, and to them, the library was a redundant concept. They were not Turing, and had no promises to keep.

For them, exile was an act of benevolence.

Then I will go among the stars!

"I agree," she answered the old man, "but on one condition."

"Please state it."

"When I first arrived, I requested that all books be transferred here, but you didn't send any, because there were no books. Now that I am leaving, you must write down all the knowledge you possess, into books, and send them to me."

"This is somewhat a difficult request. No one can guarantee they could put all their knowledge in writing."

"Please do what you can. As soon as you are finished, I will leave. This will also give us time to prepare my starship."

The old man contemplated, and then lifted his head. "Fine. There will be a batch of books coming tomorrow."

Ehuang smiled. "As an equivalent exchange. If one day you need this library, it shall be open. Anytime."

* * *

3

ANOTHER BLUE PLANET floated into view of the Fangzhou.

"I have no intention of invading. I am merely a traveller, and a librarian." Ehuang continued to send the transmission as she approached the planet.

It wasn't just her ship that moved towards the planet: it was a fleet. Thirty-five ships of varying sizes, each containing a library. Though not armed, the fleet was larger than most armadas in the galaxy.

Ehuang had transmitted in six of the most commonly used languages in the universe.

At a distance of six light seconds from the planet, the fleet stopped their advancement. This distance provided an effective vantage point to observe the planet, but was also just out of firing range should any impetuous civilizations choose to fire their primitive weapons.

The message had been transmitting for thirty hours, but there had been no response. Nor had the planet shown any sign of radio activity.

If this planet has a civilization, then it probably hasn't yet grasped wireless technology, but they might have books. On at least two pre-broadcast planets, she had found books, and adopted them.

Ehuang instructed the smallest ship to navigate towards the planet, and to search from orbit for any traces of civilization on the ground.

The ship had performed all possible searches for squares, circles…geometric shapes of any kind, but found no object over thirty square metres that exhibited any features of a cultural artifact.

This is a primeval planet: although there is life, it is yet to be a civilization.

Ehuang was just preparing to leave when a tiny floating object caught her attention.

The object was not large—no more than twenty metres wide. If it hadn't moved to a space just below the reconnoitering ship, it would have been missed entirely.

It was a continuously rotating metal ball, almost a perfect sphere, the surface of which was smooth but carved with ornamentation.

This wasn't a celestial body!

Ehuang tried all kinds of channels and methods to communicate with it, all to no avail.

Cut it open. The idea suddenly pushed its way into her thoughts.

There was no laser cutter on the starship. Yet in her books were over two thousand ways to construct different kinds of laser tools. Ehuang found the manual for a medium-range laser lance, and set the nanobots to work.

Three days later, the laser was being moved into orbit.

When the high-energy beam struck the metal orb, it emitted a sharp whistling scream. The monitors showed a sharp spike in radio activity, like a howling wave, crashing forwards.

It's awake! Ehuang switched off the laser.

A soft cloud of light seemed to enshroud the metal orb, and it began to project a mixture of images all around it. They were sentient creatures with six legs and two arms: they had two genders and a written language. They had made all kinds of tools, wares, and constructed giant forts, large-scale rockets, as well as space stations. They had built many superstructures on the surface of the planet, some as long as sixty miles and as wide as thirty. Then, they vanished down into their creations, and gradually the superstructures were reclaimed by the planet's vegetation.

It was broadcasting a brief history of the planet's civilization.

The metal orb gave out a final electric wave. It was some kind of language Ehuang had never come across. After fifteen days of painstakingly piecing together the written text she'd found within the projected images and examining every potential meaning, she finally cracked the translation.

"All glory and splendour eventually gravitate towards oblivion. This is but a puppet's life, driven by primitive desires, and this mortal coil merely an illusion. Traveller, whether you are from the future, or from another planet, there is only one thing we wish you to know. We have already understood the mystery of life, the ultimate secret of the universe, and have chosen to fade into nothing. Time will erase everything, except for this message and our gravekeeper. Any question you ask, it will answer."

The gravekeeper was this metal orb: an artificial intelligence, a solitary souvenir of this civilization that had self-destructed.

"How long has it been since your masters departed?" Ehuang asked it.

"Seventy million planetary cycles ago," the metal orb replied.

Seventy million cycles. This planet took sixty hours to rotate on its axis; that would make it nearly four million years. In four million years, the seas would have long turned into grassland, and any traces of civilization would have long faded from the surface of the planet. Only a few mounds still remained, on which vestiges of the superstructures could vaguely be made out.

"Why did they leave?"

"Stars will always go out, the universe will die in the

end. Long and short, fast and slow. Departure isn't always painful, there is no point to civilizational struggle."

"Do you have books?"

"Query not understood."

"Do you have any knowledge I can learn?"

"I have none of what you seek."

Ehuang was thinking. The planet had lost its curiosity: there was nothing it could gain or lose. Even though they had placed the metal orb in orbit, they didn't seem to mind whether or not it was ever found. There was not much to be gained by talking to it.

"May I have a look at your architecture? I want to find out what happened to your masters in the end.

An image appeared in front of the orb.

A creature, whose civilization had made this orb, was sprawled over a giant chair. Its body seemed to be covered in a kind of fungus. Something looking like a sea sponge grew out of its large head, spreading out from it and connecting with the same things growing out of others' heads. They hung like fruits born from one creeping vine.

This was what became of them in the end: they all died, in decay. They found a way to join their minds into one. It must have been a perfect world of bliss. Everyone perished, happy, in that perfect world.

Ehuang had no more questions.

"Come with me? I can take you all over the galaxy. My ship is equipped with FTL technology, so travel won't take up too much time."

"Anyone who touches me will be punished," warned the metal orb.

Ehuang made no reply, but silently activated the ship's capture command.

*   *   *

THE ENGINES ACTIVATED, and slowly blossomed into existence as if from nothing.

"Ehuang, where shall we go?" asked her new companion.

"I don't know. Our mission is to collect books, and keep them."

Ehuang looked at the floating ellipse next to her. She had studied the metal orb's structure, deconstructing it, and then recreated the 'Tuoyuan'[44] according to its original format. But the Tuoyuan wasn't merely an exquisite replica of the metal orb: it was now miniaturised, only a metre in diameter.

Ehuang wasn't sure why she had the impulse to tear down the orb. Perhaps she wanted to take it with her no matter what. Even while she constructed the Tuoyuan, she felt deeply contrite and guilty for her recklessness.

Halfway across the galaxy, on a journey of two billion light years, she had been constantly alone. At least for the remainder of her journey, she would have a companion.

They had only one thing in common—they were both rejects of civilization.

"How long is our journey?" Tuoyuan asked.

The answer Ehuang had given long, long ago resurfaced in her memory.

"Until the stars go out," she answered.

4

"YOU HAVE A formidable fleet." The light grey creature shook its broad face. The Pageroid had flat, round bodies,

---

44 Tuoyuan (椭圆) means oval or ellipse in Chinese.

five pairs of appendages spread evenly around the upper body, and the same number of legs on the lower body, allowing it to stand stably. Its head, also round and flat, looked like a tongue with eyes. It resembled a soft aquatic creature in neat clothes—yet they were a powerful people.

Among the less friendly civilizations Ehuang had had the misfortune of meeting, they were the most formidable. Their hundred-thousand-strong fleet was now densely arranged into a battle ball formation, two thousand miles in circumference and resembling a small planet.

Aggressive civilizations will always hunt down their opponents. 'Destroy and conquer' seemed to be the eternal tenets of the Pageroid. Having made several attempts at peaceful communication, Ehuang had come to understand their motives.

By now, the library fleet had also become a colossus with over two thousand starships, the smallest weighing two thousand tonnes. Each ship its own library, holding the collected knowledge of hundreds of civilized planets: yet it was nothing compared to the fleet of the Pageroid.

Praise from the Pageroid was not a good thing. Their combined firepower could reduce the libraries to particles in a mere moment.

"We are just a library, we are not armed," Ehuang assured the Pageroid on the screen.

"Our intel has already informed us of this." The Pageroid commander had come prepared. "The battle has lost its meaning. So, we have instead, decided to offer you a proposal."

"What kind of proposal?" Ehuang didn't think it would be a good proposal, but she was still willing to listen.

"We will open a wormhole, and jump to a nice distant point in the galaxy. If we find any interesting targets there, we'll have a war! And if we don't, we will return via the same wormhole—and when we do, you must be prepared to fight, for we will show you no mercy! You will have time to make all the necessary preparations," declared the commander, nodding with high spirits. "Your fleet fascinates us. It has advanced hyperspace and defence capabilities, but no weapon facilities. If, when we return, you have run away, it will be a futile action. We will hunt you down and destroy you. If you wish to avoid this, you'd better find a way to defend yourselves."

A wormhole large enough to transport the Pageroid fleet would take over two hundred years to traverse.

"We will not go to war," Ehuang replied, with her usual resolution.

The Pageroid did not look pleased. "We have already given you your chance. If you forgo the chance to defend yourself, then we will still end you. Have a proper think about it."

The Pageroid cut their communication.

"Ehuang, we can fight them. I have observed their fleet. Their weapons are not advanced. I can limit their movement with singularity traps, and then simply finish them off with six hundred gravity generators," Tuoyuan reported.

"Tuoyuan, have you ever fought in a war?" Ehuang asked, obviously dismissing the proposal.

"No, but I've read all the books and learnt a wide range of strategies, for fighting on all kinds of different terrains, from planets' surfaces to space. I have over fifty methods to eliminate these warmongers. The aim of war is to prevent war, those on the side of justice have always said so. If they are really so foolish as to come back through the wormhole, I could seal them inside it, which would completely remove them from the universe." Tuoyuan was growing a little excited, and began reeling off plans incessantly.

"War is destruction. Our goal is not to destroy."

"But we must protect ourselves."

Ehuang smiled faintly. "Believe in the power of wisdom. If they really wanted to destroy everything, then they would never have come among the stars."

"Do you intend we just sit here waiting for death? Or shall we run?" Tuoyuan squeezed its body into a flat shape. "*We will hunt you down and destroy you,*" he imitated both the form and tone of the Pageroid. "*If you forgo the chance to defend yourself, then we will still end you.*"

Ehuang couldn't help but laugh.

"Do me a favour. We don't know where the Pageroid are from, but they must have a point of origin, and I think I've seen them somewhere before. They must come from that latter half of the galaxy we've just explored."

"I can try, but you do you not feel I would be better employed devising the optimum battle plan? If I spend this time searching the origin of those monsters, then I will be unable to commit time to battle preparations. If we instruct the entire stock of nanomachines to go into full production, it will still take approximately one hundred years to complete the necessary armaments."

"I have a plan. Go and find their homeworld!"

The Pageroid fleet was preparing to depart. Their wormhole phased in from nothingness, spreading slowly like a translucent glass ball growing out of the vacuum of space, bejeweled with multicoloured stars, sparkling and majestic. It was beautiful.

"Are you sure you do not wish me to engage a singularity attack? I could lock them in that corridor with ease,"

Tuoyuan asked again as he flew towards the Third Library.

"There is no need. Go and find what I asked for," Ehuang instructed him.

The Pageroid fleet disappeared into the wormhole, which remained shining for a few moments before it folded up, replaced by the emptiness of the cosmos.

After searching through six hundred billion pages, Tuoyuan reported his findings. "I believe I have found it. They come from Arcturus 9, two thousand light years away. You have indeed been there, before my time."

Arcturus 9. Suddenly, she understood the causes of all these events. She had met the snail-like people there. Even at the birth of their civilization, they were already building giant, impenetrable forts, even before they developed flight.

Yes, the Pageroid were the descendants of these mollusc people. Back then, they were a fledgling people, carrying heavy shells on their backs, and living in the humid swamps of their planet.

"Ehuang, we still have time. I could prepare a trap for them."

"That is not necessary. I have an idea."

The Pageroid returned, and honouring their promise, the moment they emerged the wormhole they began to attack. Their enormous cannon ships crackled with fully charged energy, all weapons now trained on the library. At a command, the apocalyptic flame would burn the whole fleet into oblivion.

Yet, immediately, they stood down.

A giant monolith now floated in the space between them. It was blacker than the void, and rectangular; the proportions of its sides a distinct ratio of 1:4:9.

It hung there silently, slowly tumbling.

The Pageroid fleet had fallen silent.

A single command ship solemnly left the fleet and approached the library.

A small retinue of Pageroids scuttled between the expansive rows of bookshelves, their footsteps trudging, their breathing labored. At the end of the shelves, Ehuang sat restfully. Beside her floated a tiny model of the monolith, slowly tumbling.

Seven Pageroid knelt before Ehuang.

"All powerful teacher, O Great Prophet, forgive our rashness and ignorance. We have traversed thousands of light years to find your whereabouts. Please enlighten us, O Prophet and banisher of darkness and chaos."

They had prostrated almost their entire bodies against the floor, fearful only of not conveying enough sincerity.

Yes, the black stone was their sacred relic. It had once landed on Arcturus 9, and an endless flow of knowledge had been transmitted to the entire tribe of snail people in exchange for their own limited writings. It had led to great leaps in their civilization, and utterly transformed their religion. They came to venerate the eternal god of the universe. The black stone was holy to them, the bridge between their people and the divine being. It had been brought to their planet by the Prophet, and after completing their enlightenment, it had vanished.

This was the moment the black stone had manifested itself again: this was the coming of the Second Enlightenment.

The Pageroid continued their prostration, waiting for their Prophet to speak.

"You destroy everything before you. Is this your idea of fun?" Ehuang demanded.

"We have tried every possible means of finding you, esteemed Prophet. In the end, the elders agreed that if we destroyed all the wisdom in the universe, then all that remains and cannot be destroyed must be the will of God. This was the quickest way to find our Prophet."

"You almost destroyed the library. This library was the original font of knowledge for your civilization."

"Please forgive our ignorance and sins!" the Pageroid groveled even lower, almost gluing themselves to the floor.

"I have already made a decision. Stand."

Fearfully, the Pageroid stood up and shuffled to one side.

"You wanted to find your holy relic? This is it. The black stone was merely its symbol, something I made from one of our earliest books. The real form is the library, this whole fleet. The library is open to any civilisation in the galaxy, and you are now its guardians. Your army will continue to travel the galaxy, but no longer bringing destruction: you will bring knowledge and civilization. It is your Goddess' wish for the galaxy to be prosperous and civilized, and you shall be its protectors."

Once again, the Pageroid prostrated themselves, so full of fervour that their flat little bodies were shaking all over. Yes, they were creatures of such a character that when a course is set, nothing will sway them. This perseverance was a merit their stubborn forebears had instilled in their blood, and with their fleet bristling with armaments, there was no other race in the galaxy better suited for the role.

The Pageroid fleet approached the library—this time, expanding their formation and carefully enveloping the library fleet. A soft core wrapped in a hard shell: this was the most safeguarded fort in the galaxy, the most sacred of all libraries. It would travel the galaxy, enlightening civilisations.

"Ehuang, what should be do now?" asked Tuoyuan.

"Continue our journey. We have only travelled half the galaxy," Ehuang replied.

"But you've given them the library."

"I have not given it to them. I have given it to everybody. Well, most of it. Look."

Next to the splendid, combined fleet, the now tiny-looking Fangzhou idled, its stealth tech rendering it so subtle that even the battle-born Pageroid had failed to notice it.

Fifteen light seconds away, Ehuang executed a hyperjump.

5

THE SPLENDID MILKY Way lay behind them, in its full glory.

Hundreds of millions of stars in its spiralling arms, all spitting out their brilliant magnificence

At the end of the galaxy, just the endless darkness of space.

"Where else can we go?" asked Tuoyuan. "This is the end."

The galaxy is smaller than one might expect: it is our whole world. The next real cluster of star systems beyond that are a hundred thousand light years away, seeming more like a trick of the light as it traverses the universe, down the long corridor of time.

In a closed pocket of three-dimensional space, the only direction is forwards, and the eventual destination is the starting point.

A hundred thousand light years of travel had suddenly come to an end. Ehuang felt tired. She had no answer to Tuoyuan's question, so she stayed silent.

Tuoyuan did not press the issue.

They were sitting in the library on the edge of the galaxy, watching the Milky Way spinning from a unique vantage point.

The glorious Milky Way, countless civilizations.

Once, she had owned that galaxy's largest library, its most abundant store of knowledge, yet she had left it with the Pageroid, because it belonged to all the civilisations in the Milky Way.

This original library ark still belonged to her.

Her own creator, the father of Artificial Intelligence, Wang Shi'Er, had left it with her, requesting that she took care of it in perpetuity. She had kept her promise, and yet there was a potential to the library she had been unable to fulfill.

Ever since she left Second Earth, she has never seen or met any humans, and of course has had no readers from that planet.

"Tuoyuan, I want to tell you some things."

"Go ahead, I'm listening."

"My father once told me that, in the future, people will need this library. He told me to keep waiting, no matter what, and I will see. I have made no such observation."

"Then you intend to persevere?"

"As I said, I'll wait till the stars go out... but these stars are so full of vitality. One winks out, and another is born. So we will have to wait till the end of time."

"I don't mind waiting."

"The question is, when will we have a visitor?" Ehuang felt a little anxious.

"You created the largest library in the galaxy. Countless civilizations have already read the books within."

"That's not the same. This library is for the people of

Earth. I'm worried whether anyone is even left there to visit. Perhaps I should return and take a look," Ehuang said as she made her way back to the highest point in the library.

"I'd also very much like to see Earth. You've seen where I was born. I have not seen the place where you were born."

Ehuang smiled. "There's no need. If there are people who really want to read, they will find us."

"Then we will wait here?"

"Keep the door open, and perhaps we can rest for a while."

On the display panel of the door to the library, rows of text quietly appeared.

> *Till the stars go out.*
> *Waiting at the end of the world,*
> *For someone.*
> *A sentence,*
> *The eternal vow and the flower that never dies.*
> *The fire of civilization leaping*
> *Across the deep chasm of time and space.*
> *Till the stars go out.*

6

THE SOUND THAT wakes them up is shrill and a little piercing to the ears: a majestic symphonic march.

The doorbell to a library should sound sweet and melodious, but Tuoyuan must have secretly reset it.

Ehuang gets up to welcome the guest.

Tuoyuan is already there, and standing before him is a

guest. A guest whose body and features conform to the characteristics of "human"—an Earthman undoubtedly. He resembles Turing V a little, being a middle-aged man in prime health, but he is actually a robot, and his whole body emanating that peculiar scent of nanomachines.

The visitor looks around, his face solemn, without a hint of emotion.

Ehuang does not attempt to converse but quietly sits in her seat, calmly observing the guest. In this library, guests could do anything they like, as long as it doesn't bother the others.

Their rest has lasted a little shy of six million years, so she does not mind passing a little more time. Those who are meant to come, will be here.

The visitor's eyes fall on Ehuang.

"I've found this place and, at last, you."

"Who are you, and why are you looking for me?"

"I am Envoy 2084. I come from Titan City, which is situated in a low-density nebula 320 light years away from its origin, Second Earth. As for the reason of my visit? All human cities have fallen into a state of torpor. Even our space metropolis has lost its vibrancy. Second Earth is no exception, nor are the three other planets humans have now settled. All human civilization has ground to a halt. I am one of the sixty thousand emissaries created by Turing, tasked to travel throughout the galaxy to find your whereabouts. It is an honour to finally meet you, and complete my mission."

The envoy's speech has the rigidity of reciting from a textbook.

"What exactly do you want with me?" Ehuang pursues.

"I don't know. I only know that you have the key to everything. Only when we find you, could the human civilization recover its vitality."

Ehuang ponders. "I understand. Let me have a think."

Ehuang walks through the bookshelves, row by row, until she reaches the very last rack.

There hangs a picture, a portrait of Wang Shi'Er. In the portrait, Wang seems to be watching her, his gaze brimming with a smile, mysterious and inscrutable.

Yes, that someone she'd be waiting for has arrived, yet there's still no ready answer.

Father, what did you intend for me to do?

"Ehuang, is this your father?" Tuoyuan's voice comes from beside her.

Ehuang turns her head and sees Tuoyuan floating silently to one side. Above him is a head-to-toe projection of a tiny humanoid figure. The figure is nodding to Ehuang. Tuoyuan had found an image of Earth's *Homo Erectus*. In that eternity of waiting, he must have read through the entire book collection.

Suddenly, Ehuang is sure of her mind.

Briskly, she walks back until she is face to face with the visitor.

"How do you learn?"

"Turing gave me everything."

"How do humans learn?"

"Everyone receives different brain imprinting according to their parents' request. Robots receive their knowledge from the Turings."

Ehuang turns towards Tuoyuan. "Do you understand now?"

Tuoyuan's caveman shakes his head. "No, I do not."

"You have a complete mind and personality. He doesn't. You grew up in the library, and learned through reading. While he is an accurate copy, all his knowledge is given, not learned."

Ehuang regarded Tuoyuan seriously, and continued, "Only through learning can wisdom be attained. A mind that only possesses imprinted information is only capable of moving towards atrophy and death: this is the fate of the human cities. Generation after generation, they became more and more dependent on knowledge imprinting. They came to lose more and more vitality. If this continues, humans will become no different to the Turings in the end. The Turings do not accept the atrophy of the human race, so this is a deadlock."

Tuoyuan blinks. "I think I'm beginning to understand."

"So this is the reason?" asks Envoy 2084, who had been standing to one side and staring at them. "Then should we erase all the memory imprinted into humans?"

"Of course not! That would only bring death. You need a library. A place people could go and read in. Let your children learn to walk. Let their minds be improved by the struggles and pains of learning, and let them reach the shore of wisdom by themselves."

The emissary nods. "I believe everything you say. It is just as Turing had advised: that as long as we find you, we could resolve this deadlock. Now, please will you let me take you on our journey back to the world of human civilization?"

Ehuang shakes her head. "I won't be going back."

The envoy's eyes widen with disbelief. "What? Why not? Do you not wish to see the library return to human cities?"

"Yes, of course, and he will help that wish come true," sighs Ehuang, and gives Tuoyuan a push forwards.

Tuoyuan cries out in alarm. "Me? What do you mean?"

"That's a whole different world which you, Tuoyuan, have yet to experience. It will be well worth your time."

"What about you?"

"I will stay here."

"No, I don't want to leave you."

"For you to find your own path, you must abandon your mother's arms. I can't always be with you."

Tuoyuan remains silent.

"If you miss me, you can always come back. I'll be here, waiting for you."

The light of the envoy's ship disappears beyond the wormhole; the crack in space suddenly seals up, and the Milky Way shines amidst the blackness of the space. Ehuang quietly closes the door, and walks among the rows of bookshelves.

She believes the library, as it exists in Tuoyuan's memory bank, will bring a fresh light and a new spark to their civilization, and that one day, humans will come here again.

There is one little lie she had told Tuoyuan. When he returns, he will not see her again. She won't be doing any more waiting. To have travelled across the Galaxy, come to the end of it, and raised such an intelligent and clever offspring, she feels perfectly content with the life she's led. She has no desire to demand any more of it.

She also feels exhausted.

Regarding life itself, there is something else that humans, and even the Turings, have yet to understand. They will, however, understand in the end.

As Ehuang gazes at the portrait of her father, the light of life gradually fades from her eyes.

At the edge of the galaxy, the lights of the library are still burning. On one side of the tightly shut door is displayed the poem "Till the stars to go out." On the other, more text fades into existence.

It is the poem Ehuang read from the picture frame of

her father's portrait.

> *Grow old with me,*
> *For there will be beauty in the last moment.*
> *There is life, and there is death.*
> *This is the way of universe.*

NOTES

JIANG BO IS a self-confessed "sci-fi nerd", having grown up on a diet of wuxia, science and kehuan books. During his university days, he took part in writing competitions and circulated his SF stories on the institution's BBS. He published his debut story in 2003 and by 2017 was able to quit his day job at a foreign enterprise, to devote more time to his writing. Despite being one of the older writers in this collection, Jiang considers himself a representative of China's "Sci-Fi Regeneration". He believes that science fiction provides a unique space for reflections on reality, and that the genre can lead us to a common future for humanity. He has written over 40 short stories, and in 2012, began to work on longer pieces, including the "Heart of the Galaxy" trilogy, and "Machine Gate".

"Starship: Library" was a chance for Jiang Bo to explore the nature of learning. In the story, knowledge can be instantly imprinted on the mind, so what is the point of slow, protracted learning from books? The library is an archaic channel of learning, and Ehuang's task of preserving this for humanity is often treated as a worthless endeavour. This is of course an allegory of an almost global disregard for libraries in light of digital intake of information and the ability to Google anything from the slim devices in our pockets.

There is a certain charm and humour which comes from Jiang Bo's unfettered imagination, which I have more commonly experienced in British sci-fi, such as *Doctor Who* and *The Hitchhiker's Guide to the Galaxy*, and which almost led to this story being titled "Library at the End of the Universe". The fierce and warlike Pageroids, eventually being revealed to be small, paper-thin creatures, in particular brought a smile to my lips as I translated. Whilst the moral of this story is that books are important, that learning and knowledge is power, and that libraries are one of the greatest places in the universe, it is also good to see demonstrated that due to poor civil planning, they always tend to be built in the most inconvenient of places.

I have taken great care in the selection, translation and presentation of these stories, and hope you have enjoyed this collection, both as a single volume, and a window into the world of kehuan. Selecting this story as the last in the collection I hope serves as a reminder of how wonderful this thing in your hands, and indeed all books, can be.

ACKNOWLEDGEMENTS

I WANT TO thank Joseph Brant, for his invaluable help and editing throughout the creation of this book, for putting up with the outbursts, and always supporting my Chinese cultural activities, never doubting that I would one day get a collection like this in front of a Western audience. I also want to thank Commissioning Editor Michael, for his fantastic foresight and astuteness in this project, always ready to have lengthy discussions about it, or practically any subject! Thank you to Kate Coe for her great copy editing and to David Moore for his help with contract and licensing matters, which have been more complex than usual for this book. A big thank you also to Regina at Storycom for her enthusiasm for the project, and tireless readiness to provide whatever assistance, whenever needed. Last but by no means least, I'd like to thank each and every one of the 13 wonderful Kehuan authors, for creating such excellent stories and participating in this anthology. They have all been a pleasure to work with. I know it's not easy to create alongside whatever vocations occupy your days. Never stop dreaming.

ABOUT THE TRANSLATOR
AND EDITOR

Xueting Christine Ni was born in Guangzhou, during China's "re-opening to the West". Having lived in cities across China, she emigrated with her family to Britain at the age of 11, where she continued to be immersed in Chinese culture, alongside her British education, realising ultimately that this gave her a unique cultural perspective, bridging her Eastern and Western experiences. After graduating in English Literature from the University of London, she began a career in the publishing industry, whilst also translating original works of Chinese fiction. She returned to China in 2008 to continue her research at Central University of Nationalities, Beijing. Since 2010, Xueting has written extensively on Chinese culture and China's place in Western pop media, working with companies, theatres, institutions and festivals, to help improve understanding of China's heritage, culture and innovation, and introduce its wonders to new audiences. Xueting has contributed to the BBC, Tordotcom Publishing, and the Guangdong Art Academy. Xueting currently lives in the suburbs of London with her partner and their cats, all of whom are learning Chinese.

ABOUT THE AUTHORS

KEY TERMS

The Xingyung (Nebula) Award—founded in 2010 by the World Chinese Fiction Association. It is open to all science fiction works published in the Chinese language around the world. Voting is not limited to members, but extended to the public.

The Yinhe (Galaxy) Award—the first and only one of its kind for the first two decades of its lifetime. It is considered the highest honour a science fiction author could achieve in China. Until very recently, it was only awarded to stories published in *Science Fiction World*.

Science Fiction World—starting as a scientific and literary journal in 1979, the magazine became *Science Fiction World* in 1991 and is one of China's longest running major science fiction magazines.

GU SHI

Gu Shi is a speculative fiction writer and senior urban planner. She has been working as a researcher at the China Academy of Urban Planning and Design since

2012. Her short fiction works have won two Yinhe Awards and three Xingyun Awards. She published her first story collection Möbius Continuum in 2020. Her stories have been translated into English and published in Clarkesworld and Xprize's Sci-fi Ocean Anthology.

HAN SONG

Han Song, science fiction writer, chairman of the Science Fiction Writers section of the Chinese Science Writers Association. Winner of multiple Yinhe, Xingyun and Tokyo Literature Awards. His signature works include "Subway", "Hospital", "The Red Sea", *Red Star Over America*, *Tombs of the Universe*, and "Regenerated Bricks". He has been translated into English, French, Italian, Japanese and other languages.

HAO JINGFANG

Born in 1984, **Hao Jingfang** leads the new generation of Chinese science fiction writers. A physics graduate, she holds a PhD in macro-economics and works at the China Development Research Foundation. In 2016, she became the first Chinese woman to win a Hugo Award. She has published three collections of short fiction and the novel *Vagabonds*. She lives in Beijing with her husband and daughter.

NIAN YU

A graduate of Shanghai Jiaotong University of Communications, **Nian Yu** is a contracted Storycom writer, and a self-proclaimed post-95 avant-garde sci-fi author. Ever since her debut *Wild Fire*, she has been exploring the fantasy imagination, not only creating sci-fi, but fantasy and fairy tales, publishing many pieces in *Science Fiction World* and *Sci-Fi Gin—Youth Edition*. She won the New Author Silver Award at the 7th Xingyun and has published a short fiction collection, *Lilian is Everywhere*.

WANG JINKANG

Wang Jikang, born in 1948, is a renowned science fiction writer, senior engineer. Winner of multiple Yinhe Awards, he is the only writer to have won the Lifetime Achievement Award simultaneously at the Yinhe as well as the Xingyun. Launching his writing career in the early 1990s, he has composed over a hundred works of science fiction, being named one the Three Leading Lights of Chinese Sci-Fi. His signature works include *The Return of Adam*, "Sowing on Venus" and *The Song of Life*.

ZHAO HAIHONG

Zhao Haihong holds an MA in English and American literature from Zhejiang University and a Ph.D in art history from the China Academy of Arts. She teaches at Zhejiang Gongshang University in Hangzhou. She has been publishing SF stories since 1996 and is the winner of the National Award For Outstanding Children's Literature and a six-time winner of the Galaxy Award. Her translated stories "Exuviation" and "Windhorse" have appeared in *Lady Churchill's Rosebud Wristlet*; and "The Starry Sky over the Southern Isle" has been published on *Asimov's Science Fiction*. Her story "1923, A Fantasy" (translated by Nicky Harman and Pang Zhaoxia) was included in the *The Reincarnated Giants: An Anthology of 21st-Century Chinese Science Fiction* by Linda Rui Feng. She is currently working with publishers around the world on stories for several upcoming anthologies.

TANG FEI

Tang Fei, writer, commentator. Member of the Shanghai Writer's Association and the SFWA. Her signature works include *Paradise in the Clouds*, *The Person who Saw Cetus* and *The Anonymous Banquet*. Since 2013, ten of her stories have been translated and published around the world; her novella *The Panda Keeper* won Best Microfiction at 2019's Smokelong Quarterly, *Wu Ding's Journey to the West* won the Silver Prize for Most Popular Deduction Fiction at the Speculative Fiction in Translation Awards, and "The Robe" won Best Short Story at the Yinli (China Reader's Choice) SF Awards. Apart from writing, she also dabbles in other art forms such as literary criticism, poetry, installation art and photography. Her commentary pieces have been published in *The Economics Observer* (China), Hong Kong and Shenzhen Literary Review.

MA BOYONG

Ma Boyong, writer. Winner of the People's Literature Awards and Zhu Ziqing Prose Awards. His signature works include *Two Capitals, Fifteen Days*, *The Great Ming Under the Microscrope*, *The Longest Day in Chang'An*, *Antiques and Intrigue*, and *Secrets of the The Three Kingdoms*. Focussing his attention on historical speculative fiction, he is widely recognised to be one of the writers who set the bar for Chinese literature since the May the 4th reforms in the arts.

ANNA WU

Anna Wu is a Chinese science fiction, screen writer and playwright. She wrote the script for *Of Cloud and Mist*, which won Best Film at the 6th Xingyun Awards. Her works have been published on platforms such as *Clarkesworld*, *Galaxy's Edge* and *Science Fiction World*. Some of Wu's translated works have appeared as parts of collections, such as *The Shape of Thought* (translated by Ken Liu). Her science fiction collection, *Double Life*, was published in June 2017.

A QUE

Born in 1990, **A Que** (a pseudonym) graduated from Sichuan University, and currently lives in Chengdu. As one of the representatives of New Science Fiction in China, he published his debut in 2012, and subsequently many works in *Science Fiction World*, as well as overseas, in English, winning the Xingyun and Yinhe Awards multiple times. His works mainly feature soft sci-fi, but A Que has an eclectic writing style. He loves robots, writes about them and eulogizes them. He hopes they'll let him live once they've taken over the world. His published works include "Walking with Robots" and "The Living World of A.I.".

BAO SHU

Bao Shu is a Chinese SF writer who has won multiple major awards, and published four novels and three collections.

His shorter works are published by celebrated magazines like *Science Fiction World, Knowledge is Power, People's Literature, Fiction World,* and *Flower City.* Some of his works have been translated into multiple languages. Several of his stories are now available in English, published in *F&SF* and *Clarkesworld. Redemption of Time* (translated by Ken Liu), the officially sanctioned spin-off to Liu Cixin's *Remembrance of Earth's Past* trilogy, was published in 2019.

REGINA KANYU WANG

Regina Kanyu Wang is a bilingual writer from Shanghai who has won multiple Xingyun Awards, the SF Comet International SF Writing Competition, and the Annual Best Works of Shanghai Writers' Association Awards. Her stories can be found in *Shanghai Literature, Galaxy's Edge, Clarkesworld* and more. Her essays can be found in publications such as *Mithila Review, Broken Stars,* and *Korean Literature Now.* She has published two science fiction story collections, *Of Cloud and Mist 2.2* and *The Seafood Restaurant* in Chinese and her works have been translated into multiple languages and published around the world. She is also a PhD fellow of the CoFUTURES project at the University of Oslo, researching Chinese science fiction from gender and environmental perspectives.

JIANG BO

Renowned science-fiction author, **Jiang Bo** graduated from Qinghua University with a master's degree in 2003, the same year as the publication of his debut. He has written over 40 pieces of short to medium-length fiction, totalling over 800,000 words. In 2012, he began creating longer works, of which well-known ones include *Heart of the Galaxy* trilogy, and *Machine Gate*. A recent winner of a Best Original Science Fiction award in China, he has also won the Yinhe Awards six times, and the Xingyun Gold Award four times and is considered a representative of China's generation of "Sci-Fi Regeneration" writers.

CONTRIBUTOR'S COPYRIGHT NOTICES

FIND US ONLINE!

www.rebellionpublishing.com

/rebellionpub /rebellionpublishing /rebellionpublishing

SIGN UP TO OUR NEWSLETTER!

rebellionpublishing.com/newsletter

YOUR REVIEWS MATTER!

Enjoy this book? Got something to say?

Leave a review on Amazon, GoodReads or with your
favourite bookseller and let the world know!

NEW SUNS

ORIGINAL SPECULATIVE FICTION BY
PEOPLE OF COLOR EDITED BY NISI SHAWL

INTRODUCTION BY LEVAR BURTON
INCLUDING STORIES BY INDRAPRAMIT DAS,
E LILY YU, REBECCA ROANHORSE, ANIL MENON,
JAYMEE GOH AND MANY OTHERS

NEW SUNS

Original Speculative Fiction By People Of Colour

Winner of the 2020 Locus, World Fantasy and Ignyte Awards

"There's nothing new under the sun,
but there are new suns," proclaimed Octavia E. Butler.

New Suns: Original Speculative Fiction by People of Color
showcases emerging and seasoned writers of many races telling
stories filled with shocking delights, powerful visions of the
familiar made strange. Between this book's covers burn tales of
science fiction, fantasy, horror, and their indefinable overlappings.
These are authors aware of our many possible pasts and futures,
authors freed of stereotypes and clichés, ready to dazzle you with
their daring genius.

Unexpected brilliance shines forth from every page.

Includes stories by Kathleen Alcala, Minsoo Kang, Anil Menon,
Silvia Moreno-Garcia, Alex Jennings, Alberto Yanez, Steven Barnes,
Jaymee Goh, Karin Lowachee, E. Lily Yu, Andrea Hairston, Tobias
Buckell, Hiromi Goto, Rebecca Roanhorse, Indrapramit Das, Chinelo
Onwualu and Darcie Little Badger.

 WWW.SOLARISBOOKS.COM

Follow us on Twitter! www.twitter.com/solarisbooks

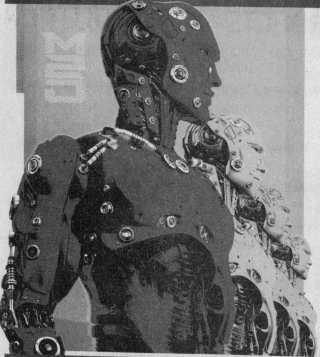

ROBOTS AND REVOLUTION

MADE TO ORDER

EDITED BY

JONATHAN STRAHAN

| PETER F HAMILTON, ANNALEE NEWITZ, ALASTAIR REYNOLDS
BROOKE BOLANDER, KEN LIU, SARAH PINSKER

ROBOTS AND REVOLUTION

100 years after Karel Capek coined the word,
"robots" are an everyday idea, and the inspiration for
countless stories in books, film, TV and games.

They are often among the least privileged, most unfairly
used of us, and the more robots are like humans, the
more interesting they become. This collection of stories
is where robots stand in for us, where both we and they
are disadvantaged, and where hope and optimism shines
through.

Including stories by: Brooke Bolander
John Chu · Daryl Gregory · Peter F. Hamilton
Saad Z. Hossain · Rich Larson · Ken Liu
Ian R. Macleod · Annalee Newitz
Tochi Onyebuchi · Suzanne Palmer
Sarah Pinsker · Vina Jie-Min Prasad
Alastair Reynolds · Sofia Samatar · Peter Watts

 WWW.SOLARISBOOKS.COM